ALSO BY A.K. WILDER

THE AMASSIA SERIES

Crown of Bones
Curse of Shadows

CURSE OF SHADOWS

A.K. WILDER

Entangled Publishing, LLC
644 Shrewsbury Commons Ave., STE 181
Shrewsbury, PA 17361
rights@entangledpublishing.com

Entangled Teen is an imprint of Entangled Publishing, LLC.

Visit our website at www.entangledpublishing.com.

Edited by Molly Majumder and Heather Howland
Cover design by Bree Archer
Stock art by fergregory/GettyImages,
Kesu01/Depositphotos,
WarmTail/Depositphotos,
AntonMatyukha/Depositphotos
Map art by Kim Falconer
Chapter graphic art by Anna Campbell
Interior design by Toni Kerr

ISBN 978-1-64937-108-9
Ebook ISBN 978-1-64937-154-6

Manufactured in the United States of America

First Edition December 2022

10 9 8 7 6 5 4 3 2 1

entangled teen
an imprint of Entangled Publishing LLC

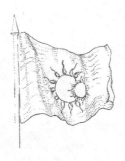

This book is for you, Nic,
with your heart and soul in every page…

HIERARCHY OF THE ROBES

BLACK ROBE

RED ROBE

ORANGE ROBE

YELLOW ROBE

GREEN ROBE

BLUE ROBE

BROWN ROBE

NON-SAVANT

Si Er Rak Tablet - Fragment XI & XII

Natsari, Natsari, where hides the crown?
The forests are burning, the children are drowned.
Natsari, Natsari, bring the dark sun,
Kiss us farewell, the Great Dying's begun.

Natsari, Natsari, call up the shades,
long-cursed shadows of warrior blades.
Natsari, Natsari, unearth the bones,
Raise Er's crown, lest we turn to stone.

MARCUS

Blood pounds in my temples. I should be used to betrayal by now, but something about having a mentor do it is particularly enraging. I almost give in to the urge and raise my phantom in a rush of seething bulk, letting him explode through the floorboards and bring down a rain of splinters and bricks. I turn to Master Brogal, the High Savant of Baiseen, not waiting for permission to speak.

"My brother's taken over the realm, our enemies could be anywhere, and you expect me to do nothing?" My fists clench tight.

Wrong question, De'ral, my phantom, rumbles deep in my mind.

"Quiet!" I don't need his advice on this.

Master Brogal pierces me with dark, strained eyes that don't seem to blink. His phantom, a bird-of-paradise *caller,* perches on his shoulder and watches me with the same unblinking gaze. "Petén is our ruler now, Marcus. Accept it."

"Accept it?" I've earned my yellow robes. Despite Father's doubts, I'm finally fit to take the throne.

"Marcus, it's understandable—"

"The only thing to understand is that my brother is not the rightful Heir. I am! Petén doesn't know the first thing about running a realm. How could he?" I take a breath. "He's non-savant."

"He'll learn." Brogal sighs and lowers into his chair. The phantom grips the High Savant's red robes to keep balanced. Brogal looks tired, his round face sagging, his usually golden skin sallow.

If I weren't so angry, I'd be worried for him. He's gone rangy since the attack, white hair thinner. Strands escape the tie when he leans forward to roll up a map.

"Have you spoken to your father?" he asks.

Now there's a question. "The healers tell me the same thing they have since I returned. He's too ill for visitors, even his own sons." I take the chair opposite Brogal, stretching my legs out long and staring at my muddy boots. I should have stomped them harder at the door.

The High Savant's chambers are large, though the shelves overflow with books. The window behind his desk gives a full view of the terraced city, some streets pristine, their cobbles swept, tall houses and landscaped gardens still intact. Others are pitted, charred black and piled high with wreckage.

"Do you honestly think Petén is fit to rule?" I ask.

Still the wrong question. De'ral can't keep his comments to himself.

Brogal turns to gaze out the window toward the sea. "You're doing an excellent job with the restorations."

More topic changing? Heat rises to my face as I think of Petén's latest idiocy. "Did you hear? He plans to go ahead with the solstice eve celebrations." It's the wrong choice. We haven't recovered from the attack. It's no time to be stuffing ourselves with the winter's cache and dancing under the new moon. "People are still homeless, and Petén is running us into the ground with his spending. He's an incompetent non-savant—"

"Careful, Marcus." Brogal waves me quiet.

But it's true. Petén *is* incompetent, and non-savant, meaning he doesn't raise a phantom. Never could and never will. He has no business on the phantom throne. There is nothing for the woodcutters to carve into it, marking the start of his reign. I take a deep breath to say it aloud.

Brogal hushes me again. "The Magistrate has ears."

Ears? He means Rhiannon. How that conniving daughter of darkness attached herself to my brother, I'll never know. Is he completely blind? Well, no, because she is beautiful, but that's beside the point.

"I've other meetings." Brogal rises, signaling the end of my interview.

"That's it?" My chest tightens. Why was I even summoned? So he could dismiss my petition to reclaim the throne in person? How considerate.

He's not on my side. Few are after my brother's poisonous words. Instead of honoring me and my company for warning the city and leading the defense to victory, I'm shunned in my own palace. Humiliated. Faces turn away when I walk past while Petén rides through the streets, Rhiannon at his side, horses prancing, robes flowing—

Crowds cheering, De'ral adds in a dry voice.

"Shut up."

You still haven't asked the right question.

"Continue to supervise the repair of Baiseen, Marcus." Brogal motions me out the door. "Those are your orders, for now."

My jaw tightens. "I *will* put Baiseen back on her feet, don't worry about that. But hear this, I cannot tolerate my brother's rule. There has to be a way to—"

"Let it go, Marcus!" Brogal slaps the desk. The mugs jump and his phantom squawks, fanning its wings for balance.

So this is how it is? Fine.

I erase the scowl from my face, dip my head in a nod and walk out the door, barely resisting the urge to slam it right off the hinges.

Interesting... De'ral says.

"What's that?" I snap. *"His complete lack of concern for my plight and that of the realm?"*

No. De'ral snorts. *His fear.*

I stop as a chill prickles my scalp. *"What is the High Savant, red-robe of Baiseen, afraid of?"*

Finally. De'ral exhales. *The right question.*

• • •

I leave the Sanctuary deep in thought, my heart sinking as I pass the boarded up windows and abandoned shops. The battle's over, and we won. But the toppled homes, fallen trees, and destitute people begging for food say otherwise. Baiseen was once a beautiful city. The shining pearl and capital of our realm.

Not anymore. We are vulnerable now, open to another siege. Is that what has Brogal anxious?

I reach the row of burnt trees on High Street and wave at the others working there. *"Ready?"*

I don't wait for him to answer but touch one knee to the earth and raise my phantom. The ground in front of me cracks and from it he springs. De'ral - a *warrior,* three times my height and weight, fighting fit, though today we don't face an attack but the repair from one. As he shakes dirt from his broad shoulders and long, dark gold braid, I send him to the other side of the street to remove broken beams and slabs.

This part of the city caught fire during the invasion, leaving black stumps and gutted buildings that have yet to be cleared. Behind, the granary lies in ruin. Its roof collapsed during renovations last week. Not everyone got out in time. I hoist a log and throw it on the pile. "Tann did this!" I spit his name. Tann, the red-robe warlord, who invaded our shores.

Samsen, Belair, and I, and other savants, have been working for weeks to rebuild. Everyone pitches in but there's still a long way to go.

"Marcus! Over here." Belair waves from the side of the street where the granary fell. They've managed to unearth a quarter of the main wall and continue to haul away what grain is salvageable. "Someone's buried under a slab."

I scramble to understand as I run toward him. They might still be alive? After five days?

Belair holds a thin, gray hand, all that's visible in the rubble. "I thought I felt a pulse, but now–" His red hair falls into his eyes as he shakes his head.

"Make sure." My heart pounds as I wait.

Belair's eyes glaze as he communes with his red sun leopard mind-to-mind. The *warrior* cat phantom pricks its ears, not moving save for a twitching tail.

I hold my breath.

A moment later, Belair exhales. "There's a heartbeat. But faint."

"Samsen!" I call over my shoulder. "Get Piper!"

Samsen dips his head. From the *callers* working to draw grain from the ruins, his phantom, in the form of a sea eagle, arrows to the Sanctuary.

"Help me!" Belair kneels, pulling away rocks.

Other savants–the blue-robe novices, and mid-level green-robes under my supervision–drop everything and follow me. We scramble over the rubble to the victim.

"You three"—I point at the brown-robe children who hang back, eyes wide—"run to the healer's hall and fetch a stretcher."

They bow and rush off, boots splashing up the muddy street.

Larseen, a yellow-robe friend from childhood, joins the rest of us to pull loose stones from the mound. "They're trapped," he says, only stopping to tie his ropy hair into a knot on top of his head. "The slab's huge."

"De'ral, we need you."

My phantom emerges from the other side of the street dragging a beam. He drops it, the ground shaking under his giant footfalls as he races toward us.

"Make room!" I shout.

The other savants scramble away in a flurry of colored robes. They don't have to be told twice.

De'ral picks up a marble column, the stone easily tall as a tree and weighing five times as much. He hefts it aside like a twig. Next he shoves over two cracked slabs of the wall, splitting them apart like halves of a melon. He's angry, my phantom. But his anger is not directed at me.

"Someone should've discovered this victim sooner."

Yes.

"Careful now," I say to him.

De'ral grunts in my head and unearths the last pieces of mortar and debris.

"What do we have?" Piper arrives out of breath. Her twin-headed snake, a *healer* phantom, coils around her neck, tasting the air with bright blue tongues.

We brush aside the last of the dirt, revealing a girl. Average height, long dark hair. At least I think it's dark. It's hard to tell with the thick film of rock dust covering her from head to toe.

"I don't recognize her." Piper takes her pulse as she speaks.

The others shake their heads. "Too much bruising. Her face…" Samsen's voice trails off.

"Bring the stretcher." Piper waves the youngsters in. She rolls up her sleeves, the orange of her robe—the color reserved for highly accomplished savants—contrasting the dark skin of her forearms. The healer's many braids are frazzled and coming out of the wooden beads. But her eyes are steady and focused.

We lift her onto the stretcher. When Piper's phantom sinks fangs into the wounded girl's neck and then releases healing elixir, the victim's eyes fly open and she gasps.

"You're safe now. Just breathe." Piper motions us to carry her to the healer's hall, inside the heart of the Sanctuary.

But first, I dip one knee to the ground, bringing De'ral back in. He growls but complies. I'll not leave my phantom up to stomp around unsupervised. Learned that lesson long ago.

"Are there any others?" I ask Belair and Larseen. The injured had been rescued days ago. So we thought. I shudder, trying to imagine how we could have missed the girl, buried here for so long.

Belair's eyes lose focus as he silently instructs his big cat. The beast jumps from slab to boulder to broken column, ears pricked, nose to the wreckage, sensing for signs of life as other phantoms had done after the collapse. Larseen does the same with his *caller,* a jackal with black ears and tail that leaves trails like smoke from a chimney.

"She was the only one," Larseen says, and Belair confirms it.

I nod, and Belair and Lars kneel to the ground, bringing their phantoms in. The four of us lift the stretcher and follow Piper, jogging up the street and through the Sanctuary gates at the top of the city. Repairs are in progress here, too, but we have to detour around a giant boulder lodged in front of the library doors. They need me and De'ral to move that one, but we haven't gotten to it yet.

"Tann and his catapults." My jaw works side to side.

De'ral rolls under my skin. *We'll make him pay.*

I don't know when, or even how, but I mentally nod in agreement.

The air in the healer's hall is warm and smells of herbs. I scan across the rows of beds for Ash's cot, the one she's laid in every day for the last month. My spine chills when I see it empty. "Where is she?" I say it louder than I mean to. But this is Ash I'm asking after. I can't catch my breath at the thought of…

Stop worrying, De'ral says. *It's not like she's lost.*

"Where is she then?" It's only been a few days since she's recovered enough to hold a conversation. What are they doing letting her wander around the city on her own?

Not wandering either. De'ral answers. *She's at the lookout.*

How my phantom knows her whereabouts, a non-savant no less, is unexplainable. But he always does.

"She's up and about," Piper says. "Looking for you, I think." Piper scans the hall for another empty bed. "Set the stretcher down here." She turns to her new patient and shoos us away.

I head for the door, but Samsen lays a gentle hand on Piper's shoulder, whispering something before he follows me out.

"Back to it?" he asks.

I hesitate. "Meet you there. I'm checking on Ash."

Samsen, Larseen, and Belair thump their fists to their chests and bow before returning to the work site. The three of us are near the same age, late teens. And the same rank, yellow-robes, but my friends still show me the respect due only to the Heir of Baiseen. Even though I've been stripped of that title. My eyes sting as I salute back. Their loyalty is all the more reason to repair the city and regain my throne, before Tann, or anyone else, threatens our shores again.

I leave the healer's hall in search of Ash.

Of course, she's right where De'ral said she would be, alone and looking wistful.

There's still no explanation for her condition. On the day of the attack, Brogal told her to meet him in his chambers but she never appeared. We found her, hours later, unconscious on the training field. It might have been an *ouster* wind that knocked her out, or a blast from the catapults, but if so, why were there no injuries? The healers couldn't find a mark on her, nor explain why she didn't wake for days. And now, the bouts of memory loss?

What happened to you, Ash?

2

MARCUS

I trot up the steps to the platform and walk toward my friend. Ash stands at the far edge of the observation deck, facing out to sea. Her dark auburn hair glistens in the sun, strands catching in the wind. Her elbows are propped on the railing, hands clutching a piece of parchment paper. She sighs and smiles at the vast ocean.

It's not hard to guess who that smile's for.

Kaylin, our guide to Aku, formed an attachment with Ash. How far it went, she hasn't confided, but I know she cares. I was jealous at first. Protective. But he turned out to be an uncanny guide on land and sea. And a brilliant swordsman. He saved our lives, more than once. I have to admit, I trust him.

But you don't miss him? De'ral chides me.

"Not like she does," I admit.

Ash turns at the sound of my footsteps. The lookout is above the palace courtyard and takes in the entire Bay of Baiseen from the palace turrets, down the semicircle of terraced streets, to the shipping harbor and small islets beyond. A spectacular view, but I only see Ash—sparkling turquoise eyes, brows lifted, her build so slender I can wrap my arms around her almost twice. Ash is the only family I need, especially since my blood relatives have stabbed me in the back.

Family? De'ral questions my every thought today.

"Fine." I confess. *"She was more than that, once."* A lot more.

I reach Ash in a few strides. "What are you up to?"

"On my way to the library." She smiles at me and warmth spreads across my chest.

"Should you be back to work already?" It's too soon. She's pale, her hair, on closer inspection, is unbrushed and full of tangles. Her wrists are thin, her cheeks a bit hollow. She's lost weight that wasn't there to lose. I'm worried. It would be different if Kaylin was here. She listens to him more than me, anyway.

Kaylin will return by solstice eve, De'ral informs me.

"You can't possibly know that."

Really?

I'm not going to repeat my phantom's proclamation. It's based on nothing tangible, and the last thing she needs is false hope. Kaylin's been away a month–since the day after Tann's attack—and we haven't heard a word. Something could have gone wrong.

"I'm feeling much better." Ash folds her note and stuffs it deep into her coat pocket before giving me a hug.

"I've been worried about you. We all have." I hug her back tight. She's definitely too thin.

"Worrying about someone is like a curse." She delivers one of her favorite adages.

That's Ash. Even in convalescence, she's thinking about our advancement along the path to An'awntia–the lofty state of mind reached over many lifetimes of progress. I don't know how she does it. I've enough to think about with this current life in front of me, let alone the next one, or the next.

"Headaches?" I raise my brows and examine her face.

"Fewer and fewer." She looks away.

"Exhaustion?"

"Nope."

"Memory?"

"Um, not sure. What's your name again?" She laughs and punches my arm.

"Ha ha."

Her smile stays in place, but she shivers. I flip the fur-lined collar of her coat and do the top button. "Where did you get this monstrosity?" It's several sizes too big, hanging straight to her ankles, brushing the tops of her bare feet. Of course they are bare. In the middle of winter. Nothing new for Ash. I shake my head. None of us returned from Aku with more than the stolen uniforms on our backs. I'll have to see that she's better outfitted. Clearly Brogal has neglected to.

"And what was in that note, if I might ask." I gently bump her shoulder as I rest against the railing.

"You may ask, but it doesn't mean I'll answer." She bumps me back and then laughs it off. "I'm still waiting to talk to Brogal. He promised me a meeting, and access to the archives, but so far he's given me neither."

"That's odd."

"I don't think he's taking me seriously."

My arm goes over her shoulder and she leans into me, the feel of her comfortable, familiar, right. I mean to soothe her, but I can't deny how much it soothes *me* to see her starting to get better. "He'll come through."

"I need that access now. Have you noticed? The signs of change foretold in the prophecy?" She points to the northern coastline.

I follow her line of sight. The high tide mark cuts into the headland, eating fresh chunks out of the cliffs. The color of the Suni River Mouth is a mud brown instead of its usual crystal blue. Half the topsoil in the realm must be at the bottom of the bay. "I've seen the changes in the coastline, and the weather, but is that really what's making you sad?"

"If you think I'm worried about Kaylin, stop."

Yes. Stop. De'ral agrees. *She doesn't need to talk about it.*

"Piper said it would help her memory to talk about things."

But maybe not those *things.*

"If you must know"—Ash straightens—"I'm a little miffed. Kaylin could have told me in person he was leaving to track Tann. Instead, I got a note."

"Um, he couldn't tell you in person, Ash. You were unconscious for days."

"Was I?" Her eyes lose focus.

Has she forgotten this again? I try not to let my frustration show. Or my worry. "You were out cold for almost a week, Ash. I delivered his message the moment you woke up."

"The message?" Her hand goes to her coat pocket. "That's right, but it didn't really say much."

"I know—" My mouth snaps shut too late.

"You read it?" She turns, hands on hips. It's like I spilled ink on her new parchment paper. I freeze as she stares at me, her eyebrows pinched tight. Then I see it, that playful glint. She's trying not to laugh.

"I read it for security reasons."

"Security?" Her brow furrows deeper.

"I thought it might have vital information. Important to the realm."

She punches my arm again. "Liar."

I stop trying to defend myself and we return to staring out to sea. I want to put my arm around her again. I don't.

"Did you hear?" Her voice brightens. "Petén's going through with solstice eve celebrations."

I click my tongue. "A complete waste of time and resources."

"I don't know, Marcus. It might be a good idea."

"You sound like Brogal."

She winces briefly before changing the subject. "How's your father? The healers wouldn't give me an update."

"They aren't telling me anything either!"

"You still haven't seen him?"

"Not allowed in." My jaw clamps, making my words monotone.

She gives me a measured look. "We'll see about that." Ash loops her arm through the crook of my elbow and pulls me toward the palace.

I try to resist but she's surprisingly strong for her size, and supposedly weakened state. Maybe she's more recovered than I first thought. "They'll stop us."

"I don't think so." She tugs me along, much more her old self again.

I give up and head for the main entrance to the palace.

"Not that way, silly." She pulls me off course. "We'll have to sneak around the back."

"To my own palace?"

"Exactly."

We leave our coats and my robe in the mudroom and don servant aprons and caps. It's not the exact uniform of the Magistrate's staff, but close enough to slip by unnoticed, according to Ash. It makes me think she's done this before. Ash leads me to the pantry and hands me a tray. The ease with which she finds the bread and the cheese and the water jugs confirms it. She's definitely done this before.

"Keep your eyes down. You can't look like you f'qad'n own the place," she whispers as we walk up the backstairs. "Think servant, not—" She cuts herself off.

"Ex-heir?"

De'ral chuckles under my skin.

"I was going to say, savant. Just don't be so royal, I mean."

"Got it." I slow my stride and lower my gaze. "This will never work."

"It won't if you keep saying that."

We reach my father's wing on the third floor without being questioned. One thing is certain, when I recover my throne, I'll be looking into palace security.

The back of my neck itches as we walk under the portraits of my forebears. They stare down at me, each man and woman's expression increasingly disapproving until we reach my father's, the most critical of all. I never liked this hallway but have learned to keep silent in front of Ash. She thinks it's a treasure to know one's family line. Makes sense, her being an orphan with no memory of where she comes from.

"I'll do the talking if we're stopped," she drops her chin and whispers.

"As you please." The growing weight in the pit of my stomach isn't making me feel conversational.

When we reach Father's chambers, the door is unguarded. I knock once and push in.

Immediately, I'm slammed with a nauseating stench. Bile rushes up the back of my throat. I'm aware of Ash taking the tray before I drop it, and setting it down. She says something, but I can't listen. There's no doubt anymore. Whatever illness my father battles, it's winning.

The Magistrate's room is unrecognizable. The usually bright windows that lead to the gardens are cloaked with heavy drapes. A bat couldn't find its way out of here. The floor is littered with dressing gowns and towels are thrown over the backs of chairs. A stack of dirty dishes sit on the bedside table. Are servants not allowed to attend him? His large, four poster bed is a mound of blankets, and my father–the Magistrate–is like a stick figure smothered beneath them.

The lines in his face have deepened to crags. The once robust flesh hangs like an empty sack. "Have they not fed him?" I didn't mean to speak aloud, not yet, and not those words.

But Jacas Adicio, once great ruler of Palrio, Magistrate of the phantom throne, raiser of the mighty wolf *caller*, stirs. His white stubbly jaw works as his dry lips press together.

"Go on." Ash puts her hand on my arm, urging me forward. "Talk to him."

And say what?

"Petén? Is that you?" he asks.

I clear my throat. "No, Father. It's me. Marcus."

Jacas opens his eyes and blinks. He tries to sit up, but the effort sends him into a fit of coughing.

I reach out to help. He's all bone, like a rack of lamb in a nightshirt.

"My cup?" Jacas turns filmy eyes to the bed stand and attempts to reach for it. "Is that you, Rhiannon?" His voice takes on a softer tone. "Can you pass me my tonic? Bless you, dear."

Ash hands me the half-filled cup and I hold it to my father's lips. The smell of the medicine is worse than the reek in the chambers.

"We'll walk in the garden again today, won't we, my dear? Discuss the future of our realm." The old man pats the bed beside him as if it were a woman's thigh. "You have been so kind to me."

At least someone has. De'ral comments without a trace of his usual sarcasm.

I pause at that. Father is so frail, for a moment my heart pinches.

Jacas blinks again, his face contorting. "Marcus, you say?" The softness in his voice vanishes.

"Yes, Father. It's me." My chest tightens, my hands feel thick and clumsy. "Are you... do the healers think..." How to ask after his health when it's so obviously deteriorated? I try again. "I wanted to see you, Father, to learn–"

"Learn what, Marcus?" He coughs and dark spots spatter his sleeve. "How long I have left on the path?"

His abruptness bites, and I blurt out, "To learn why you denied me the throne." Flames rush to my cheeks. It's not what I wanted to say, at least not yet. But I can't deny it is what I burn to know.

"Simple." Jacas smacks his lips, becoming more lucid. "You couldn't control your phantom."

He's right, De'ral says.

"Quiet!"

"I can control him now! I returned from Aku a yellow-robe, fully accomplished." But I know it's not entirely true.

"No matter. It's done."

"You can undo it. Petén's not fit to take the phantom throne."

Jacas grabs my sleeve. "But *she* is, Marcus. She is high born. Raises a fine *caller* and is loyal to me."

"Rhiannon?" I can't believe what he's saying. "She's using you." I raise my voice. "Can't you see?"

"Rhiannon will be the pillar if Petén falters. And she is good and kind, Marcus. You cannot reproach her." He winces and wipes his mouth.

Kind? How is she *kind*? Seems more like manipulative. What are my brother and that snake doing?

"It wouldn't have come to this, if my first son had lived," Jacas says.

My guts tighten as I hand the empty cup to Ash.

She squeezes my arm, her comfort running through me. She knows this story, how all my life, I've had to compete with a ghost.

"That was twenty years ago, Father." Back when the Bone Throwers deemed my eldest brother marred and condemned him to the sea. "*I* am here now."

Jacas draws in a deep breath and his bony rib cage expands. "Leave me, Marcus. Send for Rhiannon—" The coughing returns.

"Magistrate?" A healer comes in. "Oh good. You brought fresh water," he says to Ash, not recognizing me as I bend to pick up dirty clothes off the floor.

Ash retrieves the tray. "We are finished, master." She curtsies and then gives me a pointed look, directing me to the door.

Father is still coughing and hacking, his body about to shake apart. The healer goes to his side.

A coldness creeps over me. I may never see him again, but I head for the door, clothes still clutched in my hands. My ears are ringing. There's not a coherent thought in my head, but my feet automatically take me to the hallway, back down the row of frowning portraits and to the stairs.

Ash walks at my side, tray held high. Silent except for her soft bare feet on the carpet and the rattle of the empty cup.

I stare unseeing at the steps as we descend to the first level. Back in the mudroom, I dump the clothes. "He's really dying," I hear myself say. "Those might be his last words to me."

"He's the father your path has given you." Ash's voice is barely a whisper. She comes closer and laces her hand in mine. "What are your last words for him?"

The coldness still sits deep in my bones.

Finally I swallow, and then, through a tight mouth, I exhale quietly to myself. "Peace be your path, Father...but rest certain. Petén will not hold the phantom throne much longer."

3

ASH

Good news! Over the last three days, since Marcus and I had that terrible visit with his father, my headaches are almost gone. And the memory gaps? I think they are fewer, too, but I write things down, just in case. I'm physically stronger, able to study again—combing the library for anything on the prophecy of the next Great Dying. Brogal still hasn't granted me access to the Sanctuary archives, but the general shelves are a start. I can't wait to discuss what I've found with the others.

Which might be tonight. It's midwinter solstice eve, and we'll all be at the feast, along with everyone else in Baiseen. Well, almost everyone. I pull Kaylin's message out of my coat pocket and tuck it into a Sierrak dictionary. I remember where he is, off tracking Tann. I remember he'll return soon, or so he promises. No need to keep the message on my person anymore like I do with other notes and reminders.

I slip in the greenstone earrings Piper loaned me, smiling at the fact that they are the color of his eyes—the ones I'll be looking into again soon. *Oh yes, I am recovering from this forgetfulness more by the minute.* I smooth down my dress and smile at the mirror before going to meet my friends.

Samsen escorts Piper and me, one on each arm, into the great hall. I should say *impromptu* great hall. The actual building fell under Tann's attack, but the pavilion they raised for the midwinter solstice eve celebrations is spectacular. Candle lanterns hang in strings over the expansive dance floor. There's an elevated platform for the musicians, and long tables so laden with food you'd never guess stores were in short supply. People are already dancing. Petén has gone all out and by the bones, he's done a fine job.

I lean across Samsen to get Piper's attention. He looks smart in his black riding pants and high boots, with a pale yellow shirt that matches his hair. There's a dark gold waistcoat with a deep navy doublet over the top. Samsen's outfit is a big improvement on his tattered savant robes, but Piper? She is stop-you-in-your-tracks stunning. Samsen can't pull his eyes from her.

Her curtain of dark braids falls to her shoulders, the ends held tight with fire opal beads. And even though her outfit is not new, she has never looked better in the elegant mandarin orange dress with its high collar, snug fit, and finely embroidered long sleeves.

"Tyche didn't come?" I ask Piper, as I look for the other girl. At twelve years old, Tyche is young for an orange-robe savant. Too young for war, and definitely too young to witness her grandmother–the High Savant of Aku–being murdered. I'm concerned at how withdrawn she is, almost a void at times. It would have been good to see her here.

Piper shakes her head, beads clinking with the motion. "I left her by the hearth with Mistress Dina." Piper turns her attention to the room. "Petén spared no expense," she adds, her tone neutral.

I wish Marcus had the same diplomacy. He's livid about wasting stores and doesn't try to hide it. On one hand, I agree, but as I look at the smiling faces of all gathered, the rich mixing with the poor, savants with non-savants, I can't help but wonder. Was this such a bad idea? I give a shrug. "You look amazing, Piper."

"I'm not the only one." Piper winks at me, then quickly leans into Samsen. "Shall we dance?"

I let go of Samsen's arm and wave them off to the dance floor where a band of wooden drums, pipes, and tambourines play, backed by a harmony of *callers* and their savants. There are even a few black-robes playing whistle bones, which is a rare treat. Most of their cult are sequestered tonight, throwing the bones to determine the best times for planting, fishing, harvest, retribution… all the important events for next year. The music reverberates in my bones, a delight, but I'm not dancing, not yet.

"Ash. Over here!" Belair's clear voice rises over the crowd. He and Marcus hover around one of the tables, piling up their plates. Well, Belair is piling. Marcus stabs at a small piece of meat like it's the enemy.

I wave back, but only Belair responds. Always affable. I guess being a Tangeen diplomat's son means he's especially good at the social niceties. I head their way, inhaling the scents—jugs of steaming apple and cinnamon cider, jars of breadsticks stuck into slow-pressed goat's cheese. It makes my mouth water. Roast game is sliced and drenched in gravy along with tubers, winter greens, whole ocean fish, and braided sourdough in rounds as large as wagon wheels. Dotted everywhere are side dishes of pickled chili peppers and freshly foraged mushrooms, baked apples stuffed with stewed rhubarb and berry tarts. My smile tilts sideways as I stare at the red syrup oozing around the crimp in the crust. The last time I ate berry tarts was on a picnic, in Aku. With Kaylin…

The memory bursts into my mind. We swam in a small bay under the

Sanctuary cliffs, though the water was shivering cold. Him gathering oysters and me panicking, thinking he'd been underwater so long he'd surely drowned. We emerged laughing. Him toweling my face dry, taking my hands and kissing me with moist, salty lips. My whole body softening… I touch my mouth as if his lips had just been there.

"Happy solstice eve!" Belair brings me out of the memory.

"Happy indeed." I hug both Marcus and Belair, receiving kisses on my cheeks in return.

"Where did you get that dress?" Belair's face is full of appreciation.

"Marcus." I curtsey. My gown is high-waisted, long-sleeved, and sweeps to the floor in layers of rich brocade. Warm enough for this winter night; well-fitting and comfortable enough to never stop dancing. If I wanted to dance, that is… I have no idea where he got it on such short notice. Hopefully, not from the back of Rhiannon's closet.

"And you?" I nod at Belair's dark green waistcoat, double-breasted with gold coin buttons and a red ruffle shirt. He's as striking as the red sun leopard phantom he raises.

"Same." He bows to Marcus who is wearing his finely tooled leather waistcoat with black pearl buttons and gold rivets over the cuffs and collar. It matches his dark brown eyes and accentuates his physique, which is tall, perfectly proportioned, and more muscular than ever, since training daily on Aku. Flawless, really. I've never seen him look more the Heir, even though he is that no longer.

"Eat, Ash. You've lost too much weight." Marcus hands me a plate and fork.

"What about you?" I nod at his meager portion.

Belair scoops up a second plate. "You two must excuse me. I'm sharing this with Hahmen." He stands. "We shall dance later, Ash. I promise."

I follow Belair as he weaves his way to a table near the music. "Oh! Who's the new friend?" Handsome is the first word that comes to mind. And the second.

"It's Hahmen." Marcus's brows pinch, like I should know the name.

I shake my head.

"The green-robe from Tangeen? The one Belair hasn't stopped talking about?"

My head feels light as I force a smile. "Of course!"

Of course what, Ash? I ask myself. It's clear I should know about this new friend, but I don't. That is, I don't remember.

Instead of saying so, I change the subject. "Petén really did have it right," I say to Marcus, testing his temper more than anything else. He's not said a word about our visit to his father, even when I pushed him to talk.

"Her idea, the solstice extravagance, I'll wager." He stuffs a tiny forest berry tart into his mouth and tips his head at the main table.

And there she is. Rhiannon. Sitting next to the new Magistrate. She's wearing the most splendid gown I've ever seen. It's as yellow as the sun with crystals decorating the bodice and long sleeves. Her strawberry curls are tied up high with strings of sparkling gems. I want to despise her after all that has happened—all that we suspect—but they say she raised her meerkat *caller* and fought with Brogal's troops, not stopping until the battle was won. Which is more than I did, passed out in the grass. "Whoever's idea it was," I say, "Their plan is working."

Marcus scowls and leads the way to a relatively quiet corner where we can watch the crowd while we eat. A stranger wouldn't be able to tell the difference between the savants and non-savants tonight, seeing as we are all in festival clothes. All except the High Savant. Master Brogal won't attend. He never does unless it's to give a speech and there are none of those tonight. He'd be at his desk, pondering all the revelations I brought back from Aku before the attack. At least, I hope he's pondering them. Oddly, the thought sends shivers across my shoulder blades and makes me flinch.

I try to focus on the delicious food, but my eyes keep straying to the entrance of their own accord. Back on Aku, Kaylin and I talked about where we might be, come midwinter solstice. *I'm here, Kaylin. Where are you?*

"He'll return, sooner or later." Marcus breaks apart a steaming loaf of bread and hands half to me.

I take a delicate bite. "Whoever do you mean?"

Marcus holds out his hand, ignoring my question. "Care to dance?"

"Later, if that's all right."

"Then I'm going to find you a cider." He disappears into the crowd, eager to be on a mission.

I cast my eyes downward, studying my hands. If I was hoping we'd all be discussing the mysteries that started to unfold on the Isle of Aku, bad luck. We've drifted a bit in opposite directions, it seems. I pick at the edge of my finger until every nerve in my body screams for me to look up. I do, and there he is.

"Kaylin!" I call to him, mind-to-mind, like I used to.

Warm waves roll down my back. The entire hall swirls around me, everyone gliding to the music, all except Kaylin. He stands still, his eyes fixed on mine, lips parting as if about to speak, but I don't hear his mental answer.

"Kaylin?" I stand.

He looks exactly as I remember him, dressed in his usual attire, drawstring pants and an open white shirt that reveals his tan chest. His curly dark hair flows around him, double-curved blades strapped to his back. He's straight off the ship, I guess. His dark gray-green eyes are curious as he strides toward me. That incredibly confident walk.

At an arm's length away, he dips his head. "Lass, you look stunning. I..."

His words trail off when Nun, Brogal's ever-present assistant, steps between us. He glares at Kaylin. "What are you doing at the feast?" He sounds uncharacteristically urgent. "The High Savant is waiting for you." Nun turns his back, expecting Kaylin to follow.

And he does, but not before his fingertips gently brush mine and he leans down to whisper, "It's here."

Sparks zing through me at the touch.

"What's here?" I wait for an answer, but still can't hear his voice in my mind.

Nun turns and beckons. "You, too, Ash. Bring the others. Quickly." With that, they both disappear out a side door.

This is not how I imagined our reunion, but I do as Nun asks.

"What's the rush?" Belair says. He's not happy leaving, um, I wrack my mind for the handsome fellow's name, but I already forgot it.

"They're over there." I spot Kaylin's silhouette on the lookout as we head for the Sanctuary. Nun is with him, and a few others. They are all gazing at the sky.

A weight sinks into the pit of my stomach. *It's here...*

"He's back, I see." Marcus leans down as we approach. "We'll have news of Tann's whereabouts, finally."

"I think it's more than that." I lead them up the steps.

"What more?" Samsen asks.

A black-robe Bone Thrower is with them as well. He gazes skyward, the glow of his phantom pulsing around him.

More gather to study the night sky. Suddenly children jump and squeal, pointing overhead. Others *ooh* and *ahh*. We make our way to Kaylin, lifting our faces to the thinning clouds. Dread washes over me as I search the stars overhead.

"There!" someone shouts.

It's hard to see at first, what with gossamer clouds floating past, but when the large star burns through to reveal its glowing red light, I have no doubts. "Rirt'n stars and stuggs," I whisper to myself, my body going numb.

It *is* here.

"A meteor!" someone calls from the crowd.

"Comet!" another counters.

Cheers go up and words like *signs of fortune* and *good omen* rise from the chatter.

My stomach sinks to my feet.

Elders shout praises and children are sent indoors to spread the news. Brogal's face tightens but he doesn't correct them. Soon the music falters and the entire hall pours out to gaze at this haunting red light in the sky, though by now clouds have covered it up again. Still, the lookout is packed tight, everyone shoulder to shoulder, trying to catch a glimpse.

I find myself pressed into Marcus's broad back. I can smell the fine leather of his waistcoat and feel as much as hear his deep growl when everyone calls to make way for Petén and Rhiannon.

"All of you," Master Brogal says, taking in our small group. "My chambers. Now."

We squeeze past the crowd, who continue with their *oohs* and *aahs*. But my mentor's face goes gray. Because he knows different. We all do.

The red star twinkling in the sky is not an omen of joy and prosperity. It's the second sun, herald of the next Great Dying.

And according to prophecy, it marks the beginning of the end of the world.

4

ASH

Brogal's chambers shrink as we all file in. He waves us to the long table where extra chairs are placed, but I hesitate in front of his desk. I've been waiting to sit opposite him and relay all my discoveries found on Aku. He'll want to hear what I learned about the second sun, especially now.

"I wish we had this confirmation sooner, Ash, before our meeting," he says, reeling me back to the moment.

I stare at him, unmoving. "Before?"

He sighs. "Sit-sit." He nudges me toward the table. "There isn't much time."

My fingers tingle as I pull out a chair and take my seat across from Marcus and Belair. Is he saying we already had our meeting? I reach for my pocket of notes and then realize I'm in my festival dress.

"Hello, lovely lass." Kaylin takes the seat next to me. "May I say again how beautiful you are tonight?"

My heart pounds so hard I think it might burst from my chest and all I can manage is, "Hi."

In answer, Kaylin flashes me his brilliant smile and winks, making me want to…I don't know…punch him as hard as I can, or maybe leap out of my chair and wrestle him to the ground. Instead, I call out to him with my mental voice, but again, he doesn't answer.

He holds my gaze, at first expectant and then, I think, confused. Is he calling to me, mind-to-mind as well?

"It's the second sun," I say in a rush, stating the obvious.

"Aye lass, it's here." But he still looks confused.

I catch Marcus staring at us, a hint of his old possessiveness showing through layers of other worries.

A fresh headache starts to build at the back of my skull. I thought I was through with these.

Making it worse, the Bone Thrower pulls out the chair on my other side. The hem of his black robe swirls over the floor when he sits, brushing the edge of my new boots. His presence suddenly makes the high ceiling feel too close, the walls close in. I swallow and try not to stare at his profile. Unsuccessfully. He pushes his cowl back and ropes of dark hair fall to his waist, many wrapped in colored cloth, braided with feathers, shells, and small bones. It's the mark of a black-robe well advanced along the path. He smells dry, like desert sand.

I'm wedged between the black-robe on one side and Kaylin on the other. This would be the perfect time for my inner voice to pipe up, pointing out things I might otherwise miss, coaching me as to what to say. I haven't been able to hear it of late, either. *"Where are you?"*

There's no answer from within. Nor is there one from Kaylin when I bombard him with my thoughts. We used to be able to speak freely to each other, mind-to-mind. What's happened now that we can't? I sneak another glance at him, but he's turned away, talking to Piper. She has no problem chatting to him. We're all friends here. What's wrong with me?

Panic rises and my heart pounds.

I take some deep breaths to settle myself.

When Master Brogal steps to the head of the table, a chill trickles down my back. It steals my breath. For a moment, the room tilts and I imagine him close in my face, shouting, forcing me to drink from a cup. He chants harsh words that make my skin crawl. I gasp more than once before I have my breathing under control. And then I notice Kaylin staring at me. Piper, too.

"I'm fine," I whisper, though neither asked, at least, not that I heard.

Brogal's my guardian. Has been for ten years. He's reserved, sure, but still my mentor. He would never harm me. I don't know what would make me feel otherwise.

At the head of the table, he unrolls a map. "First up." He taps the coastline northwest of Baiseen. "Tann's fleet is here, beached for repairs." He looks at Kaylin. "Thank you for your assistance." He bows slightly and goes on. "And, as you warned us Marcus, it seems Tann's goal *is* to gather the original twelve whistle bones from their guardian sanctuaries, by force or persuasion, in hopes of reforming the crown. Fortunately, he did not get Baiseen's."

The room goes still.

It's about time someone believes us. But I want to point out it was Tyche who revealed Tann's intention when we first returned from Aku. I wish she were here. She belongs at this meeting. Especially now.

As if my thoughts conjured her from thin air, Tyche appears at the doorway. Her long black hair is in a single braid, her quilted orange robe freshly cleaned. She doesn't smile, exactly, but her eyes do shine as she comes purposefully into the room and takes a seat beside Piper.

Brogal nods to her, and then continues. "Further, if any of you had doubts, the red 'star' pulsing overhead is neither comet nor meteor but nothing other than Amassia's second sun."

"Herald of the next Great Dying," Kaylin and I whisper at the same time. He catches my eye, and the stone in the hollow of my stomach turns into butterflies.

"True." The black-robe speaks. "We have reached the end of another great cycle, as foretold."

We stir, murmuring to each other before Brogal calls for silence. I close my mouth and listen.

Master Brogal talks about the urgency of the moment, choices to make, but it's hard to follow as the black-robe's phantom wafts toward me. Black-robes don't raise phantoms from the earth to take solid form like other savants do. Theirs are more curtains of light, just under or over their skin. This one shimmers in smoky wisps of tangerine and yellow, forming a face that dissolves into a finger that points at…me.

I blink but can't look away.

The Bone Thrower notices. He clicks his tongue and the ethereal phantom snaps back to his side. "We will consult the bones for the next step along the path," he says to Master Brogal.

I've never been this close to a whistle bone reading, not that I remember. Of course the black-robes visit all children of Amassia soon after birth to throw the bones and deem if they have the potential to be savant. If not, they are classed as non-savant, like me, which is common enough. Then there are the rare few found *marred*—that is a terrible fate, for certain. Our realm only recently banned the child sacrifices. Other realms have not.

According to Brogal, the Bone Thrower saw potential in me, but turns out it wasn't enough. Try as I did, I never raised a phantom. I don't remember my early childhood, or my parents disappearing, or even Brogal adopting me. It's all a blank page until I began my wordsmith apprenticeship at age ten. Trauma, I guess. What else would explain it? My shoulders tighten at the thought. I wonder what explains it now, my not always remembering things?

"This will be telling," Kaylin says softly in my ear.

"Indeed," I say, trying to stay poised. His proximity chac'n unravels me, but he's right. The throw of the bones will help reveal what to prepare for next. Hopefully it will show the steps along the path each of us must take. But there is more I would like to know, things that came up in my studies over the last few days that I can't find answers to. I need a meeting with Brogal. I also want to ask Kaylin a thing or two, but this is hardly the time. The reading is underway.

The black-robe lays out a worn hide and rubs his tattooed hands together. He opens his bag of bones and plunges his fingers in deep, chanting to himself. His voice is rumbling and makes the back of my neck itch. In moments, he has a handful of whistle bones in his grasp.

"That's a lot of bones," I whisper to Marcus. He needs to pay attention to this. "One for each of the original sanctuaries?"

Kaylin counts heads. "Aye, lass. And maybe one for each of us, too."

Before I can respond, the High Savant stands and directs a question to the Bone Thrower. "What is the best course of action to take, now that the second sun is visible in the sky?" He nods and the black-robe releases the bones.

They bounce and skip over the hide until stopping in a jumbled pattern. The Bone Thrower stares at the spread for a long moment, then finally speaks. "It is seen." He falters a moment, reaching out to steady himself. It's the price of divination, life force taken for the ability to *see*. "The twelve original whistle bones must be gathered and kept in our hands if there is any hope of protecting the allied realms." His eyes fall on Marcus.

"Gathered?" Marcus says. "You mean *taken* from Tann? The ones he has in that sealed and guarded chest?"

"Those, yes, and the remaining ones from the sanctuaries that still harbor them." The Bone Thrower sinks back into his seat. One of his gnarled fingers traces an invisible line across the cloth. "And they must be gathered by you, Marcus."

"Me? How in the green lands and blue skies does this fall on me?"

The Bone Thrower's eyes are sharp as swords when they cut to Marcus. "*You* are the initiate who passed Mossman's Shoals on your journey to Aku, are you not?"

"We were run off course by soldiers and forced into the river." Marcus's throat bobs as he swallows hard. "We barely survived the Falls. It was the only way."

The Bone Thrower nods. "The how or why does not make the way less true."

"Marcus?" I clear my throat, trying to get his attention. The Bone Thrower certainly isn't explaining it very well. I nod to the whistle bone pointing off the edge of the hide, the one leading the others. I don't know how I can read the meaning, but my heart skips a beat when I know in my soul that I do. "Marcus, it was always meant to be you." I gasp as the full meaning dawns. "You *are* the initiate of the prophecy."

Before any of us say another thing, the High Savant lifts both arms and cheers, "Hail Marcus Adicio, hereafter to be known as the Bone Gatherer!"

5

MARCUS

As Heir, I was trained to be ready for anything: attack, flood, famine, corruption, pandemic, earthquake, tidal wave. Anything but this. "Hereafter known as the *what*?" I push back my chair and stand.

"You, Bone Gatherer, must set out before first light," the black-robe continues as if he didn't hear me.

"Before first light?" I'm shouting now. "Absolutely not! The city comes first. I won't abandon Baiseen!"

The black-robe's face softens for a moment. "So goes the path, Marcus." But then he hardens. "We've come to a point unexpected, and everyone must do their part."

"What unexpected point are you talking about?" I pinch the bridge of my nose. I can't have heard right.

I'd be more concerned about that part they want us to play, De'ral says.

I can't fathom what that might be. My legs weaken and I sit back down.

"How can we make it any plainer, Marcus? The ancient prophecy is fulfilled by you. The path is set by the return of the second sun."

"We never realized it meant—" Ash tries to speak again, but this time she's interrupted by the Bone Thrower.

"There's more," he says, still studying the spread. "We'll witness changes in the land that precede the next Great Dying. Drought, floods, rising seas. That's already happening. But the crucial thing is this..." He indicates the bone covered hide as if it makes perfect sense. "The warrior bone points straight to you, Marcus. The prophecy is fulfilled...*in* you."

"I can't see it."

I can. De'ral doesn't seem upset at all. If anything, he's excited.

I study the spread, trying to understand. There, alone, is a single bone shaped like a spear. It points northwest. I guess that's at me. Seven of the other whistle bones follow in its wake. One is a little farther behind than the others.

"You *are* the Bone Gatherer as foretold, Marcus, rising with the second sun to gather the bones and protect the realms from the next Great Dying."

Goose bumps prickle my arms as it sinks in. I lean toward Ash and Kaylin. "You both could have made a stronger case for your discoveries, back on Aku." Sure, they had explained their beliefs about the second sun with its wildly eccentric orbit, and how, according to ancient lore, its return would herald the end of all life as we know it.

They had even spoken of a crown of bones made up of the original whistle bones, the first ones ever carved. Twelve of them, I think, made from some unfortunate Sierrak King. There was a war, or disaster, and the crown was dismantled, the bones spread far and wide, but the prophecy says they will be gathered to form the crown once again, when the second sun reappears.

So you do recall?

"I thought it was some future event, happening eons after our own bones are dust."

I turn to Brogal. "You are saying that I'm to travel the realms convincing the foreign sanctuaries to give up their first whistle bones? And battle Tann, who leads an army the size of a small realm, for the ones he holds? Speaking of, how many, exactly, does he have now? I assume we need all twelve?" Brogal really is losing his mind.

"We don't know his count, but yes. As I've told you already, all twelve must be gathered," Brogal says. "To rebuild the crown."

"What about the Mar?" Ash speaks up. The shine in her eyes tells me she's more than a little intrigued.

He doesn't answer so I repeat her question louder.

Master Brogal barks out a laugh. "This is no time for children's stories, Marcus. The last known Mar disappeared from Amassia long ago." He glares at Ash. "I explained this yesterday."

Ash's face flushes pink.

I'm not sure what meeting Brogal's talking about, but the half smile on Kaylin's lips and De'ral chuckling in my head are welcome. I'm going to enjoy having one up on the High Savant, just this once.

"About the Mar," I say, keeping my voice even. "The operant word there is last *known* Mar."

Brogal's white eyebrows form a peak. "Go on."

"Ash is right. They still exist."

"That's preposterous." The High Savant scoffs. "What in the name of Er makes you think so?"

"I've met one."

Salila. De'ral's voice turns smoky.

"She saved my life. More than once," I add. It should have been in Ash's report, but the bound journal was lost to the sea, and it seems Brogal didn't believe her recitation.

I think he might believe her now. De'ral chuckles.

Brogal looks like stampeding horses are galloping straight for him. "You were tricked. Misled."

"I don't doubt Salila could both trick and mislead us, but, by the bones, she is Mar." Samsen comes to our aid.

"She guided us across the channel from Aku," Piper chimes in, "calling up an uncanny fog so we could escape Tann's fleet."

"She saved us again off the coast of Gleemarie when our ship went aground," Belair adds.

"You didn't think to explain this clearer in our meetings?" He directs his anger at Ash. "I thought you were relaying folktales."

Ash opens her mouth, but no words come out. The hurt is plain on her face.

"This is no folktale." I look to Kaylin. "Our sailor knows more, so you might ask him, though I can report that the Mar are a cantankerous race. Decidedly dangerous, yet intriguing." I try not to think of Salila's naked body when she first leaped out of the sea onto the deck of our stolen ship.

I can feel De'ral smiling inside me.

"You know more?" Brogal asks Kaylin.

He gives an off-handed shrug. "Aye, maybe. Though I'm guessing the last thing Mar care about are the landers' whistle bones."

"Landers?" Brogal says.

"Their word for us."

"And you think they don't care about the second sun? The next Great Dying?"

"I'm not sure it affects them."

I will ask Salila, De'ral says. *She will help.*

"*Don't be ridiculous. You can't commune with a Mar. Not without me knowing.*"

Can't I?

I ignore him though my spine burns. "Mar aside, is this all the guidance you have? Gather the original whistle bones from the remaining sanctuaries? Which ones? I have no idea. And what then?"

"I wrote the entire reading out for you." The Bone Thrower waves parchment back and forth, drying the ink before he hands it over. "To aid you in your quest."

How welcoming. De'ral snickers. *More vague and clouded instruction from a black-robe. Just what we need.*

My head spins. It's all happening too fast. "But my throne—"

Brogal meets my gaze, his eyes burning with an intense fire. "Leave Baiseen and the realm to others, but know, if Tann gathers the whistle bones first and rebuilds the crown, he will not use it to protect us."

The thought of Tann enslaving our *callers* and destroying our lands, our people, turns my stomach sour.

"Choose your company wisely, Marcus, and walk the path." He signals Nun, who nods and leaves the room.

Choose my company? The walls seem to close in around me, but Piper is quick to my side, shifting my attention. "Think about it, Marcus. Maybe you were *meant* to lose the throne—"

"What?" I won't believe that.

"—in order to free you for this greater purpose."

It's a lot to take in.

The idea of a *greater purpose* grows in my mind like a giant, uncoiling serpent. It tries to warp around me, choking the breath from my lungs. Then De'ral appears. He pins it to the ground, crushing it until the light goes out of its eyes and its bones crumble, all but twelve, which I hold in my hand.

When the vision fades, I feel gut-punched. Still, I say, "If the task truly falls on me, I'll go. I'll face Tann and protect the allied realms, but this is no initiation journey to Aku and back." I square my shoulders. "The path is mine and my phantom's alone." I'm careful to avoid everyone's eyes. "I will not risk the lives of anyone else."

The air becomes thick as my words settle over the quiet room. Brogal's eyebrow twitches, but he nods with what I hope is respect. My companions are stunned until Kaylin's voice rises, speaking before anyone else.

"I will be your guide again, Marcus." He stands and gives me a bow. "If you'll have me." His last words soften as his eyes shift to Ash. "Otherwise, I will dog your every step, as I daresay the others will, too. This is not your path alone." He nods to the bones in the wake of the warrior arrow.

"Hear, hear!" Everyone jumps to their feet. Piper, Samsen, Tyche, Belair, and Ash. Oh gods. Ash.

She comes around the table and squeezes my hand. "You'll need a recorder by your side, and a translator. I'm surely the only one who can put up with you."

"You'll need a healer, too," Piper adds. "No telling when you'll get another knife to the chest or stumble off a cliff." She reaches her hand out to Samsen and he puts his arm over her shoulders.

"And a guard," he says.

Belair salutes me and pledges himself as well.

"And a *caller* that will not fail," Tyche adds, sounding more like her confident self.

As they gather around me, a deeper voice cuts through.

"I'm coming, Marcus." A member of the honor guard crosses the threshold of the chambers, followed by Nun. He wears the tall captain's helmet and salutes me.

"Rowten!" I call out.

"Captain!" the others chorus.

Everyone greets him cheerfully, including Belair, though I can tell Kaylin is on guard. Tyche hangs back, too. "This is Captain Rowten," I explain. "He's an orange-robe who leads the Magistrate's Royal Honor Guard."

Rowten wears black leather armor and an orange cape, clearly coming straight from patrol. His phantom—a lynx with sooty ear tufts, bob tail, and long fangs—bow stretches toward me, then goes straight to Ash.

She holds perfectly still.

Kaylin leans my way. "You know each other?"

"All our lives," I answer. "He's Baiseen's most renowned hero."

Rowten ruffs his phantom's head and chuckles. "Leave the lovely Miss Ash be." He pulls off his helmet, revealing close-cropped brown hair and an equally short beard. "Hail Marcus and company of the Bone Gatherer." His voice is official. "I trust you have room for one more."

Heat stings the backs of my eyes. I don't think any of them realize what they are committing to, aligning with me. Not sure I do myself. But deep in my heart I am grateful for it. Only one thing bothers me. "Master Brogal?"

He looks up, brows lifted.

"Now that the second sun is visible, won't savants outside the allied realms be seeking the twelve originals, too? I mean, as well as Tann?"

"Oh yes, Marcus." His face darkens. "That is why you must leave at once, otherwise we are doomed."

I rake my hand through my hair, trying to understand.

"It's simple. Whoever holds the crown, holds the future of all the realms in their hands."

6

ASH

My horse is anxious, poor thing. I can't seem to calm her. She snorts and tugs at the reins, pulling them through my frozen fingers as we thunder along. *"Settle. Settle."* I'm talking to both of us as we race away from Baiseen as if our tails are on fire. According to Master Brogal, they are.

I look over my shoulder at the city lights, tears blurring them into streams against the night sky. The dak'n deep, empty feeling that stabs at my chest is still with me. I keep telling everyone I'm fine, but the truth is I'm missing something. More than Kaylin, who has returned, though the old gods know I miss his voice in my head. Not my inner voice with its gems of wisdom and sharp quips, though that I miss, too. It's like I've forgotten something precious, a treasure left behind with my old books and outgrown boots. A presence so familiar, I can hardly breathe with it gone…but I don't know what it is!

My mind is …*fractured*. That's the only way to describe it. Like a vase dropped and some pieces hold their shape and others are shards, sharp and small and requiring glue. Some memories are intact, and others…gone.

I hate that part of my past is missing.

I hate that I can recall six languages and easily twice as many dialects, but I can't recall what happened amid the battle. Or the details of my day yesterday. I hate that I remember Kaylin's voice in my head, the deep lilt and cadence of it, but I can't hear it now, so I doubt myself that I ever did.

My inner voice, if it were audible, would say, *true, true, but there's much more to think about now.*

No argument there. Master Brogal finally gave me access to the information I've been asking for. A year's worth of reading in the form of books and manuscripts. I only had time to scan the titles as I carefully packed them to take on the journey. I can't wait to dive in, but really, what took him so long? I press my fingers to my temple. I guess I haven't been all that well. Still, equally exciting but somewhat daunting is the bronze medallion that hangs around my neck. It's not a parting gift from Master Brogal. I would never mistake it as that. It's a communication tool, imbided with amplifying powers.

Imagine it! Me, a non-savant recorder, wearing a device forged in the mines of ancient Sierrak. The purpose is to heighten thoughts, pushing them along the ethers between two or more receiving medallions so the wearers can communicate over great distances.

It's an uncomfortable idea, Master Brogal and I conversing mind-to-mind. It's hard enough talking to him aloud. But, as our brief trial not an hour ago proved, it's different from the mind speech I am used to. That I *was* used to. Different from Kaylin's sweet missives, my dry inner voice, even De'ral's pictorial images.

I look at Kaylin riding beside me and feel the comfort of his nearness, the anticipation of our next shared moment. I'm grateful for his return. So grateful. *"Kaylin?"*

From his mind, there is no answer. Not a mental peep. It pinches my heart so much I have to look away.

When Marcus brings us down to a walk, Kaylin reins his mount close to mine.

In front of us, Marcus and Rowten converse without any reserve.

"Bless the path." Rowten lifts his chin, turning to say to us all. "But you'll have to educate me as to what that path is exactly. There was no time."

"It's simple," I speak up, as is my role as recorder. "We ride with all urgency to the Bone Thrower's cave to collect Baiseen's first whistle bone. Then, we sail to Nonnova in hopes of collecting theirs. Beyond that—"

"Save the details for later." Marcus glances to the east. "Dawn's coming. Let's not keep the ship waiting."

"You've secured a vessel?" Rowten asks.

"Kaylin has," I say. "We're meeting Captain Anders of the *Dugong* at sunrise, at the mouth of the Suni River."

Rowten salutes and we continue at a trot.

Kaylin keeps his mount shoulder to shoulder with mine and leans toward me, his voice lowered.

"So, Rowten?" he asks. "Anything I should know?"

"Pardon?" I wrinkle my nose.

"His phantom's fascinated with you, for one."

"Oh, that happens. Remember—" Meaning dawns and I laugh the notion away. "It's just I…everyone really…loves him." That didn't come out right. I take a breath and start over. "His younger sister Lilian befriended me, long before he became captain of the Guard. I spent time in his family home." I study Kaylin's thoughtful expression. "He's an asset to the group, I promise. And that is all."

Kaylin gives a nod after a few moments of silence. "Good he has joined us then." The words are cheery, but his brow remains pinched. I wonder if he's testing our mental communication in these long pauses, like I have been. A test that is failing terribly. What is wrong with us?

We ease to a walk as the road turns steep. "The Bone Thrower's cave isn't far." I have to say something, and none of my questions seem right for the moment.

"Cave?" Kaylin asks.

"It is, but not the way you might think." *You'll see,* I add but again, there's no sign he hears me.

The trees become sparse, the grass thinning as the grade turns steep. "There they are!" I lift my voice and point. The pillars that mark the entrance to the Bone Thrower's cave stand out stark against the cliff face. They are only reached by a sheer, single file track. It reduces the possibility of a surprise attack of any force. We dismount and form a long, snaking line as we climb toward the stronghold.

Thousands of years ago, the ocean lapped at the foot of the pillars, hugging the contours of the mountainside. Not anymore. The water receded over eons, sucked up into Amassia's frozen poles. It left oddities, like these stairs that begin halfway up the cliff face at a rocky shelf, the remnants of a stone pier now miles from the shore. Farther along the cliff wall, side doors open outward and are lit from the inside, but they are impossible to reach save by an eagle. I count myself lucky to see any of it.

The general population, non-savants that is, are not usually allowed entrance into the Bone Throwers' domain. I am the rare exception. Well, me and Nun, Brogal's trusted assistant. But that is only by the direct request of the High Savant himself. Even the Bone Throwers must defer to Master Brogal, the reigning red-robe of Baiseen. But otherwise, this is *their* sanctuary where they keep the records of the realm, train their initiates, carve the whistle bones and, of course, throw the bones.

"Halt," Rowten and Marcus say at the same time. They frown at each other, both accustomed to giving orders.

This will be interesting. As I think it, a shadow falls over me.

"What is it, lass?" Kaylin whispers.

Quick as lightning, the feeling is gone. I shake my head. How can I explain a premonition when there is no evidence in sight? "Probably nothing."

He raises his brow, but I don't know what else to say.

Two black-robes, a man and a woman, greet us at the gate. I can tell by their expressions we are expected.

Well, they are Bone Throwers after all. They should see things coming.

We tie our horses at the watering trough and follow the black-robes up the final steps. The walkway to the upper level is lined with clay pots, each with a dwarf citrus tree. They have such a beautiful fragrance in spring, and are grafted with every known citrus—lemon, lime, orange, mandarin. But now they are bare and thorny. We reach the top of the steps where the tall pillars stand. They mark the wide entrance into the cave. More like a marble palace, spacious and dry. The walls are covered with tapestries, floors with plush rugs. No hint of dirt or roots.

"Stay here, please," the black-robe guard says to Marcus. "We will retrieve the Ancient Shearwater for you."

A shiver straightens my back. The Ancient Shearwater! I don't need Brogal's books to tell me what it looks like. Carved from a shoulder blade and etched with seabirds in flight, it represents the third lot or path to An'awntia, Awareness of Mind. It was given to the Sanctuary of Baiseen to watch over and has been hanging in our meeting hall for generations, until Tann's attack that is. Then they sent it straight here for the Bone Throwers to guard.

"Wait here?" Kaylin asks.

I nod. "There's no ceremony required in this instance. Brogal informed them and sent our Bone Thrower to see to the transfer of guardianship." Was it only a few hours ago we were all sitting in his chambers?

We mill about the high-ceilinged foyer, warming hands on the open braziers and studying the wall hangings. The scenes on them vary, but all include the sea in deep greens and black, sometimes calm, sometimes wild and stormy. I recognize Baiseen on the nearest one, and the waters between here and Nonnova, our next destination. I walk on, my eyes unable to pull away from the tapestries. When I come to one with a volcanic eruption, I stop.

There, on an island in the Nonnova chain, is a horrendous scene. A mountain explodes. Molten lava flows like fire down to the roiling sea, consuming everything in its path. A magnificent coastal Sanctuary is buried alive. Savants flee, their faces twisted into frozen screams. I swallow a bitter taste in my mouth and reach out to touch the painting, my fingers brushing lightly across the mass devastation. "When did this happen?" I have no recollection of such an eruption in our histories.

"Not that long ago, child."

I jump and look around. There's no one near me.

"This way, and hurry."

I find the direction of the voice just as a figure disappears down a hallway. White-robe? There is only one I've ever met, the fabled white-robe of the Aku Sanctuary, but it couldn't be her, could it? "Talus?"

I turn a corner and see her clear as day.

"Finally," Talus says as I meet her face-to-face. She's obviously been traveling. The hem of her white robe is muddy and torn. But her pale gray hair is neatly braided and her handsome brown face is serene as ever. She smiles a familiar, motherly smile, and no matter how shocked I am to see her here, only weeks since the attack on Aku, I feel compelled to smile back. "It's really you?" I drop to one knee before rising. "How—"

"No time for that. Listen to me, child. They'll return soon."

"With Baiseen's first whistle bone, yes and then we—"

"No, it's not. But that doesn't matter yet."

"What?"

"Baiseen's whistle bone. You mustn't be fooled. It will appear later, though, so don't worry."

"Um…" I'm too confused to worry. "Talus, can you slow down?"

"The next one you seek isn't where you think it is. Use your instincts, girl. You had it right when studying the mural. Do you remember the name of the island?"

"The one destroyed?"

"Bakton, Ash. Remember that. It will call to you."

I'm pretty sure the Island of Bakton doesn't have a voice, and if it did, it wouldn't direct it at me. I shake my head.

"Instincts, Ash. Use them. Go where they lead, and know that I will guide you whenever I can."

"Ash?" Kaylin calls. "We're leaving." His footsteps pad down the hallway after me.

I put my hand out to stop him but when I turn back to Talus, she is gone.

"Who were you talking to?"

"You didn't see?" I look up and down the hall but it's empty, as if she'd never been there.

7

PETÉN

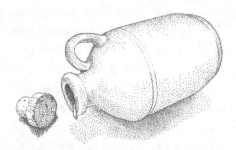

I pull on my high collar, starved for air. When did it start feeling like a noose around my neck? One minute I'm hot, the next shivering... I can barely follow Brogal, his face flickering behind the candlelight. Next Great Dying? First whistle bones? It's incomprehensible nonsense at the best of times. And I am not at my best before breakfast, let alone before the roosters crow, especially with this head cold. I haven't been sick in years. Who could I have caught it from?

I try to pick up the thread of conversation, but the entire war council is crammed into the map room, and I can hardly breathe. One thing is clear. Rhiannon thinks it's rubbish—this Great Dying business. I see the annoyance in her eyes. I should recognize it. She's been giving me the same look for days. Ever since we announced our engagement. Which doesn't bode well.

I must take charge of this room before she loses faith in me altogether.

"Let's drop the ancient lore for a moment and focus on our immediate danger, shall we?" Rhiannon takes the words right out of my head.

Brogal's jaw tightens, but he doesn't protest. How can he? She's my wife-to-be, savant, and taking an active role in overseeing the realm. Too active, I'm beginning to think.

"One more sweep will do it." U'karn, leader of the war council repeats his earlier report. "We'll have the last of those Aturnians lurking on the borders dead and buried."

"We must ride through the city again and remind the people who their new Magistrate is." I stifle a groan. Horseback is not going to be comfortable, the way I'm feeling. I cough into a napkin, and wipe sweat from my brow.

"That is perhaps best done tomorrow, when we've heard back from the scouts." U'karn saves me.

"If you insist." I speak before Rhiannon can argue for sooner. "Meanwhile, we should chase down Tann's ships. Keep track of his whereabouts."

"I agree with the sentiment, but what do you propose we chase him down with?" Rhiannon shoots piercing eyes to Master Brogal, the one who insisted a strong navy would never be necessary, what with his army of *phantoms*. "Shall we net them with our fishing trollers?"

"The criticism isn't helping, butterfly," I say to her under my breath. To the others, "Tann's attack came without warning and that's our hard lesson here."

Brogal clears his throat. "Marcus warned us," he says into the silence.

We're all thinking it, of course. "About him…"

Rhiannon touches my sleeve. "Not yet," she whispers. To the others she says, "Those watchtower guards who failed us should be hanged, not to mention the Bone Throwers who had no warning of their own."

The room gasps.

"Dear, let's take stock before we start killing our own, shall we?" I say back.

The woman is ruthless beyond my wildest dreams.

And stunning.

My bride-to-be dresses not in her usual court finery but in her savant robes—yellow quilted pants and robe with a dark fur-lined cape over it all. Her strawberry hair is still in ringlets, but they are bound in a ponytail at the back of her head. The savants' attire suits her. Everything does, and even better, nothing at all but her ice-blue eyes.

Rhiannon raises a *caller* phantom, a furball with teeth. Unlike me, who raises nothing. She's reminded me of that more than once lately. Every phantom and their savants have been put to work to restore Baiseen, hers no exception. And the snappy creature is up, I notice. It's an unusual ability, keeping it raised throughout the day, at least for a savant of her intermediate level. Most of her rank are exhausted in a few hours, their phantoms sent to ground, but Rhiannon has energy to burn and keeps hers at the ready from dawn to dusk. To protect me, she says. More likely I need protection from it, the way it growls, following my every move with its eyes.

She calls it her *lovely*; I call it a pest—a large meerkat with tawny fur and black tipped ears, feet, and tail—always underfoot, though I have seen its value firsthand. Still, the thing makes me want to down a jug of wine, which I won't do, not with my promise to Rhiannon. All phantoms have this effect on me, but hers is predatory. I guess that's no surprise, given her own appetites.

"The primary directive henceforth must be a powerful, indomitable army and navy." I take advantage of a lull in the discussion. "We have the people and resources to do it."

U'karn runs his hands through his thick dark hair. The leather of his armor plates squeaks with the movement. "I agree we must design better defenses for our city, and all of Palrio. There are also some environmental issues to consider. The floods. The odd migration patterns."

"Signs of the next Great Dying," Brogal puts in.

I'm about to say more about that but am hit with a spasm of coughing. It's the worst time to be sick. I should be firming my position as Magistrate, but instead Rhiannon must take over for me again.

"Sweetheart, let me get you more tonic." She snatches up my empty cup before I can pull it away.

"A servant can do it." I don't need them to see her doting on me.

She pats my hand and stands, the entire table getting up with her. "Let me, Magistrate. It'll only take a moment." Rhiannon turns to the others. "Gentlemen and women of the council, I'll return shortly. Meanwhile, have we considered the possibility of a large threat from the west? Marcus's report about Gollnar seems exaggerated, but…"

"Scouts report no more signs of Gollnar troops." U'karn shrugs.

"To be safe," Rhiannon says while I continue to cough, "we should have them sweep the northwestern borders again."

"See to it," I manage, but U'karn is already sending a runner.

Rhiannon gives a quick lift of my empty medicinal cup and leaves the room. I feel a strange relief with her gone.

The council members return to their seats. They have no problems taking direction from her. To be honest, I'm relieved she's on our side. She'd make a formidable enemy.

"The report of a thousand Gollnar troops is ludicrous," U'karn's aide says.

This is my moment. "You agree my brother is delusional?"

"Delusional?" He shakes his head. "I didn't mean that."

"I think your brother returned under a great strain, what with the attack on Aku and riding nonstop through Aturnia," U'karn answers for his aide. He folds his calloused hands in front of him. "But he did warn us of attack and fought for Baiseen. He and his companions won back Flat Tail Beach against all odds. These are not acts of a delusional savant. He's been overseeing the repairs of the city ever since."

"True, to a point. And this task of Bone Gatherer?" I direct the question to Brogal. "He is fit for it?" Any regret I might have felt when Father abdicated the throne to me vanished the moment Marcus returned. He was supposed to be dead! There had been no word of his arrival on Aku. Of course, there couldn't have been since the messages were intercepted, ships sunk, the Isle attacked. But how were we to know? On our end, there was no news for many months, and the Bone Throwers couldn't *see* him. *Lost in a fog,* were their exact words.

We presumed him dead.

My relationship with my brother had been tumultuous at best. But in those days when I'd finally accepted him gone, I'd *mourned* him.

And when he did return, instead of thanking me for taking over on his behalf, he lost his temper and raised his giant phantom right up through the palace floor, threatening us all. Crazed, he was, and is still, if you ask me. Point him at an enemy, maybe, but put him on the throne? I think not.

"The Bone Throwers approved Marcus as the Bone Gatherer of Baiseen," Brogal says.

He doesn't exactly answer my question though. And those Bone Throwers? They will be the first thing to go with my new reign. Brogal, the old bastard, will be next.

Rhiannon returns with my drink. I take a sip and it burns the taste buds right off my tongue.

"Hot," she warns me too late.

It's actually a blessing. Now I can't taste the revolting brew.

Master Brogal nods out into the hallway where a messenger hovers, trying to catch his breath.

"What word," U'karn asks as he waves them into the room.

"A red-robe is at the west gate, bearing a white flag. He says he will only speak to Rhiannon."

"Pardon?" at least three of us say at once, Master Brogal included.

"Oh, that's Atikis." Rhiannon waves it off before the room erupts in protest.

"Atikis rides?" Brogal is on his feet.

"Don't worry. It's nothing dramatic, I am sure. We met on the way to Aku. You remember? It's in my records."

"What could he want?" I ask. *With you?* This wasn't part of the plan, at least not the one she shared with me.

"He's probably here with news of Tann's movements and is uncertain of the leadership, what with rumors flying about."

Rumors of Father's illness, or Marcus's return?

"He's Gollnarian," the Bone Thrower says in a dry voice. "Maybe he leads troops to our doorstep, despite the white flag."

"Nonsense. He's a mentor to me," Rhiannon replies. "We've kept in touch. Besides, he owes allegiance to no Sanctuary. Certainly, he has no army."

If this is the same red-robe Atikis discussed by the council last year, his phantom *is* an army, and he's likely rogue. "But…"

She holds me in her gaze, and I don't let my eyes flit away, though I want to.

"He may have vital information. I'll go now—"

"Not alone," I insist before she's out the door.

"I'll take the entire palace guard, husband-to-be, if that pleases you." She heads for the door, not waiting for Brogal's or U'karn's approval. Or mine. The husband-to-be and the Magistrate... As she walks past me, she stops to feign a kiss and whispers, "I'll deal with this; you take care of Marcus."

My head throbs and I drain the warm, sticky liquid to the bottom of the cup. Take care of Marcus. That I can do.

"Don't worry, Magistrate. Rowten's men will escort her."

"I am sure she'll be protected, but the situation with my brother does worry me."

No one speaks for a moment. "A contested throne is not what we want right now..." U'karn lets his voice trail off.

"Contested? I am the Magistrate, decreed by my father. There's no contest."

"As you say, Magistrate," U'karn agrees with me. "But there could be talk of reinstating Marcus, especially if he returns with the twelve whistle bones. He's savant, after all, and his *warrior* has won some respect. *They* may want him back."

"It would destabilize the realm, and I won't let that happen."

Brogal doesn't dare contradict me, but I see turmoil behind his eyes. Or maybe that's his phantom peering out of them. I shrink back.

The High Savant steeples his hands. "Marcus has a greater task ahead than ruling Baiseen. Must I remind you all that the second sun has returned? We are on the brink of the next Great Dying."

I want to argue that, but the black-robe is sitting right there, red and gold wisps of her phantom floating about her shoulders, so I hold back. Everything in good time...

"Where is Marcus now?" I ask.

"Collecting the Baiseen whistle bone, hopefully the first of many."

"I want to be kept updated of his progress." There's hope yet that this will be easy.

Master Brogal bows to me and gives U'karn and the rest of the room a nod. "I will see for myself what Atikis wants."

He's up to something, that much is obvious.

I excuse myself and duck out after him. "Master Brogal, you aren't thinking to support Marcus's reinstatement when he returns, are you?"

He looks me up and down, no doubt reminding himself of my non-savant status. "Ultimately, the throw of the bones must decide."

"Really?" I narrow my eyes.

Brogal goes still, and I feel his anger build. "Do not presume to command me, Magistrate, in matters of the Sanctuary. You have no idea of the magnitude of the situation."

I stay calm. "Perhaps. But think that through." I pull down my cuffs and straighten my waistcoat. "And while you're at it, think how long you will remain red-robe without my support. Are you willing to risk so much to go against me, and my father?"

He doesn't answer, though his tightened face says enough without words.

I lean in. "Side with me on this, because if you don't, I will cut off the Sanctuary and any modicum of power you have left to control it."

Master Brogal hesitates, then finally gives a curt bow and hurries away.

I mop my brow. This solves the problem of my brother, Marcus Adicio, and his claim to the throne of Baiseen.

Rhiannon will be so pleased.

8

MARCUS

Baiseen shrinks behind us as we gallop away. Into the dark unknown.

Dramatic, De'ral says.

I groan. Phantoms are meant to sleep, resting until needed, but this one never does, not completely. *"We're leaving Baiseen without so much as a salute. I have to mark the moment somehow, even if it's only in my head."*

Anyway, it's true. The road is dark. The moon wanes. The second sun has set. At least, I assume it has because I can't find it.

I cast one last glance at my city. Over the bay, fireworks pop, marking the midwinter solstice. It's eerie, how they burst across the night sky in silence, the booms reaching us a second later. I can't hear the cheers, but I can imagine them. How many years did Petén and I sneak onto the roof of the highest turret to watch? I clamp my jaw tight. Another in the long list of things I will never do again. Not with my usurping brother.

I force myself to turn away. Look ahead, not behind.

This is me now, the Bone Gatherer, racing against Tann and the second sun.

Herald of the next Great Dying, De'ral adds.

"Do you even know what that means?" Because I don't.

De'ral paces in the depths of my mind. Brooding. He still wants to stomp Petén into an early grave. To be fair, I do too. What will happen to the realm with him in command? And my father? I know in my heart I'll never see him again.

I call a halt at the crossroads, waiting for Belair who brings up the rear.

"What exactly did the Bone Thrower record about the reading?" Samsen asks and nods to my pocket, knowing the list is there. "Can we hear the additional notes?" As usual, he's giving me something productive to focus on.

I pull out the short scroll and unroll it, angling it to the moonlight. It's not necessary. In the hours since the momentous reading in Brogal's chambers, I've memorized it.

Make your journey from the youngest sanctuaries to eldest—Baiseen, Nonnova Isles, Kutoon, Tangeen, and Asyleen.

Not until spring renewal will the quest be complete.

A curse of shadows blinds all but one.
A sea dragon lies in the depths, changing the path of every shore.
The smallest phantom extracts the highest price.
A ruler from the exalted throne will cause deception.
When the red sun lights the world on fire, the true journey begins.
Only arrows from the sea can pierce the Heir's heart.

"Marcus? Anything helpful?" Ash prods when I don't speak.

"The main thing, we already know. I am designated Bone Gatherer. After that, it's mostly rhymes and riddles, as usual."

"Try us." Samsen rides up beside me.

I take a breath. "We have the order of the journey, as promised. It runs from the youngest sanctuary to the oldest—Baiseen, Nonnova Isles, Kutoon, Tangeen, and Asyleen."

"Asyleen? In Sierrak?" Ash's eyes light up.

She's itching to go there. "It's what it says." I run my thumb down the list. The rest is nonsense.

You're surprised?

I ignore De'ral and give them the gist. "We'll be gone well into spring. Something about a curse of shadows. Great. Just what we need. Oh, and sea dragons exist, apparently, because one will change the path of every shore." I stop to roll my eyes. Belair laughs outright. "Then, it's look out for small phantoms, deception, rulers on high, and when the second sun sets the world afire, well, that sounds like the end of the world to me."

"Is that what it says?" Ash asks.

"No. It says that's when the true journey begins."

I omit the last prediction because it names me specifically and I don't like what it says. Last thing I want is everyone trying to protect me from hypothetical arrows every time we near the coast.

Maybe they are metaphorical arrows.

I wrinkle my brow. It's not a word I expect from my phantom. Metaphorical? *"Have you been talking to Ash?"*

I haven't. De'ral sounds oddly confused about that admission.

I roll up the list and tuck it back into my deep pocket. These details change nothing. Mollify nothing! I gaze up the road, toward the Suni River mouth. In that direction it's all dark headlands and a darker sea. "Ride on," I command and nearly doze off until Piper's declaration startles me.

"Is that our ship?" she asks when we halt on the last ridge. Between us and the sea is a steep ride down a cliff, across the headland plains for half a mile, and then down the sandy dunes to the beach. I squint at a tiny light winking at us not far out to sea.

"I imagine so," Rowten answers before I do.

"Aye, it is," Kaylin says at the same time.

Ash yawns. "We made it." But then she sniffs the air. "Do you smell that?"

"Flowers?" I don't usually mind her attention to the details of nature, but this isn't really the time.

"Not flowers," she protests. "More earthy like—"

"Freshly turned soil?" Kaylin says as he lifts his nose. His horse shifts nervously.

"I don't smell it," I say.

"I do." Piper is alert. "Fresh rain on newly turned fields."

We all look up to a now cloudless vault overhead. No rain for miles.

"Let's go," Rowten says. His voice is light, but I hear the undertone of concern.

"You suspect something?" I ask.

He shrugs it off. "We want to be across that field before sunrise. Less exposure."

It takes a moment to sink in. "You fear an attack?" I don't give him time to answer. "We ran off Tann's horde, and the one from Gollnar. This is Palrion soil. None would dare trespass."

Aturnians dared. Gollnarians dared. The—

"That was before we sent them packing!" I shout aloud. It echoes over the hills and the constant background of chirping insects suddenly stops. My company all stare. It's obvious I'm responding to a jab from my phantom, not something I like making public—the prods or my need to defend myself. All tell-tale signs of poor control. My face flushes hot. "Do you fear an attack?" I repeat my question to Rowten.

"It's unlikely." But still, he points his horse's nose toward the goat track and heads down the hill. He's not even waiting for me to confirm the plan. It's starting to rankle, but Master Brogal would say that line of thinking won't take me further along the path. Ash would say it, too.

"Shall we spread out? Not all take the same track?" There are other goat paths, pale in the dim light, winding to the bottom. "Safer that way." I have to say something to save face.

Ash would say—

"Do. Be. Quiet, De'ral!"

"Good idea." Piper comes up beside me and gives me a salute. "In case one of us brings a landslide."

She couldn't have said it better if I'd planted the words in her head. I'm glad she acknowledges my leadership.

While the others disappear over the edge, I take a final look behind in the direction of Baiseen. There's nothing to see anymore, but it doesn't stop my skin from prickling. *Brother of mine, be sure of one thing. If you misguide the realm or threaten the Sanctuary, I'll take back my throne, by force if necessary.*

9

KAYLIN

"*Ash, lass? Can you hear me?*"

I've been calling to her in my mind, over and over again since we sailed into Baiseen Harbor. Surely she has recovered enough. But no matter how many times I've tested our mental link…nothing. Not a whisper of her sweet voice. I'm doubled over by it. Gutted. Why can't she hear me? We'd built a pathway between us as wide as the Cabazon Straits. Our thoughts flowed back and forth, at first to my shock and then my delight. What lander has such talent? But since Tann's attack on Baiseen, not a sound. At first, I assumed the worst. If she was gone, if Ash just wasn't there anymore… I don't know what I would've done. I might as well be off the path myself.

I can't describe the moment when I found her in the festival hall. Our eyes met and a wave of heat rose through me. My mind went numb after that. Uncertain. Was it really her? Of course it was her, but as the warmth evaporated, my chest became too tight to breathe. My lass was alive and well, thank the Ma'ata. And as beautiful as ever, but she still did not hear me.

I'd planned to sweep her up into my arms the moment I saw her, and tell her everything. *Everything!* She must know who I really am. *What* I am… The consequences be damned. But at that moment, Nun stepped between us. He knows, of course. His ruse as Brogal's assistant doesn't fool me. How could it? I've been aware of him since the start, before his role in the Sanctuary began.

"*Ash?*" I try again.

All I can do is resign myself to the archaic method of speaking aloud. "You first, lass." I hold my horse back so she can head over the cliff before me.

I pat the animal's neck, sending kind thoughts. We've ridden hard over the last hour, and Ash encourages me to show appreciation to the beast. "*Stay connected and listen,*" she said right from the start when teaching me. "*They communicate through touch and are smarter than you think.*" I call this mare Ginger, which, if it isn't her name, it should be. She's the color of sunrise, and as fast as lightning. I'm fairly sure we could beat anyone here in a race, but that's not important now. There's a steep cliff to navigate, a wide field to cross, and a ship to meet if I'm to deliver this company safely to Nonnova. Let the others believe Marcus or this Captain Rowten is in charge. I know who really is. Who has to be if we are to survive.

I cluck to Ginger and lean back in the saddle, keeping my weight to the rear as she sinks her haunches low. "Take it slow, lass," I say to Ash as her pace quickens into a slide.

"Riding instructions from a lad who couldn't tell a fetlock from a forelock when we met?" she calls over her shoulder.

I smile into the dawn. "One's on the foot, right?"

"I think you mean hoof." Her sweet laughter tumbles down the trail. "Did you forget *I* taught you how to ride?"

"Never." I laugh as well. Ginger assumes a fishtail gait, half walk, half slide down the cliff face. Even without the growing dawn light, I'd have no trouble seeing the path all the way to the bottom. There's a steep drop, an overhang, and then the trail splits, going around either side. Rubble and loose dirt fall with each step, the sound of shuffling hooves, squeaking leather and trickling rocks rise up the ridge along with the dust. We're nearly to the bottom when I hear a distant sound. It's faint yet eerily familiar. "Mother of Ma'ata, it can't be," I say louder than I'd meant to.

"Kaylin?" Ash pulls her horse to a stop and turns sideways to the cliff face. "What's wrong?"

"Hold!" I call to everyone. Ginger responds instantly to my command, but it takes a while for the rest of them to stop. They all take up awkward, right angles to the slope. While they settle, I listen. The sound is clear, a definite churning and roiling. It's loud enough for the others to hear as well. But it's not just the sounds in the distance. The smell, like Ash noticed earlier. Damp earth. Fresh rain on a churned field. I should have paid better attention. I should have known!

"It definitely smells like rain," Ash says quietly as she looks skyward. "Still, not a single cloud."

Curse the tombs of the deep, it's nothing to do with the weather.

"Troops behind us?" Rowten asks.

"We'll soon see," Samsen says as he jumps off his horse and touches a knee to the ground to raise his phantom. It erupts from the earth in the form of a brown hawk and takes to the sky.

The churning stops, and there's a minuscule chance that I am wrong. Please let me be wrong. I wait for his phantom's report. It will come in a matter of seconds.

"False alarm," Samsen says as he brings his phantom to ground and mounts back up on his horse. "No sign of troops. Just a single rider on a warhorse heading this way. Perhaps a message—"

"Not a false alarm," I shout. "To the bottom. Everyone, fly!" I urge Ginger down the hill assuming they will obey.

For a moment, no one but Ash does.

"Ride, if you value your lives!" I shout over my shoulder, cursing their bureaucratic process. I agree, the forum of equality is inspiring, but we don't have time for this. "Ride, all of you. To the bottom, now!" I hold back, allowing them to pass.

Ash leads the way and finally the rest follow, steadily increasing their pace to match hers. Any care in choosing the path vanishes as they tear down the cliff. Rowten reaches the bottom after Ash, then Marcus and Belair. I hold back to let Tyche pass me, and Piper too. Samsen and I dovetail in behind them all to bring up the rear. "Keep going!"

But Rowten doesn't lead the escape across the field. He holds his fist up, gathering us under the ledge, an overhang that forms a shallow cave flush with the hillside.

"We can't hide from this," I say to him. "We need to get to the ship."

He cranes his neck around the overhang. "It's only a single rider. What is the panic?"

"No ordinary single rider," I say, chafing. We need to go!

Judging by everyone's expression, contradicting the captain of the Honor Guard is not often done. I sneak a look overhead. Backlit by the breaking dawn, a solitary rider sits on his dark horse. His long cape wafts in an uncanny breeze and the trace of multiple phantoms spark around him.

Marcus comes to the edge and follows my line of sight. "What is it?" He keeps his voice a whisper.

I nod and turn to Rowten, knowing he's the one to convince. "I've seen it before, the likes of a Gollnar savant I promise you don't want to face."

"Who?" Marcus asks.

"Are you familiar with the name Atikis?"

Marcus pales and a murmur runs through the others but it's Rowten who recovers first. *Finally.* "Best meet the ship quickly then, as your sailor advises. Better safe than dead."

Marcus nods at me and then gives the order. "At the gallop!"

Our horses throw their heads high, ears pinned. They bunch their hindquarters and explode across the field at a dead run.

10

MARCUS

"Gee up!" My mount thunders over the ground. Kaylin's red mare is the fastest by far, though he holds her back, guarding the rear with Samsen. I give him a quick nod. He is our best sword. Though against this rider, would it be enough? A non-savant, no matter their skill, could not hope to best a red-robe. I'm a warrior savant and know I wouldn't have an old god's prayer. I mean, a yellow-robe against a red?

De'ral roars under my skin. Retreat is not his favorite tactic.

Fortunately, the way to the headland is clear, the open field covered with dry grass and a few scraggly trees. It offers no cover from the pursuit if arrows start to fly, but the ground is flat and good for a gallop. I take another look over my shoulder and am stung by the yellow rays of sunrise. No sign of pursuit. Did we get it wrong?

De'ral growls. *Not wrong.*

I look behind again as a single savant on the black charger makes his way down the cliff. He's unhurried, almost casual, like someone who knows the stampeding herd is going exactly where he wants them to. Cold shivers down my neck.

Trap, De'ral spits out the words.

My horse slows. "You don't know that," I snap at my phantom, but the words are aloud.

Rowten turns at my outburst, his face questioning.

I tap my heels against the horse's sides, speeding him up again. *"Stop distracting me, De'ral. We're here to catch a ship, not fight a red-robe."* If half the stories are true, and this is really Atikis, well, he's more than just an ordinary red-robe. Kaylin is convinced of it, too. "Straight to the river mouth?" I ask, riding neck and neck with Rowten.

"To the river mouth," Rowten repeats over the pound of hooves.

If we keep up the pace, we'll reach the shore, signal the ship and be gone before the threat catches up.

De'ral huffs.

"I suppose you have a better idea?" I ask.

We fight!

"Too risky. We have non-warriors with us. We have Ash."

I will protect her.

"I have a better plan. We'll reach the shore and signal the boat."

How?

De'ral has a point. I'm not dead sure of how we get a message to the waiting vessel, short of jumping up and down on the beach, or sending Samsen's bird, which can only be received by another savant with a raised phantom onboard. That's highly unlikely as phantoms can't be raised over water and are seldom left up for a voyage of any length. *"If all fails, Kaylin can swim for it."* I slap my horse on the rump. "Get on, old man," I say. "This is no time to nap."

Rowten takes the lead. I'm behind him, flanked by Piper on one side, Tyche on the other. *"Where's Ash?"*

He guards her.

A quick glance over my shoulder shows Belair, with Ash, Kaylin, and Samsen right behind. We move into a tight pack and gallop hard. The sound of hooves pounds out as fast as my heart, and I scan the coastline ahead.

"Pursuit!" Belair cries out.

Sure enough, the red-robe has started to gallop after us, the warhorse faster than I expected.

Now we fight?

"No!" I urge my horse on, but instead of giving me more speed, it slows. The others behind me charge past.

"What are you doing?" Kaylin shouts as I ease back next to him.

I realize then that I am reining my mount in. *And why not?* I think, suddenly seeing it differently. He's a single rider. De'ral and I could put him down in a matter of a minute and be galloping on again, catching up with the others. Threat gone.

In the back of my mind, I know these are De'ral's thoughts, not mine, but it doesn't matter because I agree. "See the others to safety," I say to Kaylin. "I'll be right behind you."

I'm nearly to a halt when Kaylin stops, spins his horse over its hindquarters and charges back to me. "Bad plan, Marcus. Ride!"

"We can handle a lone rider." The voice, again, is De'ral's, not mine and he's champing at the bones to rise.

"Have you forgotten the lone rider is a red-robe? You can't fight him."

I draw my sword and face the enemy. Why is Kaylin in such a hurry to escape? It's just the one horseman, a tall figure. A red-robe, more a cape, in the style of Gollnar High Savants. I shake my head. What am I doing? The savant controls the phantom, not the other way around. I've seen what destruction my phantom causes when I lose control. *"De'ral, are you insane?"*

We fight, De'ral grinds out the words.

"No, we do not!" I cry and sheathe my blade. I rein my confused horse toward the sea and Kaylin does the same, relief on his face. We dig in our heels and the mounts find a fresh burst of speed. "Keep running!" I holler to the others, but they are far ahead now, including Kaylin on his bolt of lightning red mare.

I'm poised for the run, leaning forward, hands far up the animal's neck, but instead of putting distance between me and the red-robe, the horse slows again. Not my doing this time. I stare down at his shoulder as he tries to race away. But as each hoof hits the ground, the earth caves in like sand down a sinkhole. Suddenly the hard-packed field crumbles beneath us until my mount is swimming in sand. Sweat beads my brow when I look behind. The red-robe savant has caught up. Around the solitary horseman, the ground begins to erupt. "Phantom rising," I yell, but I'm the only one who can hear over the grinding, churning earth.

The sound is like bones cracking apart. Then I smell it, wet soil and rain. All the while, out of the ground erupts a phantom just as Kaylin had warned, the likes of nothing I've ever seen.

True to the stories, it's multiple in aspect, a troop of horsed warriors that look part animal, part human, and part earth. They rise up on their steeds and arch over the ground only to dive back in again, traveling toward me as if the earth was the sea. Closer they come, rising and falling, earth spraying, explosive sounds booming across the field, and everywhere the smell of wet loam. I make out the vacant eyes of the phantom riders and the saw-edge blades they carry, but it's the beasts that terrify me the most. They transform as they rise and fall—one moment snakes, then four-legged galloping steeds, then serpents again. Dirt falls from their slick wet hides and fanged teeth. I spin back and fix my eyes on the coast, begging my mount to find solid footing and flee.

De'ral scoffs, pacing corner to corner in the confines of my mind, pounding the walls to be released.

"It's an alter *phantom, ten times our size and a thousand times our training."*

De'ral answers me with a challenging roar that comes out of my mouth.

"Great. Let's provoke the red-robe who controls a phantom that's fifty beasts in one. Just the plan."

My horse gives a mighty leap and goes down, pitching me out of the saddle.

I hit hard, taking it mostly on my sword arm, curse the bones. I see no choice but to run on foot, though by now I'm surrounded by quaking ground and an undulating phantom. I turn to face the Gollnar savant. The cut of his robe proves it, as does the livery of the phantom riders—black leather armor and red capes.

Let me rise! De'ral yells between my ears.

Like there's a choice? I stop and drop hard to my knees.

Sand shoots skyward as my massive *warrior* explodes from the ground in front of me. Three times my height and width, ten times my bulk, he is a power unto himself, but a match for this red-robe? Not likely.

"Just block him, De'ral. I'll run to the coast," I shout. I'm on my feet, ready to run the last leg to the shore. It turns my stomach to be fleeing, but De'ral and I don't have the many years of training or the absolute power that red-robes achieve. "I'll call you to ground when we reach the wharf and head out to sea. Even a red-robe can't follow us there."

Subtle, Marcus, De'ral says and then bellows a challenge at the churning phantoms.

I admit, it might not be the best thing to shout my strategy, but there is so much noise and turmoil around I can hardly think straight. *"Just do what I say!"* I lower my head and run.

Or try to. The multiple phantoms undulate around me, tearing in and out of the earth, tunneling beneath the surface and rising up in columns of rock. Debris flings to the sky, choking my lungs and blinding the way. *"I'm trapped."*

Or soon will be.

The earth shakes in waves, sweeping me up and dropping me flat on my back. I can't move, can't catch my breath. The world blurs, but I struggle to stay present. I can't risk losing consciousness while De'ral is up. But even as I think it, my control wavers and De'ral pushes me down. I freeze as a dark well looms before me. *"De'ral? Don't do this!"*

Do what? he whispers as he boots me over the edge of my mind.

An endless fall, leaving me in total darkness.

"Noooo!" I wail. But the void closes in and the outer world disappears.

11

DE'RAL

Chains snap in half. The cage door swings open, and a thousand blackbirds fly free. They turn into arrows and fly for the sun. I follow them. To my freedom. *He* is under now and I'm in control. Rank means nothing. I am De'ral! I will fight and win!

I roar, not caring if the ground falls out from my feet. Strength bounds through me.

"Red! Robe!" His voice is desperate. Nagging.

I trip and fall. Does he have a point? The enemy is a worthy opponent.

His body lies near. Best not let it be crushed underfoot. Not good for either of us.

I sweep up his body and run with it over my shoulder, dropping it out of the way. He will not take charge, but he will not die either. It's a good choice.

The ground he just occupied erupts into a column of rock. More shoot up, massive fangs rushing toward the clouds, surrounding me as the phantom riders tear through the earth. Leaps. Dives. Plunges. The threat tightens around me.

My arms whirl, cutting, pounding, and smashing the phantoms down. Warning. As fast as I crush one, another appears, taller and wider, fencing me in. I slam my fist into the neck of a phantom horse. A meat-eater with fangs dripping blood. My arm goes straight through it. The horse falls apart, a storm of earth. More rise. Faster than I can put down.

Another pillar rushes up and I leap back. It turns into serpents. I chop it in half, but the pieces find each other and reform, rising as something new. Suddenly I'm face-to-face with a *warrior* twice my size, its cavernous mouth open, rocks falling off the tongue. It booms louder than the cracking earth. "Puny phantom! You dare to challenge me?"

I dare.

But the wind from its mouth throws me. I swing at the midsection, but it's faster, long arms grabbing my throat. Its fingers spread wide. Clamp hard. I'm forced to my knees. It speaks again, bone-cracking vibrations shaking the ground with each word. "I will crush you."

You won't! I shout in my mind as I can't speak aloud.

He groans in the depths.

I club with balled fists. No good. It raises me up and slams me down. Over and over. Then it dives, still strangling my throat.

It's winning.

I'm dragged through darkness. Rocks and wet earth and rivers of mud rush by until I burst back into daylight. I'm close to where *he* lies, his body in danger again.

Maybe his plan was better.

If you die, I die, we say to each other.

I twist inside my skin, a cat held by the nape of the neck, and lay into the enemy.

That's when the sailor's horse comes to a sliding stop just in front of Marcus. If I'm going to do anything, it has to be now.

As the phantom dives into the earth for another turn below ground, I stick out my arms and legs at right angles, slowing the downward motion. But my bones strain. I can't stop it for long.

But it's long enough.

The phantom releases me and dives back into the earth alone. I spring up to my feet and face the red-robe.

He sits on his horse, watching from a distance. Smirking. He feels no threat from me.

I raise my fist and run toward him.

All I have to do is kill the savant and the phantom is gone. The sailor throws *him* over his horse's shoulders, vaults up, and gallops away. Safe.

I turn back to the red-robe as again the earth crumbles underfoot. "Say goodbye to your path," I challenge him, but am answered only with his laugh.

Pain slams through me. My face is smashed against the pounding shoulder of a bright red horse. Kaylin's. My head rings like a harbor buoy. The scent of horse sweat and leather rushes up my nose as the ground rips by at breakneck speed. I lift my head for a better view, hair falling away from my face.

"Don't move." Kaylin pushes me back down.

I want to argue, but he's right. How this horse runs so fast carrying both our weights, I don't know. I need to hold still or it'll lose balance.

"You can call your phantom in, as soon as we hit the beach."

The sailor turns out to be a good rider. Too bad he has no idea that my phantom has taken over control. There's no way for me to call De'ral back. I'll never live this down, having to be rescued by Kaylin, yet again.

I try to look behind but all I see is blinding sunlight. I try to move into phantom perspective, to find out what's happening with the red-robe, but there's nothing there to touch or push against. I think for an instant that De'ral has gone to ground but I don't sense him internally either. It's like not having a phantom at all. I tense and start to shake.

"Hang on, Marcus. We're nearly there," Kaylin says.

My inner voice cracks as I call out. *"Where are you?"*

"Your *warrior's* holding off the red-robe, but it won't manage for long. Best get out of his perspective entirely. Otherwise, you'll drop like lead when you call it in."

Just what I need. More advice from a non-savant. The sailor has no idea of my true predicament, and I'm not going to be the one to enlighten him. Then again, everyone will find out soon enough. There's no way I'm crossing water without my phantom.

"I'll have you on the ground in moments."

"Thanks," I mumble. But De'ral's up, facing a High Savant with an army of an *alter* all on his own, and I have no way to bring him back.

13

ASH

"**M**arcus has gone b'lark-the-bones crazy," I yell to Belair who gallops hard beside me. Stopping to distract the red-robe while we escape may seem brave—noble even—but really, this is too risky. "He's taunting a red-robe for demon's sake!"

"And now Kaylin's gone after him. If this goes bad, our search for the whistle bones will be over as it starts."

We look at each other and shake our heads before focusing on the nearing river mouth. *"Kaylin? What are you doing?"* I reach out to him but touch only air.

"Ride." Rowten waves me and Belair on. "To the beach!"

I have no problems following that command. It's not like I can do anything to slow the red-robe. I have to trust that Marcus and Kaylin somehow know what they are doing. *Please know what you are doing!* I think to them both.

The coastline looms ahead, the smell of moist earth whisked away by the salty onshore wind. I reach the headland above the mouth of the Suni River first. Belair is right behind me, with Tyche. Rowten, Samsen, and Piper brings up the rear. The riverbanks are wide and ragged. They barely contain the mud-brown flow. This has always been a crystal blue waterway. But there's no time to ponder it now.

"Where's Marcus?" Piper twists around in the saddle. "Kaylin?"

"Right behind us," Rowten says, and it better be true.

We trot along the mud banks until we find a path down to the beach. It's another long and winding goat track, and the horses skid and slip, sides working like bellows to catch a breath as they make their way to the white sand beach. Halfway down, I see the ship. It's waiting for us in deep water. "Rowboat?" I ask the others, trying to catch my own breath as well.

"Don't see one," Rowten calls out, standing up in his stirrups at the top of the headland.

The swell is large with a pounding shore break. I don't know how a small vessel will make it in, or back out again. Please don't say we have to swim for it. My horse reaches the beach first and the others follow, bringing half the trail worth of sand down with them.

"There it is." Belair points to the small boat being tossed toward shore. It's manned by a single sailor. They'll need a lot of skill not to capsize.

"Marcus," Piper says. "And Kaylin." She makes to climb back up the trail, but Samsen stops her with a touch.

"I'll check on them." Belair dismounts and drops to one knee.

The ground beyond him rumbles and shakes. From the churning center springs his red sun leopard, gaining height as sand falls from its hide. It lands lightly and snarls, muscles rippling as it bounds up the dune, tearing the ground with churning paws. In a few long strides, it crests the top and disappears over the other side.

Belair's still breathing hard as his eyes glaze and then widen. "They're challenging the red-robe."

"Distracting him so we can all get away." Rowten pulls our attention back. "Dismount and turn the horses loose. Quickly!"

I go to work on my mount's saddle first, unbuckling the girth and pulling it off. While still undoing the tiny clasps on the bridle, Rowten helps Tyche, his own horse already freed.

"Imp?" Tyche's hands fish deep in her pockets, becoming more frantic by the moment. "I lost him!" Her eyes well as she makes to kneel in the sand. She's going to raise her phantom and *call* the stuffed toy back to her.

I understand. It's all she has left of Aku, of her grandmother Yuki, of the life she knew before the attack, but Piper is having none of it. She pulls her to her feet.

"No time." Her voice is stern, but when Tyche closes her eyes, tears falling down her cheeks, Piper pulls her into a quick hug. "Nothing for it, sweetheart. We have to run."

"Grab the saddlebags," Samsen commands as he slaps the horses' rumps, moving them out of the way. "And the packs."

I hoist mine while searching the cliff face for Marcus and Kaylin. They should be coming down the track by now. Why aren't they? As I wonder, a boom peels through the air. It sounds like a volcano exploding. "Marcus! Kaylin!" I shout.

"They're coming," Belair says and dips his knee to the sand, bringing his phantom back to ground.

Captain Rowten grips my shoulder, forcing me to look into his eyes. "Take gear to the waterline and help land the boat. We're right behind you." He frowns at Tyche. The girl's eyes are glazed as she stares at nothing we can see. "Take her, too, and mind the tide!"

"Tyche, this way." The words are not harsh, but they brook no resistance. I trudge through the deep sand, pulling the girl along, watching the rowboat wink in and out of view. It's behind the crashing waves one moment, then thundering toward the shore the next. Again and again, the cliff face, like a magnet, pulls my head around. *"Kaylin. Marcus. Please hurry. Please be safe."*

A slow smile lifts my face when I hear a response, loud and clear.

"To the rowboat, fast as you can!" Kaylin's voice rings out over the beach from the top of the headland. His mount tears down the cliff at a reckless speed, Marcus like a sack of bones over the horse's withers.

"What happened?" I shout but my question is swept out to sea by the rising wind.

Kaylin hits the beach and jumps off his mount while Marcus falls hard in a heap. The horse shies away, Rowten catching the reins just in time. "To the shore!" If I didn't know better, I would think there was actual fear in his voice.

I take Tyche's hand and bolt to the hightide mark. "Stay here," I tell her as I drop the gear. "Keep your eyes on the rowboat, hands in the air to give him a marker." I lift her hands high and when she holds them up, I sprint back to the others.

"Is he hurt?" I try to get to Marcus, but he's surrounded by Piper, Samsen, and Rowten.

"I'm unharmed," he says, but his ragged voice tells me otherwise.

"Untack her." Rowten hands Kaylin's red mare to me. She's shaking, sweat pouring down each leg, turning the sand brown at the base of each hoof.

"And that one." Rowten points to Marcus's mount trotting down the trail toward us, dragging her reins. "Get the saddlebags."

Belair has her as she joins the other mounts. I untack the red mare, heaving another pack over one shoulder.

"To the boat," Kaylin commands again, leading the way toward the surf. "He'll need help beaching it."

"Kaylin, wait." Piper stops him. Samsen and Rowten are trying to pull Marcus to his feet, but he has collapsed. "Has his phantom gone to ground?"

Kaylin shakes his head. "Not last I saw, but surely now?"

Piper nods and we all jog through the deep sand toward the rowboat, Samsen and Rowten dragging Marcus between them.

That's when warmth rushes up my arm and floods my body. Kaylin is beside me. His hand takes mine in the next breath. "Hurry, lass. We're cutting it close."

Heat sparks through my fingers where they entwine with his. It's a heat that I am sure reaches my face. "You saved Marcus," I say, wishing I had a free hand to brush away my tears. As I speak, a massive shadow arcs overhead.

Kaylin frowns. "Not yet. Run!"

14

DE'RAL

*"*D*uck!" he* shouts at me from within.

I drop, but not fast enough. The phantom smacks my chest. The force is a charging bull. I fold in two, the punch throwing me into the sky. His warning came too late.

"It wouldn't have been too late if you had bones-be-damned let me out of this hole sooner. What are you thinking? Picking a fight with a red-robe and shoving me into the dark?"

A string of curses and threats rise, which I ignore.

I'm still flying. Over the headland. Over the shocked company on the beach. Out to sea. Not good. Then, the flying stops. I turn into a falling stone.

"You dead stump of an idiot." He blames me. Always. *"Now look what you've done."*

The criticism never ends, but this time he might be right.

Ducks float; phantoms sink.

I don't know much else other than he fears water. Unless it is to drink. This ocean is not that.

He panics as the surface rushes to meet us. *"Help! Help!"*

Calm down.

"Help!" he cries louder.

Who does he think will answer? I slam him back into the darkness of our shared mind.

But he won't stay.

He's too panicked.

Is there any confusion about why I don't put him in charge?

I'm dropped from the sky. A wall of whitewater explodes as I sink.

"Let me out!" Marcus bangs on the trapdoor of our mind.

I won't let him out. Not yet. Though at a given point, I may have to.

Rushing seas fill my lungs and salt burns my wounds. I know he feels everything. It makes him wilder.

All right. Come out.

Marcus has a logic to him that could serve, but when I reach for the trapdoor, pure terror hides on the other side of the barricade. This–drowning– is his nightmare come to life, and it renders him useless. The logic is gone and I close the door. It's up to me now.

Light fades from the surface as I continue to sink. The water is cold, crushing.

Can I go to ground? It's not meant to be possible, but is there a chance? Marcus must call me in. At this moment, he can't call his own name. His fear soaks into me. It catches. I am as terrified as *him*.

Limbs flail, stirring up sand clouds, distorting sight. A chick stumbles after mother hen, but too slow, trod on by all the siblings until it's crushed. The push of the sea knocks me flat on my back. I flail more. Unguarded, the trapdoor swings open and I watch *him* rise, clinging, clawing, desperate to take control.

"Breathe!" Piper pleads with *him* where they sit together on the shore. *"Marcus, you have to breathe!"* The sound of her voice calms us both, a little, but breathing can't happen here. We both know that.

And then I see her. Hovering close, but not so near that I'll smack her into the seabed with floundering arms. I still myself, even though Marcus continues to thrash within. She stares into my eyes. I feel each grain of sand settling on my skin, in my hair, my eyelashes as I hold perfectly still.

She found us.

"De'ral?" she says, ivory hand touching my face.

"Salila." I send an image of the sunrise over the sea.

She laughs and my chest expands. I lie against the seabed and she leans over me. *"What in the dark demon's Drop are you doing under water?"*

A slight misstep. With a red-robe. I smile. She is exquisite in every way.

Marcus screams and I push him down with one hand, not taking my eyes from her. *Quiet. She's talking.*

Salila kisses my face before releasing it. *"Get back to shore, you glorious beast of a phantom, before you both drown."*

"Salila?" Marcus says. In my distraction, *he* has taken over my voice. He has taken control.

"Ah, the ex-heir is here as well?" Her words tease. *"Did you know there's a quest to accomplish, Bone Gatherer? I think you might be off track."*

I respond before *he* can think of what to say. *"Help us?"* A lion cub watches the huntress in awe.

She stays near enough for me to touch her. And I do. A single finger gently to her cheek.

"There is solid ground beneath you, De'ral. With your height, all you have

to do is stand." Her words are warm honey.

I see the move, but *he* is still near hysterical and unfortunately sharing control.

Salila knows it and speaks directly to him. *"Your phantom is tall as a tower, Marcus. Find your feet. Bend your knees and stand up."*

Survival is more important than control. I declare a truce. Together, we turn skyward to the surface, ignoring the drag of the current. We tuck feet under and raise arms high. He's frantic for air, and overbalances. I fall back to stare at the sun. A yellow orb rippling beyond the top of the sea.

I cling to invisible vines, kick up to a squat, then straighten my legs before he can think about it. My head breaks the surface. I draw in a breath, filling phantom lungs. It reminds *him* to do the same. Waves smash into my shoulders and back, lifting me, but I stay upright. The motion drops me down closer to shore. Now my chest is exposed.

"I'll make a swimmer of you yet, my love." Salila is nowhere to be seen but her voice rings in my mind.

Come back? The surface ripples, leaves in the wind. It covers her path.

"I will."

I want to explain before she goes. *You tell her,* I say to Marcus. *This is your fault.*

"How in the end-of-the-eternal-bones is this my *fault?"*

"Listen, you two…" Salila hesitates. I stand immobile until she speaks again. *"Mend your argument. The others are waiting for you, and there's still the little matter of the red-robe."*

She's right.

I blink seawater and stride through the waves, using arms like paddles to pull to shore. When the last wave smashes me into the hard, wet sand, I bound to my feet and charge. The others back away, staring. I scale the cliff, rip a tall sapling from the ground, and find the red-robe. He's still mounted on his warhorse. Still smiling.

Let's see how long that lasts.

"No!" Marcus shouts. *"To ground, I said!"*

I ignore him, building speed. In a thunderous stride, I launch and impale the nearest phantom warrior rising out of the ground. The sapling spear hits, the armor shatters. The shaft of the tree slides through up to my fists while the phantom convulses.

"Watch out," Marcus cries. Its razor-sharp sword swings toward my face.

I lunge and retreat. Lunge again. Impaling until several warriors are stacked onto my spear. Where they belong. Mud runs down my wet arms and covers my chest. "Let's see if *she* can teach you to swim," I boom and whirl around.

Sand flies when I stop dead and double grip the spear. The impaled enemy launches off the shaft. They sail out to sea. It's my thank you to Salila. She might enjoy the offering.

He disagrees, says it's barbaric, but I know.

She will understand. She will know I am thinking of her. I hoist the dripping spear and charge. Back for more. But the red-robe is waiting for me.

15

MARCUS

My eyes fly open, and I gasp for air. I know this feeling, the rush of healing venom coursing through my veins. Piper hovers, her snake recoiling, but I can't see right. I'm shaking, head pounding like a sledgehammer hit full force. I think I'm going blind.

"This is no time for glory in battle, Marcus. Bring it in," Piper commands.

My eyes close and the darkness surrounds me. *"De'ral, return."* I break out in a sweat. Nothing. The link is gone, my *warrior* disconnected. *"Bones be damned, De'ral. Listen to me. Come to ground before we're both flung off the path."*

Rowten and Samsen grab a shoulder each and help me stand. They assume the job's done. "Wait. I can't—" But they take off at a jog, dragging me between them.

"You have him back, right, Marcus?" Samsen leans in to make sure.

"There's no link," I whisper into the tunnel of darkness.

He drops me like a hot rock. "Bring your phantom to ground, Heir of Baiseen!" Samsen shouts at me. At me! I thought Brogal was the only savant who could speak to me that way. "Bring it back. Now!"

The sound of the surf is close, the sand wet and hard. I'm on my knees, but nothing is happening.

"He's injured," Ash says, coming to my side. She pushes hair from my ear and lowers her voice. "De'ral? We are making our escape. Will you please join us?"

Chills wash across my skin. Ash is the only other person who knows my phantom's name. It was an accident, her finding out. I let it slip when he first took solid form, but she promised me she would never speak it, never remember she even knew it.

"The cliffs!" Rowten's voice rises above the waves.

Through blurred vision, I watch an avalanche of sand roll down the cliff, the headland breaking apart as De'ral careens along the goat trail.

"Bring him in!" Samsen shouts.

Ash's hand on my shoulder gives me more strength.

"Return," I command him again. *"If you don't come now, Ash could die."*

De'ral stops as if slapped in the face and melts into ground. He rushes, painfully fast, back to my core, bringing a tidal wave of emotion with him.

"Well done," Samsen says.

I nod but my eyes go to Ash. There's no time to thank her as Samsen and Rowten drag me into the water and toss me into the rocking boat like so much luggage. The cold revives me and I right myself on the bench. Kaylin's up to his chest in the swirling whitewater, keeping the bow pointed out to sea. Belair and the other sailor hold the stern while the current rips past their legs.

Ash slides in next to me. "Where are you hurt?" She starts searching for wounds.

"I'm fine." I push her hand away not wanting her to realize there are no phantom wounds, since I was not in phantom perspective when De'ral took his beating. I was locked out.

My thoughts slam to a stop as Tyche shouts. "Look there!" She stares behind us, open-mouthed as she points to the cliffs.

We all turn as one to the headland. The red-robe savant sits on his dark horse, watching, while on the beach, just lengths away from the water's edge, columns of sand spray into the sky. His phantom rises again, within arm's reach of us all.

"Row!" Kaylin cries. He's shoulder deep in the wash, pulling the bow into the oncoming waves with all his might, which is surprisingly substantial. "Belair, get in."

He and the sailor scramble up the side and take the back bench.

"It's coming for us!" Tyche cries out again.

"It can't," I tell her, trying to soothe the hysteria I feel as well. Deep down, I'm not so sure what this red-robe's phantom can do.

The beach erupts and as the sand blows away on the wind, a form takes shape, the undulating column sprouting arms, a head, and powerful legs. I stare, fists tightening. It's a phantom *warrior*, twice the size of De'ral, but near identical in shape—a hulking, massive force, roaring after us in a subterranean voice as it thumps its fists against its chest.

Kaylin leaps gracefully from the crashing waves and into the boat, splashing us all. He grabs the aft oars and rows hard, his white shirt soaked and clinging to his chest, dark hair dripping down his back.

The phantom, enraged, stops at the water's edge. His savant still sits on his horse, high on the headland, his robes blowing in the wind. The morning sun backlights his form, making it impossible to see his face, but I feel as if the red-robe is staring straight back at me.

"Baiseen's whistle bone?" Ash asks. "Do you still have it?"

My limbs go weak as I reach for the pouch tied to my belt. It's there, and I feel the outline of the bone still inside. Ash seems about to say something, but her eyes go back to the beach watching the red-robe's phantom pounding up and down the shore.

All any of us do while we crash through head-high waves is grip the rails and hang on, except for Kaylin and the crewman who work the oars. Ash turns pale and I think she will be sick. It's not out of the question that I might join her. Even Piper is looking a little green.

Each time we gain ground, a new set of waves hammers us back toward shore where the enormous phantom waits. But the sailors know their craft and finally, we punch through the swell and reach deep water beyond the breakers. It takes a moment for any of us to exchange a glance. By then, Ash is a sickly shade of gray. I swallow hard and look to the shore, watching the phantom slowly go to ground.

Kaylin turns the boat west, toward our waiting vessel. As he does, he leans close to Ash and clamps his free hand over her wrist, pressing hard. She smiles weakly at him, taking over the pressure herself. "I forgot," she says, already looking better. He taught her that on our first voyage together, how pressure to the inside of the wrists keeps the nausea at bay.

I'm about to speak when Kaylin clicks his tongue before whispering, loud enough for me to hear, "Now I've saved him, lass."

Spontaneously, she kisses his cheek — *kisses* it — before turning scarlet red. They share a private moment. Private, that is, except for me and everyone else watching. I start to turn away, but he's not through.

"And, little lass," Kaylin says to Tyche as he pulls a soggy stuffed impala out of his pocket. "This belongs to you, I believe."

"Imp!" Tyche's mouth opens as she takes the wet stuffed toy from Kaylin and holds it to her cheek. "You saved him, too," she says, her eyes lingering on Kaylin.

Ash whispers something to him, so softly that this time, I don't catch the words. I rub the back of my neck and look away, noticing that Rowten is still watching Ash. My frown deepens for a new set of reasons I can't yet name. Phantoms, sailors, captains. Do all have eyes for Ash?

"I've never seen anything like that," Captain Rowten says, bringing our attention back. "Your phantom came roaring out of the sea!" He presses his fingers into his temple. "And that monster phantom? Was that really the legendary Atikis?"

"An *alter* phantom, for certain," I say. "And red-robe dressed in the tradition of Gollnar. It has to be him." I shake my head. "Definitely not something I've ever faced before."

Water sloshes against the hull and, for a moment, all I can hear is the sound of the bow gliding through the waves and the creak of the oars.

"But I have," Kaylin says under his breath. "Atikis, it is. Originally from the Sanctuary of Goll."

"Atikis," Ash repeats the name, saying it slowly. "He broke ties with his home sanctuary, as I understand it." Her cheeks are still pink as she glances at Kaylin.

"Went rogue." He nods. "Rides alone, they say."

"Then what does he want with us?" Rowten asks.

"Should be obvious, aye?" Kaylin shrugs. "He's after the whistle bones, too."

16

ASH

My legs are jelly as I clutch the galley bench and try to match the sway of the ship. Nope. No sea legs yet. And not much rest, either, unlike the others who have been snoring like farm dogs since we boarded the ship. I took a short nap after we settled in, but who can sleep when new books are calling? Not literally *calling*, of course, but the thought of those treasures waiting to be read sends a buzz to my belly and brightness to my mind that makes it impossible to stay in my hammock. They cover the galley table now. "Treasures." I smile at them.

So far, I've checked each book, text, and scroll Brogal supplied. All stayed dry, thanks to the waterproof satchels he wrapped them in. I make a mental note to ask the next recorder I meet where I can procure more of the material. The illustrated books with the twelve original whistle bones drawn in fine detail, in particular, must be protected. Tyche needs to memorize them. We all do, but callers must visualize what they *call,* without hesitation. I want to make sure that when we best Tann, we can steal the bones quickly.

I frown at the thought, wondering where this journey is taking us along the path. Not the physical route, though that may be unpredictable as well. But what about the path to An'awntia? Our highest advancement. Tann wants the bones for himself and demon's stuggs to the rest of us. And Atikis? I don't know his intent, but how different from either of them are we if we take the whistle bones by force?

Right about now, my inner voice would say, *you won't take anything anywhere if you don't rest. At least, have a cup of tea.*

It's good advice, even if I can no longer hear it like I used to.

I brew a fragrant tea of sarsaparilla, fenugreek, and orange blossom. "Off we go to Nonnova," I whisper to myself, wondering if Talus's words will make more sense once we reach the islands. I've not had a chance to think about this strange encounter, or search the new books for mentions of white-robe savants. I need to do so soon, before her message fades away.

"Piper," I say when she appears. "Good rest?"

She starts to speak but puts a hand over her mouth and turns away, gagging a bit.

"Piper? Are you sick?" I've never known her to succumb to seasickness. That's my forte onboard.

It's a moment before she can speak. "Let's add these to the pot." She hands me a piece of ginger root and a vial of dried herbs. I pop the cork and the smell of basil and clover wafts out.

"Of course." I take them but hold her gaze. "So, you *are* seasick?"

She hesitates for a moment, trying to keep her face bland. "No Ash. It's not the sea." A small smile escapes despite her efforts.

I look to her and then to her belly, my eyes going wide.

Piper's already holding a finger to her lips and shaking her head. "Not yet."

Not yet? That's ridiculous. Everyone will want to know, and celebrate with her and Samsen. They have such a special bond.

Ever since that day in the woods, four years ago. He was only a green-robe at the time, yet together they turned back a Gollnar scouting party. They bonded immediately, though no one thought it would stick, her being an orange-robe and five years older. Time has proven the doubters wrong, and now this good news? That I must keep to myself?

But I nod my head and agree.

When I turn back to the teapot, the dark haired, thick-set chef arrives. He has a fresh sea bass held up by the gills. Dinner, I assume. He goes to work in the galley after donning a well-worn apron and hat.

Belair is up next, his red hair springing in all directions, sleep in his eyes. I gather my books and stow them away so he can sit.

"Ochee Tea?" he asks and slides all the way down the bench to the wall.

"Not exactly, but close." I pour him a cup, add honey, and slide down the bench to sit next to him. Before he says a word, Kaylin appears from topside and sits next to me. Very close though there is plenty of room on the other side.

Heat burns my face. I straighten and say hi to Kaylin but it comes out as more of an exhale. *Poised, Ash. Really poised...* As he turns to me, it all comes rushing back. *I kissed him.*

In front of everyone, I kissed him.

It was on the cheek, and friendly, of course...but it was a kiss, nonetheless. Completely outside the bounds of a journeying wordsmith's conduct toward, well, anyone.

What was I thinking?

In my defense, I wasn't...but I was so relieved for finally reaching the safety of the sea. And, by the cracked bones of the gods, grateful for all that Kaylin did to save Marcus from certain death. I mean, De'ral was launched out to sea. I may be non-savant, but I know the rules. If a phantom dies with the savant still in its perspective, the savant dies too. And phantom under water equals phantom death, right? So yes, I was feeling particularly appreciative of Kaylin and showed it. That's all.

My inner voice would say something like, *those are a lot of words to describe a simple thank you.*

But then, I suppose spewing over the side of the rowboat a few minutes later erased the spontaneous kiss from everyone's mind. Good old seasick Ash.

"Did you catch the bass?" Belair askes Kaylin.

"Aye," he answers, leaning past me, my face still heating.

The chef, busy dicing onions, suddenly has all my attention. "He's not making Klaavik, but something close. Dinner should be good." I say it like I'm describing the weather.

"Sounds delicious," Kaylin says into my ear, sending shivers down the entire left side of my body.

It's safe to say he didn't mind the kiss.

"Marcus, you're awake!" I bark the words when he comes in and pours himself a cup of tea.

Then Samsen, Tyche, and Rowten join us at the table. Once we're all there, I put my mind firmly on the tasks ahead and bring up the question I've been wrestling with. "What exactly was Atikis after?"

"Our whistle bone," Marcus says.

"I think it could be more than that," I say, but Marcus isn't finished with his thought.

"Maybe, but how did he appear there, at that exact moment, without foreknowledge of our plans? We only just knew ourselves."

No one has an answer until Rowten speaks. "Bone Thrower?"

"Makes sense," Marcus says. "He could have known that way."

"We'll have to be vigilant." Kaylin clicks his tongue. "Especially if…" His face is thoughtful and I raise my brows, inviting him to say more.

"If Atikis is tracking one of us as well as the whistle bones?" He crosses his arms over his chest.

"One of us?" I think about it and my gaze falls to Tyche.

"Tann was after callers on Aku. It's not a hard leap to think he may use them to *call* the bones from anyone else who doesn't want to hand them over." Kaylin says it softly but I see her wince.

"Tyche is one of the most powerful callers in the allied realms," Piper says. "If Atikis knows she's with us…" Her voice trails off and she starts over. "Taking the Baiseen whistle bone from Marcus would have just been a bonus."

Tyche blinks, her eyes wide.

"If that's the case, you are safe now." Samsen pats her back. "Atikis can't follow us to Nonnova without a ship. We're ahead of the game."

"And we best stay that way," Rowten adds. "Can we see it on the map?"

I rise to retrieve the world map, and the illustrated book of the twelve original whistle bones for Tyche.

When I return, I pass the book to our young caller and spread the map in the space they've cleared, each of us holding down a corner.

Kaylin takes several spoons and tucks them halfway up the southern coast of Tangeen, below Kutoon. "Tann's here, rebuilding his fleet after the damage Baiseen delivered, and he's decimating a fair few farms to feed his troops while at it."

"Would Tangeen send a defense to protect the farmers?" Marcus asks.

We all turn to Belair.

"Probably already done," he says, "but it would take time to reach them."

"Another concern," I say and trace a line straight south to the main island in Nonnova. "Couldn't Tann take a single vessel and beat us, claiming the whistle bone for himself?"

"He could." Kaylin taps Nonnova, his hand brushing mine. "But he hadn't as of two days ago."

We all pause when our fish soup is served, but I linger on the chain of islands that make up the Nonnova archipelago. I spot it, the volcanic isle depicted in the Bone Thrower's tapestry. And there's the name written beneath it, *Bakton*. It's between Nonnova's main island and the channel crossing to the northern mainland. We'll practically sail right over the top of it if I have my bearings right. I close my eyes. This would be the perfect time to relay what Talus told me, but my throat constricts, and I hesitate.

Not yet, I say to myself. I'll see what happens in Nonnova first. See if it can make more sense.

Marcus breaks the silence. "I still don't understand why there are twelve whistle bones to collect. Not ten, or fifteen or even twenty. I've seen more varieties than that in the Bone Thrower's bag. Definitely more than an even dozen."

All eyes turn to me. "True, but we seek only the originals, the first twelve whistle bones carved from the skeleton of Er."

"Er?" Belair asks.

"The first savant."

"First *known* savant," Kaylin says softly but I'm the only one who hears.

I keep going. "The tradition of the Bone Throwers began in the far northern mountains of Sierrak, Si Er Rak, or simply Er. That's the name of the savant who first used bones for divination."

Marcus turns to me. "Why bones?"

"Same reason they are used today—they retain a certain force, helpful in divining the future and offering guidance," Piper answers.

"But that's not *why* they created the bones known as the original twelve." I have the table's full attention.

"Tell us, lass," Kaylin says, but the light in his eyes makes me certain he already knows.

I take a deep breath. "It began with the death of King Er, an eccentric ruler, said to be a musician and empath who only wore black."

"Why black?" Rowten asks, looking up from his bowl.

"For protection and containment. Black keeps other people's life force out." I don't know how else to describe it. "When he died, they carved from his skeleton twelve whistles and etched them with symbols, one each for the twelve lots or paths of An'awntia."

"Ah." Marcus nods. "So that's why."

"But those whistle bones were bound into a crown?" Samsen asks.

"The exact translation is, they were formed on a crown, but the story gets even stranger. Apparently a Sea King stole the crown. It caused a huge battle so that when the black-robe followers of Er managed to take it back, they split it apart. Back into the original twelve whistle bones."

"For safekeeping," Kaylin adds.

"Exactly. To protect them further, Er's black-robes sent each whistle bone in a different direction, one for each sanctuary across Amassia. There they have been guarded ever since, kept safe until the Bone Gatherer comes to collect them."

"When the second sun returns," Kaylin says softly.

Everyone takes a moment to let the story sink in.

"Good retelling," Rowten says, and they all agree.

It only makes me want to dive into study more as I wonder about this crown, and this Sea King. It only now makes me think he was Mar.

After dinner, the conversation dies out, each of us retreating into our own thoughts. Piper suggests we turn in early and get more rest. There's no telling when our next chance at a warm, dry bed will be. I roll up the map and stifle a yawn. Just a little more reading tonight.

Kaylin heads for the hatch. "I'll check our heading." He climbs out of the hold without another word.

I turn to the table and help Belair clear.

"Have you talked?" he says quietly and tilts his head toward the hatch.

"About the kiss?" I can't seem to whisper it without blushing. "It was no big thing. Just a peck. A thank you."

"More like a spontaneous burst of—"

I shush him. "He's well aware of the protocols."

"More so than you, it seems." Belair ribs me again and I give him a shove.

"A stroll topside?" Rowten asks Marcus. "Ash? Join us?"

"I'll be right there." I'm mostly talked out, but a chat with Rowten on deck would be lovely and I do have a question for him. I haven't seen Lilian in months. There must be news. Once our bowls are rinsed and the table wiped, Belair gives me a quick hug and retires to his bunk in the bow. I climb up out of the hatch, and the fresh sea air hits me.

The breeze fills the sails and keeps the ship, a fine sloop, gliding smoothly over the water. I draw in a deep breath and gaze at the stars. It's quite beautiful, the open ocean at night. Kaylin is nowhere I can see. Neither is the second sun, but there are crew members on deck, hauling sails and scrubbing the fittings. I hurry to catch up with Marcus and Rowten near the wheelhouse, under the main mast. Maybe this is the right time for me to share Talus's cryptic message, but I'm still hesitant. Part of me thinks I imagined the whole thing, what with the way my thoughts have been of late. Maybe I should research the books first? Find out more?

If only my inner voice would wake up and weigh in on this! It's the part of me that would know for certain what to do next.

17

NATSARI

Hard walls of iron press in. Twisting. Suffocating. They pin me, crushing scales and stabbing soft underbelly skin. The red-robe's curse took hold when I wasn't looking. Always be looking! From now on, always be looking. If I ever escape.

His binding came at me, a thousand strands of liquid iron, splintered from a single strand of his soul. Wrapping and twisting until I couldn't move. Unthinkable, but the High Savant thought it anyway, his fear was so great. Fear of me, Natsari.

I was ready to forgive him for the first atrocity. He will not be forgiven for the second. If I survive.

The torment consumes me and takes away my voice. Still, I try. She must hear me.

Ash, listen. I am here.

But as I speak to her, I forget myself and who I am. Only when slammed back into the torment do I realize, I am Natsari.

I draw in a breath, believing it is my last. Hoping it will be my last and end the pain, but no. That is not my path. I must breathe again, and again, bound for eternity in a shadow-cursed prison made by a foolish, misguided savant.

Unless I find a way to break free.

Unless she does.

Ash… Her name wails through me, as thin and stretched as my heart, but the sound doesn't escape the darkness.

Ash…please hear me.

There isn't a flinch or flicker behind her eyes. Not even a cock to her head. Her mind is on the stars over the sea, in conversations and remembrances. She laughs, remembering some things, forgetting others, over and over while I twist in agony. I understand. We are sundered, but it will be the end of us both unless I break these cursed bindings.

I wrench myself around to find a new position in the airless cracks of her mind. Knives gouge flesh with every movement, each one more hurtful than the last. When my head points to where I think her heart lies, I send my voice again. A scream, this time, shrill enough to shatter glass. My body trembles apart with the effort, but I keep it up, hoping against hope she will hear me.

Before it is too late.

18

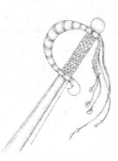

KAYLIN

Quiet! I need quiet.

There are too many thoughts on the wind tonight. They needle my mind, but I won't block them. Not when there's a chance one might be Ash's. It's a risk, leaving myself open with nothing but a wooden hull between me and the sea. There's not much any Mar wouldn't give to know where I am. That tidbit would assure the Sea King's good graces for a fair time to come. The Sea King with whom I was meant to check in with again before now. I need to seek Teern out myself, to make things right, but it would mean abandoning my companions. More to the point, it would mean abandoning Ash, and I won't do that to my lass. I look skyward at the stars winking between the masts. Surely, I can't be in that much trouble with Father, could I?

"Ash? Can you hear me?"

I keep trying, keep listening, and still no answer comes. It has me uncertain. What if I have it wrong about Ash? What if she *can* hear me but chooses not to answer?

I give myself a mental slap. Come on! Think it through. Doubting Ash? That's b'larkin absurd. She'd say it that way herself. I just wish I could actually hear her say it. In my mind. It would be such a relief. Our vocal conversations aren't the same.

But can I blame her holding back? I vanished when we reached Baiseen, virtually without a word of explanation. Gone to track Tann? It was only partly true. I couldn't exactly say that Teern had found me, since I had yet to tell her the truth of who I am. Teern had called. I answered. It wasn't something I could avoid. Will she ever understand? Will my explanations make matters worse?

I climb the mast to the crow's nest to be alone with my thoughts.

"I'll give you a thought, brother." Salila's voice jars through my head. *"Teern blames you for just about everything these days."*

The mast sways in widening arcs as I swing over the railing and stand on the small platform. So much for being alone. "Hello Salila." I lock my inner thoughts down tight. "Come to gloat?"

I was not expecting to see my sister here so soon.

That's not *sister* in the landers' sense of the word—related by blood—but only in the way that all Mar are connected through the Ma'ata. She stands in the center of the crow's nest, her long honey hair dripping down past her hips. Her skin is so fair it glows a pale blue in the night and her limbs rest at ease, lean and graceful. Her face, the one that melts landers' hearts, men and women alike, is curious, almost teasing, until her green eyes darken. "Surprisingly, not to gloat." She glances below and smiles, the whimsical look reappearing for an instant. Then her features smooth out. "I came to warn you about something."

"Don't tell me. Teern wants to chat?"

She outright laughs. "Not as much as he wants to skin you alive."

"And you think to hand me over?"

"Oh Kaylin." Her look is pity mixed with I-told-you-so. "You are incredibly naive sometimes."

I growl in the back of my throat. "Stop talking in riddles and say what you came to say."

She blows out a breath. "Have you forgotten you were chest-deep in the sea just hours ago? Be sure Teern knows exactly where you are, and more importantly, who you are with."

Damn the bones. I had hoped to avoid detection, at least for a little while longer. He did release me to perform a task, just not the one I am currently performing.

"The next time you dip a toe, he'll pull you down and stuff you under a rock. I doubt you'll see the suns for a very long time to come." She examines her fingernails, testing for sharpness.

I ignore the theatrics. "It's good you're here, Salila. I need you to deliver a message."

She picks her tooth with the longest nail. "I'm listening."

"Tell Teern I'll see him at sunrise, off the west coast of Nonnova." It's a risk, especially if he is as perturbed as she makes him out to be.

Well, what did I expect? I disobeyed him, again.

She *tsks*. "Will do, brother, but meanwhile, you best pay closer attention to your charges." Her eyes go to the deck below.

I follow her gaze. Ash climbs up the hatch and makes her way across the deck toward Marcus and Rowten who welcome her cheerily. "Why's that?"

"Trouble's brewing." Salila blows me a kiss and leaps to the railing. "Ta-ta, little brother, or should I say, chop-chop." She swan dives and disappears into the sea without another word.

19

MARCUS

I lose the thread of conversation when Ash approaches. "You look like you're feeling better." Ironic she's so fond of a sailor, what with her terrible sea legs.

"I'm cured." She smiles and taps her wrist.

"Reminds me of the day you cured Marcus of the hiccups," Rowten says, trying not to laugh. "Using Lilian's pet skunk."

I grimace. "No need to bring that up, Captain."

"Very angry pet skunk, you mean." Ash's laughter rises toward the sails. "I thought if I startled you, they'd go away. Didn't think the skunk would be more panicked than you." She tries to say "Sorry," with her hand over her mouth, holding in the giggles.

"I don't think you're sorry at all. The story gives you too much pleasure." I cross my arms.

"I'll never forget your face!" she says.

"I'll never forget the smell." Rowten chuckles.

"Such bad timing, with the visiting savants from Aku arriving." Ash has tears in her eyes. "And that girl. What was her name?"

"I don't recall." How did we get on this topic?

Her name was Sophia, De'ral supplies. *I liked her.*

"No one asked you." Heat burns my cheeks.

She and Rowten chuckle until the ship hits a trough. It slams down hard, and I grab the wheelhouse for support.

When it smooths out, Ash wipes tears from her eyes and asks Rowten, "What of your sister, Lilian?"

"You haven't heard?" He seems surprised.

I frown at her. Just last week I shared with her the good news of Lilian's baby. I hesitate before trying to explain. "Ash has only just been released from the healer's hall."

"And it's not like I dropped in for a cup of tea before we fled Baiseen. Tell me!"

Piper warned there could be more lapses.

Ash doesn't even realize anything is amiss as she shakes a finger at Rowten. "Give me the details, immediately. I want to know everything."

"Baby girl! They call her Roxanne."

"Exact birthday?" Ash takes a deep breath, not waiting for an answer. "Has the Bone Thrower been? *Alters* run on her dad's side, and *callers* on yours. How much did she weigh? Black hair like Lil's or red like Dev's?" Ash shoots one question after the other.

"Hold on." I smile at them both. "Before you launch on this story, I'm turning in. You should, too, Ash. Healer's orders." I clasp Rowten's hand and give it a shake. "Really glad you're with us, Captain, and congratulations again for Lilian."

"Again?" Ash says and gives me a haunted look. "I'll be a moment, Marcus." The vibrance fades from her smile, then lights back up.

Rowten doesn't seem to notice. "I won't keep her long." He nods, and I head to the hatch. I can hear their conversation resume while I climb down to the galley. It is a boon, having the captain of the Royal Guard along on this journey, raising our morale, protecting, and guiding. And if we must fight, he and his phantom are no small menace.

My boots click on the polished wood ladder as the walls of the hold rise over my head. The air turns warm from the galley stove and the close quarters below. I reach the bottom step and hear the scream.

Ash!

The cold fear in her voice sends De'ral shooting to the surface, roiling under my skin as I spin around and race back out of the hatch.

Time slows to a near stop, like in a dream. Each rise of my foot takes forever before I can plant it down on the next step. I grip the railing, hoisting my bulk upward. Damn the bones. My sword. I've left it behind in the hold.

"Attack! Arm yourselves," I cry out to the others in the galley. Sweat beads at my temple as my eyes come level with the deck. It gives me an unobstructed view of the mast. I make out Ash's boots and as I climb higher, and her black riding pants appear.

Her knees bend in a crouch, the scream trailing off. Her ponytail flies upward as she ducks. A sword swings straight for her neck.

It's Rowten's blade. Rowten's hands gripping the hilt.

He swings in a steady, relentless arc, cutting downward, an inevitable connection approaching as it slices through the air. Unstoppable, save by her skin and bones. My boot hits the deck, as Ash tries to drop lower, her bangs flying up off her forehead. I will never get there in time.

"Ash!" My eyes beg to shut out the horror. But I keep them open and run as time snaps back to normal speed.

A whistling sound falls toward the deck, joined by a bolt of lightning. The blur of white light streaks down from the crow's nest. A man? With a blade? He plummets, feet first, sword in front of him like a cross pinned to his chest, point down. Before Ash's neck cracks under Rowten's blade, the other weapon finds its mark. It slices Rowten straight through from the top of his shoulder to the hip, piledriving his body into the deck. The captain's sword clatters harmlessly to the side.

Ash's savior lands on one knee, still gripping his sword double-handed. He pulls it out of Rowten's prone body. Splinters fly from the deck with a spray of blood and gore.

Kaylin.

Who just killed Rowten.

Kaylin, who saved Ash's life.

My stomach's in my throat as I sprint toward them. When I reach Ash, she's sitting on her heels, trying to breathe. Her face is drained of blood and her eyes stare blankly. I hold her shoulders, gently lifting her, shaking her, trying to snap her out of it. "Ash! Ash! Look at me."

"Don't break the lass's neck after I just saved it," Kaylin says. He pulls himself from the splintered deck to stand. I'll be surprised if his legs are not broken, along with his spine, but he stands unharmed.

"Kaylin?" Ash asks, eyes welling. "What happened?"

Before either of us can speak, Samsen, Belair, and Piper arrive. They take in the scene, Rowten's skewed body stuck into the deck, Kaylin's blood splattered clothes, me holding Ash in a crushing grip.

They hazard a guess, draw their swords and point them all at Kaylin.

"Hold," Samsen commands him. "Hands where I can see them."

Kaylin shows the palms of his hands but doesn't let go of his sword hilt.

"It wasn't him." I step between the sailor and the others, dragging Ash with me. "Kaylin saved her."

"Saved who?" Piper keeps her sword trained on Kaylin's throat.

"Me," Ash manages to say as she pulls herself out of my stronghold. "It was Rowten. He tried. He…he…"

"He attacked her." I finish the sentence she can't get out. "He would have sliced her head clean off if Kaylin hadn't been there."

"Been where?" Belair tries to make sense of the scene.

I point toward the crow's nest high above. "He jumped, feet first."

Slowly the others sheath their swords, their faces pinched, eyes glancing from Kaylin to the hero of Baiseen's body pooling in his own blood.

Kaylin speaks softly to Ash. "Are you hurt?" He brushes hair back from her forehead, examining where Rowten's blade chopped a corner of her bangs short.

"Ahoy! What's this?" Captain Anders arrives on the scene with his first mate. "Kaylin?" He waits for an explanation but seems as concerned with the damage to the teak wood deck as he is with the dead man embedded in it.

Kaylin ignores him, his attention only on Ash.

I flank Ash, too, ready to help her, bent on understanding what I witnessed, but Captain Anders, getting no answer from Kaylin, holds me back. The rest take Ash below. I want it to be my protective hand on her back, my voice offering reassurance. I must deal with Anders first.

She is safe with Kaylin. De'ral seems to prefer me topside, watching for signs of further threats.

"And she wasn't with me?"

De'ral doesn't answer. He doesn't have to. Ash was not safe with me. I walked away and she nearly died.

We were betrayed.

My jaw tightens, fists clench. *"But why?"* I swallow over the tightness in my throat.

Truth is, Rowten is dead, cut down while trying to kill Ash. This journey is cursed from the start.

20

ASH

"I don't f'qad'n know," I say again. My voice is shrill in my ears. "If I did, I would tell you." Heat burns behind my eyes.

They've trapped me at the galley table. Not that I want to escape, but I do need a moment to think. It would be nice to stop shaking, too.

"You must remember, Ash." Piper is urgent.

I try again, if for nothing else than to make them leave me alone. "We were talking about Lilian's new baby and then…" I skip the part where my inner voice shouted a warning. It was like the side of a mountain erupted in my skull. Unfortunately, the shock paralyzed me.

"Opposite to the desired effect," my inner voice says.

I see that now, but tell me, where in demon stuggs have you been?

"I…can't say. Inside, I know, but when I try to speak it, I can't say."

I know that feeling of late.

"Go on, Ash." Piper draws my attention back to her. "You were talking about Lilian?"

"I couldn't believe my eyes." I swallow hard. "Rowten drew his sword and…"

"Let her be." Kaylin attempts to end the interrogation. "She doesn't know the assailant's mind anymore than we do."

"She must know something. Otherwise, how are we to make sense of this?" Samsen's voice is stern, too, and I realize they are scared. For me and for themselves. "Was it something you mentioned? You offended him gravely? Threatened his family?"

"Pardon?" *They don't really think I would do something like that, do they?*

"Maybe it's better than the alternatives." My inner voice is calm. Soothing to me in so many ways.

Don't disappear like that. Ever again. Promise?

My inner voice gives a mental shrug. *"It was out of my control."*

Marcus joins us from topside. "Threaten his family? You can't be serious," he says. "Ash doesn't go around threatening people."

At least he is sticking up for me. *Hey, wait. What alternatives are you talking about?*

My inner voice drops to a whisper. *"Rowten could have been instructed to kill you."*

I squeeze my eyes shut and relive the seconds before the hero of my childhood was nailed to the deck by Kaylin's sword. An image pops in front of my eyes. "A look came over his face."

"What kind of look?" Piper asks.

"I don't know..." I wring my hands. "Resolved? Then he said he was sorry and started to chant." I find Kaylin's blood-spattered face and pretend I'm speaking only to him. "I asked what he was sorry for, but when he raised the sword, I knew."

"What did you know, Ash?" Samsen prompts.

My eyes stay on Kaylin's. "That he was going to kill me."

It's not completely true. My inner voice knew an instant before me. I was in disbelief, frozen to the spot. I screamed, yes, but was barely able to duck. "If Kaylin hadn't been watching from above..." My head falls into my hands, and I scrub my face as if that will wake me up from this horrid dream, or at least, erase the last fifteen minutes of it.

I lift my eyes back to Kaylin. "How did you know? You were so far above."

"I heard you," Kaylin answers. And then, in my mind alone, *"I finally heard you."*

My lips part. The rest of the room disappears.

Finally, *finally*, it's just the both of us. Like it used to be. Alone together in the crowded world. I take a soft, shaky breath. *"Kaylin? You heard me?"*

"Aye, lass. I did." His smile is full of secret treasures.

My heart beats double-time as it suddenly becomes too big for my chest. I'm light-headed, so much so, I think I will float up to the rafters. Kaylin's back. I have him back! The words tumble between us so fast they spill out with our excitement. *"I've been trying, but—"*

"—been trying, too, since docking in Baiseen."

I turn to my inner voice, ready to jump up and down. *Kaylin hears me!*

"So it appears," my inner voice says with great patience. *"But do you really want him to know your every giddy thought?"*

My face heats and I remember to be selective, but the excitement takes over again.

"I have so much to tell you," we both say to each other at the same time. Despite everything going on around us, it evokes a bubble of laughter from my lips as I watch his eyes dance.

Then I feel the others staring at us. How long have we been conversing in silence?

Marcus clears his throat. "You say you heard her?" He directs his question to Kaylin.

Kaylin nods, his eyes still on me.

My lips twitch, turning up in a smile until my inner voice brings me back to the night's terrifying events.

"They will want to know about the chant."

Do you remember it?

"You don't?"

"This would be a whole other discussion if Kaylin had been wrong," Samsen says, frowning at Kaylin.

"As it would be if I hadn't acted when I did."

No one argues with that, and we sit in silence until the sound of the crew on the deck, and the slow breaths of Tyche asleep in her hammock, become loud in my ears. Belair hands me a warm mug and I clutch it in both hands. "I still can't imagine why Rowten would try to kill me."

"A madness must have taken him?" Piper suggests. "It can happen, with some illnesses."

"He seemed in good health to me," Marcus says.

"Could Tann's influence have infiltrated the royal guard?" Belair asks.

No one wants to answer that, but we all know it might be possible. Red-robes have inexplicable powers. "Still, why target me?"

"Maybe it was Atikis from the headlands, directing from afar," Samsen says.

"Any of these possibilities put us in more danger than we realized," Kaylin says when no one else speaks. "You said he started to chant. Do you remember what it was? It might—"

"We have enemies," Marcus cuts him off. "But it still doesn't explain why Ash was singled out. Why would he try to assassinate my non-savant recorder?"

I turn to him and narrow my eyes. "Truly, why?"

"No offense," Marcus adds quickly.

"Of course not." I say it so he knows it is offensive whether I take it that way or not, to me and all non-savants of Amassia. He makes it sound like an affliction. And it's not the first time. But I guess, in the wider scheme of things, the question needs answering. Why the non-savant recorder? Why me?

"The chant?" A rush of energy tingles through me as Kaylin's voice fills my mind.

"You think it's important?"

"I do."

"The chant…" I try to fill my lungs with a deep breath but only manage a few quick gulps. "I think it was the Warriors' Decree."

There are gasps around me as I speak the words.

"Aye, lass. That is why I killed him before he could touch you. I heard that, too."

"Are you sure?" Piper whispers. "The Warriors' Decree is only evoked—"

"When embarking on a rampage," Samsen finished for her.

I focus again on Kaylin and begin the chant. "Sing, my blade—"

"Stop!" Marcus's face is white. "Don't repeat it." He turns to the others. "It was the Warriors' Decree."

"Still doesn't explain why." Piper frowns.

"It could only make sense if he was planning on killing us all and I was the first. A gift, really. Didn't have to watch you lot die." I try to smile but it's more a grimace.

"Kill us all, and then what?" Belair asks. "The ship's captain would have him in chains, even if he claimed the whistle bone."

"Maybe he was going to slay himself at the end. If it was a compulsion, consequences wouldn't matter." Marcus shakes his head.

"Was it as simple as him wanting the whistle bone?" Belair looks unconvinced. "Is a ship waiting for a signal to collect it?"

"I'm not the keeper of the bones," I say. "Rowten knew that."

"Peace be his path." My inner voice says the words I cannot yet form. Or will not.

Marcus stands. "We can't know his mind, but we must be careful. Palrio has more enemies than guessed, and as long as we are traveling the realms collecting whistle bones, we're targets, too." He holds everyone's eyes. "All of us are."

I exhale the breath I'd been holding in.

"Come," Piper says. "Sleep."

"I don't think I can."

"I'll watch over you." Kaylin's voice is soft in my mind.

"I'm not sure that's going to make me want to sleep." My face warms with the inner thought.

"Drink this," Piper says, lifting the cup to me.

I drain the contents and already my lids are heavier. Piper leads me to my hammock and tucks me as Kaylin steps back to the wall.

"You aren't seriously going to stand guard while I sleep," I ask when Piper is gone.

"Aye, lass. Be sure that I am."

21

ASH

"*Marcus is about to wake you,*" my inner voice says.

I rise from a deep sleep, one crowded with images of Rowten's blade swinging toward me, the Warriors' Decree rumbling deep in his throat. How could he do it? Why? I was a friend of his family, of his sister–which reminds me, Lilian was expecting. Has she had her baby yet?

"Ash, wake up." Marcus's warm breath tickles the side of my face. Behind him, I see Kaylin nod and slip away. He stood guard all night…

"What the Balargk, Marcus?" I try to shove him away. "Do you know how long it took me to go to sleep last night?"

"It's morning now and we have to talk."

I sit up, rubbing my eyes with the heels of my hands.

"Come with me." Marcus is urgent. He takes my hand and pulls me out of the hammock, none too gently.

"Where are we going?" I ask as he leads me to the hatch.

"Topside."

I wrench out of his grip and go back for my coat and boots, blinking away sleep while doing up the buttons. The deck is the last place I want to be.

"*It nearly was our last place on this path,*" my inner voice says quietly.

Marcus leads me onward, oblivious.

The deck is crowded with crew, men and women putting up more sail. Some of them pause to scan the sky. *What are they searching for?*

"*You don't remember?*"

My head throbs when I tip it back to follow their gaze. A red pulse of light, bigger than the morning star by double, shines down at me. For a moment, I'm confused.

"*Confused? Really?*"

Is that—oh! Memory fills my mind like a basin. *The second sun. Of course.* I'm more tired than I thought.

The crew points at it and whispers to each other, but a bark from the first mate has them quickly back to work. I feel the ship pick up speed under my feet. It's a straight shot to Nonnova's big island now, and it looks like we're going to make good time, judging by the wind streaming through my messy hair and fluttering the sails.

"This way." Marcus leads me to a more secluded spot on the starboard railing. The air is moist and salty. It beads on my eyelashes and upper lip as I watch the sea transform from deep purple depths to the flame-red reflection of sunrise. Off the port side, a pod of whales breach. They're traveling fast, spouting geysers before diving again. My smile fades. They are early if they are journeying north as they appear to be. Much too early. But when the morning light trumpets across the sky to the far horizon, I suddenly lose my train of thought. "Thank you, Marcus, for showing me. It's so beautiful."

He shakes his head. "Not that."

"What then?"

He avoids my eyes, which is never a good sign with Marcus. His golden hair blows in the wind as well, strands catching on his chin stubble. "You have Brogal's medallion?"

I pull it out from under my coat and dangle it in front of him. The bright bronze catches the sun and flashes light over the polished wooden deck. "Right here." My mouth goes dry, recalling how we tested it, how little faith Brogal had in me. The shock when I heard his doubting thoughts in my head.

"Then your mouth might be about to get drier," my inner voice warns.

"You want me to use it now?" I ask Marcus.

"To try and contact Brogal. He needs to know."

"Try?" I frown, for more than one reason. "It's premature, wouldn't you say? Nothing has really happened yet."

"That doesn't even make sense to me," my inner voice says.

Apparently, Marcus is equally confused.

"Nothing has happened?" He raises his voice. "We were attacked by a red-robe, Rowten is dead, killed while attempting to assassinate *you*. How is that nothing?"

I don't have an answer but, inexplicably, I'm reluctant to contact Master Brogal with this medallion. "He told me to check in when we secured Nonnova's bone. We haven't done that yet."

Marcus pulls his hair back from his face and ties it with a leather thong. "Contact him now, Ash, if you can." His voice is decidedly Heir-like for someone who has lost their throne. "If nothing else, I want to hear if my father still lives."

That shoots a dozen holes in my resistance, and I lower my head. "I will, of course. Just give me a moment."

"I'll be in the galley." He stomps away, not looking back. I guess we are all dealing with Rowten's betrayal in our own ways. His is anger; mine is…

"Avoidance?"

Thank you. I bite the gratitude in half.

Looking for more privacy, I make my way to the stoop. Part of me knows I can do this, and the other part is terrified to try, in case I can't.

"Make up your mind. Capable or incapable."

Capable. I blow out my breath. *I'm capable.*

After sitting in silence, back against one of the water barrels strapped to the deck, I pull off the medallion and clasp it in both hands. *"Knock, knock."* If there are more formal words for activating it, he didn't bother to teach them. Or I don't remember. *"Master Brogal? A moment of your time?"*

My scalp prickles as any lingering doubts vanish on the wind. Brogal's undeniable presence is here. I can sense him at his desk. My body tenses, as if for a blow. *Relax,* I coach myself, expecting my inner voice to chime in, but it seems to have vanished, too. I wait for whatever greeting, or lack of greeting, he'll offer, but he's distracted. I don't think he knows I'm here. There are thoughts coming at me from all angles as the sound of shuffling scrolls and books fill my mind. Is he looking for something? Conversing with his phantom? I certainly can't hear that.

"You knew it would be dangerous, Master, using slips of your own soul for the binding. I warned—"

"Quiet, Nun!" Brogal growls. *"You want the whole Sanctuary to know?"*

"Of course not, but Master, it already wears at your mind. You said it would be undone by now, freeing the bonds to return to you. But they have not, and you're suffering because of it."

Undone? Suffering? None of this makes sense.

"There's obviously been a delay." He sounds agitated, not his usual contained self.

"Master Brogal? Can you hear me?" I keep my voice light, as if I'd just arrived. No eavesdropping here… *"Marcus, I mean, the Bone Gatherer asked me to contact…"*

"…should have taken care of it from the start." Brogal says it with self-reproach. *"But I couldn't with it watching my every move."*

"It's too late for that now," Nun says. *"But if what you say is true, you'll be whole again before the night is out."*

What's too late, I wonder? *"Master Brogal? It's Ash."*

There's a pause, some swearing, which surprises me because the High

Savant never swears. I mean, never—probably one of the reasons I adopted the habit early on, though only in other languages. I wanted to be as much unlike him as possible.

"Ash." His voice is curious. "Did you not meet the boat?"

Why would he think that? "We're a day and a half from Nonnova, if the winds hold. But I must report ahead of time."

"Continue."

Butter wouldn't melt in the sun near him.

I take a deep breath. "The Gollnar red-robe Atikis attacked us at the Suni River flats."

"Are you certain it was Atikis?"

"We think so. His phantom made that clear."

"Casualties?"

"We escaped."

"Marcus still has the Baiseen whistle bone?"

"Indeed, Master, but he's concerned about the state of the city, and he asks after his father."

"Jacas Adicio passed last night." It's like he's giving a weather report. Cloudy skies with a storm of hail and then, the magistrate died... "Peace be his path."

I repeat the traditional well wishes for his soul's journey. "Peace be his path." Deep down, I realize this completes the transfer of power to Petén. Poor Marcus. We knew it was inevitable, but it will not lessen the pain of his losses.

"Again, was anyone injured?"

"No injuries of consequence." I follow his example and am blunt. "But, and this will sound bizarre, Rowten tried to kill me."

He doesn't speak and I feel a jumble of thoughts unexpressed, like chickens frantically pecking after too few grains.

"Kaylin stopped him," I add.

"How?" He hits me hard with the question, and I want to drop the medallion and back away.

"Rowten was an assassin, Master." I don't think I'm making this clear enough. "He tried to kill me."

"That's impossible." Brogal pauses and asks Nun to fetch Dina.

I want to protest. But I hardly believe it myself, so why should he? "If it hadn't been for Kaylin, I would be dead."

"Has he confessed anything?"

"Rowten confessed? Um... No."

"Why not? Piper should be able to dose him, make him talk."

"He's dead, Master Brogal. Peace be his path…"

Brogal's voice lowers into a growl. *"The captain of the honor guard is dead? Why?"*

Am I not saying this right?

"Because that's how Kaylin stopped him."

Brogal pauses again. *"What provocation did the captain of the Royal Guard have to kill you?"*

My thoughts exactly, but the way Brogal puts it, to the exclusion of any comfort or concern, makes my stomach sink through the ship's hull and into the sandy seabed. *I should be used to this by now.*

"No one should ever be used to such a thing," my inner voice says as if from very far away.

The truth of that somehow helps. *"We think he planned to kill us all,"* I say to Brogal. *"He evoked the Warriors' Decree."*

"How would you know that?"

I want to say, because I am a wordsmith. Because I have read every book in the Sanctuary library, at least the ones not banned to non-savants. But I don't. It's simpler to repeat the cursed thing which suddenly rises clear in my mind. *"Sing, my blade, fast and true. Find your mark, through and through. Take the heart and the soul. To the core, on you go—"*

"Stop!" He is silent for a while. *"Who else is aware of this event?"*

Not the question I expect. *"Everyone onboard the* Dugong.*"*

"It must be Tann, and if he got to Rowten, he could get to anyone." There is a series of sounds, his chair scraping, him standing, orders given… *"Ash!"*

"I'm here."

"Make haste to Nonnova. Secure the next whistle bone. Trust no one. Do you understand?" He doesn't wait for my response but keeps talking. *"Toss the body overboard with all his possessions. Leave no trace. There is to be no evidence left behind."*

Toss the body? *"But his family, his sister Lilian. They have to be—"*

"No trace. Do. You. Understand?"

I don't, not at all. *"Yes, Master."*

"Then walk your path." There's an audible clank as if he's shut the medallion away in a drawer.

"Master Brogal?"

My hands shake as I stand, putting the medallion over my neck and tucking it under my coat. The wind tugs at my hair, now missing a chunk on the left corner of my bangs. Thanks to Rowten's blade. It blows away the single tear rolling down my cheek. If Brogal thinks no more of an attempt on my life than that... When I trust my heart can't be lower, it sinks deeper again.

"If he thinks no more...then so be it," my inner voice concludes. *"His loss."*

"Aye," I say the way Kaylin would, which comforts me as well. I straighten my back. There is news to deliver to Marcus, and that's the priority. I palm moisture from my cheeks and go below.

22

KAYLIN

The water rushes over me, the sensations like fingers chilling my skin. Finally, I can breathe. The dawn sends light to the depths like curtains of gold. Schools of bait fish flee at my approach. There are hundreds of them, all changing direction in a snap—shift left, halt, sudden right, and left again. Their scales are mirrors reflecting the kelp and reefs, luminous under the rising suns. Herding the silver fish from behind are big-mouthed groupers and green sea bass. A vast landscape unfolds before me, and my heart swells. I am home. I am in my sanctuary.

This is the world I want nothing more than to share with Ash. And this is the world she cannot enter for more than a glimpse. She is a lander. Her allegiance belongs to the air she breathes, to feet on the ground, food on the table, and books in the libraries. To the people she loves. To hopes and dreams that do not exist under the waves. This home of mine is something Ash will never know and it breaks my heart to think of it.

I clear the emotion from my head with a shake. What I must do next cannot be clouded with sentiments. *Sentiments?* Who am I kidding? I am harboring a long-sight more than sentiments. I love her!

As I swim, my shadow falls over the reef fish and they disappear into the safety of the corals. I want to stop and imbibe the memories of this region but swim on, knowing Teern has tracked me since my head went under the waves. Mustn't keep the Sea King waiting.

"Kaylin." Teern's voice booms around me.

I stop short, my hair fanning out as I search the seascape. He's impossible to miss, even as a shadow rippling on the surface a hundred yards away. Here we go.

He streams toward me. *"Father, I can explain everything."*

"Can you?" Teern circles me once, like a shark, and doesn't say more.

His silence is a knife to my throat. I really may have miscalculated how much trouble I'm in.

"Follow," he says and dives deeper.

I swim in the Sea King's wake, entering a dark well that cuts through the currents. When we reach a cave thirty fathoms down, the water turns cold as the poles. I shiver, but not because of the temperature. Teern leads the way into the darkness, kicking past nurse sharks sleeping under the shoals. They line the entrance like guards. We glide over large slabs of granite, ruins from an ancient time when the continents were seven, the sea level much lower. The slabs are encrusted with anemones, sponges and urchins, and slow-moving herds of giant starfish. I feel my way more than see, until bioluminescent creatures light the cave walls like a cityscape. I must admit it. I have missed this these last few months.

We emerge into the air pocket of the underwater cave, climbing huge steps out of the water. Pocket is wrong. It's more the size of a king's hall. Probably was one, once. The light makes me blink, its shimmering glow like a thousand tiny suns. It is beautiful, under the right circumstances, but today Teern has called the bioluminescent creatures to this cave, so the density is unnatural and eerie to my eyes. Somehow, on land, with Ash by my side, this inevitable meeting with Teern seemed more manageable.

Now that I face him, I'm a child who lost his father's favorite hunting dog and is about to be taught a lesson in responsibilities. A child that keeps a secret, one I can't allow even into the edges of my thoughts.

Teern stands to his full height, seven feet tall. Unlike me and Salila, he would not pass on the streets of Baiseen, not as a lander, even if dressed in savant robes. There have not been giants on Amassia since long before the continents rejoined.

Teern chuckles, plucking that thought right out of my head as he crosses his arms over his massive chest. Water runs off his hair and beard, like he's a statue in the rain. I know there is something important to divulge, for him to choose a cave insulated from the ears of other Mar. Here, when we speak aloud, no one on land or in the sea will hear. As if any lander has that skill. Which makes me acknowledge that Ash does. It's not a morsel for the Sea King to chew on today, if I can help it. I shove the thought away.

"Feeling a little paranoid?" I ask Teern. My voice is chiding, arrogance to the fore. He expects nothing less from his favorite son.

But I might be pushing it. And it remains to be seen if I am still his favorite.

He moves fast, a blurred hand reaching for my throat. The Sea King slams me against the urchin encrusted wall, squeezing tight while my feet hang above the cave floor.

"You better have a mother-of-fine-pearl excuse for disobeying me."

I gasp, unable to speak aloud. *"I'm no good to you with a broken neck, Father."*

"I suppose." The Sea King grudgingly loosens his grip. "But thus far you are not terribly useful without one."

Released, I hit the wet rock floor. "I know Brogal's plan," I say, trying to clear my throat, and my mind.

Teern harrumphs. "That knowledge is not what I'm after." He moves to the center of the cave and takes the ancient throne, a high back and wide seat carved from granite and covered with runes. He lounges in it, his considerable bulk laid out like a sculpture. He motions me to his feet. His eyes are blue-black orbs in the luminous light of the cave. His chiseled jaw clamps tight and then relaxes into a smile. "Salila," he says without looking at the steps. "You're late."

I don't have to turn around to know she's coming out of the water behind me. I'd sensed her the moment I immersed. *"Traitor,"* I say, sending her the thought privately.

"You should talk," she says back.

"Speak aloud," Teern booms. "Why do you think I've brought you here?"

"To keep the little non-savant out?" Salila spits out a wad of fish bone she's been rolling around with her tongue.

"Don't call her that." I bare my teeth.

Her canines flash right back at me.

"Come." The Sea King motions Salila to sit to the side of the throne. "I want to clear a few things up before deciding your fates."

Neither of us interrupts.

"Kaylin." He taps his fingers on the throne.

I meet his eyes.

"You were to drown the Heir and his followers on the way back from Aku. But you rescued them instead. I asked especially that the orphan girl, Ash, not make it to shore, yet to shore she went, alive and well. Tell me one reason why I shouldn't send you back to the Ma'ata and crush the landers myself." His voice is calm, almost quizzical, but I don't let that fool me. He's dead serious.

"I understand you wanted the Heir and his companions drowned."

"If that's so, why do they live?"

"He fell for the girl," Salila says before I can speak. "Quite hard. I think it knocked all sense out of him." She takes great pleasure in delivering this bit of news.

"That's not the reason they are still alive." I keep my voice calm and deliberate, careful to speak true, but not too true, especially about Ash. "The reason they are alive is because I have a better idea." Teern waits for me to say more. "I took a risk, assuming you would trust me." I shrug my shoulders like it's no big thing.

The Sea King's face is like granite. "Elaborate?"

"You want the crown of bones, but did it occur to you that the Bone Gatherer might have a better time collecting the originals than you, or Tann for that matter?"

"Even if I wake the Dreaded?" he says in a quiet breath.

I stumble, nearly losing my calm. He can't seriously be thinking of turning them loose on the world. They were cursed to the Ma'ata by his own hand. And for good reason. I take a breath. "Look how far from the sea the journey will take them. Even the Dreaded"—I flinch saying the name aloud—"are not equipped for inland roads."

"What are you proposing, Kaylin?"

"That I continue with Marcus, keeping firsthand eyes on the Bone Gatherer and—"

"That doesn't mean we can't kill the girl, just to be safe," he interrupts.

Just to be safe? What is he talking about? "We can't kill Ash!" I blurt out the words, then collect myself. "You don't understand. If Ash disappears, Marcus will think of nothing else. He would turn over the world to find her, or avenge her."

"He'd abandon the quest?"

"I believe he would, but if you leave the party intact, when he has all the six from the remaining Sanctuaries, and then the six from Tann, or whoever else, I'll return them to you."

Teern laughs. "Now why in the demon-deep crags would I trust you to do that?"

"Because of what I want in return."

"Your freedom isn't enough?"

"It's not."

Teern rubs his bearded jaw. "What more then?"

"Ash," I say softly. "You'll leave us be and never threaten her life again. Ever."

"Ha!" Salila says. "Told you."

"Does it matter with the next Great Dying upon us?" I say, trying not to let my desperation show. "Admit it, this is a sound plan. The Bone Gatherer's company has as strong a chance of gaining the twelve as any team of Mar, especially with the little caller from Aku."

The Sea King's eyes grow distant as he considers it.

"Do we have an agreement?" I press, hoping the perspiration on my forehead isn't about to start dripping.

"All right, Kaylin." Teern slowly nods. "You bring me the rest of Er's bones and I'll grant your wish, assuming you and the girl survive."

"Excellent." My shoulders lighten, until I catch his wording. "The *rest* of the whistle bones?"

Teern's lip curls in a half smile. "You'll not need Baiseen's."

So ours is a fake? I don't ask how he got his hands on it. Nun, no doubt, when it should have been spirited away to the Bone Thrower's cave.

Teern chuckles. "You surprise me, Kaylin, but know this, if you let Ash out of your sight, even for a moment, our deal is off."

His interest in her makes the hairs at the back of my neck stand up, but I nod. "Done."

It'll be fine. I know her through and through. She is special, no doubt unique. But she can't be who he suspects her to be.

"Done." Teern answers back and then waves me away. "Go. Retrieve the bones and stick to your word or I'll send you back to the Ma'ata for the next ten rounds of the dark sun."

I temple my palms together and lift them to my forehead, giving him a formal bow. "Thank you, Teern."

"Goodnight, Father." Salila tries to slip away with me.

"Salila!" The walls of the cave quake from Teern's voice.

"What? I've done as told," Salila says, spinning around, her lower lip pushing out. "But I wouldn't mind joining Marcus's little party as well." She runs her tongue over her teeth. "I could just eat him up. And his phantom? I could get used to—"

"This is not a game, Daughter!" Teern's voice knocks us both off our feet. "You'll shadow Tann's ships, informing us of his actions and be ready when Kaylin calls."

"I'm under his direction now?" She jerks her thumb toward me.

"You're both under mine. If you don't want to find yourselves forever sleeping in your tombs, you best remember it." He stands abruptly, again his movements so fast they are only a blur. "Be away, both of you, and do not reveal yourselves. Yes, the rumors of Mar are good for the sacrifices. But better also they remain unconfirmed." He shakes his bearded head. "Landers…"

"I'd rather follow Marcus and De'ral," Salila grumbles, staying well out of Teern's reach as she does. "Trade?" She looks at me.

I ignore her and dip my head once more to the Sea King. As I rush back to the *Dugong*, relief floods me. Still, I wonder how Teern will take it when he realizes that Salila and I have confirmed the secret of the Mar. It's like the proverbial cat. No one on land or sea is going to stuff it back in the bag.

23

ASH

I find Marcus sitting by himself at the galley table, nursing a steaming mug. I don't know where Kaylin is, but the others must still be in their bunks and hammocks. I reach for a clean cup from the cupboard above the galley benchtop and pour tea from the pot. The scent of cloves, cardamom, and cinnamon fills the air. Looks like Belair found more Ochee. That's comforting, too.

"Ash, you're pale as linen." Marcus slides over, making room for me on the bench. "Did you reach Brogal?"

"I talked with the High Savant, yes." My voice is barely more than a breath. There was something wrong with him, but I don't know what.

"And? My father?"

I clasp both his hands in mine. "He died last night. Peace be his path." I watch as a cascade of emotions storm through Marcus's eyes. The one he chooses makes me shudder. It's empty, like a bottomless void. I let go of his hands.

"Not unexpected," he says, barely moving his lips. "His advice about Rowten?"

"Marcus, your father just died." I soften my voice. "Tell me what you need."

He straightens his back and looks beyond me. "What I need is to hear Brogal's advice about Rowten."

I remind myself he's in shock and doesn't know he's lashing out. I stiffen anyway, and use my most formal voice. "Brogal said we were to commit Rowten's body, and all his possessions, into the sea. Leave no trace. We aren't to tell anyone, or waste time going through his things."

"Like he was never here? That's madness."

"Brogal didn't seem himself." I nod. "We're to carry on, collect the bones but trust no one, not even each other."

"That's it?" Marcus is tense as a lyre string.

"He wondered if Tann was controlling Rowten somehow."

"You told him about Atikis?"

"He didn't seem that concerned." I hold my cup with both hands to keep them from shaking. "He also wasn't concerned about my—" I don't want to say near-death but can't think of another word.

Marcus studies my face for a moment, some of his familiar self coming back. "Not all fathers, surrogate or true, care for their offspring, past a usefulness." The declaration ends with a quick shrug.

His bluntness punches the wind out of me and my eyes well.

He frowns and tries again. "Brogal isn't an emotional man, but he trusts you, Ash. He approved of you for this quest and gave you the medallion. Hold on to that if you need something from him."

The welling tears spill. Marcus's newfound coldness has me leaning away, tightening my arms to my sides.

"I'll make eggs." He takes a frying pan from under the benchtop. "Want some?"

"No," I whisper. We don't say another word until Kaylin comes trotting down the ladder and into the galley. His hair is wet, shirt damp. His eyes go to me first.

"How was the morning swim?" I ask.

"It would have only been more glorious if you'd joined me."

I give him a mock curtsey and he bows. I want to thank him for watching over me, and savor this first hello of the day, but not in front of Marcus. Not now. *"But did you even sleep?"*

"I had a beautiful night." Kaylin says it loud as a tower bell. *"Guarding a goddess among wordsmiths while she slumbered."*

He's a poet this morning. I blush and beam at him, warmed by the attention. Our sailor is completely recovered, not a splinter or bruise from his death drop that saved my life. It doesn't surprise me anymore. He's the most resilient person I've ever met.

"What says Brogal, lass?" He slides onto the bench seat beside me, putting his arm over my shoulder.

I love the way he has complete faith in me, that there was no chance, in his mind, that I didn't reach the High Savant. *Kaylin cares.*

"They both do, but Marcus is in pain." My inner voice is uncharacteristically compassionate today, and I know the words are true.

I share again what transpired in my short conversation with the High Savant while Marcus whisks eggs in a bowl.

I decide that from now on, any sympathy I need because my guardian takes no interest in my life or death, can come from me. And here it is: *too bad, Ash. You deserve better. Now stay alert because all may not be well in our Sanctuary.*

I take a moment to deliver that message to myself, accept it and let out the breath I keep holding. A very small smile touches my lips as I gain strength from my own thoughts.

When I return my focus to the room, Kaylin is talking to Marcus. "Condolences, Bone Gatherer, for your father," he says. "Peace be his path." He gets up to fill his own mug. "By all rights, you are the new Magistrate of Palrio, holder of the Phantom Throne of Baiseen." He lifts his mug to salute. "And even if delayed, the carving of your *warrior* will be added to your ancestors' when you take power."

I join Kaylin in the salute, my mug raised high. "Hear! Hear!"

"Maybe, someday." Marcus looks away, barely allowing the honor we give him. "But for now, we must follow Brogal's course: secure the whistle bones, keep our eyes open, and trust no one."

"Agreed," Kaylin and I say together.

And for me, that distrust now includes the High Savant of Baiseen. Not just because he thinks so little of my life, but because of what he said before he knew I was there.

What didn't Brogal want the whole Sanctuary to hear?

"Indeed, what?"

I don't have an answer. Maybe it will be clear by tomorrow when we dock in Nonnova. But somehow I don't think it will.

24

MARCUS

How does she stay so positive?

Ash holds the railing, bouncing on her toes as we glide over the turquoise water into the harbor of Nonnova. "It's as stunning as ever."

"Hmm." If I say more, it will come out harsh, and I don't want to dampen her spirits. Not after what she's been through. I can't believe she isn't crushed by the betrayal. Doesn't it take more than two nights' sleep to get over that?

Betrayal? Really? De'ral rumbles.

My phantom is right. Assassination attempt. On her life! I expected her to be devastated, but she's not. It's almost like she's back to her old self, from before the attack on Baiseen. Today, at least her spirits are strong. I wish I could say the same for mine.

"I have the documents all in order." She pats her satchel, trying again to strike up a conversation.

"Good." The documents Brogal signed, sanctioning our purpose in gathering the whistle bones, should give me confidence, but all I can do is roll through the turmoil in my mind. I can't make sense of anything. But I have to try.

First, there's no grief in me for Rowten. He lost all rights to that when he tried to lop off Ash's head. But the fact that he did it? I would be a fool not to be alarmed. Second, Father. I don't miss his doubts and disapproval. If anything, I'm relieved he's gone. Relieved, and furious that he left Petén to rule the realm. Devastated that the last chance to prove myself is gone.

He put Petén and Rhiannon on the throne, De'ral interrupts my thoughts.

"Don't remind me of that alliance," I growl aloud in response.

Third, there is my phantom. Even after the extensive training on Aku, and stepping up from green to yellow-robe, can I honestly say I am in full control? Ever? The battle with the red-robe Atikis shouts a loud and clear no.

Salila would say no, too…

"*Not helping, De'ral.*" But then, there is no evidence of my phantom wanting to be helpful.

And then there's Salila, a Mar I can't get out of my head, literally. How can I hear her?

You don't.

"What are you talking about? We had a conversation, under the water no less."

I have conversations with her. You were a fly on the wall.

It's De'ral who hears her, not me? Of course, it is. But how can he do so on his own, as if we weren't one and the same?

Ash squeezes my arm. "Are you all right?"

"I'm the one who should be asking you that." I soften toward her.

"I asked first." She nudges me with her shoulder. "Everything is happening at once, Marcus, roaring toward us like a herd of Aturnian long-horns. I feel it, too."

She waits for me to look at her.

"Just choose one out of the many overworked thoughts in your head. Share that, at least, with me." She raises her brows. "I'm your friend, Marcus. You talk with your friends."

"All right." I draw a deep breath and let it out in a rush. "I'm either going mad, or I can hear Salila in my head. Well, my *warrior* can, at least, and I hear her when he lets me." My face heats and I turn back to the sea. "It's unnerving."

Ash doesn't answer right away and when she does, I'm surprised.

"I've heard Salila in my head, too."

"You have! Why didn't you say?" I can't believe this. "You mentioned getting images from phantoms, from De'ral especially." I whisper his name. No point pretending Ash doesn't know it, but I don't need the rest of the world to. "Is it like that? Images?" I don't give her time to answer. "Because for me, Salila's voice is clear with her bold, if not rude thoughts." It strikes me that the Mar woman is so well versed in multiple languages. I've recognized her use of several, not that I could understand much. I wonder how she was educated. Can she read all the languages she speaks? I mean, books in the sea? That's impossible.

You are always asking the wrong questions, Marcus.

"Go back to sleep."

I listen when Ash speaks.

Another perplexity I cannot fathom—De'ral's fascination with Ash. All phantoms' fascination really...

"Calm down, Marcus." She puts her hand on my shoulder.

I take a breath and let her go on.

"Salila's voice in my head is not like the pictures phantoms send. It's actual conversations, or it was back on Aku. I haven't talked with her, mind-to-mind or otherwise since."

"Well, I have." And I guess I really needed to share that.

She pats my hand where I have tightened my grip on the rail. "How does your *warrior* feel about it all?"

"Loves it." I laugh grimly.

"Well then, maybe it's a gift."

"A gift?" I dismiss the idea but then backtrack. "Maybe you're right." I put my arm around her shoulder. "But for now, as long as you are safe and well, we best focus on what's ahead."

She blows out her breath. "Honestly, I won't say I have made peace with Rowten's attack. Not sure I ever will, but I agree. We focus on what's next. Are you ready for Servine?"

"As ready as I can be." I haven't seen the High Savant Servine since her red-robe ceremony four years ago where I demonstrated, to humiliating levels, how inept I was at raising my phantom. Father had little to say about that, but he didn't need to. I was disappointed in myself enough for us both.

"You've come such a long way." Ash smiles. "And she probably won't remember the last visit."

"I should be so lucky."

De'ral laughs and I try to ignore him.

From the deck of the *Dugong*, it looks like nothing's changed in Nonnova. Mountainous island, crystal water, white sand, and tropical fruits ripening on trees. Young women and men gather in small groups on the beach, husking coconuts. Weaving. Children rushing about with buckets and fishing nets. Ash is right. Nonnova is as stunning as ever.

"We should purchase dried coconut and dates for the journey," I say. Small talk seems much easier now.

"You just want to go meet those girls." Ash nudges me.

"I will join you, Marcus," Belair says as he comes up behind us.

Ash gives him a friendly shove, too. "And you just want to meet those boys. Make sure, in all the meeting, you don't forget to buy the coconut and dates."

For a small moment, the three of us laugh together and my burdens lift. Then I sober. "We should also measure their temperament as regards to the second sun."

"They don't look too worried to me," Belair says.

He's right. They don't.

"Here comes the welcoming party." Ash tips her head at the entrance to the docks.

Orange-robe savants trot down the steps and along the wooden pier toward our berth. They're too far away to make out faces, but their stride is purposeful. Formal.

"They've received Brogal's message, I presume," Kaylin says as he joins us. "Or did their Bone Throwers know we were coming?"

"Both, I imagine." I roll my shoulders, refusing to tense up. My feelings toward Kaylin are a little uneasy since Rowten's death. He slaughtered him mercilessly, after all. If I hadn't seen the attack with my own eyes…

He saved Ash.

"That's why I didn't run him through on the spot, but still, sailor or not, the dive from the crow's nest seems impossible."

Then be glad it wasn't.

"Hopefully Tann hasn't beat us here." Ash's cheeks flush as Kaylin leans against the railing beside her.

"No sign of battle." I keep up the small talk. "The harbor is clean and peaceful."

"No fires, no sunken ships. And the youths on the beach seem unfazed," Kaylin adds.

"Looks like Servine's honor guard," Belair says, pointing at the additional troops coming down the dock to meet us.

Ash's spine stiffens. She lets go of the railing and takes a step back.

"Nothing's going to happen to you." Kaylin puts his arm around her and draws her into his side.

"That goes without saying." I take her free hand and pull her over toward me.

She drops my hand while squirming out from under Kaylin's arm. "Thanks, both of you, but we're here on official business and I am your wordsmith, not a child who needs coddling." She gives both of us a measured look. "I will admit, though, I'm very lucky to have such fine champions at my side."

"Ever the diplomat, lass," Kaylin says and tips an imaginary hat to her.

Of course, it makes her laugh. I want to pull her back to my side where I know she is safe—I nearly lost her to the assassin—but I can see no valid reason to smother her.

Who needs a reason?

"Quiet, De'ral."

I'm close enough, and besides, Kaylin is a master warrior. I have no problem admitting that he can protect her, too, though Ash would probably say I'm missing the point. She is not an object in need of protection.

But could she have defended herself that night? Could any of us, under such an unexpected attack?

She couldn't have.

I step closer. Between the two of us, she has the best bodyguards on Amassia.

The three of us, De'ral says.

Again, I find it uncanny that my phantom thinks himself separate from me at the moment, but apparently, he does. I'm not going to fight it. *"The three of us will keep her safe."* In that, I will trust.

The *Dugong* crew jumps into action as we glide into the vacant berth. Along the dock, men and women are waving and catching ropes. In short order the long lines are tied, the gangplank down, and I lead our company to meet the welcome committee of orange-robes.

"I'm Marcus Adicio, here by the request of—"

"Yes, yes. Brogal has sent word. Follow us." A woman directs us with a wave of her hand.

Before I can say more, we are all staring at the retreating backs of the savants. There is nothing else to do but follow them up the broad steps and along a wide, tree-lined thoroughfare.

"Customary welcome?" Kaylin asks me under his breath.

"Not really."

But Ash doesn't seem to notice with her nose to the sky. "Jacarandas," she says, a ghost of a smile on her lips. "They're beautiful in spring."

I take her word for it. The trees are bare this time of year and like the orange-robes, not particularly welcoming. Also, we're headed in the wrong direction. The Sanctuary is to the left of the harbor, not right.

Ash tugs on my sleeve. "We're going the wrong way," she whispers.

"I noticed."

Kaylin's hand rests on the hilt of his sword.

I speak to Samsen out the side of my mouth. "Eyes open, everyone."

Samsen's hand goes to his sword as well as he passes the warning to Piper, Belair, and Tyche.

I clear my throat. "Masters?" The orange-robes had offered no introductions so there is no other way to address them. "Excuse me, but you're taking us to the High Savant Servine?"

The woman in the lead turns her head and lifts a shoulder. The gesture is ambiguous, but she continues until the street narrows and we head inland toward the heart of the isle. The sun rises higher, flies buzz around my face, and I begin to sweat.

"I forgot how warm it is here," Ash says, unbuttoning her winter coat, the one that was covered in Rowten's blood last night. Looks like the deckman got it clean. But her words don't sit right. I'm about to comment that she's been making several journeys a year to Nonnova, and her memory must be failing, but I stop myself.

As we approach a shady pathway that leads to a carved wooden gate, Ash comments on the wall. It's made of pale clay bricks and extends in a long curving line until it disappears into the jungle. We're entering the Sanctuary, but not by the main gates. Good to know, but why?

Ash frowns at me and grips my hand.

I look again. Much of the wall is covered in trailing vines but a section in the distance is being worked on. Several blue-robes are scrubbing the surface clean. A yellow-robe savant directs them.

"What happened there?" I ask.

Our guides neither turn to look nor answer. I want to push for an explanation, but Ash squeezes my hand again and shakes her head as if she's read my mind. In her eyes is fear and I realize I shouldn't have been so quick to trust even our sovereign ally, the High Savant Servine.

25

ASH

I slow my pace as we are led into the Sanctuary, the heavy wooden side gate clapping shut behind us. Something's not right.

"There is more than one lie in the air."

I forgot how little sense my inner voice makes at times. *Care to elaborate?*

"Two or maybe three deceptions are flowing over one another. Tied up in knots."

I don't know what that means, but it doesn't sound good. Without warning, a chill snakes through me, and my heart beats wildly out of rhythm. I can't breathe.

"You have to breathe," my inner voice coaches.

I take a gulp of air. This is Nonnova, I remind myself. Our allies since the realms were formed. We are safe here, for viz'n's sake. I try to laugh it off.

"Breathe, Ash. Let it pass."

Now you're an expert on my panics?

"You forget. They are mine, too." My inner voice gives a mental sigh. *"Notice the little things."*

I try, but my eyes dart everywhere at first, seeking the source of my growing anxiety. Where are these knots of lies? I can't tell, which makes everything worse. The gardens are well kept, not a shade or shadow in sight. Though the twisting trunks of the wisteria look like they are hungry for something to choke.

"What else do you see?"

I focus on the landscape of freshly pruned hibiscus, orange angel trumpets, and small leafy azaleas that are already covered with pink and white buds. *It's beautiful,* I admit.

"What do you hear?"

I take another breath and listen. Tiny hummingbirds beat their transparent wings, dipping into the trumpet flowers. They move more like buzzing bees than birds. As I expected, spring in Nonnova is not far off, though there are only two seasons here, hot and dry and hot and wet. I take another deep breath and let it out.

Kaylin steps nearer to walk beside me. His fingers release the hilt of his sword and brush the back of my hand. *"I'm here,"* he whispers in my mind.

I focus on the sound of his voice, the lightness of his touch, and expand my lungs. They fill with the sweet, scented air. When I let out my breath, my shoulders relax. I'm back in the present moment, but I keep up the observations, allowing my awareness to take in everything around me. It helps.

The pathways are meticulously swept and blue- and green-robe students — healers mostly, I assume — are at work with rakes and brooms. From the higher branches of surrounding umbrella trees squeaks, whistles, and chatter waft down from the pandemonium of lorikeets roosting there. Then I see it, a group of orange-robes training on the far side of the garden pools.

"Kaylin, do you see what I see?"

"Aye. Callers."

Tyche notices, too. Her eyes narrow, and she looks at me with confusion. Piper takes her hand.

I catch up with Marcus and tug on his sleeve for the tenth time since disembarking. It may be starting to annoy him, but this is important.

He bends his head to me. "What now?"

"Callers," I whisper.

He studies the orange-robes as we walk by. The phantoms are various creatures, bird-like and four-footed beasts, all of them vocalizing. I can't see what they are practicing with until weapons fly through the air, the savants catching them in outstretched hands.

Marcus furrows his brow and I know he understands.

"This is unusual, right?" Kaylin asks, his lips brushing my ear.

His proximity makes my breath catch. "Nonnova isn't known for their callers and those…" I shut my mouth. *"They don't look like Nonnova savants."*

"Nonnovan savants have a look?"

"Yes and no. They vary in color and conformation like we all do. But did you notice the girls on the beach this morning?"

"Aye!"

Does he have to be so enthused? *"Well then, did you notice the way they…"*

"Smile? And move like they walk on clouds? And laugh like—"

"I can see you studied them in depth. The point is, accomplished as those orange-robes are, they don't have the same way about them."

"I see your point."

We make a hard left and enter the main building, but again from a side door. *"And what of this indirect route?"* Our boots sound on the tile floors as I orient myself. We must be in the left wing, behind the reception hall. Interesting, because that is the hall where their first whistle bone usually hangs. I've seen it enough times on my visits here. The Tree of Eternity, symbol of physical life, a whistle carved from a neck bone and decorated with images of root to trunk to stem to bud to flower to seed and back to root. I feel very certain it is no longer hanging there. But how can I know that?

"Talus said to trust your gut."

I'm trying to!

They lead us down the corridor and into a small waiting room. No refreshments are offered, and the guards are left behind, effectively blocking any way out. Their phantoms are up and armed, looking nothing like *healers* in this light. I jump when the door on the opposite side of the room opens.

"Calm yourself. In moments, you will be translating for the High Savant."

I take another measured breath and lift my chin as I exhale. *I'm ready.*

"This way," the approaching savant says and disappears into the darkness. He leads us down a torch-lit corridor made of uneven stone steps.

"Where are we going?" Tyche asks in a loud whisper.

I squint at the windowless walls and looming ceiling. "Somewhere secure."

Piper takes Tyche's hand again and keeps ahold of it.

I lose count of the steps before we reach the bottom where the corridor opens into a large, vaulted room with a hundred blazing candles. It's the most beautiful meditation hall I've ever seen. The warm glow, colorful cushions, the low central table all make it familiar and inviting. "I had no idea this was here," I can't help myself from saying.

"Sit," the savant says. "The High Savant will be with you shortly."

There is water on the low table, and we all sit cross-legged around it. I barely have time to fill my glass and bring it to my lips when Servine enters the room. I make to rise along with the rest of our party.

"Stay seated." She waves us back down. She's young for a red-robe, in her late thirties. Her skin is dark brown, her face round and open, her lips full. But her eyes don't miss a thing. "I will join you," she says in Nonnovan. Her voice feels like a warm breeze on a hot summer night, the accent sultry. I ready myself to translate. Whenever I've conversed directly with Servine in the past, on errands for Master Brogal, we speak Nonnovan.

I square my shoulders and keep my hands in my lap while Servine settles on a crimson cushion at the head of the table. The High Savant pours herself a drink, holding her sleeve back with an elegantly manicured hand with brightly painted nails. "Welcome to Nonnova Sanctuary." She smiles. "You'll have to forgive the lack of fanfare. It's been an eventful day, and it's not even half over."

Servine slips out of the Palrion common tongue and into her own. "Quite the eventful week, actually, with the appearance of the second sun."

"Indeed. With your permission, High Savant, I will translate?" I offer.

Servine dips her head once. "Please do, Ash."

My face warms. I didn't expect her to remember my name. I take Brogal's official scroll out of my satchel and pass it to her, but Servine's eyes are not on me. She reads through the document and then turns quickly to Marcus, who, to his credit, remains completely composed. One of the many benefits of being groomed for the throne, he knows how to handle himself in a formal setting.

"I had word of your arrival, Marcus Adicio, or should I say Bone Gatherer?" The High Savant addresses him as if he can understand her. "Your presence surprises me. Last I was told, you perished on your way to Aku. But now I see you are alive and well and have advanced to yellow-robe. This is good news. I thought, at one point, the day would never come. Congratulations."

I turn to Marcus. "She's relieved to see you alive. Good job on gaining your yellow robes."

He clears his throat. "Tell her thank you, and that my death was a false rumor, one that was carried on phantom wings, or so it seems."

"Phantom wings?" I say out the side of my mouth.

"Just translate it." Marcus keeps his eyes on Servine who nods when I pass along his words.

"No doubt there are those who would benefit from such a loss," Servine says. Of course, she knows about Petén's ascension to the throne. "Your father's health is failing? Tell me that is a rumor as well."

"She knows your brother took the throne and asks after Jacas," I say.

Marcus shakes his head. "My father is dead."

I turn to Servine. "Sadly, the Magistrate has passed. We had news of it only this morning." I pause before adding, "Peace be his path."

Her eyes go to my medallion chain. Was that a slip? For me to admit we received news mid-seas? Am I meant to keep my communication abilities to myself? Brogal hadn't instructed me on that matter, but he did say to trust no one.

"My sympathies to you, Marcus Adicio. Peace and serenity on his next path." Servine switches to Palrio for a quick second. "We could have used his wisdom, on this verge of the next Great Dying."

"Thank you." Marcus presses his hands together, touches his forehead and gives a bow. "Then do your Bone Throwers confirm the validity of the second sun and what it heralds?"

I translate and she nods. "They do."

"We saw no signs of concern. The people seemed unmoved either way."

Servine holds out her hand. "We adhere to strong divisions in Nonnova, keep separate the matters of the Sanctuary and those of ordinary non-savants. The lore of the second sun is Sanctuary business and stays within our walls."

It's true to some degree in Palrio as well, with hundreds of years of Magistrates all being savant, up until Petén that is. But back home, there has always been more flow of knowledge. In any case, I don't see how Nonnova will be able to keep that up. It's a seaport and news travels. People talk, especially us non-savants, but I translate her words faithfully.

Marcus bows again, avoiding the topic of segregation. I don't blame him. We are here for the bone, not political debate.

Servine takes the next few moments to run her eyes over each of us. She rests them uncomfortably long on Kaylin. Well, uncomfortable to me, at least. There's no sign of him being bothered, but I can understand her scrutiny. He stands out. Poised and attractive, emanating confidence but not in savant robes. She must wonder what his role is in our group.

"Tutapa?" she asks him directly.

Or maybe she already knows.

"Aye, High Savant. That is where I was born."

The meaning of their short conversation is obvious, so I don't translate for the others. Kaylin speaks beautiful Nonnovan. Is there a language he hasn't studied?

"Could be said of you, too," my inner voice reminds me.

"And where is Captain Rowten? I was told he journeyed with you. Back on the ship?"

"Not on the ship," I say, looking her straight in the eye. "He stayed back." I wave out to sea, which also happens to be the direction of Baiseen. I'm not going to lie to a red-robe, but I am not going to disobey one, either.

"Ah, I see." Whatever she's thinking is hidden behind her tranquil face. She turns back to Marcus. "So you are the Bone Gatherer, as spoken of in the ancient scripts?"

"She knows you're the Bone Gatherer," I say.

Marcus tilts his head slightly to confirm it.

"Unhappily," Servine says, gently stroking long dark hair back from her face. "My news for you will not be well received."

I hold my breath and tell the others, "Bad news."

"I'm afraid I cannot pass Nonnova's first whistle bone into your care."

I tell Marcus and he keeps his face neutral. "Why not?"

She doesn't need a translation for that, either. "It was *called* last night, snatched from its place of honor." She lets out a sigh and turns bewitching eyes onto us all. "To be true, we thought it might have been you, hence the cautious greeting. There were casualties. Can you confirm the new Magistrate of Palrio is not declaring war on Nonnova?"

"What's she saying?" Marcus whispers.

"Bone's gone, *called,* it seems. People murdered. She thought it might have been our doing. Petén declaring war."

"Set her straight!"

I hold my hand out to hush him, not the most diplomatic gesture, but I need to keep my attention on the High Savant. "There were casualties, you say?"

"They *called* the hearts from my guards' chests before we saw them coming." She hoods her eyes. "An Adicio trait."

I remember the stains on the garden wall and my stomach drops. "It is not the intention of Palrio to threaten the Nonnova Isles in any way, but the red-robe Sierrak, Tann, who has taken callers captive, also pursues the original whistle bones," I say and turn to Marcus. "Tann got here first, and none too gently."

"Yes, Tann." Servine echoes the name. "My advisors suggest he is the most likely culprit, but our whistle bone was *called*, not *ousted*. We all heard it, and Palrio is the realm of *caller* phantoms, so you understand our concern."

"We've been your staunch allies for over five hundred years," I point out. "And Tann has been abducting—"

"Callers. I know that now. Our Bone Throwers collaborate your claims, but still, it's a bad coincidence. Could I not have been informed of Tann's attack sooner?"

"Our apologies, High Savant." Why hadn't Brogal told her? All the allied realms should know.

"In any case, the Nonnova whistle bone is gone and cannot be passed to you."

I translate, and everyone starts talking among themselves.

"I can offer you a midday meal," Servine interrupts, "and some supplies for your journey, but it looks like in this race, Tann is well in the lead, which bodes badly for the allied realms."

Marcus grimaces when he understands. "Please tell the High Savant that we will help here in any way we can."

She appreciates the offer but declines. While she and the others exchange information about Aku and Baiseen, keeping me busy with the translating, our meal arrives.

"I'm starving," Tyche says, her voice small.

Kaylin smiles at her. "Me too."

Unfortunately, everyone keeps talking while they eat, and I feel obliged to make sure Servine isn't shut out of the conversations. When the talk is more on the meal than our strategy, Kaylin takes over so I can eat. *"Thanks!"* Seems I have an appetite, too.

Servine brightens as Kaylin translates. Her eyes never leave his, even though they are talking about things as inconsequential as the delicious pineapples cut in half and filled with bananas, papaya, and passion fruit, or the roast bird the size of a turkey, which I suspect is a peacock, or the fresh coconut water drunk straight from the shells. The various dishes are served on woven mats covered in squares of green banana leaves. I'm glad for the break and the chance to enjoy the meal, but predictably, it doesn't last.

Soon, the table animates and both Kaylin and I are translating. Samsen and Marcus have much to say about stopping Tann in his tracks, and Belair is openly sharing his skepticism about the true meaning of the second sun and the next Great Dying. It seems that within the walls of the Sanctuary, anything can be discussed.

In it all, Servine ends up encouraging us to go on to Kutoon in Gollnar in the hopes of arriving ahead of Tann, if indeed that is his next destination. It's still not easy to translate with food in my mouth, so by the time everyone else is scraping their plates, Kaylin and I still have a fair way to go. I roll my shoulders, trying to loosen up whatever has me increasingly on edge again.

"An attempt on one's life can unsettle the nerves," Kaylin says to me privately.

I shiver, still not used to the return of his voice in my head. *"As would executing said assassin,"* I say back. *"But here you are, calm as ever."*

When my plate is finally empty, I say, "Tann's probably happy to let us gather what we can, for now, biding his time until he *calls* them from us. It's what we plan to do to him. But if there's a way to prevent that from happening, we need to uncover it."

That gets me murmurs of agreement from everyone. I quiz Servine on the matter, finding sympathy for our plight, but no new information on retaining the whistle bones.

"Perhaps Zakia, High Savant of Kutoon, can advise." Servine looks deep into her mug before draining it. "Be careful there. She could have ties to Atikis, rogue as he is, and it seems from what you've said, that he seeks the bones as well." She leans toward me. "There's a faster route to Kutoon, you know? Not many captains do."

Kaylin perks up at this.

"You'll have to skirt the north isles and hug the coast. There the current runs like a torrent to the north. Then, on the way back, take the southerly stream, five miles off the coast," she says as the woven mat plates are cleared, and we rise to leave.

"Skirt the north isles?" I frown at that, the Bone Thrower's mural coming to the forefront of my mind, bringing with them a nagging headache.

"Yes, the chain of—"

"Bakton!" I say, interrupting. Everyone turns my way. "Bakton is in the north island chain." I try to sound calm but it's probably too late for that. All while we talk, I feel an increasing restlessness in the pit of my guts as my head pounds harder. It's like a thought, or proclamation, is trying to erupt.

"Ash, are you all right?" Marcus asks.

I nod, keeping my eyes glued on Servine. "That's the isle destroyed by a volcanic eruption?"

"Centuries ago, yes." Servine gives me a curious look.

"The isle that was once the Sanctuary of Nonnova?"

"Indeed."

"Ash, thank her and let's be on our way." Marcus grips my shoulder, trying to turn me toward the stairs.

"Wait." I brush his hand off. "Servine, what's left on Bakton? What survived?"

The High Savant shakes her head. "There are only ruins. A few pillars and totems slowly being engulfed by the sea. The rest is a volcanic wasteland, save for the gull nests to the north."

"What of *their* original whistle bone?" I whisper. "Did they have one?" I know the twelve originals are accounted for, at least, Brogal's text says they are. And I have seen the Tree of Eternity hanging in its place of honor in their meeting hall, but what if it was first given to Bakton?

"Indeed." The High Savant lifts her chin. "They first held our original whistle bone. It was brought here to safety, only to have Tann steal it last night."

"Are you sure it was brought here?"

"As sure as the ancient scripts. Besides, how could Tann's *callers* take it if it were not indeed the original?"

"But is there any chance it wasn't?"

Her brow furrows, and I know she has doubts. "A replica so good that it fooled all the High Savants of Nonnova, ever since the island blew? Fooled Tann? I guess it could be possible."

"Thank you." I give her a ceremonial bow, hands steepled and pressed to my forehead. When we're back to the harbor, walking up the gangplank, I whisper to Marcus, "We have to go to Bakton."

"What in the world for?"

"We have to check that their original whistle bone isn't still there."

He pulls me to the side, out of the way of longshoremen loading crates. "Are you saying there's a chance Nonnova's first whistle bone wasn't taken by Tann? That it's buried on some island under a ton of lava?"

My body prickles as Talus's message finally makes sense. *The answer you're looking for isn't where you think it is. Use your instincts, girl. You had it right when studying the mural. Do you remember the name of the island?*

"Not just some island, Marcus," I say. "It's called Bakton, and we have to go there."

Why are we still arguing? The *Dugong* is underway and my debate with Ash takes over the galley table. "How could the bone be on Bakton?" I ask her for the fifth time. "The black-robe named Nonnova as our second destination."

Earlier, I thought Ash was becoming more herself again, but this insistence on changing course is not like her. I blame it on this journey. She wasn't ready for it, not to mention the assassination attempt. It's enough to put anyone off-kilter. I'll give allowances for that, sure, but it doesn't mean I'm going along with this unsubstantiated detour.

"The Bone Thrower named the Nonnovan *Isles*, Marcus, of which Bakton is one." She shakes her head. "And a replica whistle bone could have been hanging in their Sanctuary hall for centuries and none the wiser."

"You know this for certain?"

"Servine admitted it was possible." Her eyes have never looked so fierce. "You have to trust me. I just *know* it's there."

I want to, but Ash doesn't "just know" things. She finds proof backed by research and clear thinking.

Maybe you don't know her well enough.

"What's that supposed to mean?" My phantom needs to stop interrupting this conversation.

Ash is more than the girl you met ten years ago. More than the recorder who set out for Aku.

I ignore De'ral. "You need to give me a reason beyond your gut feeling, Ash." My voice is close to a shout.

The others avert their eyes. Samsen studies the map, his hand resting on Piper's shoulder, hers on her belly as if trying to calm an inner storm. Tyche has her book of original whistle bones opened to the Tree of Eternity, Nonnova's first whistle bone—the one Tann already has in his possession. Why are we still discussing this?

"Really, Ash. You have to give me more." I slap my hand over the Nonnova archipelago. "Bakton could be a trap, a trick of Tann's or maybe even Servine's. I'm not sure I trust her."

"I don't trust anyone after last night, Marcus," Ash snaps. "But I know this. We have to go to Bakton."

"Who says?"

"Talus does," she blurts out then presses her lips tight.

Tyche's head comes up, but she doesn't speak.

My whole body heats. The choice I make could put all our lives in danger. If Brogal is right, though I question it, my choice could put the whole realm in danger, too. "Who's Talus?"

"I told you about her, on Aku."

"Refresh my memory." I lean back and try to relax. We're both getting too worked up.

"She's a Bone Thrower."

Tyche keeps her nose in the book but makes a harrumph.

"Ash, I don't have time for this. The captain is at the helm waiting for me to give him a new heading." For now, the *Dugong* points northeast toward the Nulsea Gap. If any are watching from the heights of Nonnova—and I'd be surprised if Servine's people aren't—we appear to be off as intended, to Kutoon.

Ash levels her eyes on me. "Tell him the heading is Bakton."

"Because Talus said what, exactly?"

"I believe she said we'd find the whistle bone there, not on Nonnova."

"How? When?" We've known for less than two days that we are seeking them at all. "Wait a minute. You 'believe,' as in you're not sure?"

"Talus gave me a message in the Bone Thrower's cave, while I was waiting for you and Rowten. It didn't make sense at the time, but as soon as Servine mentioned the Isles, the meaning fell into place. I can't explain her presence in the Bone Thrower's cave—"

"What do you mean? Where's she meant to be?" I interrupt.

"Aku. I told you. I met her on Aku."

I shake my head. "She could have sailed with Tann's fleet, which makes her an enemy. In that light, Bakton is the last place we should go."

"But you're wrong." Ash outright contradicts me. "She's not with Tann. I feel it in my heart." She rubs her eyes and looks up. "Maybe it was the medallion or a vision. I don't know, but we can trust her, Marcus. I'm certain."

"Like we trusted Rowten?"

Ash bites her lower lip when it starts to tremble. "She said the whistle bone would call to me, and it has. Loudly!"

"Call to you? A non-savant?"

Ash jerks back as if I'd slapped her.

"I didn't mean—" But I stop myself because I did mean it, just not in the way she thinks. Not as ridicule. "It's not—"

Before I say more, Kaylin leans in and whispers, "Maybe try to be less of an arse."

Everyone stares at me while my guts sink to my feet. He's right. She's my journey recorder, my best friend, deserving of more respect. "I only meant, a non-savant is least likely to feel connected to a whistle bone because that is the realm of the black-robes."

"All true," she says, recovering. The only sign of her taking offense is the redness in her darkening face. "But I hear it just the same."

I let out a rough breath. "If you think Bakton is so important, why are you only telling me this now?" I look to Kaylin but he's surprised, too.

"I wanted to understand it myself first. It was an unusual experience."

The room goes quiet until Tyche speaks up. "Talus was the First Bone Thrower on Aku," she says quietly while keeping a finger on the page she studies.

Well, that does it. But I check my impatience and rise, pouring myself more tea. "So, an ancient Bone Thrower from Aku is dropping sage advice? And only to you, a non-savant?" At this moment, I am doubting everything. "A message from a black-robe half the world away?"

"She's a white-robe actually." Ash's lips thin into a line.

Before I can backtrack, yet again, from making *non-savant* sound like a curse, or ask her what she means by a *white-robe,* Tyche butts in.

"You don't understand." The girl shakes her head. "Talus was *the first* Bone Thrower on Aku."

Everyone stares at her.

"The *first*, as in the original?" Piper asks.

Tyche nods.

"So now we're taking orders from a shade?" I can't believe it.

Belair lets out a hiss not unlike the sound his red leopard makes. "This argument isn't getting us anywhere."

"Listen!" Ash barks. "They share the same name, obviously." After a few breaths, her face softens, the red fading, and I know she's begging me to fathom something I clearly do not. "There's no way to explain it, but if we go to Bakton we'll retrieve the lost whistle bone. If we don't go, it may stay buried forever, then nobody reforms the crown of bones."

I take a gulp of tea and choke as it burns my tongue. "I need fresh air." I put my cup in the holder and head topside, knowing Ash will follow. When I reach the port railing, I turn, expecting to see only her, but everyone has come, too. So much for a private conversation.

"It's more or less on the way," Kaylin says, his eyes frowning at the western horizon. "Nothing but an afternoon lost in checking this out."

"If anyone can *call* the thing, it's Tyche." Samsen dips his head toward the girl. "Even if it is buried deep."

The young orange-robe nods. "I can get it, if it's there."

Kaylin turns to me, rubbing the back of his neck. "It grows larger every day."

"What?" I snap at the distraction.

"The second sun."

I find it low in the west, about to set. The dark red sun winks through streaming clouds, an orb, like an eclipsed star, black in the center with flares of crimson and gold. It's nearly doubled in size since solstice. I watch in silence as it disappears behind thick clouds.

It's real, De'ral says. *All is real on this path.*

"*As real as Ash's intuition?*"

Yes.

I rub my shoulder, still sore from the fall when fleeing Atikis. It clicks and settles into place. "*If* you're right, Ash." I give her a slight bow. "And *if* things are on the brink as they say." I open my arm to the second sun. "We will need to act on even the remote chance Nonnova's whistle bone is there." I gaze at the others. "We set course to Bakton."

"Thank you," Ash says in a rush of breath.

The others continue to watch for the second sun, measuring the angle between it and our bright yellow sun. Kaylin has gone to talk to Captain Anders, and I finally have Ash to myself for a moment. I rest one hand on her shoulder. "One of my reasons for hesitation is the time a detour will take." I tilt my head to the sky. "We've problems to solve and will need time in the libraries of Kutoon, perhaps, and most definitely in Tangeen."

"I know." Her smile is grudging. "Like how to keep the whistle bones from being stolen out from under us. The true nature of the Mar and how they might help or hinder us. The gathering of the crown of bones and how it will protect the realm."

"Yes. Like that."

"I'll find the answers, Marcus," she says. Her face relaxes, the smile becomes genuine. "I promise."

And like that, our fight is over.

"Marcus?" Ash grabs my arm and pulls me closer. "Look." She points to the second sun as it sinks below the horizon and turns the sky crimson red. "You know what this means?"

I frown. "What?"

"You read it to me just last night, from your list. *When the red star sets, lighting the world on fire, our true journey begins*." She smiles.

Nothing wrong with her memory now. "So be it, Ash. Let the journey begin."

Though deep down, after all that has happened, I feel it began months ago when we first left for the Isle of Aku.

27

KAYLIN

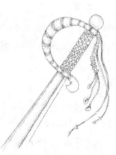

Ash standing up to Marcus! It's spectacular to see. Her tenacity. The faith she has in her feelings. She challenges his choice, as any respected journey recorder has the right to do. I'm proud of her, and tell her so, sending an abundance of sweet whispers to her mind. But there is more for me to say. So much more. I can't wait any longer.

I want to reveal the whole truth. Of course, I do, and I need to before she finds out on her own. It's past time to tell her who I am, no matter what Teern hangs over my head. But will she understand, or run from me in horror?

There is no denying it. I have done horrible things.

I head for the bow to think. The ocean spray hits my face square on as I climb down to the rope netting that spans the bowsprit. It's instant relief. The sea washes over me until my hair drips down my back and my eyelashes are weighted with salt. As I lie against the roping, staring up at the clouds, a call comes down from the crow's nest.

"Land ahoy!"

"Bakton," I whisper, a shadow falling over me. As much as I think Ash is right, they don't know what they're getting themselves into. I'm not even sure I do. So many savants died there, suddenly. Without warning. Yes, the mountain smoked, but it had been doing so for centuries. Who knew it would blow its top that day? No one, not even Teern. Such a place of death doesn't bode well for us.

Bakton remains a mystery, a volcanic isle that, since the last eruption, takes the shape of a black sea dragon. It was once the heart and soul of the Nonnova archipelago before the disaster. I remember the lush tropical foliage ringing the deepest blue lagoon imaginable. Now it's an obsidian mountain with a conical, still smoking peak. I squint at the horizon, identifying the craggy outline. It might be long after the next Great Dying before the isle is habitable again, if it's even an island then. But no matter. The whistle bone must be found and Ash is right. It could well be there.

"You're coming, aren't you?" my lass asks as she climbs the netting toward me.

Looking into her turquoise eyes, the memory of her kiss on my cheek lands all over again. "To search for a whistle bone on a smoldering isle with you? Wouldn't miss it."

She leans back, joining my study of the sky. "It's so sad, what happened there. I can't get the images from the tapestry out of my mind. Did you see it?"

"Aye." We all watched the island erupt that day, from a safe distance.

"Lava covered everything, but before that," Ash goes on, "According to records, the Sanctuary of Bakton would have rivaled Baiseen."

"It did..."

"Pardon?"

"So the records say." I turn, and her familiar scent covers me like a silken tide. Lilacs and summer seas. My shifting weight dips the netting and she rolls up against me.

"Kaylin," she whispers. "There is so much to say. I don't know where to begin."

My lips are a breath away from hers. Now is the time to start telling her the truth of what I am, why we met, how it all came to be. Not by happenstance, but by design. I don't know what kind of future I can ever have with Ash. Our worlds are sundered, our paths crossing for the briefest moment in the eternity of being. But I also know I'm bound to her in some inexplicable way. Ash, the girl I was sent to kill. The girl who yet lives. The one who holds my heart in her hands. I part my lips and whisper back, "Aye, lass. Let me start."

"Bring her about!" the captain shouts from the helm.

I wrap my arms around her, pulling her against my chest as the boom swings. The ship stalls before it lurches onto a new heading. For an instant, we are suspended between the rise and fall of the prow as if time has stopped.

Then, the bowsprit netting sways, and we roll right to the edge, stopped only by my finger and big toe hooking the rope. When the going is smooth again, I don't let go. Instead, my lips touch hers gently as I whisper, "First, I want to kiss you."

She doesn't pull away as her eyelashes flutter against my cheek. "Then kiss me."

I close my eyes and softly brush her lips again. We melt into each other and time stops, a rush of energy consuming me. I give in to it, to her, letting down every guard and caution.

Our kiss is a starburst showering me in droplets of golden light. The ordinary world is gone, replaced by our own universe. Here there are no sounds of the sea against the hull, the beat of the prow over the waves, or the wind billowing the sails. All I sense is her heartbeat and mine, her breath and mine, her touch and mine. I ache for more as my hands tangle in her hair. This is what I want. She is who I want...

Ash ignites me, awakening every sense, every desire, every nerve and cell. I am falling from a precipice that has no bottom. Ash is the only thing that can save me, but she wraps her arms around me and falls, too.

When time snaps back to its usual flow, it takes all my willpower to release her.

She catches her breath and smiles. "That was unexpected."

"But not unwelcome?" A part of my mind insists we stop and have our real and necessary conversation before we go a moment longer, but I'm too single-minded, waiting on her next words, to pay heed to it. I must not misread or misunderstand. I have to know that she feels it, too.

"Not unwelcome at all, but..." She shakes her head, the smile fading. "Protocols," she whispers. "They haven't changed."

"Remind me what they are again?" I release her from the intensity of my grip.

She straightens a bit but doesn't move away. Her voice becomes a tutor's. "Official recorder must take heed of certain social and civil restraints while performing their duties, including no wandering, no distractions, no hobbies, no hunting, no hobnobbing—"

"Hobnobbing?"

"Yes, that word specifically." She takes a breath and continues. "No pastimes or forming intimate relationships of any kind while in service to the realm." She smiles and lays her cheek on my arm.

"Is that what I am? A pastime."

She inches close, her lips near my ear. "You are many things, Kaylin of Tutapa, but never just a pastime to me." She curls a strand of hair behind my ear. "But we both serve the Bone Gatherer on this journey. The protocols must stand."

"I think there has been a serious lapse then." I don't try to correct it.

"Very serious." But her shining eyes start to fade.

Reluctantly I sit, pulling her up with me. "Then for now, we will be upstanding. We will abide." I trace along her brow where the bangs grow unevenly. "I can straighten that up for you."

She shakes her head, letting her hair fall naturally into place, with the chunk sliced by Rowten's sword forming a gap-toothed smile over her forehead. "I think I'll leave it for now, as a reminder of how serious this journey is." Her gaze is on Bakton. "Do you think Talus spoke true?"

"Maybe. You said she warned you of Tann's attack before I found you in the Aku library."

"Moments before the tower fell."

"Hard to see that as an enemy's action."

"Yet her appearing at the Bone Thrower's cave is inexplicable."

I inch closer again; can't help myself. "Second thoughts?"

"Not exactly. We need to explore Bakton." Her breath is warm and sweet, like pineapples and honey. "But I'm nervous just the same."

I take her hand. "Promise you'll stay close on the island?"

"I promise." She smiles up at me. "And I'll wear my sword, though the danger there may not be frightened by it."

She's right. I take the moment to lean forward, cup her face in my hands and decide that I must begin. Because how can I tell her I love her without being honest about myself first? "Lass, when we met in Toretta—"

"Ash!" Marcus's voice booms over us.

We jump away from each other abruptly and look up to see him leaning over the bow.

"What are you doing down there?" he says. "You're soaking wet."

It's an exaggeration, but I don't mention this. He's jangled enough as it is with what he witnessed two nights ago, and the news of his father's death, the fight with Atikis... He doesn't need me contradicting him at every turn. "Just cooling off." I shrug like it's no big thing.

"We're about to drop sail." His voice is unusually deep while his phantom glowers behind his eyes. "If you want to join us on Bakton, I suggest you both disentangle and come with me."

"Marcus," Ash says calmly though her face is red. "Of course, we are coming. This isn't what it looks—"

"Just get in the boat, you two. We're running out of daylight."

He leads the way, and we both scramble to follow.

28

ASH

He kissed me! I close my eyes to relive it, the strength of his arms around me as the ship lurched. The gentleness of his lips as they slowly moved closer to mine. How all the racing thoughts in my head vanished, leaving me only aware of our thrumming hearts and the exquisiteness of his touch. *What a kiss…*

It was so much more than the peck I gave him when we fled the shore at the Suni River mouth. Though that was good! Then I felt weightless, lighthearted, buoyed up by unseen currents and also a little embarrassed that everyone saw. But this kiss? It was like our first, back on the beach of Aku. It started with curiosity, a tenderness that quickly turned into a blazing fire. *What a kiss!*

"You mentioned," my inner voice says dryly. *"And the protocols? You remember those, don't you?"*

I do, and like that I come down from the clouds with a bump.

The protocols. They are in place for this very reason. I'm supposed to be focused on Bakton and the whistle bone I insisted is there. And what about poor Marcus? He's had the shock of his father's death, not to mention our journey nearly being cut off at the knees, or rather at the neck. My neck! He doesn't need to see me frolicking with Kaylin at every turn. It's completely inappropriate! This quest is deadly serious. I understand that better than anyone.

"Aren't you wise." My inner voice is snide. *"So far along the path."*

Wise? Really, if I have something to say to myself, I should just say it. *What are you insinuating?*

"Simply that you are sage beyond your years if you know what others need, or do not need, along their path."

I blow out my breath. There's truth there but I hate admitting it. *Point taken,* I mumble through tight lips. *But I don't regret the kiss if that's what you're thinking.*

My mind goes back to Kaylin, my lips still tingling. But as Bakton looms nearer, I know I have to stay focused. I remind myself, as we lower a rowboat and climb in, that going there was my idea. An idea I had to fight for.

"Actually, it was Talus's idea."

True, but if things go wrong it won't be her they'll blame.

The closer we get, the more the isle looks like a dragon poised next to a blue lagoon. Waves crash around its crouching legs and above, high into the clouds, his head tips back, mouth open in a mighty roar. Smoke rises from the hollow throat. "Stunning," I say. "So powerful."

"I don't like it." Tyche turns away.

Piper wraps an arm around the girl. "We won't stay long," the healer says, her voice light, maybe for all our sakes. We stare at the obsidian land, each stroke of the oars bringing us closer to its chilly shadow.

The sun is lower on the horizon than I'd thought, the frozen claws of lava turning gold in the late afternoon light. I lick salt from my lips. The sea is as calm as a mirror, save near the shore. That's one good thing.

"Keep her pointed at the beach," Kaylin says as he rows harder. "And stick together when we land."

"Afraid of the monster?" Marcus chides him.

Kaylin doesn't respond. We've all seen him in battle. Fearless doesn't begin to describe him. I don't like speculating on what would make Kaylin uneasy, but this island seems to.

"You aren't worried, are you?" I ask.

"Never." He winks. *"But still, let's all stay together."*

"No argument here."

"Right oars, straighten her up," Kaylin calls out as the swell latches onto the bottom of our boat and rushes us forward. Soon the black sand beach is beneath us, and we jump out, the water up to my knees. Marcus and Belair haul the rope while the rest of us push the small vessel above the tide line. It lists to the side, stuck deep in the dry sand between two long arms of lava. We're in the shadow of the dragon's belly. I find it a relief not to see the smoking head anymore.

"The temple ruins are that way, according to the map." I point left around the dragon's arm. "I think there's a path." My hands and feet tingle. "What's that noise?" I ask.

"Kelp Gulls." Kaylin indicates the birds circling in the distance.

"They sound different."

"Aye. It's rare to see them nesting this far north." He shoulders his pack and leads the way. "Unless the southern waters have frozen."

"Ha!" That's not possible…is it?

We look to the sky. Only a single sun is visible on the western horizon, but it feels ominous just the same. "Let's move."

"Are you ready to *call* the whistle bone?" I offer Tyche my hand.

She nods and then says, "Everything here is dead."

"Not those noisy birds." I try to laugh. "And not us." I stumble as I say it and fall to my knees.

Kaylin turns but I'm up and dusting myself off before he can speak. I push on the side of my temple. For a moment, my thoughts jumble and I am on the trail behind the training field in the Sanctuary of Baiseen. I'm racing Marcus to the lake and am sadly falling behind. I stumble again, and this time Kaylin pulls me up.

"Are you all right, lass?"

Everyone has stopped to press in toward me. Piper has her hand on my wrist, Marcus is firing questions. Kaylin's in my head.

"Enough!" I reclaim my hand. "I stumbled, is all. Let's go find this bone before the sun sets."

No one speaks as we continue down the path.

I follow behind, noting that this was once a great road that hugged the shore. It's now overgrown with wispy dead grass that fringes the giant arms of cooled lava flow. In places the road is underwater and we scramble over black rocks to stay dry. The desolate landscape reminds me of a cake pan, the contents burnt black and warped out of shape.

I trot to catch up when Kaylin leads us over a rise and comes to a halt.

"Great goddess of the Drop," I whisper. From the knoll, we have a full view of the Sanctuary below us, what is left of it, at least. It takes me a moment to catch my breath. Even after studying the mural, I wasn't expecting this. Despite being in ruins, the Bakton Sanctuary emanates magnificence.

The freestanding columns tower high, jutting out of the sea in the north aspect like a giant phantom's fingers turned to stone. "Is it marble?" I ask.

"Can't see how," Belair answers. "White granite?"

"Master sculptors created this," Piper says. "But look how much the sea has risen. Those distant columns are almost completely underwater."

"A warning to build on higher ground as our ancestors did in Baiseen." Marcus shakes his head.

"I don't think it was so close to the sea when it was built." It didn't seem that way in the tapestry.

Long shadows splash across the beach, giving the site an eerie feel. The ruins speak of wealth and grandeur; the relentless sea slowly swallow it whole. The water's edge is littered with fallen slabs of rock encrusted with barnacles and reclining statues that once stood upright, as proud winged guardians. It makes me think of the palace garden chessboard at Baiseen, with its life-size, finely carved pieces all toppled over. Only these are so much larger.

Opposite the statues, in the distance, is an elegant, curved structure— the remains of an amphitheater. The columns still form a perfect semicircle, a half-moon sinking into the sea, save for a few pillars broken off at the base but above the tideline. As the sun drops even closer to the horizon, the inland lava hills darken, and the ruined Sanctuary turns from gold to vermillion.

"Ready to have a go, little lass?" Kaylin says to Tyche. "Best be quick, so we aren't rowing back under the stars."

"I need to be closer," she says. "And higher," she adds. "We don't know where it'll be coming from."

"Here," Marcus calls out. He's climbed up a mound of lava.

Tyche doesn't move.

Kaylin draws his sword and walks ahead of her to the claw. "Come on, bring your phantom up and *call* the whistle bone. Marcus and I will stand guard."

Marcus takes the cue and draws his sword as well. "That we will."

Piper joins her as she finds a spot between the two young men. "You know we're after the Tree of Eternity, the whistle bone that represents—"

"The second step on the path to An'awntia," Tyche answers. "Awareness of Physicality. I studied it. I'm ready." She motions the rest of us to step back. As we do, she drops to her knees and instantly her phantom erupts from the black sand. The long-necked, elegant impala, one of the most powerful *callers* of Aku, looks calm. It shakes its coat and gazes at Tyche. If the creature is upset to find itself at the edge of the sea, on a lava black island at sunset, it doesn't show it.

Tyche's eyes go soft, focused on nothing. Marcus helps her climb higher along the rocks for even more elevation, and the impala springs after her, bounding like a kid goat up the side of a cliff. It flaps its ears and turns to face west. As the sun melts into the horizon and the sky explodes with pink and orange streaks, the phantom and savant begin their chant.

I watch from my perch at the edge of the obsidian. A beautiful melody mingles with the sounds of the sea, and I find every bone in my body tingling. After a few moments, the sun dims behind clouds and a wispy fog rolls in. "Should have brought my coat."

"Should have brought more than that," my inner voice replies.

Pardon?

"Stay aware."

But time passes, and nothing happens, so I'm not sure what I'm meant to be aware of. Tyche stops for a moment to shift her focus to another part of the ruins and calls again. Nothing.

"Over here."

I clutch the medallion through my coat. "Who spoke?"

"Look at the runes on the columns. They will point to the great hall, where the bone used to hang. That's where the girl needs to be...come closer."

"Talus?" I check over my shoulder but no one else seems to have heard her words. Am I imagining things? But the advice is good. I slip off the rock and walk down to the nearest column. It's cold to the touch and half buried in the sand. Even with the tide out, my boots make shallow prints that quickly fill with water. I run my hand along the smooth column and sure enough, I come to a row of glyphs carved into the stone.

"What have you found?" Kaylin asks, heading toward me.

"Do you recognize these?"

Kaylin studies them. "I'm not sure."

"I think we need to look for the main hall, or where it once stood."

"Good idea."

"Not mine. I..."

Kaylin straightens with a question on his face.

"I think I heard Talus suggest it. That sounds crazy, doesn't it." As soon as I speak the name aloud, a shape appears on the other side of the columns. "Who's that," I whisper, heading toward it.

"Wait up," Kaylin trots behind me.

"Look to the runes, Ash. The one with the Eternity Tree."

"Right!" I stop so quickly Kaylin nearly plows into me from behind. "We're looking for the Eternity symbol. That's what would be carved into the hall pillars." I wave to the others. "Help search, everyone."

"Ash, who are you talking to?" Kaylin asks.

"You, of course. Come on. You love the water. Check those pillars over there in the depths." I point toward the ones half submerged in the turning tide. The others join in, and we comb the ruins until I find it. "Here!" I call Tyche over. "I think it's here."

Marcus and Piper flank Tyche as they escort her and her phantom to the edge of the sea.

"This might have been the main hall." I spin around, arms wide, indicating the expanse.

"They look like old teeth." Tyche clasps her hands as she stares at the ruins.

"It's just stone, little lass," Kaylin says, kicking the nearest pillar for emphasis.

"All right." Tyche squares her shoulders and again the melodic tones rise like mist from the sea, this time dampened by the thickening fog and the sea rushing in.

"She's got something," Piper whispers.

The water bubbles and churns until it bursts like a geyser. From its midst, a whistle bone flies with such a force it leaves a spray of sand and seawater trailing through the darkening sky. Tyche turns and touches her phantom. It slows the tempo of its call and the object arcs gracefully forward and lands at her feet. Everyone exclaims, then breaks into applause.

"Are you sure that's it? The Tree of Eternity?" Marcus asks.

Tyche picks it up and studies it closely. "I'm sure."

Kaylin pats her gently on the back while everyone presses in to see. She takes the bone to the edge of the tide to rinse it clean. Indeed, it is the Tree of Eternity, the etching still vibrant black lines in the buttery colored bone. Tyche removes a tag of kelp that caught on the "wings" of the vertebrae and hands it to Marcus.

"The second one, Bone Gatherer," she says with a little bow.

As she hands it over, the nesting gulls go silent and then all take flight at once, black silhouettes in the sky.

"We need to go," Kaylin says without explaining.

Marcus tucks the whistle bone into the small bag tied to his belt and the ground begins to tremble. Twilight sucks the color from the sky and shadows fall hard across the landscape. The smooth black lava fields disappear in the fog. Marcus slips the bag into his robe pocket, but as he looks my way, his eyes go wild. He pulls Tyche behind him and raises his sword. "Look out!'

"Shades," Tyche screams. Her impala melts into the ground.

The sound of thunder explodes above us. "The mountain's blowing!" Marcus shouts.

The taste of sulfur and ash fills the air as smokey figures appear from around the columns. The ethereal forms waft in and out of view, obscured by the fog and each other's transparent shadows. They float over the ruins, slowly but unquestionably advancing toward us. My throat is so dry I can't speak.

"Back to the boat!" Kaylin commands, jolting us to respond.

"Run, all of you!" Marcus seconds it, his voice a good octave deeper than usual. His shoulders seem to ripple beneath his robe.

"De'ral?"

"Run, Ash," his phantom booms in my head. "Run!" I can hear him pounding back toward me.

I bunch my legs and launch forward, willing my body to sprint through the wet, gyrating sand as the ground continues to shake. I pick up momentum in a few strides, lift my head and slam straight into a form more tree than person. The arms are long limbs, the body a trunk, twisted knots for eyes. I've seen this kind of phantom before, on Aku. "An agapha," I gasp, my hands flying up to ward off twig fingers.

"Hello, there, Ash." It is oblivious of the turmoil around us. "Lost your way?"

The knot-like swirl in the middle of the woody face doesn't move, its thoughts sounding in my head. "No time to stop," I say, pretending I'm not terrified out of my mind as I try to run around it.

Let's make time, shall we? It moves so fast, I run into it again.

More ghostly phantoms float toward me like mist over the water. They are still rising from behind the columns and crevices in the lava fields. In moments I'm surrounded.

"I have to go," I say again, my heart pounding like a wild beast's as I search for Kaylin and the others. I can see nothing in the fog.

"There's no rush, child." They advance even closer.

"These phantoms have no manners whatsoever," my inner voice offers.

That's all you can say? I open my mouth to scream for help, but no sound comes out.

"Best not let it get too close."

You think?

The shades take more solid form as their faces turn toward the erupting mountain. They sway, their expressions warping as if tormented. Booms crack the sky and the sound of spewing lava belches from the dragon's mouth. It makes the shades retreat, thinning into wisps and disappearing back into the fog.

But not the agapha. It remains. With a long, slender twig hand it reaches out and catches me in a chokehold. "You're coming with me."

Its grip clamps around my throat, making it impossible to breathe. This can't be happening. As I think it, I bring up my right hand and slam it into the branchy arm, but it's like hitting solid iron. Pain blooms from my wrist and my thoughts scatter like frightened birds.

The agapha roils and blurs, transforming in front of me as legs shorten into animal haunches that scrabble and gain purchase on my thighs. The spine contorts into a hunched creature, twiggy hands turning into claws that move up my chest and toward my face. It's an alter. It's… "You!" I shriek mind-to-mind. My heart beats a hundred times too fast as I recognize the paralyzing creature of my dreams—the nightmares that tormented me on Aku. How did it get here?

"Don't panic, Ash."

My inner voice has no idea. It is. Time. To. Panic!

I open my mouth to scream but the creature only laughs as if it's found a secret door.

I fight back, pummeling at the snarling fangs and ripping claws. I smash its jaw with an uppercut and knock it to the ground, but before I can turn to run, it leaps onto my chest again. The creature rakes my face and I yell at the top of my lungs. "Help!"

I slam my mouth shut, but the monster has a paw halfway down my throat.

"*Let it in.*" My inner voice is calm as the Sargasso.

That's insane advice. I gag and choke as it tries to force its way inside.

"*Trust me. Let it in.*"

I won't, but try as I do, I can't stop it. The creature dives down my throat.

And then, somewhere in the depths of my core, pressure rises. A twist and turbulence races under my skin while my inner voice gives a thunderous laugh. "*Now, you are mine.*"

For an instant, everything goes still. My breath calms. My arms stop thrashing. Even the tide seems to pause until air rushes from my lungs and my vision blurs. All sounds are sucked away, and I'm caught in a swirling vortex, falling endlessly down, or up. There's no telling. From a deep place, so hidden it feels like the center of infinity, I hear a *CRACK*. It's followed by a resounding shatter that fractures the boundaries of my soul, sending jagged lines racing up a once high and dividing wall. In that moment, the path stands still, and I inhale deeper the sea air, the fog and the shade, one and all.

29

KAYLIN

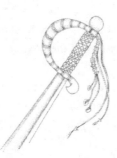

I jump to the side of the path, letting the others pass, counting the seconds until Ash catches up. But Belair brings up the rear and there's no sign of her.

I bolt back to the beach, willing my sight to cut through the fog, searching, listening with every fiber of my being for her breath, her heartbeat. Her screams? The tall columns wobble as the ground continues to shake. "Ash, where are you?" I shout, turning a full circle. I should not have let go of her hand.

Then I find her. She's close to the sea, frozen to the spot as a dark, contorted creature clings to her chest, raking claws trying to find purchase. I fly toward her as it burrows and squirms, diving headfirst down her mouth until an ear-splitting scream rips through the air. It's answered by the erupting mountain, the boom knocking me off my feet. I rise and leap toward Ash, but with each stride, the shade disappears farther down her throat. Then she stills, tips her head back, and cries out, but not in fear. This time she unleashes a fury that all but splits the mountain in half.

A shockwave slaps me down again, face first into slabs of stone. I find my feet in time to see what my mind can't make sense of. The shade is gone but with Ash's next scream comes a rain of red mist. It flies over the columns, hovers, and then falls back down. I look closer as each drop turns into a tiny red flower that quickly goes black like charred ash. The uncanny petals touch down on the sea before melting into the tide.

"Ash?" I call as I reach her.

She's choking, coughing. I drop to her side and wrap my arms around her tight. She buries her face in my chest, bits of charred petals lighting on our hair, water washing around our folded legs. "Come, lass," I whisper. "We must get off the isle."

When she doesn't respond, I sweep her into my arms and run faster than any lander can move. I don't slow my pace until we are within sight of the others. Belair is waist deep in the surf, pointing the bow of the boat toward the incoming waves which have doubled in size. Tyche and Piper are onboard, faces stricken. Samsen's at the oars. Marcus holds the stern. They are tossed about in the choppy swell while streams of molten lava appear out of the fog, flowing down the mountain's arms straight toward us.

"Row!" I call out, bounding to the boat. I push Ash over the railing and into Piper's outstretched hands.

"What's happened?" Marcus bellows.

I don't even try to answer. "Get in."

While Marcus and Belair scramble up the sides, I shove off, rowing the boat into the oncoming waves. Soaked and shaking, they man the other oars. I pull hard, using more strength than I should, but they have their heads down, not noticing how the wooden oars nearly crack in my grip. Ash is unconscious, but her breathing is slow and deep, as if sleeping. She has scratches on her face and chest, but other than that, is unharmed.

"Unharmed?" she asks me, her eyes opening brightly. *"I feel…"* She sits up, flexes and rolls her shoulders. "I'm fine. Give me an oar." She joins me on the bench and heaves to. With her added strength, which seems more than substantial considering what just happened, we pass the breakers in seconds and head back to the *Dugong*, leaving the island smoldering behind us.

But waves of emotion roll through my body, and I can't stop shaking. *"What in the demon's darkness attacked you back there?"*

In my mind, clear as spring, she replies, *"Funny. I was hoping you could tell me."*

30

ASH

I come back to myself in the rowboat, the waves parted by the cutting prow. I'm up fast, full of energy and rowing beside Kaylin, pulling the oars through the water as if a pod of sea dragons is after us.

"Sea dragons?"

Hush…we're trying to escape.

"Already accomplished."

So we have! I feel invigorated, but Kaylin has all kinds of worry on his face. He saw something on the beach, in the ruins of the ancient Sanctuary of Bakton, and wants to know what it was. So do I. It could have been a dream, an illusion.

"It wasn't either of those." My inner voice does not hush, of course.

You sound certain.

"I am." There's a satisfied murmur, like a dog who ate more than his fair share from the trough.

We reach the *Dugong* in a blink and once onboard, the captain sets a course for the Gollnar Sanctuary of Kutoon, taking the advice of Servine and hugging the coast. His eyes flash as he stares at the erupting island behind us.

"I don't know, Marcus." I watch the crashing waves around the island's clawed feet, its head thrown back, spewing lava. "This looks a lot like a mythic sea dragon changing the path of at least one shore." I nod to his pocket where he keeps the Bone Thrower's list.

"How hard would it have been for the bones to speak plain and say, Bakton?" There's no answer to that, so Marcus rallies. "Kutoon, and then on to Pandom City."

Pandom City! I can't wait to arrive. There is so much in their library I am going to look up. I feel ready to work around the clock, my fingers and toes buzzing with anticipation.

"Genealogies?"

Huh? I cock my head.

"Nothing."

You said, genealogies.

"It hurts."

What do you mean?

"I mean, it hurts to talk of it." My inner voice turns shrill.

Easy. It's all right. Just breathe.

And here I am, soaked to the bone, scratched up and more than a little rattled, telling myself to breathe…

So I do.

Below deck, I change out of wet clothes and let Piper treat my wounds.

"Did you get raked over the reefs?"

"Something like that." I am not ready to say I was attacked by a shade and swallowed it whole, but, cheers! No worse for wear. A hallucination? Has to be. "How are you feeling?" I nod to her belly which has yet to give her secret away. Anything to change the subject.

"Samsen made me these." She lifts her wrists and shows me the leather bands encircling them, a polished green stone on the underside of each wrist, pressing just where it is needed to alleviate the nausea.

"What a great idea. You could sell those at a healers' market."

"They do the trick." She smiles. "Let's eat."

When we join the others at the galley table, they are still shaken, especially Belair and Tyche who have, by the looks of them, never experienced an earthquake followed by a volcanic eruption before, at least, not one of that magnitude. They've grown up on more stable realms than Palrio.

"The earthquake was the least of the excitement."

Indeed. I'm used to the earth rolling like the sea under my feet, but having a demon of a shade trying to crawl down my throat? Could it really have happened? I was horrified, at the time, but also somehow eager, as if I knew it couldn't harm me. Was it a waking dream? That would explain why I recognized the demon as the one that haunted my sleep on Aku? I have to find out more, and the only way is to talk about it with the people I trust.

But I'm not sure I'm ready.

"Did you see them?" I ask around the table, but their only response is shock. It's not until after the evening meal, and Bakton is far behind us, that together we try to make better sense of the experience.

"They were shades," Tyche says flatly. She's sandwiched between Piper and Samsen and seems brighter now with a warm meal in her belly and Imp in her lap.

"Shades?" Marcus asks.

"The little lass means ghost phantoms," Kaylin puts in.

"We call them shadows in Tangeen." Belair looks relieved and actually scoffs. "Phantoms disembodied from their savant. You can't tell me you take the old stories seriously."

"Is there nothing you believe in?" I ask out the side of my mouth but he only shrugs.

"Not shadows."

"I know what I saw," Tyche says, more talkative than we've grown to expect. "They were shades, or shadows as Belair calls them. Hungry ones."

"Ghost phantoms, according to the literature, are extremely rare," I say after clearing my throat. If it was a ghost phantom that attacked me, the whole thing makes even less sense.

"And caused by the sudden death of the savant if they are in full phantom perspective when leaving the path," Marcus adds. "You know that." He points a spoon at Belair.

We all focus on the Tangeen. He may be skeptical, but lore of the ghost phantom is taught in the Sanctuaries, and there are plenty of scripts and firsthand accounts in the archives that bear it out.

The phantom, which effectively is a projection of the savant's unconscious, a sometimes dangerous and unpredictable projection, is freed from restraint and control, and never called back to ground. How could it be? There is no savant to return to anymore. It has left the path. The ghost phantom becomes a roaming entity, cursed, some say, to wander, growing more and more autonomous as it develops a complete identity unto itself.

"Ash, you agree with Tyche?" Marcus asks, his tone soft like I'll fall apart any moment.

Really? After what I've survived so far, he treats me like a fragile child?

"In his defense, lass, he doesn't know what you survived on Bakton. I am the only one who saw."

And I'm grateful for that. I can hardly explain it to myself and upon seeing their reactions, I don't want the others questioning me right now, asking me to relive it so they can understand, too. I need to hold this in my own mind first, and I'm not ready to do that either. But Kaylin has a point. I drop the edge that's been building on my tongue. "If it's true, we all got away unscathed."

"Meaning?" Belair asks. He's struggling to keep the doubt out of his voice.

"They were hungry," Tyche answers.

"Yes, that's what I mean."

"Hungry for what?" Marcus asks, looking confused.

"Mental stimulation, for a start," Kaylin says. "Connection. They were healers on Bakton, right? I imagine hundreds of years deprived of their trade would make them…restless."

"The result," I say, "might be a host of starved phantoms looking for a savant, and I brought them four, ripe for the choosing." I lower my head. "I'm sorry!"

"It's not your fault, Ash." Belair lifts his face and I meet his eyes. "You couldn't have known, and wouldn't we have tried anyway, to collect the bone?"

"Besides, we all have phantoms. It's not like they could take us over." Marcus leans toward Belair. "I'm with you on this. That part sounds like a bedtime story to me."

"Then you don't know your lore," Kaylin says.

"And what is your source of knowledge on this?" Marcus asks our sailor. "You're not even savant."

"I've sailed the world and been in most libraries throughout the realms. Can you say you're as experienced as I?"

"He's right, Marcus." I jump in before the argument can escalate. "A ghost phantom, or shade, as they are called on the Isle of Aku, enters a savant, flowing in on their breath, and mingling with their soul, taking it over, effectively, driving out the original phantom."

"They take their place?" Samsen asks. He visibly shivers.

"According to the texts, that is what they do." Kaylin nods.

"Whyever for?" Samsen asks.

"To be in the world," Tyche answers, tipping her head to Kaylin. "Like he said."

"I've heard they must never be allowed to touch a savant because once they do…" He rests his eyes on mine but can't finish.

"They attach," Tyche finishes for him. "The savant can't shake them loose and are eventually lured back to where the phantom was disembodied. That's where they have the power to drive out the original phantom for good."

"Can't the savant fight it?" Marcus asks.

I can tell he's starting to worry. "Sometimes the savant isn't even aware until it's too late."

That has them all gasping.

"Did the shades…" Piper turns to Belair. "Touch anyone?"

"Not me," Belair and Marcus say at the same time.

"That you know of," Kaylin adds.

Piper and Samsen shake their heads. "We were the first away, Tyche between us."

I feel Kaylin's eyes on me, and I tilt my head. *"What is it?"*

"Why aren't you telling them what happened to you?"

"I'm not ready to relive it."

"Fair enough." Aloud he asks, "Could a ghost phantom take over a non-savant?"

I hold my breath, leveling my eyes at him. *"What are you doing?"*

"Asking a question."

"Don't see how," Piper says.

The others murmur their agreement.

"You'll need to inform Master Brogal," Marcus says, bringing us all back to the present.

I pull my knit cap out of my pocket and put it on, trying not to bite my lower lip. "At least we have some good news. The Tree of Eternity is ours."

"Aye, lass." Kaylin studies me curiously. "Another whistle bone in our possession." He frowns. *"Will you tell your guardian all of it? He might know more about the shades."*

Tell the High Savant I don't trust? *"I don't know."*

But of course, I must. He's my guardian, the High Savant of Baiseen. It's my duty to report everything to him, even things I'm not ready to reveal.

I weave my way through the cargo boxes strapped to the aft deck and find a private nook, out of the wind, and the lantern light. The medallion is hot to the touch when I pull it out, like it was when I thought I heard Talus on the island. Just thinking about conversing seems to set it off. I hold it up to eye level. "You have a mind of your own, don't you friend?" I clasp it in both hands and close my eyes before it can answer. Not that it could, but just in case. I don't need to be further unnerved.

The ship cuts through the swell and we ride the waves in a gentle up and down glide. "Let's get this over with."

"Yes, let's."

"Hello? Master Brogal? It's me again." I listen hard and detect the low buzz of conversation and the ruffling of papers. Like last time, I don't think he knows I'm here. I blink. And blink again. *Am I imagining things?*

"Only if I am, too."

It's impossible, but I can see him. The medallion nearly falls from my grasp as I peer into Brogal's chambers, stifling a gasp. I float upward, weightless, my back brushing the rafters as I look down. *Are you seeing this?*

"Hmm." My inner voice sounds far away.

It's definitely Master Brogal's chambers. No doubt about that. There's his phantom perched on his shoulder, tailfeathers waterfalling down his back in brilliant blues, contrasting the master's long red robe. I can count the creases in his brow, read the map on the desk. This is bizarre and amazing all at once. I lean in to take a closer look. On the map, all the Sanctuaries are marked with a dark X and annotated. Larseen, Marcus's friend, sits opposite Master Brogal, in his orange robes. Wait, when was he promoted? Yesterday? The scene feels tense. Agitated. I try to get Brogal's attention again. *"Excuse me? Master Brogal?"*

His phantom tips its head sideways as if to look up at me. Its eyes are piercing. Suddenly I'm glad the medallion doesn't allow thoughts to flow between me and Brogal's phantom. I have enough in my head as it is, and those eyes are sharp as knives.

"Sir? Can you hear me?"

Brogal startles. *"No need to shout, Ash."* He waves Larseen out of the room.

"Sorry to interrupt." I can tell immediately he's not had enough sleep—the wrinkled brow, dark circles under his eyes. I wonder what is going on there, under Petén's rule. *"I've news for you, Master Brogal."*

"The Nonnova whistle bone?"

"Yes and no. Tann got there first, but we went to Bakton."

"Whatever for? You need to beat Tann to Kutoon now."

"Master Brogal, please listen. We were successful on Bakton. We called, that is, Tyche called, *the original whistle bone that was buried in the Sanctuary ruins."*

"The Tree of Eternity? Are you sure?"

"Yes, we have it."

"And Tann has what?"

"A replica, we think."

"He'll know by now, on close inspection, that he didn't call the original."

"It had fooled the Nonnova High Savants, but I want to report something strange about the Isle of Bakton. Hard to explain—"

"Is it important?"

"Um…"

"Don't waste my time with inconsequential details, Ash. Go on to Kutoon and report back your results there."

My stomach hardens. *"It's important."* I spit the words out before he can dismiss me again. *"In the ruins, rising from the ground, were shadows, shades, unformed like a black-robe's phantom,"* I say, realizing the comparison as I try to explain.

"Ghost phantoms?" His voice rises in pitch.

"We think so. They surrounded me." I'm going to tell him. If anyone understands what happened, he would.

"None touched a savant, did they?"

I narrow one eye. *"No, the shades didn't touch any of the savants, but one of them took form as an agapha and—"*

"Did it speak?"

"Yes!" The words from the creature come back to me. *"It said, 'let me in.'"* I go on in a rush, afraid if I pause I won't be able to continue. *"It altered and tried to take me over."*

"Altered?"

"Into a dark hunched creature." Like the one that haunted my dreams on Aku, but I don't think I say that aloud. *"It tore at my mouth and choked me.*

Tried to dive down my throat." A wave of nausea rises as I relive the experience.

"Did anything else happen?" he asks, tapping his thumb ring on the desk, taking a sip from his mug.

Because being attacked by a shade isn't enough? *"The one clawing my chest turned into a hot, burning energy, pouring into my mouth. I thought I was going to be consumed until—"* I stop mid-sentence. I don't know how to say more.

My inner voice gives no advice.

But Brogal is my High Savant and I need his help understanding, if he can offer any. *"Until something cracked."*

"Cracked?"

"There was a fracture somewhere deep in my core, and then the pressure was gone, and most of the fear. It didn't hurt anymore."

"What happened to the shade?"

"It flew out of me in a red mist. Tasted awful, but I'm fine."

Silence.

"I'm more than fine. I feel vitalized even, except for the horror of the event. Obviously."

He's still silent, but I can see him. He doesn't move. He hardly breathes. He holds the mug so tight I think it might crack under his grip.

"There's one last thing." I've gone this far. Might as well say the rest. *"As the mist fell, it turned into…"*

"What, Ash?" His voice is an icy whisper.

"Tiny red flowers that fell like flakes of snow. Red snow."

His phantom lets out a squawk and wings to the top of the bookshelf, knocking over a vase. It breaks into pieces that scatter across the floor.

"Master Brogal?"

He clears his throat. *"Tell Marcus congratulations on a successful retrieval of the Tree of Eternity. He has done well."*

I press my lips together and hold my breath so tight I sputter my next words. *"Marcus didn't do anything in this instance, Master Brogal, other than help row the boat. It was I who insisted we go to the Isle and Tyche who retrieved the bone."* I don't mean to be petty, but I'm sick to death of my guardian thinking nothing of me, let alone ignoring my increasingly frequent brushes with death.

"Of course, Ash. Well done for you all." He says it as an afterthought. *"I want you to continue with your chants. You remember them, don't you?"*

"My chants?" What's he talking about? *"The chants to help me raise my phantom?"* I haven't practiced them since before leaving for Aku. A light goes on inside me. *"Is it still possible? I might raise a phantom?"*

"No, of course not. We know you are non-savant, but chanting will settle your soul. After your ordeal, you need it."

So he does recognize the trauma. *"Chanting will help me?"*

"Clears the head and eases the mind. Please begin immediately and keep it to yourself. It's more powerful if no one knows you are doing it. Understood?"

I'm sure he means well but he says it as if I'd caught my finger in a drawer, not swallowed a demon whole. *"Yes, sir. I understand."*

"Contact me when you have the next whistle bone. Mistress Kazia of Kutoon may take some convincing to hand over the Arrow of Nii, but she'd rather him than Tann or Atikis. Tell Marcus to use whatever means to persuade her."

Again, the audible click snaps in my head and the vision is gone.

I don't move for a moment while my body shakes. Finally, I close my eyes and tears spill. I should know better by now, hoping for something, anything, from my guardian other than vague indifference.

"Sleep, lass. I will keep watch."

I tip my head up to the crow's nest. It's too dark for me to see, but I assume Kaylin is there. *"Did you hear?"*

"No, but I see it was hurtful."

"You're right. I will go to sleep…"

I blink back the emotions, head down the ladder to the hold. The others have already gone to their bunks and hammocks, so I do the same, saving the less than insightful words of the High Savant to share in the morning.

I close my eyes to find sleep, but not until repeating the chant Master Brogal taught me when I was a brown-robe potential, when I'd first come to the Sanctuary and failed to raise my phantom. And it does help my mind relax, so much so, my inner voice seems to have fallen asleep before me.

"That's all he said?" I prompt Ash when she finally joins us for breakfast. She's not looking rested, and the bed hair isn't helping. I put a plate in front of her and she pushes it back.

"Just tea, thanks."

I push the plate in front of her again. "You need more than a few stems and leaves."

She picks at the edges of the bread.

"Surely Master Brogal would have said more about Tyche's shades."

"They aren't mine," the child says, looking up from her book.

Ash holds her mug in both hands when I pass it to her, looking at the tea as if it might have all the answers. "Master Brogal said to say *well done* to you, Marcus, and to head for Kutoon next. Their whistle bone is the Arrow of Nii." She glances at Tyche, a question on her face.

"I know everything about that bone." Tyche brightens. "The Arrow of Nii was named for Ra Gin Nii, the last monarch of his line. As a boy, he was blinded in the right eye by an arrow. Being Heir, they gave him a 'right-hand man,' a boy his age bound to his right side for life. The arrow was remade and kept in Nii's quiver until Er took it from him in battle, gaining control, for a time, of what is now Gollnar." She smiles. "I'll be ready, when you need me to call it." She pats the illustrated bone book.

"*If* we need to," I say. "Hopefully it will be handed over directly." The last thing I want to do is start a war on Gollnar soil. "What else, Ash? I can tell there is more."

She takes a sip of tea and relaxes a bit. "Brogal was relieved that the ghost phantoms didn't touch any of the *savants*."

"As am I," Belair says, missing her emphasis.

But for once, I catch it. "Your guardian is a cold sod. I'm sorry you have to endure him."

"Ash, I'm sorry, too, if—"

"Can we please return to the discussion on the Letters of Er?" Ash cuts

Belair off.

Clearly, she doesn't want to dwell on her relationship with Brogal. Fair enough. I'm no fan of the red-robe, either. I take a bite of my scrambled eggs and shrug. "Please, Ash, tell us more. You think the Letters of Er can help us obtain the bones."

"More than that," she says. "The Letters of Er may tell us how to keep the whistle bones from being *called*. But there was only one of them in Brogal's resources. It will help if we can find them in the sanctuary libraries we visit."

"Won't they be reserved for red-robes only?" Samsen asks.

"True. Translated copies are not generally available," Ash says. "But I don't need translations. If I can find them in the original archaic Sierrak, I'll translate them myself."

"Would they be in the Tangeen Sanctuary's archives?" Piper asks Belair. He looks paler than usual, his eyes distant. "Belair? The Letters of Er?"

He jerks back to attention. "I guess, though they may be hard to find." He blinks and gives Piper his full attention.

"Why hard to find?" she asks.

"There has been a slow dissemination of Sanctuary knowledge in all Tangeen. High Savant Havest is losing, um, releasing some control."

"As Brogal seems to be doing in Baiseen," I say, and no one contradicts me. "Are you saying the letters could be in the city library archives?"

Belair brightens. "If so, all the easier for us to find." He's about to say more when he yelps and draws his knife. He flips it in his hand and stabs straight down into the table. The blade reverberates as he releases it, jumping as far from the table as the small space allows.

"What is it?" Piper says, springing back as well.

"Ant," Belair answers, shaking his left hand. "It was about to bite you."

"Exploding islands, assassination attempts, red-robe battles, the whistle bones to gather and you're worried about an ant?" Samsen laughs.

I take a closer look. "Stabbed it dead center. Good shot, Belair, but peace be its path."

"It's not dead!" Tyche clutches her book against her chest. "Pull it out. You're hurting it."

"Do you know how bad it can sting?" Belair doesn't move.

Kaylin comes trotting down the ladder. "I heard a scream."

"It's an ant," Ash says, eyes lighting when she turns to him.

I come around to Belair's side to get a better view. Pinned down, the large green ant with golden legs wiggles and squirms.

"That's not an ant," Kaylin says as he sticks his nose close to it as well.

"You're an expert on bugs now?"

"Ants aren't bugs," he and Ash say at the same time.

"Let it go," Tyche says again. She puts her hand on the hilt to remove it herself. As she does the six struggling legs go still.

My mouth opens as I watch the ant slowly dissolve until nothing is left.

"Where is it?" Ash asks, and everyone looks to me.

"That's interesting," Kaylin says. "Must be —"

Before he can finish, the first mate shouts down the hatch. "Captain wants a word."

"Aye," Kaylin says, and I follow him out of the hold.

33

ASH

"What the chac'n stuggs was that?" I ask Marcus and Kaylin when their meeting with the captain is over.

"Just a heading adjustment. Kutoon may not take kindly to us sailing into their harbor unannounced so we will—"

"I mean the disappearing ant."

Marcus leans against the rail, staring out to sea as the sloop cuts through the waves at high speed. "I'm not sure what I saw, thinking back. You were all blocking my view."

"I'm sure." I hold the rail lightly and rock with the sea. "It melted away, like a phantom going to ground."

"Just like that." Kaylin joins Marcus in his gaze of the horizon.

"So it was a phantom?"

He nods again.

The thought makes me lightheaded. "Who's ever heard of one so small, and on top of that, we're at sea. It can't go to ground. Can it?"

Both Marcus and I wait on Kaylin's response, but all he does is shrug.

"Not a phantom of a shipboard savant, obviously," Marcus speculates. "But what if it came onboard by itself, from Baiseen or Nonnova?"

"Or Bakton?" I shiver. "But how could a savant keep their phantom up that long, from that far away?" I exhale hard.

"It would have to be a red-robe," Marcus says.

"But it's too small."

"Ask Kaylin," my inner voice says.

I lock eyes with Kaylin. "If you know something about this, it's time to say so." I realize I'm snapping, but really. Between yesterday on Bakton, Master Brogal's cold words, and the headache pounding between my temples, I'm not feeling patient. My people need to say what they know. Right now.

He nods, a hint of a smile lifting one side of his face. "Phantoms cannot be raised on the sea."

"Already discussed," Marcus says, crossing his arms.

"But," Kaylin goes on. "Phantoms can be killed anywhere."

Marcus scratches his stubbled chin. "How would they return to their savant?"

My question exactly.

"We're still hugging Tangeen, on the shore side of the deep-sea trench. The water is only a few fathoms deep, so maybe it could have gone to ground. Another possibility is, if it be a phantom, the savant could have been fully with it," Kaylin says.

"Meaning the savant died, and there was nothing to return to?" Marcus looks even more puzzled, but the thought sparks an idea in me.

"Kaylin, have you seen this kind of phantom before?"

He studies the sea, brow pinched as if trying to remember, but I can tell he's deciding on how much to say. I wish I knew what it was that holds him back. Surely if he could, he would tell me all, wouldn't he?

"Much like it." Finally, he nods. "It was a type of *alter*—"

"But the size," Marcus interrupts.

"Small, I know. I came upon it in the far northern waters just shy of the frozen pole. The *alter* could fragment," Kaylin says.

"Fragment?" Marcus says.

"Break into multiple aspects of the one?" I whisper at the same time, rolling the concept around in my mind. "You're saying that little green ant was a part of a larger phantom?"

"I've seen it," Kaylin admits.

"Well, I haven't," Marcus says, "and I'm the savant here." His face contorts for a moment. "The smallest phantom extracts the highest price."

"What the Bone Thrower said?" I whisper.

"That might fit," Kaylin says. "But such a small fragment doesn't look like it could do more than give a nasty sting or bite. Not a very high price. And if they disperse, even in opposite directions, it can take years to fully return to the savant and reform."

"How do you know that, exactly?" Marcus wrinkles his nose like the milk has gone sour.

"Learned it in Avon Eyre. There was a fragmenting *alter* there, among their clan."

That shuts us both up. No one in our lifetime has ever gone to the Sanctuary of Avon Eyre and returned. Most think it's a mythical place, reserved for stories and tales. And indeed, it seems in a different location in every map I see.

"Only a red-robe or higher can direct a fragmenting *alter*, from what I gathered," Kaylin says as if he didn't just speak casually of the far northern isle of mystery that may or may not exist.

"Higher than a red-robe?" I ask. "You mean, a black-robe?"

"Aye. A master Bone Thrower. There are none on land more powerful."

On land? It's an odd way to put it.

"He's like that, isn't he?" My inner voice sounds whimsical, and I roll my eyes.

If you mean cryptic and evasive at times, then yes, he is. But I admit, I'm more intrigued than irritated. Much more.

"I'll tell the others." Marcus looks determined. "We have to be alert, in case there are more of them about."

"Perhaps ask if they recall seeing these creatures along the journey." Kaylin says it lightly, but it startles me like a splash of cold water.

"We have!" Why didn't I remember this before?

They don't answer, and I realize why their brows go up. Viz spit'n memory gaps. But I have it now. "Belair was bitten." I turn to Marcus. "In Clearwater, at the blacksmith's shop. We had the horses checked on the way to Aku?"

"Don't recall, but there was a line of green ants in Baiseen while we were making repairs." Marcus rubs the back of his neck. "I don't know if any were bitten. Piper might."

"There are green ants almost everywhere in the world, you know," Kaylin reminds us. "It's just a theory, that it might be a fragmenting *alter*."

"But this ant on the galley table…" My mind whirls with the possibilities. "It vanished like smoke on the wind."

"Or a phantom called back to ground," Marcus says. "Over the sea—which means it died?"

"Your phantom was underwater for longer than you can hold your breath, and he didn't die." I tap my chin. "Is it possible that everything a phantom can and can't do isn't common knowledge, even to savants?" I ask.

"Aye, lass. It's possible," Kaylin answers before Marcus can. He pushes off from the railing. "I'll talk to the captain and see if he's noticed these insects. Perhaps there's a nest."

"I'll go with you." I step out to follow Kaylin, but Marcus holds me back. "I could use you when we tell the others. We want to alert them, but not alarm. You're better at that than me."

I'm torn between missing an opportunity to talk with Kaylin alone and wanting to support Marcus. "All right, Marcus. Lead the way."

He puts his arm over my shoulder and guides me below.

The predawn sky sparkles like bioluminescence while the filling moon heads westward. It'll be under the horizon soon. Its diluted light paints the water, and above, it picks up a cast of red from the second sun in the east. The nemesis star grows brighter by the day.

"Drop anchor," commands the captain. We are just south of Manta Bay, the gateway to Kutoon Sanctuary. The shore of this small inlet is over half a mile away.

Time for a dip.

I pull my shirt over my head and hand my weapons to Marcus, all but my short knife. The plan is for me to swim ashore, scale the hundred foot sea cliffs to the tableland above, and scout Kutoon's sprawling Sanctuary without being seen. Easy enough from the cover of junipers that line the southwest headland. It's a precautionary venture, in case Tann and his warriors are traveling over land. I'm also keeping an eye out for Atikis. He's as likely to acquire, or steal, Kutoon's whistle bone, as Tann. He is Gollnarian, so he could still have strong ties to the Sanctuary.

"You can be back before sunrise?" Marcus asks. His jaw is tight, eyes darting to the distant shore and the dark sea cliffs that must be near invisible to his eye. "That's no small distance."

"Have you seen him fly up to the crow's nest?" Belair asks, blowing warm air into his hands. "He can do it."

Marcus keeps his eyes on me. "You don't want to be caught out there in daylight, if things go wrong."

"There is no catching me." I put my hand on his shoulder. "Don't worry."

Ash comes up out of the hold, bare feet padding straight for us. "You said you'd wake me."

"But you were so peaceful, lass."

She punches me in the arm, and Marcus laughs. Then she punches him for good measure. "You said you'd wake me, too." Her look is severe until she turns back to me. "Be safe." Her eyes go to the coast and the silhouettes of forested hills. Smoke rises from the edges in wisps, like young phantoms unable to take form. All week, in our sail up the coast, it's been the same. The forests burn. Rivers choke with topsoil. Amassia's resources are being consumed, even with the second sun so distant.

It won't be long before it hits them, the full extent of this Great Dying.

"Please promise me you'll be safe," Ash says, drawing my attention back to her. She's underdressed for the morning chill and her hair dances in the wind. Beautiful and wild, my lass…

"By the Serpent, I promise." I gaze straight overhead at the constellation of the Serpent twining around the Lone Hunter's arms. I know the cluster by other titles, going back to when the stars were named for the wilder gods. Before that even, when they were called by their *charms* and the people of the great island of Atlas drew on them for spells and alchemy. That didn't go well for any of us, in the end, but the names were good. Melodic, like the sound of the sea.

Will Ash understand my history when I reveal it to her? Or will she be horrified? These are the questions that keep me mute, but I must risk it all. And soon.

The *Dugong's* anchor line pulls taut. She drags the weight for a few dozen yards, then the rope strains and the ship holds steady, the current rushing by her hull. "I won't be long." I jump to the railing and dive overboard.

The shock of cold hits first, followed by myriad sounds amplified by the sea — waves lapping the *Dugong's* flanks, the strain of her anchor line and clank of metal on the reef, the chitter of a distant pod of dolphins, the susurrations of water over the sandy shore. It mixes with the rolling swell, sleeping sea lions and the tiny clicks of crustaceans harvesting algae in the dark. If I listen hard enough, I can hear the thoughts of other Mar far away. Salila is probably lurking nearby, but I shut them out. The need is expediency, not communication.

I swim for shore and surface at the end of a pier. The rose glow of sunrise lights the bay as westward stars disappear from sight. I float under the dock, silently waiting for the telltale sound of boots striking the wharf above me. With reports of Tann's attacks, and a visible second sun, it is only common sense for a coastal town to post guards. They would send a man out to scope the *Dugong* at the least. From this distance, she passes as a small merchant ship, perhaps carrying spices from Cabazon, or fruit from Nonnova. She would be welcome either way.

As expected, boots clomp down the pier, then pause. A slight thump follows, like the guard falls and remains silent. Odd. I grip the underside of the wharf and crab crawl to the edge of the beam. Before the lander can register movement,

I'm out of the water and perched on the tall piling, looking down at—nothing I ever thought I'd see.

"Teern?" A shudder runs through me and I grip my narrow roost.

The guard is face down on the dock, his left foot twitches once and then goes still. Blood drips from his wrist, throat and ankle.

"You didn't have to kill him." The last thing I should be doing right now is reprimanding the Sea King, but here I am, doing just that. "All you need is a drop, if you plan to watch the sun rise."

"What makes you think he is dead?" Teern stands to his full height, broad as a bull and even more menacing on land than in the sea. His hair hangs in thick black ropes down his back. His legs are the size of tree trunks. He crosses his arms over his chest. "Let's talk, Son."

My eyes dart to the east. "Is that advisable, Father? It will be light soon." More to the point, is it sane? Or is this part of his plan to increase the ambiguous Mar sightings? I still can't believe it. Unheard of for millennia. Square before me, water dripping down his limbs, stands Teern, King of the Sea. On land. Inviting me to talk?

He lifts one massive hand, a gesture that drops me to the deck in a bow.

Teern's power bends my head to the ground. He is no man, savant or otherwise. No lander blood flows in his veins, not now or ever. This is Teern, the oldest child of the sunken continent, from days so long ago even the sea's memories of them are lost. Teern reigned before the Himalayas fell, before the great river to the east sprouted the City of Lights, before the library that held the wisdom of the world burned down. Some Mar say he is one of the old gods, the sole survivor of the making of the Ma'ata. I don't know for sure, but it wouldn't surprise me.

After a respectable moment, I rise, and he motions me to walk beside him. Who am I to argue? The pier groans under his footfalls until we reach the sandy beach, and he leads me to the end of the cove. Under the shadows of the headland, we watch the second sun glint, no longer dull in the light of day, but bright as the moon.

Teern sits in the sand and digs up the white grains, letting them fall through his fingers. It's a novelty to him, dry earth. The moment softens, and as it does, the impending Great Dying seems eons away. We have all the time in the world. A father and his son.

That vision breaks apart when he speaks. "There's trouble over the tombs." He glances out to sea.

"Tann?"

"He's nosing around."

"That's not good."

"I've called Salila to help but I'm making it your responsibility."

"Mine?"

"You'll have to anchor there, correct? In Manta Bay?"

"Aye. We visit Kutoon Sanctuary next." I keep my face calm, waiting for enough information to make sense of this.

And then he says, "The Dreaded must not rise. At least, not yet."

"The Dreaded?"

"See to it. This is crucial, Kaylin."

The intensity of his gaze makes it impossible for me to speak, so I nod my agreement.

I rise as Teern does, our little chat over. "Off so soon," I manage when his focus turns elsewhere.

"I'm making a quick run northeast, or is it northwest today?"

My eyes widen. "Avon Eyre?" I whisper.

His lips curl in a smile. Elusive Avon Eyre, the only remnant of the sunken homelands. "Guard the tombs, Kaylin. Track the bones. And for dead gods' sakes, keep an eye on the girl while I'm away."

I give him a formal bow, hands steepled at my forehead, feeling the earth shudder at his passing. When I look up, he's gone, only a ring of foam remains beyond the breakers. "Teern?" I swallow the lump in my throat. It's not like him to come onto dry land, speak with his voice. He never does it.

Unless he's hiding his thoughts from the sea itself. I roll my neck as the sun's rays creep farther over the coast. No time left. Strength from even the quick dip, and the shock of seeing Teern, sends heat and energy through me. I streak up tall sea cliffs that form the south headland wall of Manta Bay and scan the entire coastline, up and down. Behind me and far below is the sleepy fishing village where Teern and I had our little talk. To the north and below is the home harbor of Kutoon. In front of me, spreading out over the grassy plains, lies the Sanctuary.

The view lies unobstructed, and it holds no threats. There's not a single sloop flying Gollnar colors or those of Aturnia, or Tann's Twin Suns in Manta Bay. A few fishing boats rock in their moorings along the wharf, but that's it. The access road to the Sanctuary is empty, the hundred steps from the sea to the top of the cliff, and the Sanctuary gates, empty save for two guards. No sign of enemy camps. No black warhorse in the corral outside the stable. Tann may have been and gone, but he is not here now. Nor Atikis.

All clear.

I swan dive from the cliffs into the sea and swim back to the ship. So far, there is no evidence of Tann and his threat to the Ma'ata, either. But in the long ages of the world, Teern has never been wrong about our tombs. If he says they are in danger, then I must offer my life to protect them. *All without losing sight of my lovely lass.*

35

MARCUS

Damn the bones, this path is steep. I started the climb regal enough, clean robe, smooth and pressed, hair tied back. I even got the dirt out from under my nails. Ash put her documents in order, and all our diplomatic smiles were in place. That was a waste of time. Between these endless steps and the offshore wind, we've turned into sweat-stained, wind-blown wrecks. Not that I don't appreciate Kutoon's logic in putting the Sanctuary at the top of a four-hundred-foot cliff face. No surprises can come by sea, and if they do, they'll likely collapse from heatstroke before they reach the top.

Of course, we're not a surprise attack, as Ash keeps reminding me as she pants at my side. Her headaches are back. That's obvious. I wish I could have left her onboard, but it's not an option. We are the party of the Bone Gatherer, as foretold in the ancient prophecy. My recorder must be present. To be honest, I'd prefer that Kaylin was with us as well, but I left him shipside to keep an eye out for Tann.

"Marcus," Ash says, yet again. "Keep the flag visible. We don't want to be picked off by archers because of a misunderstanding."

I save my breath for the climb but hoist the pole higher against my shoulder. The black and white ribbons of truce strain in the breeze.

"There's one other thing." Ash sounds serious.

I keep my eyes on the deep cut stones. One leg in front of the other. "Can't wait to hear it."

"Don't be cranky." She punches my upper arm. "But if Tann's been here first, and there are no signs of struggle, it's likely they've already given their whistle bone to him."

"Obvious."

"But if aligned with Atikis—"

"I know. If the High Savant has taken his side, it won't go our way."

"She will try to stop us. Perhaps even take us prisoner."

"Thank you, Ash. I'm keeping it in mind."

I can crush Zakia, De'ral says.

"You don't even know what she raises."

I can crush her.

"Let's hold off on the crushing, to start with. We aren't Tann. We're not taking these bones by force."

Not even from him?

I frown at that but keep climbing. There is so much I haven't had time to think about. We all slept through most of the sail here and I still don't feel rested.

When we reach the top of the headland, we follow the well-manicured boardwalk, a raised path in a sea of flowering ice plant, to the main gates of the Sanctuary. Surprisingly, they are wide open, flanked by a small company of guards. I wonder how long they've been watching our approach. I didn't notice any phantoms in the sky.

Because you were watching only the steps.

"And be glad because one slip could have been the end of the path for both of us."

He grumbles but thankfully shuts up as a savant steps forward. He wears an orange-robe with two scimitars strapped to his back. His brown hair is cropped short, in the style of our honor guards. My mind goes immediately to Rowten until I jerk it back.

"I am Endaro, commander of the first guard of the Sanctuary of Kutoon." He offers a small bow. "Welcome, if you come in peace."

I bow back, guessing what isn't relayed—*if you don't come in peace, be ready to die.* "We do indeed come in peace," I say. "I am the Bone Gatherer, Marcus Adicio of Baiseen, sent by Master Brogal, red-robe of Palrio." I introduce the others formally. Ash has a strange, distant look to her. I want to ask what's wrong, but it's not the time. "We seek counsel with High Savant Zakia, if it is her pleasure." All very diplomatic.

"She's expecting you. This way." Endaro eyes us all. "No raised phantoms. You understand."

We follow past the row of guards and into the Sanctuary. It's designed for training. On one side is an open field of close-cropped grass. Students are scattered about it, mostly with *ousters* but *alters* and *warriors* as well. I'm impressed by their discipline, but I also catch a couple of blue-robes stealing glances at us until their instructors pull them up. It makes me smile. No different in Baiseen, or even Aku. I slow in front of a high arched gate that marks the access to the training field. De'ral churns just under the surface.

As I catch up with Endaro, the gateway morphs, and the entire field of savants and phantoms close in. "Trap!" I shout and drop to raise De'ral. I draw my sword at the same time, but brute hands clasp my arms and keep me upright before my phantom can rise. My weapon falls to the ground. The same happens to the others, all but Ash. They leave her alone.

De'ral roars to the surface of my mind, and searing pain hits the back of my skull. The last thing I see is a flash of brilliant stars winking out in front of my eyes.

"*Ash! What's happening, lass?*" I can feel the shock of adrenaline run through her as I drop from the crow's nest, sending the first mate up to replace me. I pace the deck, waiting for her response.

Finally, she answers. *"Not sure. It seems all very formal and correct. We're being escorted to Zakia."*

I search the cliff face, waiting. "*Lass?*"

"We're in. I'll let you know if we need help."

But something seems wrong. I'm about to dive overboard and race up the steps at Mar speed and see for myself. I shouldn't have let them go without me. But Teern had other ideas.

"Guard the Ma'ata, Kaylin. Keep Tann away at all costs, but don't lose track of the bones," he'd said, and of course it's important. But so is Ash. I can't lose track of her, either!

"A little wrinkle, brother." Salila shoots me a warning from the northern mouth of Manta Bay.

"What now?"

"Tann is headed your way."

Before she says more, shouts from the crow's nest raise the alarm. "A turnian ship. Twin Suns."

I'm at the wheelhouse in a heartbeat. "Tann's vessel." I point toward it appearing out of the fog. *"Salila! You let him through!"*

"What did you want me to do? Sink his ship on sight? Teern said there could be none of that, not so near the Ma'ata."

I grip the hilt of my sword and address the captain. "We need to pull anchor and prepare for—"

"Do we? Last time I looked, laddie, you were a passenger and I, the captain."

"Fair enough, but Tann will not negotiate. We must prepare to—"

"Follow my orders or go below!" Anders bellows so loud, I take a step back. My fingers itch to draw both of my swords, but I'd have to slaughter the entire crew to take over the ship, and that could be hard to explain to Marcus and the others when they return. Harder still to explain to Ash. Plus, we are trying to avoid blanketing the Dreadeds' tombs with life-giving lander blood, instead of flooding them with it.

The captain runs up the truce flags and proceeds to watch, and wait. That's not going to work, but I keep my mouth shut.

Tann's ship tacks hard to starboard, the crew moving fluidly through the maneuver, the vessel luffing only a moment before catching the wind and picking up speed, away from us at first, then straight back to the *Dugong*. I know what's going to happen, and I wish to the fossilized old gods that Anders would listen to me.

"Sir, if—"

"Below with you, now!"

That's it. *"Salila, be ready."*

"Always." She clicks her tongue. *"What do you have in mind?"*

"I am going to stop Tann, and do it before he reaches the Dugong, *or we'll be picking bones and planks out of the Ma'ata for the rest of the year."*

"I thought you'd never ask." The battle lust in her voice bleeds into my mind, catching like fire corals. *"Where do you want me?"*

"Take the little caller to shore. I am not sure this vessel will be spared, and she is guarding the gathered bones."

"You want me to babysit the imp?"

"Yes. Thank you."

"That's not—"

"Salila!" Teern's voice blasts in our minds, nearly dropping me to the deck. *"Do as he says. I'll be there as soon as I can."*

Dead silence drifts between me and Salila until I'm under the waves, streaking toward Tann's vessel.

"Fine." She gives in. *"But you better save some of the fight for me."*

"Priorities, Salila. And please don't frighten the little orange-robe, or her phantom. We need them alive, and sane."

"Aye, aye, Cap-i-tán."

I can taste the sarcasm, but ignore it.

I'm nearly upon the Aturnian warship when I realize there is one good thing in all this. My lass and her company are safe from harm, high up in the Sanctuary of Kutoon.

Why didn't I warn Marcus?

I felt something was wrong the moment we walked through the Sanctuary gates. My inner voice warned me, and Kaylin sounded nervous, which he never does. I think I might have also heard Talus send a caution as the medallion warmed against my skin. Now inside the Sanctuary, it all feels so vague, nothing I can put my finger on. Still, I go to pull on Marcus's sleeve to get his attention, and the entire archway erupts, restraining everyone. Everyone, that is, but me.

"We mean no threat or harm!" I say it loud and sharp with my hands in the air, so they can hear me in the terrible commotion. Savants come off the field to surround us, their phantoms rising like arrows shooting out of the ground. Even a small *alter* can stir a lot of dust as it changes shape but the one holding the others is huge. I'm blinded by the swirl of colored robes, blades, phantoms, and red, headland dirt. "We are diplomats from Baiseen!" I shout again.

"What's your name, non-savant," Endaro asks when the dust settles. Beside him hunches his phantom, its curved spines nearly as high as his shoulders. It's a demon of a creature with the face of a monkey and wings of a bat, not unlike the one that terrified me at Mount Bladon, on the journey to Aku. An *alter*, no doubt. I want to keep my distance, but I can't say the same for it.

"Harmless." My inner voice clearly has no concept of what may or may not cause me harm.

Are you kidding? Harmful, my friend. Harm-chac'n-full!

That gets me a chuckle but not from Endaro. He's too busy frowning at his phantom. It stretches its short monkey neck my way and chitters like it's found a ripe bunch of bananas.

I inch away, accustomed to such behavior, but not happy with it. "As you were asking," I say, gaining Endaro's attention. My shoulders go back, chin up. "You may call me Ash, recorder to Marcus Adicio, the Bone Gatherer from Baiseen. I bring documents from High Savant Brogal to explain our presence. Please allow me to deliver them?"

He nods but has to slap his thigh hard to keep his phantom from reaching out and touching my leg.

I pass over the documents, stamped with the Sanctuary of Baiseen's seal, and the Magistrate's.

"Lost his throne, did he?" Endaro nods toward Marcus.

My jaw tightens. "He did."

"Understandable. He was reported dead." He nods to the second sun over our heads. "Changing times. We must all adapt, yes?"

I have no answer for that.

While he studies our papers, I look to the others, all held tight by the giant *alter*. Then, I feel Endaro's phantom tap the back of my hand with a hooked claw, not unlike a cat testing to see if a mouse is still alive.

Other phantoms from the surrounding savants move toward me as well, snake forms, reptilian *ousters* like crocodiles walking on hind legs, bat-winged birds. A creature half cactus, half rock. They tighten the circle with me at the center.

"Kaylin? Little situation here. I might take you up on that offer of help."

My best chance with Tann is the element of surprise. It shouldn't be a challenge.

I slink aboard his vessel unnoticed, race up the rigging, and hide in the sails. This sweet ship is not going to be needing them soon. We're still half a mile out, in the center of the bay. If I stop her here, the Ma'ata will be safe, and none the wiser on how I put the vessel to a watery rest.

I shudder as Salila's voice tries to arrow into my mind. It's the tenth time since I asked her to take Tyche ashore. How difficult can it be? *"Manage your own job, sister. I have a boat to sink."*

I click my mind shut, cutting off any further distractions from land. A deep breath later, I swing across the rigging, slicing through ropes, dropping every bit of sail she has. It falls hard, folding over the deck, knocking crew to the ground. Unfortunately, my sword fouls in the last bit of rigging and I am jerked from my purchase, falling with the last one. I hit the boom, sword tearing from my grip, and land flat on the deck. I blink to find half a dozen Aturnian warriors drawing blades and pointing them at me.

"Kaylin?" Ash's voice lilts.

"One moment, lass. Little busy here." I kick up, flipping through the air before the crew has time to skewer me. I land on my feet, cross my arms in an X and spring, somersaulting out of the circle of swords. I touch down behind the Aturnians, kneeing a guard in the back before he can turn around. Bones crack, and as the man drops, I catch his blade. In a single leap, I'm on the boom, standing above the onlookers' heads.

The Aturnian captain shouts and three guards sheath their swords, jumping to grab the boom. They circled their hands around it and swing up to stand, two in front of me, and one behind, swords quickly redrawn. Their weapons become a blur of metal, singing through the air. The Aturnians, with their broad curved blades, are fast and quick on their feet. I shoot a glance at the tilting deck, distracted by the sound of cracking timber.

"Salila? What did you do?"

"If you had stopped to listen, you'd realize, I made a little hole earlier. Is it getting bigger yet?"

Taking advantage of my distraction, the guard behind slices my shoulder as the other two press me in. "Now you've just made me angry, mates."

Faster than the eye can follow, I cut in long sweeps left and right, taking out the front two before dropping to a crouch and skewering the one behind. As I straighten, more guards swing up to the boom. I cut them down as fast as they do, my bare feet slipping on their blood. Bodies roll away as their ship lists farther to port. Meanwhile, two sailors drop like spiders from the rigging, landing square in front and behind me. They charge, weapons leveled.

I reverse my sword and impale the sailor behind, then spring to the mast, cutting the other man down on the way. I rebound off the mast and land back on the deck, sword first, impaling the last of the guards through the midsection. But when I pull my weapon out of the sailor's chest, hundreds of green ants race up the blade toward my hand. I curse and fling them away in a whip-cracking motion. The impaled sailor, far from dead, turns into a writhing mass of insects, taking on the undulating form of a man. Ants spill from the chest wound, animating the body in jerking movements. A knee bends, the head comes up, then drops back down, mouth open. This is the source of our mystery ant? I drive my sword into its heart and more insects rush up, bubbling out like water.

"You should have stayed down, Sea Prince. My quarrel isn't with you." The ant phantom's mouth is covered in insects, the lips moving in sync with the words.

"Seems like we are quarreling now," I reply, scanning for the savant that raises this thing. I don't recall being addressed as Sea Prince for quite some time. Is it Tann? He raises a reptilian *ouster*, and this is not it. Who else could it be?

A smile of ants lifts the creature's face, spreading cheek to cheek. "If it's a fight you want, I will oblige." The ant phantom is on its feet and charging.

I tuck and roll, coming upright farther down the sloping deck, sliding a few feet before finding purchase. The phantom is right behind me. I turn, swinging high, connecting with the creature's neck. My sword cracks into carapaces and soft tissue, coming clean out the other side. The head flies off and arcs out to sea, trailing a stream of ants behind it.

I track the path, frowning when it splashes down. The remaining, headless phantom doesn't fall but drops hands to the deck and brings both feet up. Before I can block, they strike me double barrel in the chest. I sail backward into the wheelhouse, splintering the wood to bits. The ship groans and tilts more, the deck turning into a vertical wall. Water runs down the hatches, making it sink faster. "Ant savant?" I shout over the rushing sea. "Are you watching me turn your phantom into fish bait?"

The decapitated mass charges, grabbing a sword rolling down the deck. Out of its neck stump pours more insects, spinning like a tornado, forming a new head, with unmatched eyes and an oversized mouth.

I tear a plank from the smashed wheelhouse and block the blows, but each one pushes me down the tilted deck until I reach the submerged railing. By the time I run out of room, waist deep in the wash, the ant phantom's head has completely grown back. It chops at me like a lumberjack with an ax. "You're the fish food, Mar Prince."

"Whoever it is," Salila sings in my head, *"they know exactly who you are."*

"I noticed."

I let go of the plank and cartwheel over the phantom, grasping the hilt of its blade as it readies for another blow. Midair, I do a half-twist and, reversing the sword, point it straight down. I drive the blade through the top of the phantom's newly formed head, sinking it to the hilt. The curved tip punches out between two ribs. From both wounds, green ants spill into the swell rushing past my legs.

The phantom falls to its knees and yanks the weapon out with a single pull. The head tilts back, mouth wide to roar out a thousand more insects. They shoot straight at me. The dark cloud throws me back and before I gain my feet, the ant phantom is on top of me, screeching, fingers tightening around my neck.

I drop my chin to my chest, tuck my knees and kick. My feet strike the phantom's gut and its body flies back, but the arms stretch, the layers of insects thinning out to strings while the iron grip on my throat remains unbreakable. I try it again, kicking to the left and then the right, but the phantom stretches farther each time and then snaps back. On the fourth try, I get a stranglehold on its neck and instead of kicking, I slam my feet down hard on the submerged deck, shoot into the air, and dive over the side of the floundering ship. I sail toward the sea, splashing down, insect phantom still in my grip.

"Kaylin, what progress?" Teern's in my head the moment the water closes over me.

"Preoccupied, Father." Apparently cold water makes the ant phantom constrict, fingers tightening. It limits my neck movement considerably.

"Have you stopped Tann? Gathered the whistle bones? Protected the Ma'ata?"

"Do you not understand the word 'preoccupied'?" But at the mention of the Ma'ata, I strain around the bulk of the phantom. *Damn the abyssal plain.* Corpses, too many of them, drift through the turquoise expanse, dark blood trailing as it leaches from their wounds. And the Mar tombs? They are much closer than they were when this fight began.

"Kaylin?"

"The plan is underway, Father." But the ant phantom shows no sign of going to ground and I can't just ask it to wait while I remove the bleeding bodies.

I roll head over heels, exchanging punches, knocking off bits of its body until it is half the original size. Underwater, the ants can't seem to regenerate so quickly, and the sparkling green of their bodies are attracting fish, not to mention the sharks that come for the blood. Streaks of silver and gray flash in and out, and open mouths tear into dead flesh making for more blood, attracting more sharks.

"What are you playing at?" Teern asks, clearly still listening to my thoughts.

I pull the next punch and take one on the chin. *"I'm having a bit of trouble with a phantom. Parts of it, anyway. It was aboard Tann's vessel and—"*

"Dispatch it," Teern's voice barks in my head. *"Send it to ground and see to the Ma'ata."*

Exactly what I've been trying to do!

I drag the undulating phantom through the water back to Tann's ship. I'll need a clear view of the coastline to launch the mangled thing through the air and send it to ground, far from Tyche and Salila. As I climb aboard, stranglehold still on the writhing thing, I raise my free hand to ward off a blow. Standing over me, sword high, is a red-robe warlord and there is no doubt. I've come face-to-face with Tann.

The Sierrak leather armor and color of his robe give him away, along with the salt and pepper braids and close-trimmed beard. He narrows black eyes at me. I'm sure he's not expecting a Mar on board, especially with a squirming phantom in tow. The damned-to-the-deep thing is *altering* again, taking the shape of the warrior staring me down. Great. Soon there'll be two of them.

"There you are, Lord Tann." I slip and then gain my footing on the half sunken deck. "Finally, we meet."

But while I'm ready to engage in fine banter, he brings his sword crashing down. The blade sings through the air, straight for my neck.

On instinct, I pull the ant phantom's sword, now honed into a solid, keen weapon as the *alter* replicates the High Savant. In a single move, I block Tann's attack, the clash of metal reverberating through the air. Then I reverse my new blade and drive it into the High Savant's chest. It slices easily through his leather armor, the fine red robes, and into the bony sternum beneath. On reflection, this may not have been the wisest choice.

The sword hits his breastbone, yes, but on contact, it dissolves, turning back into hundreds of swarming insects. Tann's chest blooms red as he falls to his knees and bows his head to the rising water but only ants expel from his mouth as he coughs, not blood. The wound gaps wider for a moment and then seals shut, the insects trapped inside him. I hold tight to the rest of the phantom, run up along the deck, and hurl it in a high arc to the northern end of the shore. The phantom disappears the moment it hits dry sand, finally gone to ground.

"Now, about those whistle bones," I say, turning back to the savant.

But Tann is gone. His guards have hustled him overboard and are rowing away from the ship.

No time to deal with him now. Not with all these bodies drifting toward the Ma'ata. Salila's busy, but the Ma'ata keeper can't be far away. *Taruna? I could use a little help.*

There is a gnashing answer, but it doesn't sound like words.

I dive, streaming over the drop-off and look down at the nightmare—feeding sharks, shredded bodies, inky red water. It's worse than I thought, the tombs of Ma'ata corals barely visible beneath it all. On the surface, Tann's sloop slowly sinks under the waves and drifts straight for me. *"Taruna?"* I call again. Surely she won't blame me for this mess.

"Kaylin, son of dead guts and bones. Why are bleeding bodies and an Aturnian warship falling on my Ma'ata?"

"I'm taking care of it!"

"If one polyp is touched, one tendril damaged. If a single drop of blood falls upon the Dreadeds' tomb, I'll skin you alive."

She means it, too.

I streak like lightning to make sure none of it comes to pass.

39

MARCUS

"*Wake him up, for Er's sake!*" It's Salila, unmistakably her. Her less than soft voice blasts into my mind, sending my hair on end. "*Tell him, this is no time for a nap.*"

I snap awake. "*I hear you just fine, woman. No need to shout.*" I'm in a torment of pain, body aching, head pounding. And Salila's speaking to me?

No, she's speaking to me.

This happened when De'ral was with her under the waves, at the Suni River mouth, but why is it happening again? "*I'm certain she's speaking to me now.*"

She's not.

"*Will you two stop arguing and tell me what's going on up there?*" Salila cuts in.

I try to wipe sweat from my eyes, only to discover my hands are stretched out high overhead, my shoulders screaming for freedom, toes only barely able to touch the ground. "*There's been a misunderstanding.*" I force my head left and right, spotting the others. "*Seems we're all tied up.*" I exhale. "*Except for Ash.*"

De'ral passes my thoughts along, none too eloquently.

"*Ash?*" Salila says. "*Don't lose that one or you'll really make him mad.*" She laughs, and it sounds like chimes. "*Need my help?*"

"*No! Say no, De'ral.*" I can't have her rescuing me, us, at every turn. Besides, swords won't help here. Only diplomacy and Salila has none of that. "*But ask her to help Kaylin keep an eye on the ship. I'll see what they want.*"

She says they want your guts on the ground, obviously. But not to worry about Kaylin. He can handle a little kerfuffle.

"*Kerfuffle? What about?*"

They both talk at once and I can't understand either of them. Something about dreaded, the color red. "*Are you talking in rhymes?*"

"*We're not.*"

Salila makes no sense. Or maybe I just can't decipher her through De'ral. "*Are the bones safe? Tyche has them and—*"

"*Tell the ex-heir that I am in charge of the little caller. All perfectly snug as barnacles at low tide."*

I don't like the sound of that.

"And while you're at it, give Marcus my condolences." Her voice softens. *"I know how vexing fathers are, but still, peace be his path."*

I squeeze my eyes shut. *"What?"* But there's no time to think of it.

"Marcus Adicio, the once Heir of Baiseen, lives?" A female voice sounds genuinely surprised.

It's impossible to see who is talking. I can't turn around, but my guess is that Zakia, the High Savant of Kutoon, has arrived. I clear my throat. "I am alive, and known now as the Bone Gatherer, traveling to the Sanctuaries of Amassia to collect the first whistle bones, in preparation of the next Great Dying. My recorder—"

"Ash? She explained everything. Can see why you hired her, though a non-savant. That's a surprise."

I exhale. Ash explained. It will be fine.

"One question for you, and then, however you answer, the discomfort will be over."

Or maybe not so fine.

A red-robe walks around the stock to stand before me. "Zakia?" She looks different than when I saw her last, more commanding, but that was several years ago, and she was still an orange-robe then.

"Well met, Bone Gatherer." She's a tall woman, near my height, with a high brow, dark skin, and short black hair trimmed close to the scalp. Her phantom is up, pacing next to her, a *warrior* with a bat face, large eyes, and powerful limbs. The sight of it makes me bristle. It's much like the phantom Destan raised, the savant I fought to the death on the Isle of Aku. "Forgive me if I don't bow. I seem to be unable to move."

De'ral rumbles in the depths. *We will—*

"Don't distract me." I take a breath. "High Savant." I try not to cry out as my shoulders nearly dislocate. "You have a question?"

"Did you kill any of my troops sent your way on a diplomatic mission?"

The right answer is obvious here, and in essence true. "No, I did not."

"The rumors say otherwise."

Suddenly I picture Kaylin, leading scouts to the west in the dead of night. His white shirt was splattered in blood when he returned, was it not?

Gollnar blood. De'ral sounds proud of the fact.

"How do you know for sure?"

I smelled it.

"I'm fairly sure all blood smells the same." I clear my throat. "You believe rumors? Because they also say I fell from the path months ago, on my way to Aku."

"True. Your presence, and yellow robes, prove otherwise. Congratulations, by the way. Well deserved."

I'm not going to fill her in with all the details but we're on the right track. "If, and I say this with all sincerity, any Gollnar diplomats were harmed in Baiseen, it was not by my intention or command." True enough.

"Does that include Atikis?"

Sweat drips into my eyes. "We did see Lord Atikis alive and well not nine days past. He, um, followed us to the mouth of the Suni River and certainly didn't look any worse for the journey."

She turns to a black-robe with thick gray hair and tan skin. "Stoe?"

The Bone Thrower walks forward, lays down a hide, and shakes his bone bag. His phantom is pale green with yellow flares of light so glaring I look away. I hope this isn't going to take long. My every joint's about to pop.

The bones fall and no one speaks. He's so long in contemplation, I wonder if I'll pass out while waiting to hear the verdict.

"Adicio speaks the truth. None of these savants had a hand in our diplomats' fate," Stoe finally says. "He journeys as the Bone Gatherer of Baiseen, all correct and honorable."

Zakia bows to the black-robe who collects the bones and rolls up the hide.

"Cut them down." Zakia waves a graceful arm toward us.

I think it might be the last thing I'll hear along this path, but on command, we are released, not disemboweled as Salila predicted. My shoulders scream with new pain as the stock that held me upright transforms back into a stately archway at the edge of the training field. "Clever *alters*," I say and fall to the ground face first.

De'ral starts to rise but Zakia is quickly behind me, knife drawn. "None of that, please. I've heard tell of the mammoth *warrior* you raise. I don't care to meet him so close to the meditation gardens."

De'ral's in a rage but I keep control. She releases the knife when I nod and the ground settles. "Your healer may see to you," Zakia says. "Then we'll talk."

Ash is at my side, helping me stand. Piper is allowed to raise her phantom and after the twin-headed snake sinks fangs into her, it goes to the rest of us, me, Samsen, and Belair in turn, injecting the medicinal venom. We're revitalized in moments, maybe too much so. My eyes are wide, and my heart rate pounds in my neck.

"Well done, Marcus," Ash whispers. "You didn't get us all killed."

"Not yet." I give her a dry smile and whisper, "De'ral's fit to punch the entire Sanctuary into the sea, you realize."

"Hopefully, he won't do that before we get the whistle bone."

De'ral roils under my skin and then stills. *Salila wants us to hurry it along. She says minding the child's as tedious as watching kelp curl in the sun.*

"Does she now?" What does this Mar think she's doing ordering me around?

Zakia leads us through a courtyard lined with edible plants. I like the idea, hanging baskets full of tomatoes and herbs. We cross another lawn to an open forum overlooking the sea. She walks to the edge of the lookout before turning to face us, her red-robes twirling when she stops.

"Do you remember this? You can see the city of Kutoon from the heights, and of course, all of Manta Bay." She gestures toward the cliffs and the white rail that marks the plunging drop-off to the sea. I admit, it's a decent view. There are two more distance viewers set up and I long to look through one. Maybe I'll ask later if things go well.

I gaze at the expanse of water, and the coastal city below. From this height, the ships in their far northern harbor and the urban setting are toys on a child's rug. Diminutive and peaceful. The sun rides high at midday, turning the sea turquoise over the white sand, and sapphire over reefs. Much closer to us, in the south end of the bay, the *Dugong* bobs, tethered by its anchor. No problems there, that I can see.

I frown and look again.

The water appears inky over the reef, and is that a rowboat on the horizon, heading north? I can't be sure. "The distance viewers…"

"Come, Marcus." The High Savant motions to the semi-circular benches that fan out from the rail. "Sit. Let us discuss your quest." She tilts her head at the second sun. "Who would have thought we would have to?"

I turn away from the sea. "May we speak freely?" I ask, eyeing the orange and yellow-robes joining us from the field. A green-robe sits on my other side, pen and parchment to hand. Ash joins me on my left, ready with hers.

Zakia hands our documents back to Ash. "Please do."

I clear my throat. "As you know, Tann attacked Aku, killed High Savant Yuki, and took their first whistle bone. He tried unsuccessfully to do the same in Baiseen." I rub the back of my neck. "Atikis appears to be doing the same."

"You're in a race, Bone Gatherer," she says, and the rest of the gathering murmur. "Does that surprise you?"

I shake my head. "We don't believe Tann is in possession of the original

Arrow of Nii, seeing as your Sanctuary still stands."

She looks to her phantom, and it nimbly slips away. "True, Marcus. He is not."

"Then, as the Bone Gatherer appointed by Master Brogal, red-robe of Baiseen, I ask that you give me custody of it to protect the people from harm."

Her face flinches. "But which people, Marcus, are you promising to protect?"

"All of our allies," I say with no hesitation.

I wait for her to comment, but she sits quietly, so I continue. "It's not been made clear to me, High Savant,"—I struggle for the right words—"On where you stand, beside me, or Tann, or Atikis, or another unknown."

"Then I will remedy the confusion." Her gaze makes my skin prickle. "Kutoon is no friend of Tann's. Twin Sun ships have pilfered Gollnar's towns up and down the coast, splitting our loyalties. We owe nothing to him and will not be aligning that way."

I'm sure the relief shows on my face.

"Have you many bones in your possession now, Marcus Adicio?"

"Two, within short reach and under guard."

She smiles. "It's good to see you take some precautions." Zakia claps her hands. "Where are my manners? Fruit and water for our guests."

Several blue-robes hustle off. Is she using the diversion to make a choice?

"Ah, thank you," Zakia says when the blue-robes return. "Please, refresh yourselves."

The water is sweetened with mint and honey, and most welcome after the climb. And the torture. I have a fleeting fear that we are being poisoned but Zakia drinks from the same pitcher and eats the dried figs and fresh apples. I hold my glass up to her in salute, and she does the same to me.

"Now to business." She puts her glass down. "I have the Arrow of Nii." As she says the name, her phantom appears with a small wooden box. "Gollnar doesn't want to see Tann rule the realms. Atikis, in my eyes, would be no better. He's never cared much for the people." She glances at Ash, and I know she means non-savants.

Again I feel relief.

"But, if we champion you, and fight for you, Bone Gatherer, what can we expect in return?"

I take a moment before speaking. She'd just bound us cruelly, but wouldn't I have done the same, if I'd suspected them of murdering Baiseen delegates? Wouldn't Yuki? I feel pride for earning the respect of Kutoon, but also impotence as I have no real power to negotiate terms. I can't even communicate with Master Brogal, save indirectly through Ash, and the bones-only-know what agreements my brother will uphold. But I must offer something honest to win her support.

"We could begin with an open trade between Palrio and Kutoon," Ash whispers while I am still thinking.

I repeat the proposition to Zakia and add, "Perhaps our wool, citrus, and spices for iron and bloodstock, as a start?" If we discovered anything on the race back to Baiseen last month, it's that Gollnar horses are superb.

"Agreed." Zakia raises her brows. "I'm wondering about something less conventional as well. Would Master Brogal consider an exchange of savants, at the green or yellow-robe level? We have the rare *caller* and *healer* with no higher-level savants to guide them other than text. I understand this is true for you, too, with *alters* and *warriors*?"

"I raise a *warrior*," Belair and I say at the same time.

"And I, an *alter-caller*," Samsen says. "My teacher was at a loss to help me with the shapes and transformations. As your green-robe callers do, I had to learn from text with no actual examples, until my initiation journey to Aku."

"The exchange is an excellent idea," I say, then turn to Piper.

"I would tutor your healer savants gladly, with Master Brogal's permission," she says.

"And I, your callers," Samsen adds.

"Good," Zakia says and smiles. "This could be mutually beneficial."

"Agreed." It feels like true progress! "With Tann's attack on Aku, there'll be no initiation journeys there for some time. We need to adapt."

The recorders dip their pens into inkwells and the negotiations begin. When they are through, we both sign an initial agreement. Zakia gives Ash a copy with her seal and presents me with the Arrow of Nii.

"A piece of Er's femur, etched with a fletched arrow above the whistle holes," Ash says. "It's beautiful." She looks to me for agreement and I nod.

"And to begin our sharing of resources, may I ask that my recorder have the privilege of studying in your library? There are mysteries surrounding the Great Dying that we are anxious to uncover."

"She may stay as long as she needs." Zakia turns to Ash. "Though our resources are small. The archives are in the north, in Goll."

"Thank you, High Savant." Ash gives her a bow.

"I am honored by the exchange," Zakia says to all of us, "and will lead a company of mounted savants to the gates of Baiseen when called. United, Tann will not conquer our sanctuaries. Nor Atikis."

"Hear-hear!"

We kiss cheeks as is the custom of Kutoon. I feel a little taller leaving the Sanctuary than when I entered.

You were stretched in the stock.

I don't argue with De'ral and my lips twitch. It's a rare moment of good-hearted humor. Then I ask for his help in turning my next thought to Salila. *"Can she have Tyche call the Arrow of Nii?"* I hold the box up in my hand only to have the lid lift. The whistle bone rises, hovering for a moment before it vanishes with the wind.

She's got it, De'ral says.

"Thank you. Tell her well done."

The savants of Kutoon stare at us and I realize what they witnessed seemed a feat given none of our phantoms are raised. My chest expands knowing I have impressed the living starlight out of Zakia. But the win is short-lived.

Salila says for everyone to come back. There's been a development.

"Development?" I wave Ash to me. "We have to get back to the ship," I whisper as we say our formal goodbyes to Zakia. "Ash will return when she is able." I leave it at that, leading the party down the hundreds of steps back to the beach. I don't know what's wrong. Nothing seems amiss from here. But the others are as concerned as I am. Concerned and baffled. The explanation I give for why my phantom can bespeak a Mar doesn't make sense. Why would it? I hardly understand it myself. Maybe Salila will enlighten us.

But when we reach Tyche on the beach, waiting with the bag of bones, Salila is gone.

"I don't see what the trouble is," Samsen says to me with a clap on the back. "The ship is safe and we've three bones gathered. Already halfway there."

The others give a quick cheer, but soon gaze into the distance, searching for the *Dugong*. It sits motionless in the bay and no rowboat waits for us at the dock.

There are only seconds left to avoid the unthinkable. *If the Dreaded rise…* I streak toward Tann's sinking ship first, grab the anchor line, and drag it away from the Ma'ata corals. When it is far enough down current, I toss the anchor into the middle of the Drop, a six-thousand-fathom deep trench below. It will never be seen by lander eyes again, unless the Great Dying moves things around dramatically and by then, it will hardly matter. All the landers will be gone. My fists clench at the thought, but I can't dwell on it now.

When I return, Taruna, the Ma'ata Keeper in charge of tending the Mar who lie like stone statues in their tombs, is spinning a new current to keep the blood away. The life-giving blood. One drop won't raise the Dreaded, but it might awaken them, which would be bad enough. No one wants them even so much as drowsy.

They would haunt me, especially me, and every Mar within range, begging for more blood so they might rise. It's the one thing that must not happen. By Teern's orders, yes, but I agree. The Dreaded shall remain entombed. Forever, I hope.

I join Taruna in fanning the current, sending the blood away, and then drag the bleeding corpses to the Drop where they can do no harm. *Peace be their paths,* as Ash would say. I really don't want her to see me now, in this act of…well, survival for me and my kind, but I don't think that would be her first thought.

As the water clears, fresh current replaces the murk. Taruna chants, brushing silt and sand from each tomb with delicate, loving hands. I haul the last body away and survey the Ma'ata. It looks clean. Safe. A warm and blessed feeling flows through me as I check each tomb, their occupants sleeping, including the maniacal, raging, blood-hungry clan known as the Dreaded. Teern put them down for good reason and this is no time in the world to see their rise. I don't think any time would be. *"What's this!"* I choke on my thought. At the end of the row of tombs, I find the very last one empty.

"Taruna!" I shout, a lightning shock burning under my skin.

"Now you've done it, Kaylin." The Ma'ata keeper glares at me from a

distance. Beyond her, a newly risen Mar gnaws on a sailor's corpse. She must have dragged it up from the Drop. Is that another pinned under one foot?

"No! No! No!" This can't be happening. I need Teern, and fast. He's the only one who can contain this.

But Teern isn't here, and I must do something. I chase after the Mar as she streams away, dragging what's left of the corpses behind her. *"Stop!"* I throw every ounce of authority into the command.

At the sound of my voice, she slows, and then turns. *"Kaylin?"* She drops the bodies and fishtails toward me.

I shrink back. *"Rosie?"* Why her, gods of the deep? Of all who could have awakened, why her?

"Did you miss me?" She doesn't pause for an answer. *"Of course you did. How long has it been this time?"*

I shift to the side, putting a tomb between us. Her time in the Ma'ata hasn't changed her one bit, at least, not her appearance. Her hair is still black as midnight with streaks of cobalt blue. It ripples down her back in twists that lift and float in the current around her. Her eyes are a few shades lighter, a smoky brown—like flint as she studies me. Her skin is brown, too, a flawless sepia shade. She sways in the water in front of me, her long limbs graceful, her body voluptuous as ever and her face, when she finishes scanning me up and down and licking her lips, blooms into a smile that would melt mountains into puddles of mud. *"No, Rosie Red, I did not miss you."*

She's too much, this Mar. Too beautiful. Too powerful. Too deadly.

She swims over the tomb and circles me like a snake around a pole, her hair flowing over my hands which are pressed outward to ward her off.

"But you woke me."

"An accident, I promise."

Her smile fades. *"Haven't I served out my time? All's forgiven?"* She looks over her shoulder, which makes me do the same.

I remember what she did to be put to ground two hundred years ago. Well, not so much any one thing but the culmination of many, many things, piling up on top of each other, crime upon crime. *"I can't speak to that. You'll have to talk to—"*

"Teern?" The smile returns. *"Is he here?"* Her voice slows to a sultry whisper.

"Soon."

"Well then, nice seeing you." She winks and, in a flurry, vanishes over the Drop.

"Wait!" Bones be crushed. *"You can't just take off."* I shout at the wake

Rosie Red leaves behind. *"Teern!"* I call into the depths of the sea. *"Help!"*

Taruna stares at Rosie's empty tomb. *"Wouldn't want to be you when he finds out."*

"Can you—"

"Go get her yourself, Kaylin. She's your charge now."

Visions of Teern's wrath, Marcus's plight, and most of all my promise to Teern, the one where I said I would not take my eyes off of Ash, all collide. I turn to the only one who can help me now, at least until Teern gets wind of this, though she may not so much help me as murder me.

"Salila, is Marcus back?"

"They're on the Dugong, *but I think you have some explaining to do."*

"And I will, but I need you. Please!"

"Again so soon? What's happened to your self-reliance?"

"I need you to track Rosie Red."

Salila bursts into laughter. *"You're joking."*

"It's no joke."

Slowly the laughter wanes. *"You woke her?"*

"Not by intention. I—"

"You. Woke. Rosie. Red?" she shouts in my mind.

"I didn't mean to." I seem to be saying that a lot.

"Of all the Dreaded, her?*"*

"Please. I'll give you anything…"

"The only thing you can give me is her head on a stake."

"You know I can't do that." I'm about to explain when a sonic boom rolls me end over end. I hit Salila as she approaches, and we both are thrown backward to hit full force against the side of a tomb.

Teern's voice rings in my head, rattling loose the tiny bones in my ears. *"I give you one simple task!"* The Sea King clamps a massive hand around my throat, his favorite greeting of late. In the other hand, fortunately, he has Rosie, gripped tight in the same hold. *"You raised this Dreaded?"*

Again, Teern's booming voice throws me back but there's nowhere to go with his fingers in a vise around my neck. My arms and legs flail in the current and I am fairly certain the next words coming out of his mouth will crack my skull open.

"Father, it was a mistake."

"Gods be damned right, it was." Instead of booming into my mind, he lowers his voice to a whisper. It turns my blood to ice.

I try to explain, pointing out the results weren't *that* bad. *"It's not like I raised them all."*

The error of those words becomes immediately clear as his fingers tighten, his majestic face purpling with rage.

"Looks like you really upset him this time," Rosie snickers.

Another unfortunate response.

Teern instantly drops me, turning all his attention on the newly risen Mar.

To her credit, Rosie Red does not cower, but the bravado in her eyes fades as his shadow darkens her body.

"I have no time for one of your insatiable appetites—"

"Please, Father." Her eyes go round and large as she looks up at him. *"I have learned my lesson."*

He clears his throat, a tick rising over his left eye.

"Lessons," she quickly corrects herself. *"I can be useful to you. I will be!"*

He considers it for some time. *"I may need you, in the end, but you will not be free to do as you please, Rosie Red. There will be no rivers of blood, mysterious sightings of scavenging Mar on open battlefields or sunken boats stripped of their treasures and crew, leaving only broken planks of wood and skeletons behind."*

"Battlefields? Treasures?" Her face looks hopeful.

He raises his brows at me. *"Does she know?"*

"We didn't get that far yet."

Slowly, he tilts her head at the surface where the yellow sun shines. And then he angles his view a handspan to the west. She stiffens as the red glare of the second sun winks through the clouds, filtering down to us through the rippling waters.

"Oh my!" Rosie all but squeals. *"I can be of help. Father, if I can just say—"*

"Silence!" Teern releases her at his feet and calls Salila back as she starts to slip away. *"Daughter, you will mind this Dreaded one."*

"Me?" Salila says.

"Her?" Rosie says at the same time.

Relief washes through me. That was one job I would do anything to avoid.

"And hear my decree, all three of you." Thunder roars through the water again, sending the hairs on my arms straight out.

We face Teern, listening.

"You"—he points at Salila—*"keep your eye on the Bone Gatherer. Shadow the ship. And Rosie Red, you will stay in her sights at all times, and out of everyone else's."*

"But—"

"No more lander blood for you."

"I could—"

"No walking under the sunlight. Understood?"

She glances over at the other tombs. *"What of Togen, Jenifern, Raymar, and Krew? I can't just leave them behind."*

His eyes say it all. That she can and she will.

"Yes, Father." Rosie lifts her chin. At least she has the good sense not to sulk in Teern's presence, but behind her mild expression, I sense the pain and the rage. Surely Teern does, too.

But Father isn't watching her anymore. His eyes are heavy on me. *"I thought we had an agreement, Kaylin."*

"As we still do."

"Really? You were to stick to Ash, not let her out of your sight."

Rosie frowns. *"Who's Ash?"*

"Never mind," Salila, Teern, and I say to her at the same time.

"Fine. I'll just go see for myself." Rosie makes to bolt away.

Salila releases a blast of curses, catches her wrist and streams off in the opposite direction.

"What are you waiting for?" Teern asks me. *"Keep Ash in your sights and bring me those whistle bones!"*

But he speaks to empty space. I'm already halfway to the *Dugong* before the sentence is out, determined to get there before Salila does, and Dreaded Rosie Red.

41

ASH

Kaylin's not paying attention. He keeps looking over the railing, down into the sea as if Tann will erupt any moment and devour us in a single bite. He's distracted, even as he explains, again, what happened while we were procuring Kutoon's whistle bone. I'm not sure why he's on edge, or so fixated on the water. Tann's gone. Escaped away in a rowboat, as he explained.

Kaylin shakes his head whenever any of us ask exactly how Tann was wounded. "He didn't die by the sword I plunged into him. But I don't think we'll see him for a spell."

Captain Anders claims Kaylin saved the *Dugong* and her crew, taking on the Aturnians and sinking the warship. *"How,"* I have to ask. *"With your bare hands?"*

But I don't hear Kaylin's answer.

"He had my help." Salila's honey milk voice wafts into my mind, making me jump a mile. Then I look up at Marcus's face. It is him she's talking to, or maybe De'ral. Definitely not me. Damn this medallion. I hear and see way more than I'm meant to.

"But is it the medallion?" my inner voice asks.

That thought makes me even more uncomfortable. *"I thought you were supposed to be minding Tyche and the bones,"* I cut in, so they know I'm listening. No telling what kind of thoughts the Mar might share with Marcus's phantom. I saw the attraction when we escaped Aku and there are things of an intimate nature I do not want to hear. And can't unhear if I do!

"I was minding the child." Salila laughs, the sound of a hundred tiny bells chiming. *"I can do more than one thing at a time, starfish."*

"I'm sure you can."

Captain Anders approaches. He brings a distance viewer and a dour expression. Our merriment fades as it is passed around. We sailed seven days straight to reach Kutoon from Nonnova, keeping close to the coast as we rode the northwest current. There were signs of storm damage, eroded dunes, and fires burning far inland. But now, as we sail to Tangeen, we take our last look at the shoreline before entering the southern current. The land looks worse than before. So much worse.

As I focus the glass, my heart pinches. "Why have the white sand beaches turned black? Ash from the fires?" But I know it's not that. Through the round and bobbing lens, I see the truth before they speak it. Shearwaters. Thousands of them, wings splayed, stabbing into the sand, beaks turned upward from bent necks. All dead or dying. Tears well as I hand the viewer over to Piper. "What's happened to them?"

No one can answer until Anders says, "Blame the uncanny weather for this. The sea air heats, the forests burn. Far north the glaciers melt. Affects their migrations. They left too soon."

"We've noticed changes," Marcus says. "But the shearwaters?"

"Been falling from the sky like rain, exhausted from the shifting headwinds. What you see is only what's washed up on shore."

All eyes turn skyward to the second sun. So much loss and death. "We have to stop it!" I say to them all.

"We will, Ash." Marcus puts an arm over my shoulder. "We will."

42

RHIANNON

Petén wakes with a headache for the fifth day in a row. It's tedious, considering this is our honeymoon. But really, the decline must be gradual. Slower, even, than his father's.

"Tea!" he orders his valet as he rubs his temples.

"No need to shout, love," I say softly.

"Who's shouting?"

"But my, you've awakened with a temper again. Headache no better?"

"Where's Darren?" he says and tries to sit up.

"Laying out your clothes, of course. Stop panicking."

"I'm hardly panicking."

I lean over him and kiss the air near his cheek. "Drink this, husband." I offer a steaming mug.

"It's not helping." But he takes the cup anyway. When he leans forward to kiss me back, I'm up, flouncing pillows and opening the curtains.

He blinks at the sun. "What bell is it?"

"Are we feeling better for the rest?" I skip past his questions.

"No, *we* are not. But damn the bones if I'll let that stop me from attending the council meeting." He shouts again for Darren.

"Oh, dear. Did you mean to attend?" I keep my voice light and sweet. "I would have awakened you earlier, of course, if I'd known, but you were ill in the night, and I just assumed…"

"I missed another meeting?"

All the yelling can't be making the headache any better, but I don't point it out. He's like a wounded bear today. "You can attend tomorrow's. Master Brogal has a special request but wanted to direct it to you, specifically."

Petén glugs down the brew. "I'll definitely attend tomorrow. Wake me, regardless of my state." He struggles out of bed and stands, but it takes effort.

Darren appears, quiet and innocuous, as usual. He holds out Petén's trousers and takes his robe.

"I assume you were there?" Petén asks me. It's an accusation, as if I am to blame for his ill health. Well…fair enough.

"Was I at the council meeting?"

"Yes, damn the bones, the council meeting!"

I cross my arms and raise one brow.

He rubs his temples harder. "Sorry, love. Sorry. None of this is your fault."

"We've been married less than a week. I do hope this isn't going to be how you plan on speaking to me for the rest of our lives."

"It's not. Of course it's not." He coughs and draws a deep breath. "But we were to decide on the defense tactics, specifically this year's budget for the shipyards. I wanted to push to keep taxes down and increase the watchtower rosters. We could have had warning of the Aturnian assault if…"

"Oh, my husband. Warning or not wouldn't have changed the outcome. Aturnia put a hundred ships on our shore. A few more minutes in advance knowledge is not the solution."

He winces at every word. I imagine my voice, which I've raised just a notch, is like knives at the base of his skull about now. "You're forgetting the savants, Rhiannon. If our *callers* had been ready…"

"Half measures at best. Remember what Jacas, peace be his path, wanted?" I smooth my voice into velvet cloth.

"Yes, but—"

"He wanted a navy," I keep going. "A real defense against attack by sea."

"I remember, of course. But how can we build a fleet without straining the resources of our people? They're already overburdened as it is."

"Our people are resourceful. They can give more, for their ultimate good."

He hunches, his head swiveling slowly toward me. "What did you do?"

"I approved the vote to increase the taxes and triple the workforce on the shipyards, starting immediately. It's what Jacas would have wanted."

"You what?" He tries to shout me down but coughs instead. Petén's weaker than I thought. He reels and sits hard on the bed.

I take the cup from his hand and push him back against the pillows. Darren steps up but I dismiss him with a wave. "This is why I've been standing in for you." I smooth his dark hair back from his forehead. *Such a handsome face,* I remind myself. "You'll be better tomorrow. We'll talk about it when it makes more sense."

Petén stares at the ceiling, his eyes watery and bloodshot. He tries to fight the tonic, but his lids grow heavy and close. I don't know what tendrils of dreams flood his mind, but I know by the jerks and grimaces they aren't pleasant. Part of me wishes it wasn't so, but…there's no going back now.

As he fades into a restless sleep, I open drawers and close them as quietly as I can. Where is it, damn the bones?

The one document I need in my possession and it's nowhere to be found? Looks like I'll have to enlist a Bone Thrower to find where he put the wretched thing. Married a week and already counting the days until the end…

"Black Dart's in sight," the first mate calls.

"Good," Marcus says though his voice is grim. "The sooner we reach Pandom City, the better."

The last four days have not been cheery with the memory of the coastline. Forests burning. Birds plummeting to their deaths. Our late-night discussions of the quest to gather the bones was grim. We have more speculation than facts, and Brogal was no help at all. I've contacted him twice now, once to report the addition of the Kutoon whistle bone, and then again to report the evidence that Anders has gathered on changing water temperatures, weather patterns, and currents. He barely commented on either, though I could see him as he spoke—rubbing his temples, sipping tea, and Larseen there in his pressed orange robes, sitting opposite, listening in.

As I think it, the ship rocks hard and I grab the rail with both hands, as does Marcus.

"Black Dart is rankled today. Best tell the others and stay below." The first mate nods to us and hurries away.

I climb down the ladder into the hold, knowing what the first mate means by rankled. The swell could reach toward the crow's nest, but I won't deliver that bit of bad news unless I have to. Piper looks green enough, though her wristbands are in place.

"Could be in for a rough ride, crossing Black Dart." They deserve some warning.

Tyche looks up from the table where she's holding a steaming mug of tea. "What's Black Dart?"

"It's, um…" Marcus says.

"A meeting place of waters in the Nulsea Gap," Belair rescues him. "A cross-section creating counter currents, whirlpools, and unpredictable tides."

"It's dangerous?" Tyche asks.

"It can be," Samsen says.

"Not at all," I say at the same time, not wanting to alarm her.

Piper elbows Samsen in the ribs. "Not dangerous for the *Dugong* with Captain Anders at the helm." She pats the girl's shoulder. "Just tuck your book into your hammock and stow your things. All will be well."

"Ash, you were in Pandom City a few months ago. Was the crossing this bad?" Marcus asks. "I remember when I was a blue-robe but…"

I laugh. "But you don't recall?"

He winks at me. "Had other things on my mind."

By the bones, he did. Can't believe I forgot, but that trip, when he was a blue-robe, was at the behest of Master Brogal. I was invited along to practice my translation skills. It was before anyone had found out about *us*. My face heats as I recall exactly how we spent the crossing, sitting as close to each other as we could get, talking in code and sneaking kisses when no one could see. Oh, to be twelve again. So uncomplicated.

"You didn't think it so uncomplicated at the time," my inner voice says.

That's because I was an orphaned non-savant from the harbor district, infatuated with my best friend who happened to be the Heir to Baiseen's throne. It seems so long ago now.

"He was more than infatuated with you."

Maybe. As I said, we were young. The crossing, however, must have been smooth because I wasn't one bit nauseated.

"Ash?" Piper asks. "You're flushed." She feels my forehead with the back of her hand.

I step away, laughing a little. "I'm fine." If you didn't count the blushing. "Just remembering the stories about the channel. There are quite a few different explanations for the appearance and disappearance of the standing waves."

"I'd like to hear them," Tyche says, and the others nod encouragement.

"Some say that because the realms have all returned to one continent…"

"Weren't they always one?" Tyche's eyes are wide.

I shake my head, wondering who her natural history teacher was on Aku. "Not according to maps found on fossil tablets from millions of years ago. If we've read them correctly, Amassia began as one continent, then broke apart, fragmenting into nine separate lands."

"Amassia was broken up?"

"Like the ants." My inner voice sounds whimsical, clearly a part of me unperturbed by the rising swell.

Yes, a reasonable metaphor.

I focus back on Tyche. "Each was its own realm with a surrounding sea. The waters were named, we think, for the gods they owed allegiance to—the

Peaceful One, the Atlas, the Great Bear… I don't remember all off hand. Over time, more than one Great Dying in length, the continents drew back together again, to reach where they are today. One continent, Amassia, and no gods of the sea."

"But there is Teern."

I frown at the mention. *The Sea King?* I learned of him back on Aku, but could the Mar really be remnants of the old gods?

"How strange," Tyche says.

We all grip the edge of the table as the sloop jumps a wave and splashes down hard. I push my thumb into my wrist to quell the seasickness and I see Piper do the same. "Very strange, if it's true, but they say that when Tangeen met with Southern Aturnia, they crashed into each other. Nonnova was thrown back, her mountains pushed high. She ripped a trench thousands of fathoms deep between the Nulsea gap and her northernmost isles."

"And the Black Dart Channel was born," Samsen says.

I bend to pick up a saltshaker that's rolling back and forth with the rock of the ship and put it in its holder. "There are other explanations."

"So I have heard," Belair says. His lips twitch as if trying to keep a straight face.

I ignore his skepticism. "Another tale is that Black Dart was dug by the Mar when they tricked the goddess of the sea into giving them immortality."

Belair laughs outright but Marcus hushes him.

"No records have been found," I say.

"How would the Mar keep records?" Tyche asks.

I think on that. "Maybe in underwater caves? Etched into the rock?"

"We should ask Kaylin," Tyche says.

"You're right, we should." He knows more about the Mar than any of us. I look to Marcus. Or so I thought.

"Is it really a thousand fathoms deep?" Samsen asks.

"We have no means of measuring past four hundred fathoms," Belair says. "We don't have ships large enough to carry longer plumb lines. But whatever created Black Dart, it's stormy today, and we must weather it."

Tyche looks worried again, so I add, "After a bit of rough seas, we'll be across and on to Tangeen."

She pulls her stuffed impala out of her pocket and holds it tight in her lap. The youngest member of our company has talked more today than she has since fleeing Aku. Still, she's regressed, seeking refuge in childhood. I don't blame her. As long as she can keep calling the bones when we need, it's the safest place for her traumatized mind.

"We'll be fine," I offer reassurance. "I've crossed many times and am no worse for it."

Marcus flashes me a smile. "Nor am I."

The others all nod their heads, missing the meaning in Marcus's eyes. Thank the bones. "I'm sure it'll be smooth as velvet on the way back out."

"But we will do as advised and stay below," Marcus says, serious again. "And as we're all gathered, I want to share more thoughts on this open exchange of students with Kutoon."

Just as Marcus is about to launch his discussion, Kaylin sticks his head down the hatch. "Marcus, a word topside, please? There's something you need to see."

I open my mouth to protest, but Kaylin winks. *"I won't let our Bone Gatherer wash overboard, lass. I promise."*

"I'll just be a moment," Marcus says and heads up the hatch.

44

MARCUS

"Are we in the middle of a cyclone?" I shout to be heard. The wind screams across the deck as the ship lurches over the waves. The guardrail around the wheelhouse is flimsy support, but I cling to it anyway. So does Samsen. He came topside with me, but probably regrets it. He's soaked to the bone, his pale hair limp about his face. Same with me. At least, for once, Ash stayed below. Anyone as light as her would be blown off the deck in this gale.

"Not a cyclone." Kaylin rocks with the ship. Calm or storm, it's all the same to him.

"Then what?" My knuckles go white.

"Black Dart stirs the katabatic winds."

I have no idea what that means and my face shows it.

"The Tangeen mountains push cold air down to the sea. The fog's running with it, and that's not the only thing." He points to the coast. "Have a look over there." Kaylin's tone has my attention. It's not so much urgent as concerned, an attitude he doesn't often take. When he hands me the distance viewer, I plant my legs in a wide stance and take a look, trying to focus on where the sailor's pointing.

At first, I'm sure I'll be sick. The roll of the ship doesn't match the all-too-magnified horizon that's jolting around at bad angles. My stomach sloshes bile up the back of my throat. I swallow hard and lower the viewer. "What am I supposed to be seeing?"

Kaylin silently directs the viewer a few degrees to the right.

I try again. "Wash water, high seas." I glance around the scope. "How big is that swell?"

"Triple overhead. Keep looking."

"At what?" I grimace, trying to hide the sick feeling. "The wall of fog just beyond the—oh."

Out of the fog comes the prow of a sleek warship. "Gollnar," I say in a whisper and hand the viewer over to Samsen.

"And gaining fast," Samsen says. He hands the distance viewer back to Kaylin.

"Has Zakia betrayed her word?" Even as I ask, I don't think it's true.

"Not with that horse cross-tied on the main deck."

"Give it here." I take the scope out of his hands and study the vessel. It's already twice as large. "Atikis." My jaw tightens. I'd not seen the horse the first time but as I adjust the focus, there it is, neck arched, hooves prancing, black mane and tail blowing in the wind.

Atikis, De'ral repeats in a deep growl.

"I see that," I say aloud. Sure enough, standing with a hand resting on the high withers, is the red-robe. The one who attacked us on the Suni River headland. The one who reportedly has gone rogue.

"Can we outrun him?" Samsen asks.

In the background, Kaylin and the captain have a few quick words.

"Even with every sail she's got," Kaylin says, "Atikis will be on us in no time. We need a different plan." He sees it as a challenge, judging by the grin on his face. "We'll be in range of their catapults soon."

And that's good news? I wipe salt mist out of my eyes. "Suggestions?"

"First, I would get that bag of whistle bones off your belt and stowed away, out of earshot."

"Earshot?"

"The red-robe has *callers,* I wager. Find a sealed chest, or a pressure-cooking pot with a tight lid, in a pinch."

"Right. But *callers* can snatch them from the hold just as easily as on deck." I want to cross my arms but don't risk letting go of the railing.

"Hiding them below will make it harder, especially if they're encased in metal, or cast iron."

"I guess that's true."

"And if a phantom is up over the sea, it's likely the savant is near to exhaustion. I say get the bones as far from their reach as possible."

It shouldn't bother me that he knows so many savant secrets.

Then why does it?

"I'll give them to Ash and Tyche to guard. What else do we do?" I pass the viewer back to Samsen, ignoring my phantom's question.

"Prepare for battle," Anders yells. "All able hands!"

"Battle?" I grab the viewer and stare through it. "They're not mad enough to engage us in the midst of this high sea, are they?"

"There be a first time for everything." Anders turns his back and continues shouting orders.

"More likely, they'll try to *call* the bones and sink us with their catapults from a safe distance," Kaylin says, not a line of humor on his face.

I lurch toward the hatch to find Ash and help her stow the whistle bones. But it doesn't solve the problem, even if we win out this time. Atikis will keep hunting us, as long as he's alive.

Then we'll have to kill him.

On this, my phantom and I agree.

45

RHIANNON

"I apologize again for the magistrate's absence, Master U'karn, High Savant." I nod at both men in turn and then the rest of the council. "He is still unwell."

Brogal stands, lines of worry on his disapproving face. Poor Ash. No wonder she turned out so odd with him as her guardian.

But trouble's coming. I see it in the High Savant's narrowed eyes. "Yes? You have a question?"

"I do." Brogal clears his throat. "This is the third council meeting the Magistrate has missed in as many days. The last was crucial, with the sightings of the second sun visible to any who care to lift their noses, the controversy on increasing taxation to support new defenses, and now that we are to discuss the very sensitive issue of the Bone Gatherer, the Magistrate is again absent. Are there physicians in attendance? My healers have not been called."

I can tell that oversight stings the most. Good. Now, to drive in the point. "That's because your healers are not needed. The Magistrate is non-savant, as you well know, and not inclined to have a phantom attend him."

"But his health…"

"His health is in good hands." I study him, brow raised, until Nun pulls him back to his seat. "Now shall we all get down to business?" I push on. "I am preparing a statement on the appearance of the second sun. It won't alarm the masses, no mention of the fabled Great Dying."

Brogal winces at that.

"I won't fuel their fears, especially if it does turn out to be a comet and this is all a far-fetched hoax."

"Rhiannon, I assure you this is not—"

"Interim Magistrate," I correct.

For a moment, Brogal looks confused. "Pardon?"

"This is a formal setting, High Savant. You shall address me as Interim Magistrate."

I can almost see his phantom contorting under his skin. It's soon to push, but they best get used to it. I pass the document over to him. Finally found it under a stack of novels, no Bone Thrower required. Petén must have thought it wouldn't be needed.

Master Brogal's face tightens as he reads. "This is unprecedented!"

Chrysel snarls from under the table.

"Respect," I chide softly. My darling phantom has been patient through all the tedium, but we don't want to push it when we've come this far. *"He is still our High Savant, love. For now."* I tap the second signatures at the bottom of the document. "Unprecedented or not, it is signed and witnessed by two black-robes. The document stands."

His eyes are unreadable as the Bone Thrower sitting next to him concurs.

I take the document back. "As you see, Jacas made sure the throne would not come under contest if his sons could not act. Petén is ill and Marcus is away on his most important quest, I understand?"

Brogal nods curtly.

"So you will all address me as Interim Magistrate if you please, or just Magistrate. No need to make it cumbersome." I cock my head. "You were saying?"

Brogal clears his throat. "Magistrate"—it's like he's chewing bitter herbs— "the second sun is no hoax. The signs—"

"Be there signs or no, I'll not terrify the populace with unsubstantiated stories. As far as the increased taxes, the people are rallying. Of course they want their city repaired, and defensible." I brush my hands, discussion over. "Now, what's this about the Bone Gatherer?"

Brogal is still impossible to read as he motions to the orange-robe next to him.

Larseen stands, his face composed, long ropy hair secured high on his head. "There has been no word from Marcus Adicio and his company since leaving Nonnova."

"Were we expecting one?"

"The recorder should have reported by now." He looks to Brogal for confirmation.

"You think they are lost at sea?" It's all I can do to not smile. My plan is taking shape even better than I imagined. Marcus was the loose thread, the one that could unravel my plan to save the realm.

Larseen looks to Brogal again, who nods. "I think they might be delayed or perhaps there is a problem with…communications."

"Communications?" My brows rise. Of course, I know exactly what that means—Ash, the non-savant wordsmith with no social standing whatsoever, the one who has Marcus wrapped around her little finger. She's dangerous, like a knife in a toddler's grip. The fools don't even realize it…or do they?

"Is this about Ash?"

Brogal's eyes dart to the window as I speak her name. Something shifts in his expression, almost imperceptibly. He knows something and fails to say?

Larseen stumbles a bit and then recovers. "That's right. We may not be receiving the messages sent."

"Or the messenger could be dead?" I'm careful with my tone. This is a weighty matter to them.

"Yes, Magistrate. That is possible, though unlikely, considering the protection she is under," Master Brogal answers.

We all know what that means—Rowten's as well as Marcus Adicio's phantom, and that sailor I've heard so much about. "This is serious. We must be able to communicate with Marcus."

"Hence my plan to assure we do," Brogal says and stands again.

Larseen sits back down.

"It is only as a courtesy that I inform you, Mistress Rhiannon—"

I clear my throat.

"—Interim Magistrate, as stated in the formal decree…" It's his turn to pass a document across the table to me. "I plan to send a savant, and with your leave, soldiers by sea to Pandom City where I hope to find them. It is crucial that Marcus is assisted in his task and if anything has gone askew with his journey, he will need the added support."

It's odd, and I'm not believing it. Why send Ash in the first place if she can't manage the communication? And why send another savant if she can? If they have been lost at sea that's one thing, but this? What is Brogal up to?

I stand slowly, my long-sleeved dress rippling about me in shimmering folds. I clasp my hands in front of me, a wise woman confronting her council. At least that's the look I mean to achieve. "Master Brogal, I must remind you it is more than courtesy that urges you to speak. It is protocol. Beyond that, it is necessity. I, in the name of the Magistrate as deeded by Jacus Adicio before he died…" I pause for them to all say *peace be his path*. "And in the absence of my husband, must not only hear your plans but approve them, especially when a ship of the palace is requested." I smile inwardly. That had been my smartest move yet: to gain more funds for the new navy, I suggested that the palace requisition all private boats and then hire their captains and crew to run them. At first U'karn and the others had protested until they saw that much of the wage would come back in increased taxes and more importantly it gave them full control of every ship in the harbor from rowboat to battle cutter. They may not have realized, at the time, that it gives that full control to me.

Chrysel chirrups from under the table. *Full control to us.*

"Yes, love. To us."

Brogal turns a coppery red, but honestly, how else to save these fools from themselves. As I gain power uncontested, I will be the one to protect the realm and see it flourish, Great Dying or not.

I smooth my expression. "I'm afraid that, in all fairness, I will have to say *no* to your request, unless the Sanctuary is prepared to pay for the vessel. You already have one acquisitioned for the use of the Bone Gatherer. I can't have you tying up two."

The council chambers are dead silent. Of course, U'karn won't protest. He has too much to gain by backing me. I'm putting him in charge of the new navy after all.

Brogal shakes his head, but I see in his eyes I have won. He'll not chase after Marcus on the harebrained notion of the whistle bone myth without giving due consideration to the prosperity and expansion of the realm. I won't let him. Either way, this plan of his will keep him busy and line the palace pockets with Sanctuary gold.

"We're in agreement, then?" The silence has dragged on long enough.

Brogal sits, resigned. "Yes, Magistrate, we are."

Perfect. Brogal has been shown his place and my authority confirmed with the council as witness.

But I do hope he doesn't send Larseen on this mission of his. I have so many more uses for him here.

46

ASH

"You want me to vez-spitt'n what?" I must have heard Marcus wrong with the rocking ship and pounding waves and his loud, unnerved voice. *"De'ral? Is that you or Marcus talking to me?"* I'm worried I can't tell the difference, and Marcus should be, too.

"He's worried that you hear his phantom at all." My inner voice chuckles. *I'm used to it by now. He should be, too.*

Marcus thrusts the whistle bone bag at me and starts rummaging in the galley. "Stow them in a cast iron pot and guard them with your life." He pulls a small one out of a box. "This will do."

"Because a Gollnar warship with catapults on deck is bearing down on us? Not to mention the red-robe on board who wants the bones?"

"Exactly."

"That's the plan? Hide them in a pot?" I grab his arm to slow him down. "It's not going to work."

"There's more to it than that."

"What more?" I don't know how we can go from gathered around the table sharing ancient myths to being under attack in less than a handful of minutes. His concern is catching, and I find my hands start to shake. The light dims and the walls of the galley close in.

"Ash? Are you listening?"

My eyes pop open and I nod.

"As soon as they're within clear sight of our aft catapult, we fire."

I blink a few times, the light coming back. "Have you forgotten the fact that we will be within range of them first? Gollnar warships have twice the reach of this sloop."

"Kaylin thinks we might get lucky."

"Lucky?" I look away from his strained face to watch water beat against the round port window. We might as well be inside a wash tub for all I can see. "Marcus, this is bad. What if—" My words are cut short by the deck bell ringing. Frantic orders boom over our heads.

Marcus races up the hatch. "Hide the whistle bones in the pot and seal the lid. Then find Tyche. Keep her safe, too."

"F'qad sake, Marcus," I call after him. "We need a better plan."

But he's gone, so I do what he says, stuff the bone bag in the pot, tie the lid down with spare thongs and stow it in the bulkhead with the rest of our gear. I also find my sword in the weapon's chest and buckle it around my waist. The belt is miles too long, but I make it snug by wrapping it twice. My fingers start to feel thick, and I fumble the clasp. "Tyche!" I call, ignoring the dizziness. *Where is she?*

My chest tightens as I run to the hatch and trip. My head hits the step and black spots burst across my vision. I roll to my back, my hands crossing over my head as a wall of bricks tumbles down. We must have capsized! I hold my breath, waiting for the crushing pain of the wall, the rush of icy water, but it never comes.

"Breathe, Ash. Breathe." A wisp of golden light washes over me.

I gasp in a breath and sit up, cradling my head. I'm alone in the dark and it takes me time to orient. What am I doing here at the bottom of the galley steps?

"Searching for Tyche. You fell."

I did? And then, I remember. I did! I haul myself up the steps to the hatch. "Tyche!" I call but the wind is so strong I can't hear my own voice.

Half of the *Dugong*'s crew are on the port side, their weapons drawn. The other half is in the rigging, hauling on the sails. The Gollnar warship streams toward us at full speed. I knew their warships were big, but I've never seen one this close. Board by plank, it's twice the *Dugong*'s size, leaving the "plenty of time to fire first" option ridiculous. But the *Dugong* captain acts fast. Crew haul down sail like mad, the first mate shouting out orders as I cling to the hatch railing. Suddenly, the captain gives the command to come about.

In this neck-snapping high swell? Where in it all is Marcus, Kaylin?

"Hold tight!" my inner voice warns.

As I do, the deck tilts. The boom swings like a giant arm and the *Dugong*, a small ship with a shallow draw, spins hard to port. At the same time, there's a whip-crack and whistle as the warship's catapults fire.

I can't see the prow, but the launch isn't followed by a jarring impact above the smash and churn of waves, so they must have missed.

Now we're in even closer range of the Gollnar ship, practically on a collision course. Before that happens, we come abreast of each other, the Gollnar warriors standing ready on the ropes. "They're going to board!" My breath freezes when I spot Atikis standing next to his warhorse, red robes blowing in the wind. His sword is raised in his right hand, and he lets out a battle cry.

We're done for, I say to myself.

"Or they are," my inner voice lilts back, oddly unconcerned.

How? How? How? It's a stupid question, made worse by saying it three times.

Gollnar warriors leap from their high perches and swing through the air and hit the deck fighting. Not all manage well. Some fall into the widening gap of ocean between the ships and some are tangled in the ropes, but it looks like the *Dugong* is about to be overwhelmed anyway, like a drop of honey next to a nest of ants.

Us being the honey, in this case.

"Kaylin!" I shout because I can't see him and because it might be the last thing I ever say on this path.

"Mind the bones, lass. I've got this."

"You've got what exactly? We're going to be massacred."

"Don't count on it."

"Where's Tyche?" I call out because I do seem to have more words in me.

"She's below. Don't worry." Kaylin's warm, buoyant voice fills my mind. I run back down into the hold, slamming the hatch behind me.

Don't worry?

What else in the drak'n dark can I do?

I love a good challenge, but this might be pushing it. The *Dugong* rides the high swells, straining under so much sail. It's not the cyclone Marcus fears, but not far off either. We can't keep it up. I look skyward and hand-over-hand it to the top of the mast, betting on the odds that Salila, and her new charge are within earshot. *"Salila?"*

The wind rips by and the rigging creaks. The sound of clashing swords wells up from the deck.

"By orders of Teern, and your own volition, sister. Answer me." I climb into the crow's nest, straining to hear her reply. The mast sways violently at this height, usually an exhilarating experience, but I'm too preoccupied to enjoy it. I loop one arm around the flagstaff, hair dripping into my eyes. There isn't much time to take stock.

The *Dugong* has two catapults, one port and one starboard, each with enough fodder to fire three shots, four at the most. It's not exactly a top-deck warship, but more a vessel for running messages and slipping in and out of places the larger ones can't. Including the *Dugong*'s company and the able-bodied sailors, we have thirty-one swords. Not even close to matching the warship's fighting power. Only one thing to do about that.

I strip off my shirt, jump to the railing and dive straight into the sea thirty yards below.

The impact shocks my body as nothing else can, but there's no time to revel in it.

"Salila! Rosie! Battle!" That'll get their attention. They both love a good fight. I dive straight down into the bottomless water first, then pull up in time to shoot toward the Gollnar vessel's prow. As I climb up the hull and break the surface, the cool white skin of Salila brushes my shoulder on the left, the brown skin of Rosie on the right.

"Can I play?" Rosie asks, flashing pointy fangs and dragging them across my neck, hard enough to get my attention, not hard enough to bleed.

I slam my palm into her jaw, and she somersaults away.

"When did you become such a grump?" She pouts.

I ignore her and turn to Salila. *"Watch my back, and for Teern's sake, watch her."*

"Delighted to."

Both Mar women's pupils dilate, their eyes bleeding to black.

"Mind yourselves." The wood splinters as we tear up the side of the ship. *"There's a red-robe onboard even you two might find a challenge."*

They laugh brightly. *"Not in the sea."*

"His horse is with him if it truly be an animal of flesh and not phantom. Beware."

Salila's eyebrows go up, muscles bunching as she climbs beside me. Water runs off her body, her hair streaming behind. Rosie speeds up, taking us over. Salila reaches out, grabs her ankle and snaps her back. It looks like she's managing to control her at least, though Rosie has yet to be consumed by the Dreaded's penchant for bloodlust—an insatiable craving that strikes without warning and leaves hundreds of victims in their wake.

"Pay attention, and when I say jump, hit the water fast. Dive as deep as you can. There will be an explosion."

"What about you?"

"I'll be right behind." I spring, launching over the railing to land lightly on both feet, dead in front of their central catapult. Shouts rise from the shocked sailors, as expected. Four crewmen back away, freshly stretched rope bending the catapult trigger taut. They're ready to fire the short distance to the *Dugong*, and it's lined up to be a direct hit. They point their swords at me, not following the blurs that are Rosie and Salila. Their necks are broken before they feel the Mar's touch. I leave them to it. By my count, I have five seconds left.

The catapult rests on a wooden carriage with four wheels and is restrained against kickback with a rope as thick as my arm. "Let's do an about-face, shall we?" I draw my blade, seawater spraying, and swing in a slicing arc. It severs the rope in a single, lightning-fast cut, leaving the ends smoking as they unravel. I kick the base and swivel the weapon to point straight at the Gollnar ship's mast. "Jump!" I holler and leap myself, cutting the trigger rope before I fly over the rail, my back parallel to the deck.

In a quick twist, I plunge toward the surface. Salila streaks past me headfirst and we hit the water one after the other. From beneath the waves, we both hear the boom of the warship's mast cracking in half.

"Magnificent, brother." Salila sweeps past me, a grin on her face, bubbles racing from her lips.

"I'm glad you enjoyed yourself."

She grabs my wrist, pulling me to a stop. *"That's your thanks?"*

I cock my head and try again. *"Thank you, fair sister, for your assistance. Well executed and most appreciated."*

"That's better." She bows. But her smile fades as she looks around. *"Where in bleeding landers is Rosie?"*

She disappears to find her, and I shoot back to the *Dugong* as fast as I can, hoping against hope none of us were seen.

48

MARCUS

"Ash?" Her name echoes over the deck. "Ash, where are you?" I won't sheath my sword until she's found.

My hands shake, but not from battle, or the enemy blood covering the deck. My recorder should have been below, where I told her to stay. Tyche's there, but there's no sign of Ash. The swell smooths out as we reach the end of the channel, but could she have been washed overboard?

The clang of steel still rings in my ears and my head throbs from De'ral's relentless pressure behind my eyes. Fighting with a *warrior* phantom unable to rise is not fun, I've discovered, but none of that matters now until I find Ash. Kaylin is missing, too, but I'm not worried about him. He's half fish, as far as I can tell. "Who's seen my wordsmith?" I call out to anyone within a shout's reach.

A deckhand tossing bodies over the side stops mid-stoop and points to the hatch. "Below, surely, sir."

I search the hold for the third time. There's little space down here on the best days but after the battle, wounded sailors lie across tables and fill the hammocks. There's hardly room to move. I lean over Piper's shoulder while she works and speak in her ear, none too quietly. "Have you seen Ash?"

"You mean since you asked five minutes ago?" Piper says, not looking up from her patient as she holds a thick cloth to his blood-soaked chest.

"This is a Gollnarian," I say, my eyes lingering on the man's uniform.

Piper nods again. "Of those that swung aboard, he is the sole survivor. I presume you want him for questioning."

"Thanks, but what about Ash?"

"Not now, Marcus," she says as arterial blood pulses into the cloth.

Tyche's bandaging our first mate's arm from shoulder to fingertips of which I only count three. "Ash?" I ask.

She shakes her head.

I wade through the wounded but there's no sign. Back on deck, my stomach's in knots. We've defeated the enemy who seemed to have fired upon themselves and crossed the channel in high seas but if Ash was swept overboard,

I'll never know victory again. "Ash!" I shout.

The ocean suddenly loses the last bit of chop and turns calm as a blue lake, the wind behind us. "Oi!" I shout when I see Belair and Samsen with Kaylin. Belair's red hair is soaked in blood and Samsen supports him on one side, Kaylin on the other.

"What's happened?" I rush to them. Belair had no injury when I left him on deck and that was not long ago.

"A small price for not ducking fast enough," Belair says. He's shrugging it off, but his face is ghost white.

"Damned lucky his head's made of stone." Samsen laughs. "Or the Gollnar blade would have split him in two."

"I'll be all right." Belair straightens to take his own weight, then sags back down against Kaylin.

"Aye, you'll be fine," the sailor says. "Once the bleeding stops."

I scan the deck. "Have you seen Ash?" The words are gruff, and I don't look directly at any of them. *"If she fell overboard. If she's lost—"*

She's fine, De'ral says.

"Why didn't you say so sooner?" Relief washes in, even though De'ral doesn't answer that.

"She's coming down now." Kaylin points to the crow's nest. "I sent her up there to keep an eye on the retreating warship."

"Up there? With her seasickness? The headaches? She was meant to stay below," I growl. "Guarding the bones."

"Which she did, with Tyche." Kaylin shrugs. "When the battle was won, she offered assistance."

"That doesn't mean you let her!"

"Let her?" Kaylin's perplexed. "Are we talking about the same lass?"

Before I can answer, Ash jumps from the top of the boom rung to the deck, landing light on her bare feet. The four of us stare at her, but only one is smiling, and it's not me.

"What could you see from the nest?" Kaylin asks before I can speak.

The right question, I admit. But I want to point out that she could have forgotten where she was and walked right over the edge.

She's lost some memories, not her mind, De'ral says.

Ash smirks, clearly hearing my phantom. She brushes her hands clean and pulls a small distance viewer from the deep pocket of her pants. "You won't believe it."

"Aye?" Kaylin takes a step closer. "And while you're explaining, I'll have the compass back."

"Um…" She tries not to smile. "Sorry sailor, but that's not a likely event."

They banter? I thought she was swept overboard, drowned at sea, and they banter?

"You lost my compass?" Kaylin pretends upset.

"I dropped it over the edge." She holds her hands out, her voice innocent. "By accident. It's at the bottom of Black Dart by now." She waves behind us toward the channel, sending Kaylin the smile she can no longer contain.

My fear flips into anger. I clear my throat to get their attention, and to dislodge the bitterness stuck there. "So, what did you see that we won't believe?"

She hands me the viewer and points at the coast. "Have a look."

I check, finding the shore closer than I'd thought. "Can't be," I say. "Is that what I think?"

"If you think it's the Gollnar warship beached in that cove, then yes." Ash becomes serious. Finally. "The ship took damage, but it landed all right, on Tangeen soil. And that's not the half of it. Look up."

I do, and spot it, or I should say, him, the red-robe savant, on his horse, gazing out to sea. If I didn't know better, I'd think he was looking right at me. Not for the first time.

"Our skirmish hasn't slowed him down." I hand the viewer to Samsen.

"What do we do?" Samsen asks.

I exhale. "Take Belair below to Piper, for a start." I turn my back on the other men and touch Ash's sleeve. "A word?"

She raises her brows. "Right now?"

"If it's convenient." The tightness in my shoulders won't relax. I walk her aft and wait until we're alone, save for the crew mopping blood off the deck.

She studies my face closely. "What's wrong?" she asks.

"You didn't stay below." I take a breath. "Kaylin sends you up to the clouds, where you've never climbed before, the opposite of staying below, or staying safe." I examine the side of her head. "You're bleeding?"

"Just a bump."

I empty my lungs in a rush. "You both defy me and put your life at risk. And what of the bones? I said to guard them."

Not what I would have said, De'ral comments from behind my eyes.

"Shut up." It's possible my words have come out wrong, but I don't need my phantom undermining them.

Possible they came out wrong? Try likely.

Well, yes. I see he's right and now Ash is on the defensive.

"I went where I was needed, when I was needed, Marcus," she says, not the least apologetic. Her eyes are hooded and something else is there, a challenge I've never seen before.

My tone sharpens. "I'm trying to protect you, Ash, but you aren't making it easy."

She crosses her arms and I brace for the inevitable list of reasons why trying to protect her is not my job. I feel the chuckle of De'ral's laughter deep inside. "I said shut up!"

"Pardon me?"

"Not you, Ash! Never you." Curse the bones, this is going from bad to worse. "That was a mistake."

She bristles, and I don't blame her at this point, but instead of the verbal catapult I'm expecting, she reaches up and slips her arms around my neck and hugs me. "I would have been frightened, too, if you were nowhere to be found. I'm sorry." On tiptoe, she kisses my cheek. "But we're safe and victorious, and in need of a wash. We can't come before the Magistrate's throne covered in blood. You know what he's like."

Persnickety, we used to say, and he's only gotten worse with age. "Maybe we'd be more convincing, showing up spattered in blood. Battle for the bones, and all. They *are* safe, right?"

"Safe and sound." She smiles. "But you stink, Marcus Adicio." She releases me. "I insist you have a proper wash."

"I will, but you don't smell all that nice yourself."

"You two look happy," Piper says, coming out of the hold. "Hope you can hold on to that feeling."

"Why?" We both say at once.

"The last man from the Gollnar ship just died. Peace be his path, but you'll hear no news of Atikis today."

49

MARCUS

Turns out there isn't enough water for a full body wash, so I rinse blood from my hands and face the best I can. Ash won't think it's good enough. But there are more important things, like having a word with Captain Anders. We review the battle, both agreeing that luck really was on our side. What are the odds the ship would shoot itself in the foot at the last possible moment?

"We're headed straight for the Nulsea Gap?" I ask when we run out of talk of wounded and damage reports.

He nods affirmative and I head below to join the others.

While the red-robe gets away? Pressure builds in the base of my skull.

I clamp down on it as a blinding flash of temper hits me. De'ral isn't pleased with any of my choices today. *"The sooner we secure the next whistle bone, the better. That means going straight to Pandom City."* I've said it ten times already. Why do I have to justify myself to my phantom?

The only response is the sensation of searing light burning the backs of my eyes.

"What's wrong?" Belair asks between spoonfuls of Klaavic. His head wound turns out to be minor, appetite undeterred.

Everyone at the table looks up, waiting for my response.

I slide onto the bench seat next to Kaylin. "Nothing's wrong. We're sailing straight through the Nulsea Gap and will be in Pandom City shortly after." I fill my bowl from the center of the table.

"The tide's incoming," Kaylin says, agreeing with the timing. "Should be smooth."

"And then?" Ash asks. She's brushing out Tyche's hair and weaving it into a fishtail braid. "Will we get an audience without delay, do you think?"

"Good question." I raise my brow at Belair, but the redhead is still shoveling food into his mouth.

He scrapes his bowl before answering. "It might take a day for an audience with the Magistrate. He's always busy, but we'll need to see him first, before High Savant Havest. Protocols."

Ash raises her hand, still gripping the hairbrush. "Let's put some effort into scrubbing up and being presentable." She looks specifically at me. "Like Belair says, Magistrate Riveren is big on protocols and even bigger on appearances. There's soap and water topside."

"Not much, but already done," I say.

"Oh? Can I suggest you do it again?" She picks a piece of kelp off my cheek.

I distinctly hear De'ral laughing. It's worse than his growls.

"Good idea." Belair clears his plate. "Undoubtedly, with the weight of your message, and the notice Brogal has sent ahead, they will hand over the whistle bone…" His voice trails off.

"It's called Ma'ata, for the deep corals that hug the coast," Ash supplies.

"Is it carved from them?" Tyche asks.

"From Er's femur. It represents the fourth step to An'awntia—Awareness of Feeling." Her eyes level to mine. "You remember this, Marcus?"

"I do." Mostly.

Belair nods and then beams a smile toward shore. "Can't wait to land and see my people."

"Anyone in particular?" Ash asks. Her eyes crinkle as she smiles. "Hahmen, perhaps?" She remembers him now, and I take that as a good sign.

Belair shrugs like it's nothing, but his face turns red as he laughs.

I smile, too, but my mind drifts back to the collecting of the whistle bones. "Are the documents in order, Ash? For the meeting with Havest?" The *Dugong* suffered only minor damage, but I want to be certain.

"All in order, Marcus." She ties off Tyche's braid and gives her a pat. "So much so, I could pass them to Piper. Let her act as recorder so I can head straight to the library."

It's worth considering.

"You don't need me to translate, and Brogal's letter says it all."

"Good idea." Her research skills are vital now. "We have so many unanswered questions. The multiple aspect *alters*, anything on the original whistle bones—"

"And how to keep them from being *called* from us," Tyche adds, a glint of her old impish determination in her contribution.

Be aware, De'ral warns. His voice in my head is quick and urgent.

I feel eyes at the back of my head and slowly rise, pressing a finger to my lips. "I'll speak to the captain," I say lightly, as if nothing is wrong. "Everyone remember, we stay alert in Tangeen, you especially Belair. I know this is your home realm, but—" I turn mid-sentence to look behind me. There's a shadow under the hatch stairs but it vanishes before I can make out who it is.

"Say no more." Belair stands and follows my line of sight. He continues talking normally in case the lurker is still within earshot. "I'll use my connections to our advantage."

Ash points toward the deck and mouths the words "cabin boy," when she spots the spy.

"At the least, I'll get us into the library archives. My status gives me a permanent pass." Belair nods at Ash and, unhurried, I lead the way topside.

The wind blows my hair in my eyes as I saunter to the port side. Belair follows my lead, leaning his back against the railing, chatting about nothing in particular.

"Is it all out?" the Tangeen asks as he touches his wild red locks.

I knit my brow. "What's that?"

"The blood and gore. Ash washed my hair for me, but I want to make sure."

"It's fine."

"Smell all right? She used peppermint soap and—"

"Your hair's fine."

"Excellent." He lowers his voice. "And where do you think our eavesdropper got to?"

I shift my eyes to the helm. There the cabin boy stands on tiptoe, speaking to Captain Anders and gesturing. "The sooner we're off the *Dugong*, the better." I scan the distant coastline. "We've spies everywhere."

"No argument about that." Belair points as if we're a couple of sightseers. "That's White Beaches coming up. We should get everyone on deck. The Gap's a sight not to be missed."

"Just keep your eyes open," I say under my breath.

"See if the cabin boy follows us into the city?"

"Precisely. If we out him now, they could replace him with someone we don't recognize."

"Clever ploy." Belair brushes down his yellow robe and buttons the cloak that covers it.

"Not quite how we'd planned to return from Aku, is it," I say.

"No." He touches the old scar where half his earlobe is missing. "Not what I had imagined at all."

"Holy mother of Dak, look at them!" I stare up at the great white pillars that mark the Nulsea Gap. It's an unnecessary command. Everyone has their necks tipped back, mouths open. Even Belair, who has traveled under them more than any of us, is enthralled.

"So tall," Tyche whispers. "They reach to the second sun!" She points at the red star pulsing over our heads.

"Not quite that far." The cliffs rise from three hundred fathoms below the sea, visible to the bottom in the crystal turquoise water. They race each other upward, marble white columns stretching for the top of the sky. There's no telling which won the race; both peaks are lost in misty clouds, though I know the east pillar is purportedly taller.

As the *Dugong* sails into the narrow channel between the towering rocks, a giant shadow falls across the deck. The gleaming white formations turn gray and the temperature drops. Quartz crystals inlaid in the stone sparkle like pale rose and blue stars, and it may sound strange, but it makes my skin tingle. With my gaze toward the peaks, I feel an overwhelming presence here at the entrance to Tangeen. It is beautiful, yes, but something more, like the secrets of the sea are captured in the columns, revealed to those who can decipher them. The wind whistles through them, and I could swear it calls a name.

I strain to hear it again, listening, but as we come out of the shadows, the spell breaks and the moment is gone. The others stir, normal conversation sparking up again.

"Do birds roost at the top?" Tyche asks, nose still to the sky.

"Albatross are known to. Midway up is the lookout," Belair says as the carved spiral steps come into view. "They'll hear of us at the palace before we reach the harbor."

"Do they have distance viewers?" Tyche continues staring at the peaks.

"Some of the finest Sierrak can make," I answer.

Belair catches the frown on Marcus's face. "We trade with Sierrak. It's no secret. They're neighbors, and we haven't been at war with them for over a century." He scratches his head and winces. "At least, we hadn't when I left."

"Sierrak to the left, Gollnar to the right," Kaylin comments, a question in his tone.

Marcus bristles, about to defend Tangeen's loyalty, by the look of him.

Kaylin holds out his hands. "I'm just saying, it's a tricky situation with Sierrak, Gollnar, and Palrio seeking the first whistle bones. Who will Tangeen choose to give theirs to? Or will they have a champion of their own?"

"They'll give it to us, of course." I nudge Marcus aside and step in. "We are their allies." But Marcus doesn't comment. He has the captain's distance viewer out and is watching the series of signals—elaborate waves of colored flags— coming from the lookout high above. "They're relaying our arrival right now."

The jib drops, and lines are thrown to stop us at the platform dock, an inspection area for incoming vessels. The Tangeen guards board, check our papers, and then wave us through. The whole thing takes less than five minutes. They'd indeed been expecting the *Dugong* and her passengers. Not sure if they thought there'd be fresh blood on the deck, though.

A good amount of cloth goes back up in short order and we make fair speed through the calm waters of the Nulsea. It's an inland ocean the size of Palrio, dramatically raised and lowered by the tides but rarely ruffled with more than a hand span of swell. There are deep grottos scattered across the basin, wells in the sea where the water turns ink blue, contrasting the rest of the turquoise water. Large and peculiar fish spawn in the depths, or so they say. Some have reported Mar sightings there, too. I frown at the thought, thinking of Salila. "Mar are not fish."

"Hardly, lass."

"Then what's down there that would intrigue them if the sightings are true? Treasures?"

"Memories." Kaylin sounds wistful when he answers but doesn't explain.

"Bring down the mainsail," Captain Anders shouts when we veer around a clanging buoy.

"Home," Belair says in a robust tone. "At last."

The harbor comes into view, the league long port, a gateway to Tangeen. It's full of ships of every size and description, with plenty of empty berths as well. We're directed by dockworkers and they have us moored in no time.

My lips curve into a full smile as we disembark. We've made it, all in one piece.

Tyche and I stand on the pier, packs at our feet, coats unbuttoned in the warmth of the late morning sun. We wait for the others to descend the gangplank. I've a full view of the *Dugong* and the damage she's sustained. The very top of the foremast has snapped off. The jib, luffing in the breeze, has been hastily mended and resembles holey cheese. The bowsprit is shaved flush with the hull and the wheelhouse roof is missing its overhang. But for all her damage topside, the *Dugong* sits high in the water and the crew is already busy scrubbing every drop of blood from the deck and making repairs to the railing. The new sections stand out with their pale wood, waiting to be sanded and oiled.

I wonder briefly if we will return to this vessel. Is that in Brogal's hands or their High Savant's? Or will it be up to us? I have no idea, but I think it should be discussed, at least. We're not pawns on a gameboard.

"Your entire path is in your hands." My inner voice sounds like a venerable old Bone Thrower. *"The way is there for you to choose."*

So says the ancient text. I don't want to argue with myself right now. "We've got a lot to do," I say aloud.

"More than you can yet imagine."

Is that supposed to encourage me? Far from it, the thought makes me shiver. But my inner voice is right, and not just about the Letters of Er and lore on the holding of the crown of bones.

"I'll help in the library," Tyche says. "Tangeen will surely let a savant of Yuki's descent have access."

My hand goes to her shoulder. "Surely." It's good to hear her speak of her grandmother without a vacant pause. For a moment, I feel a tinge of envy. She may be an orphan now, like me, but she knows her heritage going back a hundred generations. I know nothing of mine.

"That doesn't change where either of you are along the path."

True. I force a smile to lift my mood. "The three of us can get straight to work."

"Kaylin's going to help?" Tyche looks surprised.

"He's actually very good at languages, ancient maps, and stories."

She nods but doesn't speak.

"I know you were scared by the Mar who befriended him. We all were, but he's saved us, many times over." It's the first time she's talked so much in one conversation, so I bring up as much as I can, in case it will help her work through it all.

"He keeps secrets." She looks me straight in the eyes.

It's not what I expect her to say, but I know that's true as well.

"Who keeps secrets?" Kaylin comes up behind us.

"I have volunteered you for library research," I say quickly and take a step back to let him in. Then softer, "Where've you been?"

"Chatting with the harbormaster about repairs."

I laugh. "You know you aren't a bosun's mate on this ship?"

He winks at me. "Aye, but I know Pandom City's harbormaster. The *Dugong* will be as good as new in two days."

"That's great news." I turn to Tyche as if saying, see, he's here to help. "Our next task will prove successful in that amount of time, if we don't get lost in the library's endless shelves."

"That big?" Tyche asks. Her eyes lift.

"Not as magnificent as Aku's was." I give her arm a squeeze. "But this is Pandom City. You'll be impressed."

As if on cue, a parade of musicians appears in the street, dancing toward us. They are dressed in colorful flowing clothes and calling greetings. One carries a flag with Belair's name emblazoned across it. Others hold flags with dazzling red suns. It seems this group is happy to celebrate both events, the return of their initiate and the second sun.

"Is it a circus?" Tyche asks, her voice high.

"More like a welcoming party," Kaylin says. "Brace yourselves. I think our Belair is more popular than he let on."

I start to sway to the rhythm but the medallion heats, nearly burning my skin.

"Don't lose yourself in reverie now, child. There is danger ahead, in a place most secure."

Talus? What danger? What place?

But listen as I might, there's nothing more from the ancient Bone Thrower to be heard.

SALILA

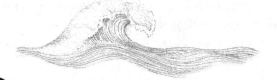

Deep, blissful depths…

Thank the dead gods! The Nulsea pools are still pristine. I wasn't sure they would be. Many currents and bays in Amassia are showing signs of decay. It's sad, really, to see it all happen again. I look for the light of the second sun as I glide just under the surface. It's inevitable, I suppose, what with the too-quick shift of temperatures. The dying reefs. Fires. Pestilence. *Must enjoy this while I can.* I glance over my shoulder and dive.

There is nothing I love more than these pools. Well, not nothing. There are—

"I'm bored," Rosie says, jarring me out of my thoughts.

I try to ignore her. There are several things I love, if not more then as much as these deep aqua pools, like the feel of drops of hot lander blood down the back of the throat, the touch of passion on my skin, the memory of life on land in the sunken pillars of Sierrak's northern realm, and most significantly, the peace and quiet of depths undisturbed for—

"Really, really bored…"

"Shut up, Rosie. My path is not to provide you entertainment."

Rosie rolls onto her back to watch the sloop sail right over us. I grab her arm and drag her with me in a headlong rush, downward like a diving narwhal, until we are a thousand fathoms deep. It's over a mile, in landers' terms. I might even have to clear my ears.

"What did you do that for?" Rosie snarls. *"I said I was bored, not seeking ambient pressure."*

And they say the Dreaded are sharp as whip cracks. *"Do you even listen to Teern? We're not to be seen."*

"Do you even listen to him?" she snaps back. *"What if we are caught down here?"*

Point taken. The pools are off-limits, as much so as land. I suppose I should surface, and report to Teern the most recent news. He'll want details on the incident with Atikis.

But the cold caresses my skin and rushes through my hair as it flows behind me, making my nerves dance. The pressure builds even more, temperature drops and the light from the surface turns to a gold pinprick. I don't need anyone to remind me not to become sidetracked. But the lure of darkness and the whisper of memories held captive in the depths are too much to resist. Also, tasty blind eels dwell here. I can hear Rosie chewing one now.

As I reach for my own slippery eel, the thought of Teern's disapproving voice shatters the tranquility. He becomes so pedantic around the Great Dyings. Still, I know what I'm doing. The ship isn't going to disappear as it tacks to Pandom City, not now that Atikis is put to land. I can fill him in on that soon enough. Teern will never know.

"Never know what, my daughter?" the Sea King booms in my head.

His voice comes from below us, rising fast. Oops.

Teern appears, his face serene, long black ropes of hair flowing away from it in waves. I don't let it fool me. One quick somersault and I am racing toward the surface, Rosie already kicking hard above me. I grab her foot and yank her back. I don't mind putting a Dreaded between me and Teern. When we erupt from the deep sea well, she tries to shoot away. I grab her wrist as Teern asks again. *"You were saying? I would never know what?"*

Fish crap on a stick.

How do I get out of this? *"Never know if Kaylin will betray us,"* I blurt out. Have to. What else can I say to deflect Teern from my little rule-breaking expedition? All Mar know the depths of the wells are off-limits. Teern won't say why, but the consequence of diving them unbidden is unpleasant, if caught. And we were certainly caught, my words possibly misconstrued as flaunting.

"Kaylin's what?" Rosie asks, trying to snatch her arm back.

"None of your business."

She growls. *"He used to be all my business."* Her face turns wicked. *"And will be again."*

It makes me laugh in spite of Teern's dark eyes on me. It's going to be so much fun when she meets the little wordsmith face-to-face.

Meanwhile, Kaylin's clever enough to handle my misdirect, and besides, the betrayal part could be true. Fifty-fifty chance, at least. *"You know he will,"* I shoot to Teern. *"He always does."*

Unfortunately, the Sea King is less interested in Kaylin's loyalty than my trespass. *"Stay out of it, daughters. These pools are not for you."* His voice is a cool whisper, more threatening than his loudest booms.

"It was Salila's idea," Rosie says, "for the eels."

"Ha! I followed her down, the sole purpose of dragging her out." It's a lie, blaming her like that, but after what she did to me, I don't care. She deserves to rot in her tomb.

Teern circles us, anger rising in heat waves. "Stay with the ship, both of you!" He knows our history. Knows her crimes. Why does he let her live?

I start to talk back, then think better of it. Why anger him more? I break through the surface, the shimmering crystal water lit by the pale-yellow sun and a spark from the red one. The wind slaps my face as I turn in circles. "Damn the bones," I whisper. The sloop is nowhere in sight.

"Lose something?" Teern asks, breaking the surface next to me.

"Not at all."

"It's important you keep an eye on Kaylin, child."

"I have been. There was a little assault from Atikis, and I helped fend him off." I frown, and then excitement ripples through my body as I catch a glint in his eye. "How close, exactly, am I to stick to Kaylin?"

"Dog his steps, I think is the term."

"On land?" I say it softly, trying not to show my hope.

"Do it well and your restrictions will be lifted."

"And mine, too?" Rosie tries to porpoise through the air, but Teern catches her shoulder and shoves her back down. "You are not to break the surface. If you do, I'll smash your tomb and end your eternal life with it."

In a swirl of current that sends me spinning, Teern tightens his grip on Rosie. He levels his eyes on me as he holds up a single finger.

All I can think of are his words, "dog his steps." "I will not disappoint."

"Leave no trace of your path, Salila."

"Not a drop, Father."

With that assurance, he turns to Rosie.

"I'll not touch foot on land." Her smokey, dark eyes rise to meet his. "Until you ask me to." She is sickeningly confident.

He nods once and is away, leaving streams of kelp and tumbling bait fish in his wake.

I wait until Teern is gone before I tear off like a barracuda, swimming just under the waves toward Pandom City harbor. "This way, Rosie. Keep up."

It's been years, centuries by the lander count, since Teern barred me from setting foot on any of Amassia's shores. Such an overreaction. One little slip-up... Well, more like thirty or forty little slip-ups, if counting individual landers, savant and non-savant alike, but I've been paying the price for eons, it seems.

I slow my speed as there's no need to rush anymore. I'll have to wait until nightfall. But then, oh then! I'll walk among the landers once more. I am so deep in revelry I don't realize until it's too late that Dreaded Rosie Red is nowhere in sight.

"Damn you Rosie! Where have you gotten to now?"

I t's nothing like my homecoming.

Be glad of it.

True. The least I can do is appreciate this reception.

Belair yells at the top of his lungs, waving his arms in the air. "Jerrik!" He nearly wrestles his friend to the ground in greeting. I'm used to his enthusiasm, envious of it at times.

Like right now?

"Yes, De'ral. Like right now."

"What a reception!" Ash shouts into my ear. Her grin is wide, but my jaw clamps shut, making it hard to smile.

I'm not jealous. Belair deserves friends. I'm glad he has them. It's just that I can't stop comparing this homecoming to my own. When we arrived at the gates of Baiseen, after a week's nonstop gallop to warn of Tann's attack, I was questioned by my own guards, ridiculed in the throne room in front of all the officials and high-ranking savants. Then—

Stripped of your throne, De'ral adds.

"Are you trying to make me feel worse?"

My phantom gives a mental shrug. *I thought we were making a list.*

"We weren't."

Meanwhile, a band of musicians beating drums, ringing bells, and playing flutes and horns dances toward us, followed by a dozen open chariots. The horses drawing them are all matched pairs. These are palace steeds, I'm betting. The crowd pulls back, making way as the lead chariot halts in front of us. The horses snort and paw the cobbled road as a robust man, dressed in finery, jumps out.

"Marcus Adicio!" he yells.

Horns blast and confetti fills the air as the loudest herald I've ever heard calls, "Hail Lord Riveren, Magistrate of Tangeen!"

And it's true. Before me strides Stein Riveren. I can't believe he came himself to welcome our company.

As I bow, the herald tries to signal silence by blowing a long, thin trumpet. It doesn't bring perfect results, but it tones the noise down, for a moment. "Make way for Marcus Adicio, newly returned from the Isle of Aku, honored yellow-robe of the Sanctuary of Baiseen, raiser of a *warrior* the likes of Gaveren the Great, and Bone Gatherer for all the allied realms." He blows on the trumpet again. "Make way, too, for Belair Duquan, son of Alvern Duquan, high diplomat of Tangeen, also successfully returned from Aku and the raiser of the famous red sun leopard…" He doesn't announce the others but no one seems to mind, judging by their smiles.

Ash tugs on my sleeve. "They are honoring you, Marcus. Soak it up!"

"So it seems." I catch her smile and keep it. Thank the bones there is no mention of me being the ex-heir in the string of titles.

"Marcus, my boy, I knew you would survive."

Does he mean the siege on Aku, the trials for my yellow-robe, or the attack on Baiseen? Could he have heard of our high-sea battle with Atikis already? Before I can comment, he steps closer, the weight of his hands on my shoulders. "We had word of your father's passing. I am so sorry, Marcus. Peace be his path."

"Thank you. I—"

"Good to see you step up for this." He waves his hand in the air and I assume he means the approaching Great Dying. "Very noble, handing the throne over to your brother so you might fulfill the duties of Bone Gatherer." He nods at the westering red star. "And not a moment too soon."

"I didn't actually—"

"And here is our realm's own son, Belair Duquan!"

I gaze out at the gathered crowd while Belair receives a warm welcome, and private words from the Magistrate as well.

"It's quite a turnout," Kaylin says in my ear. "Seems you are very well admired in Tangeen."

At this point, the Magistrate is pumping the hands of everyone in our company, even Ash's, while Belair is hoisted onto the shoulders of two friends. One of them is Hahmen, who clearly returned to Tangeen after we left. They are treating Belair like a war hero returned home.

He is *a war hero returned home.* De'ral's voice is dry.

"True. I wish they had seen it that way in Baiseen."

They see it that way here, De'ral says. *It is enough.*

Maybe he's right, but I think Belair is getting carried away, literally. "You there, bring him back. It's all fine and good to—" I'm knocked aside mid-sentence by a tall, lanky woman with shocking red hair who bounds into our midst.

"Frangelica!" Belair leaps from his friends' shoulders and wraps his arms around the woman, spinning her off her feet. Kaylin and I back away to keep from being kneecapped by her boots.

Finally, he sets her down. "Show me your new robes, red cat!" she shouts in his face, holding his cheeks.

Belair opens his coat, not bothering to explain a thing but lets his yellow robes speak for him. As he does, a blast from the herald brings our attention back to the Magistrate.

"To the palace," he cries, sweeping his hand toward me and my companions. "There will be feasting tonight!"

As if on cue, a new wave of musicians and dancers come up the street. They are clad in rainbow colors and carry hoops and juggling balls.

"Street performers!" Piper cheers and claps her hands.

Ash shouts in my ear again. "Isn't it marvelous?"

I laugh, letting go of the grudging comparisons. "Who doesn't love a parade?"

Tyche drops her gear and starts jumping up and down in time with the tunes. Frangelica, obviously Belair's sister, pulls her sibling into the middle of the riot. People traveling up and down the street in carriages and on foot are forced to a halt, but instead of protesting the delay, they applaud it. Samsen lifts Tyche onto his shoulder to give her a better view.

"I'm guessing we won't have trouble procuring this whistle bone," Samsen says, grinning. Piper leans in and gives him a quick word. His smile fades a little as he turns back to me. "We should report the battle with Atikis, Marcus. The red-robe is ashore. The Sanctuary needs to know." He scans the distance, scouting the hills behind the city.

"Agreed, but I suspect he already knows." I haven't missed the horsed guards on the fringes. Stein Riveren may be a crowd-pleasing ruler, but he is not stupid, or inept.

"You and Belair may ride with the Magistrate." His herald guides us to the chariot, Riveren grinning, holding the reins himself. "The others will follow behind."

Ash squeezes my arm and chortles her delight. She's never been in a parade like this before, only on the sidelines. Belair disentangles himself from his friends and sibling, shoulders his pack, and follows my lead. We step up to the roomy, open carriage and are off before the rest of the company, and all our gear, are led to theirs. I take a wide stand, arms crossed in front of my chest, robes billowing behind me. Belair does the same and I realize this is an exercise in diplomacy as much as a welcome ceremony.

The entourage, not dampened by our exit, trails us up the street, music, revelry, and all. We travel across the promenade, horses at a brisk trot. Their hooves clip over the wide paved walkway that skirts the Fancrest River. The design is very good, I admit, with its perfect line of trees, the circular flower gardens with blooms matching Sanctuary robe colors. All except black. Those flowers would be hard to find.

But I like how they've integrated the river into the city proper. White stone steps lead down to the water's edge, with small wharfs for day ventures. Plenty of picnic tables, too. Black swans float sedately on the current. But soon my awe turns to concern. On closer inspection, the usual crystal waters of the Fancrest are as muddy as the Suni River mouth in Baiseen. Have there been record amounts of rain this far north as well? I'll have to ask.

When we ride through the palace gates and into the courtyard, the chariots rock to a stop. "I will leave you here to be shown your accommodation. There is time for you to clean up and rest before the feast tonight."

I bow to Riveren. "Thank you, Magistrate, but we should talk. The red-robe Atikis—"

"Rides. I'm aware, and precautions are taken," he says in a low voice. "We'll discuss matters of the realms tomorrow. For now, we prepare for the feast!"

With that, he is gone, and we are left in the courtyard, the rest of the company catching up and gathering around us. Behind, the boisterous crowd, musicians, and dancers begin to disperse, but not until every single one of Belair's friends thumps him on the back and kisses his cheeks. They pump our hands, too, shouting hearty congratulations. I don't recall Pandom City being this welcoming when I've been here with Father. My gaze goes back down to the harbor and out to sea. I guess that makes sense. He only came for matters of state. I certainly don't remember dancing.

"Some reception, eh?" Belair beams as the last of the parade retreats.

"Wonderful," Ash says, a little breathless from it all. "And did I detect a certain someone among all those hugs and salutes?"

He lowers his voice to keep his answer private, but I can tell it's a yes by the dimples in his smile.

I'm happy for him. I am. But we aren't here for feasts and family reunions. We certainly aren't here for romance. I raise my fist in the air to get their attention. "It's imperative we speak with the Magistrate as soon as can be arranged, procure the whistle bone, scour the library, and be off. Let's not forget the threats we labor under." I hold their eyes until they nod back, attentive and determined.

I don't mean to be the rain cloud, but there is still so far to travel—Whitewing Sanctuary and then into Sierrak. I hold the whistle bones of Baiseen, Nonnova, and Kutoon. Tann has Aku's and possibly Aturnia's, and his home Sanctuary of Lepsea. Atikis's tally is unknown, if he has any, meaning there could be another five or more left ungathered.

"This way, Marcus." Ash turns me toward the herald who is patiently waiting to guide us. We follow through the entranceway, past a gazebo and curved garden paths. To the west, there's a parade ground and an arched bridge that spans the river. The Sanctuary is beyond, hidden by trees along the far riverbank.

"Wait here, please," our guide says. "The steward will be with you shortly."

I thank him, and a moment later, the steward arrives, a small man, non-savant by his dress, with a round face and a rounder belly.

"Welcome," he says. "All is in order, and I have put in your request for an official audience with the Magistrate."

"Request?" I echo him. "It was hardly a—"

"Thank you," Ash says, nails digging into my arm. "When do you expect the meeting might be?"

"Tomorrow morning, second bell." He registers the impatience on my face. "I suggest you take advantage of this brief interim in your travels. There may not be opportunities farther north."

He means the Realm of Sierrak, and he's right.

"Of course. Thank you."

"This way to the visitor's quarters." He sets a brisk pace. "There are ablutionary facilities there that I am certain can be put to good use." The round man lifts his nose as he speaks, as if trying to get upwind.

I guess a proper wash with hot water wouldn't hurt.

But before we reach our lodging, a green-robe messenger intercepts us. "Welcome Bone Gatherer and company." He catches his breath before addressing Belair directly. "And, well done, Savant Duquan. You are to report to the Sanctuary immediately. The High Savant awaits."

"Excellent!" Belair nods to us all, grabs his gear, and is whisked away. He gives a parting call over his shoulder about seeing us at the feast, and then he is over the bridge and gone.

I stare after him. Shouldn't we all be going straight to the High Savant? Our business is the whistle bone.

The round man reads the confusion on my face. "It is our policy. Non-citizens must meet with the Magistrate first." He sets out again. "Your quarters await."

In a few turns of the path, we arrive at a two-story building with a small courtyard at the entrance.

"Looks like we'll dwell in comfort, at least for a day or two," Piper says quietly.

Once inside, we spread out, surveying the high-ceilinged rooms.

"Attendants will see to your needs. Be sure to let us know if there are any special requirements, dietary or otherwise."

"Fancy," Ash says and flops down on an overstuffed chair. From within the guesthouse come three additional servants, apparently waiting for us. "Refreshments will be brought around shortly." One looks suspiciously at our packs. "We can launder your travel clothes as well and have them cleaned and pressed before the feast."

"Where can we bathe?" Kaylin asks.

"The communal pools are down the left-hand path, through the rosery, and adjacent to the west garden wall. I recommend you use them immediately before refreshment."

"I think he means, before we touch anything else," Kaylin whispers none too quietly to Ash. It makes her smile.

With a bow, our guide leaves us. The three servants stand in a row, awaiting orders.

"The man's right," I say. "Let's take advantage of this warm hospitality. It's the least my brother Petén can do for us." Riveren will charge him full price for board and lodging.

I turn to the servants. "If you wait a moment, we'll have laundry for you, and a light meal would be most appreciated."

One servant steps forward to show us the rooms, but we're already fanning out, claiming our own.

After I check my quarters, I make my way to Ash's. "I want you, Tyche, and Kaylin in the library first thing tomorrow. We aren't staying long, though I know it is tempting."

"Can't wait." Ash drops her gear and tips dirty laundry onto the floor. She peels out of the clothes she'd been in since Kutoon and adds them to the pile. When she's down to her underthings, my brows go up.

"Are you going to stand there gawking or come to the baths?"

I tilt my head. "I think I'll do both?"

"I think you won't!" She laughs and shoves me toward the door. "Go get ready."

"I've seen you in next to nothing since childhood. You don't need to feign modesty with me," I tease.

"Ha!" In her briefs, she pulls out her lavender-and-black lace frock, and gives it a shake. "I can finally wear this while the travel clothes are washed. And tonight, we feast!" She wraps in a white towel that covers her from collar bones to calves and deftly steps out of the rest of her clothes, tossing them on top of the pile.

Kaylin appears at the door, wearing a matching towel slung low on his hips. Ash and I both stare, but no doubt for different reasons. She's probably noticing his form which might be considered flawless. But for me, I'm surprised at the lack of scars. He's been in more sword fights since we met than I have my whole life. Why aren't there any marks? The rest of us certainly have them.

Are you going to ask? De'ral's voice is innocent.

I clear my throat and turn to go.

Kaylin offers his arm to Ash. "Shall we investigate the baths, fair lady?"

"Why, I'd be delighted, kind sir." She blushes and looks to me. "You're coming, aren't you?"

"Of course," I say, grabbing my things and hurrying to catch up. We might as well enjoy this reprieve while we can.

53

MARCUS

I can say without question, the Magistrate knows how to host a feast. I'm not sure how the rest of the city dines tonight, but the halls of the palace are overflowing with food, drink, fancy dressed courtiers, and savants of all robe colors. All in honor of us. It's a good thing we aren't trying to keep our objectives secret. Seems everyone knows our business here in Tangeen.

"Come for our first whistle bone, have you?" a well-dressed official asks. I remember him as connected to the…treasury? "And beat both Atikis and Tann to get it? We're cheering for you, Marcus. Know that!"

I thank him, but draw the line at answering personal questions, like what it's like with my brother on the throne. How does he think that's appropriate? Unless he's a wordsmith writing for the public notice boards. I'm about to ask when Belair sweeps in with Hahmen on his arm. They both know the official and with a few smiles and handshakes, the subject pivots from the throne of Baiseen to less invasive topics. When Belair and I launch into a vivid account of our first run-in with the Aturnians on the way to Aku, Hahmen's eyes brighten. The official, however, excuses himself, looking a little queasy. Objective reached.

"Dance with me?" Belair asks Hahmen and the two are off hand in hand. I'm lost in the music, watching the couples glide around the floor when I feel De'ral wake up.

She's here.

"Who are you talking about?"

Salila.

It's impossible! But as I think it, a woman lays her hand on my shoulder sending a rush of adrenaline through my body.

"Hello, Marcus." She lowers her voice to a whisper. "De'ral."

Salila wears a gown the color of dessert wine. It hugs her figure and ripples as she moves, like sunlight on water. Her brows go up, waiting for a response.

But I am speechless. My chest is dry kindling and she is the match. One twig snaps, and then another, and another until my whole core is ablaze. She's here? How? Why? *"You couldn't have given me a heads up?"* I say to my phantom.

But De'ral makes no explanation or apology. *She came,* he says simply.

"You invited her? Without telling me?" I don't listen for an answer but clear my throat. "Salila, you are—"

Beautiful. Stunning. Magnificent. De'ral has no lack of words.

I finally settle on, "Dressed."

A woman standing near us frowns at my comment. It sounds risqué, but I've never seen her in as much as a stitch. Though maybe it's best not to announce she is Mar. Is she hiding it? Has she done so in the past? My thoughts whirl. "I mean, beautifully dressed." The last word is mostly an exhale. I clear my throat again, trying to pull myself together.

Don't bother. I'm talking to her, not fumbling like a novice.

Great. Outdone by my phantom? I won't let that happen. My heart pounds as I elbow De'ral aside. There is one thing I can do that he cannot. "Salila, shall we dance?"

"I thought you'd never ask." She takes my hand and allows me to lead her onto the crowded floor. Salila is royalty among Mar, I decide. How else could she carry herself so, as if the world was hers to command. People step back, giving way in pure awe of her magnificence.

My hands go to her shoulder and waist as we join in the lively reel. It's familiar and easy for me. I may be the ex-heir now, but the sons of Jacas Adicio can dance. What really surprises me is that she can, too. "Where did you learn?" Surely not underwater.

She leans toward my ear, being of the same height, I realize, and whispers, "In a time and place so long ago, you could not comprehend it."

It's not a slight on my intelligence, but a statement of fact. "Let me try?" I'm pretty certain my heart is going to burst into a million pieces if it beats any faster, what with the feel of her in my arms, her body moving under the weight of my hands, her voice smooth like honey, her scent, magnolias riding a sea breeze—

"You *are* a poet."

I stop my thoughts, realizing she's following them, through De'ral, I guess.

"Come with me!" Salila laughs, and in a flash, she takes my hand in hers and leads me out of the hall. Her graceful walk quickly turns into a sprint.

We whisk past Ash and Kaylin who stop midbeat, Ash's jaw dropping. Kaylin's does, too, for an instant, until his lips form a thin, hard line. Disapproval? It seems we have taken them both by surprise with this little escapade. *Escapade? What am I doing?* I'm too astonished by it all to form a rational thought, or let go of her hand.

She rushes me outside, around a corner and into a breezeway. It's secluded, untouched by the light spilling from the hall. Before I can speak, I'm pressed up against the wall. Her body is so close I can feel the rise and fall of her chest as her mouth hovers inches from mine.

"Now, my lovely lander, son of Baiseen, raiser of the *warrior* De'ral." Her hands pin my arms at my sides as her lips close over mine–and then she's kissing me!

"Let me show you what I've wanted to do since—" She straightens abruptly and lets me go. "Oh, fish flipping sticks!"

"Pardon?" I gasp for breath.

"Drat you, Rosie Red. Can't you follow the simplest instructions?"

"Who's Rosie Red?" Salila speaks to no one I can see.

Then she rests her hand on my cheek so gently it hurts. "I am sorry, Marcus. Duty calls."

"Duty?" I start to say more, but she's gone, vanished, like a dream. "Salila?"

De'ral floods my mind. *She says to tell you, "We'll finish this conversation soon. But meanwhile, I wasn't here."*

"She wasn't here?" But she was. Praise to the old gods, if any still exist. She was.

It's some time before I can smooth out my breathing, and longer still before my heart steadies. I straighten my waistcoat. *"De'ral, can you believe it?"*

You mean you failing to kiss her back? My phantom churns in the depths. *Sadly, I can.* He mumbles abuse as I slide down to sit on the ground.

I lean against the wall, the feel of her lips on mine lingering. Try as I might, I can't comprehend what this encounter could mean.

Then maybe next time you'll ask.

Pressure builds at the thought, because suddenly I am sure De'ral already did.

54

"I said no killing!" Mercy, it takes strength to wrench the man out of her grasp. "Your tomb is as good as crushed now, Rosie Red. What were you thinking?"

"I'm thinking, sister, that your tomb is flattened as well."

My grip loosens. "How so?"

"Teern may have told me to stay under the waves, but he told you to keep me under control. Fine job you're doing of that." Sarcasm mixes with blood and drips from the corners of her mouth.

I grunt. It's like hauling an elephant seal up a cliff, not that I'd ever do that. Love the creatures. Still, there's a comparison to be made.

"Let go!" Rosie says around a mouth full of flesh.

"You let go!" I manage to yank the lander free. He could still be revived, but no. He tears in half, not quite down the middle. Disentangling the mauled legs from my grasp, I let them drop. "Look what you've done."

"Me?" Rosie is still chewing on her half of the body, blood soaking her bare chest. *"You too."*

I hate admitting she's right. If Teern catches us, we're both ruined. Finally, she drops her prey. Well, "drop" isn't entirely true. She gives a little twist as it falls, snapping the spine for good measure. Can't imagine why. Surely, she realizes he's been dead for at least the last few minutes. Peace be his path.

"Peace be what? Are you thinking like a lander now?"

"No, I'm… Get out of my head!"

She smiles as blood pools around the torso. *"What has you flustered, sister?"*

"Nothing!"

The alley is empty this late at night. No one has seen us, yet. They won't see if I snap her insolent neck. But Teern wouldn't be happy about that, either.

While Rosie licks her fingers clean, I sigh, catching the sound of dance music on the breeze. Landers are often so frail, but not Marcus. Not with his *warrior* phantom so close to the surface all the time. They are both strong, and… different. It surprises me.

I shake my head, coming back to the present. "I suppose I'll have to do something with this body as well," I say to the Mar like it's her fault, but I know it isn't. She can't help her propensities, or mine. We both need a drop of lander blood to walk under the sun, to keep the sea inside us at all times, but this is a sight more than one or two drops.

"Come on. Let's clean up." I scoop the body parts, with no help from her at all, and carry them to the beach. "Help me stuff it under the shoal."

"I'd rather take apart the lovely bones and—"

"Shoal. Now!"

The deep-water cove north of the Fancrest River mouth is riddled with them. Shoals, not bodies. Not yet. The bones will come loose, disarticulating as small sea creatures eat away at the flesh and sinew, but by the time bits of him, bits of them, wash ashore, there will be nothing recognizable. A femur here, vertebrae there, if that. I have the coins from his pockets and the travel papers as well. This one was rich.

"Is that important?" Rosie asks mind-to-mind.

"Of course it's important." My dress is ruined. I'm going to need a new one before sunrise.

"Me too?"

"No. You're going back to the sea."

"Make me."

If Teern finds out she killed this man—

"Um, three."

"Three!"

—three men in as many hours, while I was attending a feast in the halls of the Pandom City palace, he'll revoke my land privileges, as the least of it. But that's the beauty of being on land. Teern can't hear us. Can't track us, either. As long as no one else saw, or lives to tell if they did, I'm in the clear. Of course, a certain son of a Magistrate saw me, danced with me even, but he won't tell.

"You danced with the Bone Gatherer?" Rosie askes, her eyebrows jumping. *"What will Teern say about that?"*

I forgot how good Rosie is at picking thoughts right out of a person's head. *"No more than he'll say of your murders, when he doesn't find out."*

She takes the meaning and closes her mouth, for a moment. *"What's he like, the Bone Gatherer? Will I meet him soon? If he's caught your eye, he must be—"*

I grab her around the throat and slam her into the alley wall. "Nothing has been caught, eyes or otherwise. Say another word and I'll pluck yours out of your head."

"Test-tee." She wiggles out of my hold. *"I promise. I won't tell. I won't say a*

word. Please let me walk under the sun. It's been so long."

"Whose fault is that?"

"Mine, and I can't change it. But I promise I won't say a word, if only I can see the sun."

I crack my neck left and right, taking time to consider. "All right. You can stay, but only if you curb your appetite, do what I say, and keep your mouth shut."

"I promise." She sucks on a bone stolen from the last corpse.

"And practice using your speaking voice, just in case, the dead gods forbid, you should need it."

"Oh goodie!" she says aloud. It sounds like a bat screeching from the pits of the underworld.

"Stalking voice, Rosie. Stalking voice."

I lead the way down the street as dawn breaks and the sun peaks over the horizon. My first instinct is to duck into the shade of a tall building. Rosie's, too. It's been a while, and neither of us want to burn until we catch fire, just in case the rules have changed, though Kaylin's a sure example that they have not. Besides, I had a few moments back in Aku, but that was under cloud cover. Best be cautious.

"Is it really safe?" Rosie's voice is a little softer, but it still sounds like a barking dog.

"A drop of blood a day keeps the sunlight at bay." I repeat the rule that allows us to walk on land day or night.

To prove it, I extend my fingers, one knuckle at a time, into the light. "Ha!" It feels warm and gentle on my skin. I twinkle my fingertips and extend them farther until my entire arm is exposed. I follow it with my shoulder, upper body, and legs until I stand there, facing east, basking in the glorious gold, Rosie right beside me. I think I might cry.

When I blink my eyes open, I beam a smile, spotting just what I want. Not far away, a young girl hangs out washing in the early morning sun. The concept isn't foreign to me. The drawback of being landside is needing to stay dry. No dips. No turning up in tearooms with wet hair and soaked clothing. It just isn't done. But I quite like the outfits she pins to the line, a couple of small-waisted, low-cut dresses, one a light sea green with dark lace, the other midnight blue with tiny mother of pearl buttons holding together the cuffs.

"The blue is mine," Rosie says.

"Shh. You need to speak softly." But I don't object to her choice. The green one will match my eyes.

The washing girl herself is in a plain black shift with a white apron. I can see the class system is still well in place here in Tangeen. The moment she goes inside, I unpin the dresses, some silky underthings, and hurry away.

It's awkward, this "hurry away" motion with legs pumping over the ground. I've not done much of it in the last century. Rosie and I giggle. Despite it all, this is fun.

We carry our treasures upriver where no one is about, wash away any stubborn blood stains from skin and hair, and slip on the clean garments. Perfect fits, and long enough to cover our bare feet. We must blend in, and the hems of the dresses assure it. The little non-savant may get away with no shoes, but it's not the impression I care to make.

I scent toward the palace, the grand, heavily guarded building overlooking Pandom City, and know Kaylin is that way. A quick twist and tie secures my long hair loosely on top of my head, letting it spill over one shoulder. "Come on. And don't attract attention."

She pouts.

It's like telling a tiger shark to lose its stripes, but I say it anyway. I'm sure, at my worst, I was never this difficult.

Rosie answers that mental thought with a snort.

The gardens around the palace are adequate. Not as lovely as a Ma'ata grotto, but fair and charming. The scents bombard me though. The seasons on land are sharp and pungent, each in their own way. In the sea, it all makes sense, the migrations, the algae blooms, the shifting currents, the trade winds and whelping seals, otters, and walruses. So noisy. The hatching gulls and the traveling whales—south with gravid bellies, north with calves by their sides—but this isn't the same with its sometimes-acid tastes and clashing colors and textures. I take a deep breath and smoke makes me cough. So much to acclimate to.

"May I help you there?" a man's voice calls out.

I smile. It always starts with the offer of help.

Landers, especially the males, have no sense of caution when it comes to women.

Idiots, really, especially in this case, but it does serve my purpose. "Indeed, I think you may." I shoot a glance at Rosie. *I'll do the talking.*

"Whatever you say, sister."

The guard doesn't return my smile, but I can tell by his posture it's a struggle not to. This man remains official, restrained, and armed. A guard who will require special handling. "I'm visiting from another realm."

"Understatement."

"Shut up!"

I curtsy. "And I find myself attracted to these gardens. They are so lovely."

My arm goes gracefully out toward the greenery and manicured lawns. "Do you guard this parkland? I would so love to have your permission to walk here."

"These are the Magistrate's grounds, miss. I regret most deeply that I cannot give you leave to walk among them without invitation. May I suggest you stay close to your family? I assume they are walking along the river in the public promenade."

"Why on earth and sea would we need to stay with our family?"

"I'll explain later."

The guard takes his occupation much too seriously for my taste. "Yes, our families are on the promenade. We'll return to them at once."

"Families? I thought you were my sister."

I sigh internally. *"Stop asking so many questions."*

I give the guard another curtsy, as does Rosie and we retreat. Kaylin is still behind the palace gate. As is Marcus. I smile to myself, remembering his touch last night. The kiss… All in all, I managed a fair bit of banter and dance before Rosie interrupted. Such a spoilsport. But all is well. More opportunities will present themselves; I am sure. With that thought, I jingle the gold coins in my pocket and set out for the shops. I think I will buy a purse, and maybe a fish for breakfast.

"And one for me?"

"No, not one for you."

"Salila." She takes my hand. *"Won't you at least try and forgive me?"*

A landslide of images jolt through my mind and I jerk my hand away. It began with the tremors in the harbor. The explosions on the dock, the flames, the books and scrolls, the library itself, all consumed before I could stop it. And my Xandria? There was not enough of her left for even the Ma'ata to save. All because of Dreaded. Rosie. Red.

"I will never forgive you."

Rosie looks down. For a fraction of a second, a true emotion crosses her face. Regret, I think. Or maybe a fleeting sadness.

I exhale forcefully. "But we can, for a brief time, call a truce."

She spins back, the corners of her mouth lifting. "How generous of you." She skips beside me like a child, drawing attention. "Now, if you won't tell me more of Marcus, tell me everything about Kaylin and this girl. The one Teern was talking about. Ash, is it?" Her enthusiasm rises with her voice.

"All right, I will. But we are going into that shop." I point down the street. "And I need you to speak softly, Rosie. Please."

"I promise!" she shouts and then tries again, a little quieter. "I promise."

55

ASH

It's a fresh, sunny morning, perfect for a walk to the library.

"Perfect with one bright sun and one red not but a few hands away." My inner voice is not in the least perturbed by the twinkling red day star that I am sure has doubled in size since we left Nonnova.

We need to learn more about the second sun.

"Besides death, the changes in climate, and the next Great Dying?"

Yes, besides that. I take a serious tone. After last night's soak in the cerulean-tiled baths… My face heats at the thought. It was quite the situation, water up to my neck, steam rising as I soaked between Kaylin and Marcus. Their banter was entertaining, but I admit I felt relief when Belair arrived, followed by the others. With all of the company together in the dim, candlelit bathhouse, our thoughts turned to the tasks before us.

"And then, we feasted."

And danced. I smile and blush again. We didn't exactly have the long-promised talk, but somehow neither of us wanted to spend the night in that kind of discussion. To be sure, we hardly used words at all.

I quicken my pace to catch up to Kaylin and Tyche walking ahead. It's like I'm a new person. Red-robe attacks, hidden bones, and betraying captains seem like a distant dream. And I'm not the only one feeling renewed.

It was wonderful to find Belair having so much fun with Hahmen. I don't know why he didn't tell me they were serious.

"Sometimes, the heart is afraid to speak, for fear of breaking the spell," my wise inner voice says.

Yes, sometimes. I guess.

Is that what Marcus is doing, too? With Salila? I couldn't believe my eyes when I saw her last night. What in the world was she doing at the feast?

"Dancing with Marcus."

A bubble of laughter rises at the memory. Kaylin tried to stop me when I chased after them. I thought he was in danger! But I quickly turned back, red faced. He was not in trouble, at least not any he wanted to be rescued from. I will get the full story from him tonight even if it makes him squirm.

But for now, I'm carefree, walking under the blue sky.

"Though it is lit by two suns?"

Yes. Though lit by two suns. I am sure there is no danger on our path today. All our foes and challenges may still be before us, but for now, we're safe, and the library awaits.

As we head for the business district, I smell Ochee tea, the spiced drink Tangeen is famous for. "Let's get some," I suggest, my mouth watering. "And I want to stop there." I point to the saddlemaker's shop. "To check for waterproofing."

But Kaylin isn't listening. Tyche and I keep walking for a few steps before realizing he has stopped in front of a side alley.

"Tea is this way," I say, but he's focused so intently he doesn't appear to have heard me. I study the scene, trying to work out what has him fascinated.

A matron and several officials are firing questions at a serving girl dressed in a black shift with a white pinafore. She's in tears and I wonder who wouldn't be, the way they interrogate her. She points at a large empty space in the clothesline strung between two stoops. Another official shows much interest in the ground nearby.

"Move along." A Tangeen guard steps up to wave us away.

I grab Kaylin's sleeve, but he's glued to the spot. "What happened here?" he asks.

"Palace business," the guard says and pushes his spear arm forward. It's pointed skyward, but still, this is Kaylin. He would love a little challenge before breakfast.

"Come on," I whisper. "Library, remember?"

Finally, he yields to me, but I don't exhale until we are farther down the block. "What was that about?"

Kaylin shakes his head. "Palace business," he says, echoing the guard. Tyche and I jog to keep up as he quickens the pace, the idea of shopping abandoned.

"Since when is the palace concerned with a stolen outfit?" I ask, putting the scene together.

"Ah lass," he says, shaking off the peculiar mood. "That's one of the mysteries of Tangeen. A people obsessed with fashion."

The library is down two more streets and around a corner. When we reach it, I lift my lavender skirts to trot up the steps behind Kaylin. "Do we have to arrive breathless?" I ask. He pauses at the top and turns to me, or rather, turns to scan the street below.

"Are we being followed?" I whisper, remembering the cabin boy on the *Dugong*.

"Maybe. Let's move inside."

I glance over my shoulder but see nothing suspicious.

"After you?" Kaylin pushes through the grand doors, and steps aside to let me and Tyche pass.

The heavenly scent of polished wood, leather bindings, scrolls, and ink wafts over me. I take a deep breath and smile wide. The aromas and the echoing vastness of the building settles over us in a hushed silence. It's not my first time here, but the feeling never goes away, the feeling of being welcome, home among the books.

"Very nice," Tyche says as she takes a deep breath in. I see she takes comfort in it, too.

"Indeed." I gaze at the two-story high shelves. I don't compare it again to Aku, since Tann burnt her library to the ground, but it's good to see her brighten.

Kaylin touches my shoulder. "Ready to go to work?"

He's right. We still first have to convince the library master to let us study the reference materials that are no doubt archived under lock and key. "I'm ready." Together we walk to the reception desk.

The woman sitting on the high stool looks up from her work as we approach. It's our first bit of good luck, since Belair and Hahmen were called back to the Sanctuary at dawn. I'd been hoping for his introduction here, but don't need it. "I know her," I whisper to Kaylin. "Let me talk."

Kaylin holds back as I lead the way.

"Mistress Lucia, good morning. I can see you've been elevated." I smile at my pun, knowing the woman will appreciate it. "Congratulations."

Last autumn, Lucia had been studying for her full scribe honors, the qualification that would allow her to oversee the running of the Pandom City library, among other things. Unlike Palrio, and most other realms, Tangeen books and records are kept in a public building, not solely in the Sanctuary. It's a recent development. Still, we need to gain three access passes and show good reason for deserving them. With Lucia in charge, our chances of success are good.

"Miss Ash of Baiseen. I wasn't told of your return." Mistress Lucia studies the three of us, a hint of a smile behind the new air of authority. "Are you here with Marcus Adicio? His recorder?"

It doesn't surprise me that she, and the entire city, knows of the Bone Gatherer's presence by now. "Yes, I am his official recorder." My chest swells as I say it.

"Then we have both been elevated. Congratulations."

"Thank you." I curtsy.

Under her scrutiny, I'm glad we all bathed and donned freshly laundered clothes. Tyche makes a powerful impression in her orange savant robes, tailored after the fashion of Aku—hem to the floor, bell sleeves trimmed with blood-orange piping. I'm in the same lavender dress Lucia had seen me wear the last time I was here, and probably the time before that, but it's clean and pressed and lovely, thanks to the all-night palace staff. And Kaylin, he looks good at the worst of times, and this is hardly that. He has on a clean white shirt with an open neck and billowing sleeves—no blood stains, for once—dark sailor pants, and buffed leather boots. I persuaded him to leave his sword back at the apartment as weapons are frowned upon in the library, but I know he has long knives tucked inside those boots of his. It's the only reason he wears them. Meanwhile, I'm confident we make a presentable if somewhat unique group. "We have come at the behest of the Bone Gatherer, in search of specific texts."

"Excellent." She lets the smile out and I resist the urge to roll my eyes, remembering the infatuation she has for Marcus. She used to drill me about him until I thought my hair would stand out straight. "Will Marcus Adicio be joining the rest of your party?" She looks to the doors as if he'll walk in any moment.

"He's in conference with the Magistrate this morning, and I and my companions were directed here." I don't say by whom, but if she interprets it to be by the Magistrate, all the better. "But there is a chance that Marcus will need a pass here, too, as we have much research ahead of us, if we have time." It's not an intentional incentive, but it can't hurt. "May we acquire passes?"

Mistress Lucia's face doesn't alter. "As his recorder, I would think you'd be present at the conference."

"He assigned me to this urgent research task. May I introduce my friends?" I nudge Kaylin into her line of sight. "This is Kaylin from the isles of Tutapa and Tyche, granddaughter of the High Savant of Aku."

"Aku," she says, staying long on the second syllable. "Well met." She turns to Kaylin. "Tutapa?" She lights up.

I knew both would impress.

"Naturally, I will award you the passes. Ash, your registration is still current." She pulls out a parchment from her desk drawer and dips her quill into the ink bottle. "I trust nothing has changed between you and the Sanctuary of Baiseen since we last spoke? Still in high esteem?"

"That hasn't changed," I say, a little too quickly. It's not a lie. I am still Marcus's recorder. It's just that he isn't the Heir of Baiseen anymore. She has to know that, too.

"This is very kind of you," Kaylin says as he steps forward.

Mistress Lucia blushes. "All in line with protocol, I assure you."

Kaylin leans toward me. "We do enjoy keeping to the protocols, don't we, Ash?"

I clear my throat. "Can I slip down to the archives as well? I'm working on a historical study, the early relations between Tangeen, Sierrak, and Palrio. For Master Brogal." Now that's definitely an exaggeration.

Lucia frowns. "You will need special permission for that area."

"The authority is not still in my record?" I stand on tiptoe but can't see over the desk to look at her record book. "I was in the archive rooms last visit."

Lucia studies the document. "I see you're right." She sets it aside, convinced. "There is much in the basement on your topic. We have the journals of Bryden and Hatcheren," she says.

"Perfect! And the Letters of Er? Would they be there, too?" Knowing will save us time in the search.

Lucia's head comes up. "The Letters of Er?"

"They refer to the earliest treaties and alignments of the original realms," I explain.

"So they do." The woman finally nods. "We have some of the letters but not the entire set, you understand."

"I can't wait to read them."

Kaylin adds his smile and the keys to the downstairs rooms are handed over without further discussion. I thank her, trying not to make my way there at a dead run. But Lucia is off her stool and leading us there herself, which keeps us all moving in a stately manner.

"Let's get to work," I say when Mistress Lucia leaves. "Tyche, you search the index for anything on the original whistle bones and the formation of the crown."

"I'll look for passages about the Bone Gatherer, too."

"Perfect."

"Keep an eye out for maps more than five centuries old. Many were done with topographical drawings of the 'Bones of Er' to mark the locations of the original sanctuaries. It'll help us work out which ones Tann has already."

"I'll look for more on the return of the second sun and the next Great Dying," Kaylin says.

"And I'll find the Letters of Er themselves." I lead the way across the hall to the archives and we flow into the room, tackling our tasks. I hope that before this is over, we find out how to hold the bones we are gathering, and *call* the remaining from Tann, or whoever else may have them by then. And, why it is so important to do so.

• • •

"I think I found something," Tyche says a few hours into our research. Kaylin and I put down our work and lean toward her.

"It's a poem about Natsari. Do you know the name?"

Chills wash over me as she reads aloud.

Natsari, Natsari, where hides the crown?
The forests are burning, the children are drowned.
Natsari, Natsari, bring the dark sun,
Kiss us farewell, the Great Dying's begun...
Natsari, Natsari, call up the shades,
Lingering shadows of warrior blades.
Natsari, Natsari, unearth the bones,
Gather them all, lest we turn to stone.

"I know those verses," I whisper. "Where did you find them?"

She points over her shoulder to the shelf behind her. "It seems that there is a line of black-robes connected to Natsari."

"Connected?" Kaylin says.

"Or predicted to be? The last in their line will herald the renewal, but it doesn't say what that might be." She weighs open a scroll and reads more. *Raven Japera, black-robe of Steepwater, mother of Sul Japera—black-robe of Whitewing, mother of Ashketon Japera—deemed marred, deceased.*

Inside, my guts tighten. Where have I heard this before?

"That irony is cruel," Kaylin says.

I cock my head.

"That a black-robe Bone Thrower found their child marred?"

The thought stops me cold. "They wouldn't let a black-robe throw the bones for their own offspring, surely." I tap my chin. "But more to the point, it could mean that this Japera line threw the bones for the Natsari. Is it an ally against the second sun?"

"Old verses are often metaphorical," Kaylin says. "But the last of the line was marred. Sacrificed to the sea. Sounds like the family line ended there."

My inner voice groans like it's been hit with a shovel.

You disagree?

"No."

Agree?

"No."

What then?

"I can't say."

You've never held back an opinion before. Why now—

"You are not listening. I am unable to say."

This is the strangest conversation I've had with myself yet. I can move and breathe and speak just fine. But as my hand touches a leather tomb high on the shelf, I motion Kaylin for help.

He hoists it down and together, we read the title.

"This is it! The Letters of Er. The first ten volumes, it seems." I start reading, searching for any information on the crown of bones. An hour into it, I put my hand over my mouth. "Viz'n fqad."

"What is it?" Kaylin and Tyche ask at the same time. They are up and out of their chairs to look over my shoulder.

I shake my head and hand the tome to Tyche. As the girl reads, tears well in her eyes. Kaylin hovers. "Let me see?"

Tyche hands it to him, and I watch his expression change from curiosity to a blankness I don't know how to interpret. Kaylin silently passes the book back to me. "Explains a bit," he says. "About those cowled brothers and their bone chest on Aku."

"Brothers and sisters," Tyche corrects him.

"They call themselves the Brotherhood of Anon." I clear my throat and read aloud. "To hold the bones of Er, rendering them safe from a southern phantom's *call*, submerge them in the blood of the savant who first summoned them. It is…" The script is unreadable for a section, and I skip ahead. "…the blood of the caller binds that which is *called*. So be the path of Er's bones. So be the savant's lot."

"It's why he cut my grandmother's throat and drained it into the chest," Tyche says as her tears continue. "I won't be able to *call* Tann's bones, if he bloods each one that way. Nobody will. And the bones I call—" She looks up at us with her dark, round eyes. "You'll have to kill me to keep them."

"That's not going to happen," I whisper, but Kaylin speaks at the same time.

"But wasn't it you, little lass, who called Aku's whistle bone for Tann, not Yuki?"

Tyche holds still. "Then I don't understand."

"Is it the blood of the family line? Maybe that's what these genealogies are saying."

"We need to read the full passage." I squint at the yellowing scroll. "Kaylin, do you have a magnifying glass?"

He shakes his head.

"I'll borrow one from Lucia. Won't be a moment." I give Tyche a hug and leave. "Don't fret. We'll figure it out."

I trot up the steps, my mind hundreds of miles away, to that awful bone chest of Tann's, wondering where it is now and how many callers died to fill it with blood.

56

MARCUS

The second bell echoes through the palace grounds as the guards open the reception hall for us.

"Prompt," Piper whispers to me.

"As it should be." I'm still a little annoyed that we weren't allowed an immediate audience at the Sanctuary, but I admit the rest and food have been more than decent. And the dancing. I can't quite believe that it was really Salila.

I can. De'ral's voice rumbles through me.

"The Magistrate will see you now." The guard interrupts my inner thoughts. Piper, Samsen, and I follow him into the hall. There are courtiers and council members gathered as well.

"The High Savant is here, too," Piper says softly.

"This should speed things up," Samsen adds. "He's the one we need to speak to."

But it has me wondering. Everyone at the feast seemed aware of our business, and the significance of the second sun. Yet instead of feeling dread for the impending doom, they were swept up in the celebration. Almost rejoicing, as if this were a great opportunity. I must discuss it with Ash tonight.

For her non-savant perspective? His voice is bone dry.

"No, for her knowledge." I rub my brow. *"Can we focus on what's happening here?"*

Standing in front of the dais, I take the chance to study the visual hierarchy. Master Havest stands to the side, a tall, lean figure with white hair and flowing red robes. Stein Riveren, on the other hand, fills the throne like he rules all of Amassia from it.

Would that be such a bad thing?

I'm not sure where that thought comes from, me or De'ral, but it's true. Riveren came to the throne years ago and has improved all aspects of the realm. But does that include the Sanctuaries and savants? *"Maybe, or maybe not."* I put a smile on my face, ready for the greeting.

The Magistrate diverts his eyes as a messenger hands him a scroll. He reads it briefly and nods, then gives us his full attention. So far, this is nothing different than my father would have done. "Marcus Adicio and company! Welcome to Pandom City."

He said that yesterday.

"It's a formality," I say to my phantom. *"Please stop distracting me."* I give a slight bow to the Magistrate. Beside me, Samsen and Piper do the same, only they bow deeper. "I have come at the behest of the High Savant of Baiseen to—"

"Hold, Marcus." Riveren claps his hands, cutting me off. "We know your purpose in Tangeen. Of course we do! No one is blind to the second sun rising, after all, and I promise, our scholars are scouring the ancient text to illuminate what it might mean. Your recorder has been given access to the archives as well, if you are wondering. The sooner you gather the first whistle bones, the better, in my book. Just in case the lore is true."

Sounds like they are watching Ash and the others. De'ral is not his usual, dismissive self this morning. Actually, he's been quite talkative since last night. Since Salila. I shake thoughts of the Mar out of my head. *"Do you sense Ash?"*

She is surrounded by books, De'ral says. *But the Magistrate awaits.*

"For what?"

I don't know. I was talking to you.

"It's too raw to discuss. I see that now." The Magistrate's face softens. "Let me say again, I am sorry to hear news of your father's death. Peace be his path."

"Peace be his path," Samsen, Piper, and I say in unison.

The Magistrate goes on. "Off you go with Havest." He waves us away. "I meant it. The sooner you gather the whistle bones, the better." He gazes at me with the confidence of a man who will hear everything moments after our meeting with the High Savant ends. "To the Sanctuary, all of you, and with my blessings. But come find me, Marcus, before you set out again. I have something your father gave me. He would want you to have it."

I doubt that. Father wasn't one for sentimentality. "Of course, Magistrate."

Maybe you don't know everything about your father.

My guts tighten. *"I'm not sure I want to."*

The Magistrate motions to his recorder who exchanges a scroll with Piper, simple minutes of this audience. Guards step up to escort us out a side door.

"For setting aside formalities, there seem to still be plenty of them," Piper says. "But I daresay Ash will be making good use of her time in the archives."

"No argument there. But did you notice—"

"Marcus?" Piper touches my sleeve when I hesitate.

"Later," I say out the side of my mouth. And then louder I add, "Hopefully

Havest will have information to pass on as well."

We are led across a long fairway. It's hemmed by green circular rings surrounded by sloping sand pits. Ash described this new landscape between the palace and the Sanctuary on the sail up the Nulsea. They call it a nature strip, designed for sport, one that involves hitting a small hard ball with a long, thin club. The greens are empty of players this morning, though our guide looks warily in both directions before leading us across.

"This feels more familiar," Piper says as we enter the Sanctuary of Tangeen. "We've found the savants."

She's not wrong. The Sanctuary is a city unto itself, one filled with the colorful robes of savants and young potentials. It's much like Baiseen's, with long covered breezeways, large halls and studies, and a central field where savants raise and train with their phantoms. But different also. The buildings are all connected by sculptures. Belair would have a name for the geometric symmetry, but he knows more about architecture than I do.

As a bell rings, a rush of students spill out of the dining hall. The aromas pour out with them. It makes my mouth water.

"This way," Havest says as he waves us on. "We'll take refreshment in my quarters and discuss details there."

"That's promising," Samsen says when the High Savant's back is turned.

He's right. Maybe between Havest and Ash's time in the library, we'll have new insights for our quest. Finally!

57

KAYLIN

The little lass has warmed to me, but that doesn't mean we're easy company when left alone with each other. Especially considering the last time, when I dragged her under the waves, kicking and screaming. For her own safety, but still. The silence grows long.

Her eyes dart around the room, glancing off me, to the scroll, up to the lanterns. She ends up anchoring her sight to the text we just read.

"So." I clear my throat. "We're closer to an answer at least."

She doesn't respond to that, and I try again.

"It helps to remember we don't necessarily have a full, or accurate, translation yet."

Tears roll down her cheeks.

Mother of Ma'ata, I am not equipped for this. "Ash will be back any moment." The sooner the better. *"How's the magnifying glass coming along?"* I send her the thought.

"Kaylin, it's—" Her voice sounds excited but then cuts off.

"What's that, lass?"

When she doesn't answer, I lean toward Tyche from across the table. The girl looks up and meets my eyes. "Tyche, I know we don't quite…"

"Trust?" she offers.

"I was going to say, understand each other, but know that I will protect you, and Ash. I will not let harm come to either of you, on land or sea. It is more than a promise. It is truth."

Tyche lets out her breath.

I can tell it isn't what she expected me to say.

"I rescued your little friend there, didn't I?" I motion to the toy impala sticking out of her pocket.

She tucks it in deeper and nods. "How'd you find him?" Curiosity lightens her voice.

I smile, rubbing my hands together. "I was galloping flat-chat across the Suni headland, the giant red-robe phantom right behind us."

"Marcus…?"

"Ha! Marcus Adicio was passed out over my horse's shoulders. I can assure you; the weight of him slowed us down. But it also had me watching the turf, my cheek pressed against the animal's neck, scanning for gopher holes while pinning Marcus with my shoulder. A few strides ahead, I saw your companion, clear as a bright star on the horizon. It was the button eyes."

"Eye," Tyche says. "He only has one now." She pulls the impala out as proof. Then she cradles it in her lap, eyes welling again. "My grandma made him for me, before I ever raised my phantom."

"So Ash told me." Ash, who seems to be taking too long. *"Did you find the magnifying glass?"* I wait for her answer. "Maybe they had to send to Sierrak for it."

Tyche gives a hint of a smile back and makes to get out of her chair.

I shake my head. "I'll go see. Just be a moment." I stay calm, not wanting to alarm the little caller. It's the Pandom City Library. What harm could befall her here? But the scent of blood in the alley, the signs of struggle, it smacks of Salila, and wherever she is, Rosie Red won't be far behind. *"Salila? You best not be playing games with me."*

I bound up the steps two at a time.

The closer I come to the dais where Lucia still perches on her high stool, leaning forward, nose in a book, the more my thoughts rage. *"Ash? Did you find it?"*

Dread sinks into the pit of my stomach and I speak out before reaching the dais. "We seem to be missing Ash." I try not to sound panicked. I mean, when was the last time anything made me truly anxious?

Lucia doesn't move.

"Madame librarian? Are you awake?" But close up, I can see that she will never wake again. I hop up to the dais and feel for a pulse as Lucia tips sideways out of her chair. A magnifying glass falls from her hand and clatters onto the floor beside her. Not Salila's or Rosie's work. The body is untouched.

Conflicting thoughts scream through my head at the speed of a comet. Thoughts I can't slow down. My guts tell me to run after Ash, to head straight for the street and pick up her trail, but at the same time, it could be a trick to distract me while they…what? Assassinate Marcus and steal the bones? *"Salila! Where are you? Ash is missing!"*

There's no answer from her.

I'm tempted to call to one of the phantoms in our company, though doing that, if it even worked, would reveal me as something other than what I say

I am. It can't be risked. I clench my fists, ready to bolt, but which way? Then I remember Tyche in the basement. She's a target, too, one I'd just swore to protect by all means. I push hair out of my eyes and fly back to her.

"Get your pack," I say under my breath as I burst into the room.

Tyche startles, jumping up and tipping her chair over backward. "Where's Ash?"

"Taken." I will not lie to her.

She gasps, and I grab her shoulders, turning her to face me. "They will be watching for us, for you. We will act like nothing has happened and get out of here."

"But Ash, we can't just let them—"

"I know. And I don't intend to." I keep Tyche in my grip. "First, we leave the library, calm as a cat in summer, and lose anyone set to follow us." I stuff things into my bag, and Ash's, maps, textbooks, anything she had her eye on.

Tyche hesitates to do the same.

"We may need these documents more than anyone on Amassia ever will again. Pack 'em up."

She does, though her hands shake.

I slide all three chairs back under the table and leave the room exactly the way we'd found it, save for a few less books. Upstairs, Lucia is sprawled on the floor where she fell. I put myself between the body and Tyche, whose bag is bulging. I will have to teach her the art of packing like a thief if the opportunity arises.

"What happened to her?" Tyche asks, dragging her eyes from the body.

"She died; peace be her path."

"Did you…?"

"No, little lass." I let out an exasperated breath. "Whoever took Ash did it. Hurry." I guide her in front of me and follow her out the grand doors and onto the street, scanning the boulevard up and down as if looking for a carriage. Opposite us, near the river, are two savants, conspicuous in their artful loitering. Everyone else is headed somewhere, in conversation or working in the shops, sweeping the paths, but these two are waiting for something, or someone.

"Are they watching us?" Tyche asks as she looks the other way.

"Let's find out." I take her hand and feel her flinch but don't let go. "If they're following us, it's best we behave as naturally as possible."

"Holding your hand is not natural to me," she says out the side of her mouth, then points at a four-horse carriage.

"Can you pretend?"

"Oh look! All blacks," she says and points at the horses. "With matching white socks."

"Better, but don't overdo it." I lead her closer and bargain with the driver. Keeping us hidden by the carriage so our pursuers can't see, I open the door and then close it in front of us. "We aren't taking this one," I whisper.

"Why not?"

I tip my thumb at the carriage drawn up behind us. It's smaller and pulled by two unmatched horses, one brown and one gray. Both look half asleep. Blocked by the bigger carriage, I hand the second driver more coin than he deserves to take us to the palace, and we get in. The carriage smells musty.

Tyche makes a face. "I like the look of the first one better."

I remind myself that regardless of her orange-robe stature, Tyche is still very young.

The clip-clop from the first carriage tells me they are taking off and I peek through the blind, watching it disappear down the boulevard. The loitering savants follow. I raise my brow. "Now do you see?"

"They think we're in the first carriage."

I nod.

"The orange-robe, I know him from Baiseen," she says. "But he was a yellow-robe then. His phantom's a jackal *caller*. We fought together when Tann attacked."

I look again and she's right. "Larseen, is it?"

"That's his name. He and Marcus are friends."

Slowly our carriage pivots as the horses pull us in the opposite direction. I open the carriage door and edge toward the step.

Her eyes suddenly widen. "You're leaving me?"

"To check the harbor for ships putting out and see how far Larseen follows the carriage."

"But I…"

"Don't worry. I'll be back before you reach the palace. Just keep the shade drawn and then go straight to our apartment."

She slumps. "Find her!"

"Aye, little lass. On my life, I will."

High Savant Havest's quarters are larger than Master Brogal's, but the windows are narrow and the walls made of brick, so in spite of the size, it feels cramped. That may also be due to the number of savants squeezing in. The conference table seats twelve but there are at least twenty here, chairs edged in tight. I wish one of them was Belair, but I haven't seen him since last night.

Once Havest makes the introductions, I take a long, refreshing drink from the fine crystal cup and clear my throat. "Allow me to pass on regards, and a formal message from Master Brogal." I nod to Piper and she hands over a scroll to Havest.

He taps it lightly on his palm, then sets it down. "Excellent, but first, we eat." The High Savant waves to several blue-robes who begin serving. I glance at Samsen and exchange a look. I don't remember this much emphasis on food and drink during past visits. Good news is, there's no suggestion of failed crops or drought like we saw farther north. I make a mental note to ask about it. If I can get a word in. Every savant at the table is talking to me at once.

Finally, after a morning tea of roast goose, roots, greens, and sourdough bread followed by apple pie topped with cream, Havest breaks the seal on the scroll and reads the short message. He then folds his hands, studying them for a time. "The Great Dying. It's nothing to ignore, though the temptation to do so is high."

"Can you tell us more about it, Master? My recorder is researching at this moment, but anything you can add to our understanding would be helpful."

He exhales, shaking his head. "The lore says that if this quest of yours fails, it's the end of it all."

"All?" Piper says. Her hand goes to her belly, eyes to Samsen.

He nods.

"But Master, even if we fail, old gods forbid, to gather the bones, protect the allied realms… It would be bad, yes, but *so goes the path*. There is always the next round on the lots to An'awntia. Our next path would be—"

"Most likely gone," Havest cuts in. "According to lore."

"How can you say that?" I ask.

"When the Great Dying comes, there is no ascension, no next step along the path. How can there be, with none of our species left to carry on?"

"None left?" Samsen takes Piper's hand.

"Not for millions of years, if ever." He shrugs, clearly at peace with it, or just not believing it would really come to that.

My mouth hangs open. Ash would have a further question, but I am completely lost.

Havest sighs. "It's evolution, Marcus. How far along the path can you journey in the vessel of an algae? A mold or lichen?"

We sit with the gravity of that statement. "What then of the souls?" I finally ask.

"It's unclear." Havest rubs his forehead. "Maybe they wander the pathless voids, never reaching the end."

"Like shades," I whisper.

"Yes, perhaps like that," the High Savant says, "but here we call them shadows."

The table quiets, all the clatter of forks and cups replaced by weighted silence.

Havest is the first to break the mood. "So let's not fail!"

"Hear, hear!" The savants clink their mugs together and resume their enthusiasm.

I'm speechless. How are they so mercurial about this?

"For now, the important issue is Tangeen's first whistle bones."

"Ma'ata and Mummy Wheat," I say. Ash drilled me on both and I'm ready. "Ma'ata, the fourth lot of An'awntia, is named for the legendary coral said to have properties of regeneration. Mummy Wheat, the sixth lot, represents the power of the mind to order manifest reality."

"You've studied, Bone Gatherer." He seems surprised.

Ash is the one who studies. You can't take credit.

"I know, but let's allow him some confidence in me for a moment."

The moment won't last long. I'm already out of things to say on the topic. I miss Ash and realize how much I rely on her, and always have. I'll remember to tell her so tonight when I give her the slice of apple pie I'm saving. She deserves more recognition from me. From us all.

"Do you know about the true Ma'ata coral for which the whistle bone was named?" Havest doesn't let me answer. "Its tendrils are said to rise from the bones of the old gods."

The bones of the old gods? There are no tales of the ancient pantheon leaving their bones behind when they abandoned us.

Salila says they are the Ma'ata corals themselves.

My neck stiffens at De'ral's comment. *"You discuss theology with her now?"*

No more or less than any other day.

I don't even try to respond to that.

"But the original whistle bone isn't made of coral, is it?" Piper asks.

"No, they share a name only. The Ma'ata whistle bone was carved from Er's leg."

"And the other Tangeen whistle bone?" I ask.

"Ah, Mummy Wheat." Havest's face softens. "This bone was also linked to the Ma'ata…"

The Ma'ata and the Mar.

It makes me wonder if Brogal's message mentioned our Mar encounters. Would he speak of it, or keep silent? Should I mention it now? I wish I knew what was in the message, but I couldn't break the seal, and Brogal didn't prepare me.

Havest goes on. "Mummy Wheat is carved from the great King Er's arm bone with grains etched as if they were sprouting from an entombed savant. It's an honor just to look upon it."

I don't understand this depiction. Savants are not entombed. We are cremated. A custom fueled by the fear of creating shades. Of course, if Havest is right about the next Great Dying, we might all soon be lost to wander the pathless ways. Eternally.

"Master Brogal said we will find Mummy Wheat in Whitewing?" I steer him back on topic.

"True. Tangeen's oldest Sanctuary to the North along the coast of Nulsea."

"Bordering Sierrak," Samsen adds, though we all know this.

Havest looks grim. "Bordering's one way to put it."

"Master?"

"You think the demarcation of the realms is immutable? Over the centuries, battles have been won and lost. Whitewing has been claimed by both realms at various times in history."

I don't argue. Whitewing is known for its differences more than its similarities to other Tangeen cities. "It's on the way." I know our journey will take us to Sierrak next.

After much discussion and more ceremonial toasts, Havest finally presents me with his Sanctuary's first whistle bone, along with extensive, point-form instructions on its care and handling. Way beyond what is necessary, even for this ancient artifact. Really, I am not putting it in a glass case. There just isn't time to procure one, for starters.

Eventually, Havest bids us farewell and a safe journey. I lead the way toward the palace grounds where we will repack for our journey to Whitewing, with the promise that Belair will join us this evening. He has other duties, for now. As we hurry over the fairway, looking both ways for flying balls, Samsen grasps my arm.

"Is that Larseen?"

I peer into the distance. "I think you're right." I cup my hands around my mouth. "Larseen! Oi! Lars!"

The savant hesitates, but then jogs our way.

"Marcus. What luck to see you," he says and nods to Samsen and Piper.

I slap my old friend on the back. "By the bones, what are you doing here?"

"Military strategic council." His chest expands as he speaks. "We're negotiating tactical plans."

"Come back to our quarters," I say a little loudly. "We'll share news."

Larseen glances in the direction of the palace, again hesitating before shaking it off. "Sure. I've a bit of time. Lead on." Oddly, he takes a final glance at the palace, then hurries to catch up to my side.

On our way to the guest apartments, I tell Larseen about Atikis and his attacks both by land and sea. Piper and Samsen add their perspectives, and by the time we're inside and served a pot of Ochee tea, Larseen is wide-eyed and riveted.

Is he?

De'ral is right. I know Lars well and this is not how he normally responds to surprise. I think he already knows, which makes sense if Brogal told him, but then why pretend ignorance? "That's not the half of it," I say, hiding my suspicions. "Wait until you hear what happened on Bakton."

"The old temple island?" Larseen's jaw drops. "You went there?"

"Don't be so surprised, Lars. As the Bone Gatherer, I must enter the heart of six of the twelve ancient sanctuaries." I'm boasting about it, as much as an ex-heir who lost his throne can.

Servants bring more hot water and a plate of dried fruit and cheese. I would have thought we'd be much too full to eat again but we manage to keep Larseen company at the table. Might as well. We may not have a chance to eat our fill when traveling the roads of Sierrak.

Between bites, I describe the lava covered island until reaching the part about the ghost phantoms. "Ash will have to tell the rest. I swear you won't believe it from me."

"Where is she?" Larseen asks. His eyes go to the stairs. "Not still in bed, I trust?"

"Library. She'll be back this evening when—"

I nearly drop my cup when Kaylin bursts into the apartment.

"Is Ash here?" he shouts at me as if I'm a common servant, his voice dragon deep. Tyche sprints past him, running straight for Piper's arms. The healer holds her tight, and all heads turn to Kaylin. He's drawn his sword.

"What are you doing here?" He levels his weapon at Larseen.

"I could ask the same." Lars draws his sword in response.

I'm up so fast the table knocks over. "There must be a misunderstanding."

I give Kaylin a questioning look, but his eyes haven't left the orange-robe's. I maneuver between them. "What's this about Ash?"

"Why not let your friend enlighten us." Kaylin steps sideways to give Larseen a piercing stare. "You were the last to see her, were you not?"

"Last?" I raise my voice as De'ral fights me for the surface. "Explain!"

"I assure you; I have no idea." Larseen shakes his head. "Your sailor's been drinking."

"He doesn't drink," Samsen and Piper say at the same time.

"He's delusional then." Lars has the sense to take a step back when he says that.

"Really?" Kaylin still holds his eyes as if he can extract answers straight out of his head.

I admit he does look a little crazed right now.

"You were outside the library, moments after Ash disappeared, and the librarian was found dead."

"Ash disappeared?" I bark as De'ral roars inside me. *"Where is she?"* I snap at my phantom.

I can't hear her.

I don't want to panic or leap to what that might mean but all I can think is that if De'ral's lost track of her, she must be far away, or over water. "The librarian's dead?" I ask.

"She is, and this savant needs to explain himself," Kaylin demands.

"To a sailor?" Larseen looks to me. "I will not."

"Then explain it to me! Both of you." It's a command that shakes the room, De'ral barely contained under my skin.

"Of course." Lars speaks only to me. "I was on the promenade. Your sailor would have seen me there, but I know nothing of Ash. We didn't cross paths." His brow beads with sweat and his eyes dart away to the door.

"You expect me to believe that?" Kaylin growls at him.

While I struggle with my phantom, Larseen grips the hilt of his sword and steps around me to face Kaylin again. "I don't expect anything from you, non-savant."

"Are her things here?" Kaylin asks as he turns to me, now ignoring Larseen.

Samsen and Piper make a quick search. Ash's gear is found, just as she left it this morning. I question the servants. No one has entered the apartment, according to them, but Kaylin points out that servants can be bought.

"There has to be an explanation," I say as panic rises in my throat. "How did this happen?"

Kaylin glares at me. "She went to the library desk to borrow a magnifying glass and didn't come back. When I went to check on what the delay was, I found the librarian dead, neck snapped, and Ash nowhere to be seen."

"He was watching from the other side of the street," Tyche says, lifting her chin to Larseen.

"I don't have to account for my actions, especially to you, sailor." Larseen is defensive which makes me doubt him for the first time in my life. "What you claim is wrongfully circumstantial, I promise."

"But in the interest of finding Ash," I cut in, "you can account for them to me. This is serious. It's not like her to disappear."

I can beat the truth out of him.

"De'ral, hold your suggestions. I can't think straight." I suck in a breath. "Are you sure Ash has vanished and didn't just go to the bakery or—"

"Did you hear me? Dead librarian. Ash gone without a trace."

The full force of the situation hits me. "You let her disappear!" I know I'm roaring but I can't stop myself. "What were you thinking?"

"I was thinking Atikis and Tann were after *you*, Marcus, or at least, the whistle bones, which you hold. Not Ash. I let her walk about the library unescorted. In hindsight, a mistake. Don't think I don't know that now." He turns and punches a hole clean through the pinewood wall.

Tyche shrinks back, and the others stare at the splinters falling to the ground.

Kaylin shakes woodchips from his hand as he pulls it back. Then he grabs his long knife, kicks off his boots and straps the blade to his leg.

"We have to mount a search," I say, my eyes glued to his movements.

"Way ahead of you," Kaylin answers.

"On the Bone Thrower's head, you better be." I spit the words, De'ral held down by my slipping will. "You lost her." I know somewhere in the back of my mind that it's not Kaylin's fault, but I accuse him anyway.

Kaylin turns on me, grabs my throat, and slams me into the broken wall. His strength is astonishing, his mouth inches from my ear. "I'm going to find Ash, but you aren't coming with me."

"Like demons, I'm not!"

"You will only slow me down."

We're both breathing hard, faces contorting.

"Marcus, he's right," Piper intervenes. "But for a different reason. You're the Bone Gatherer. You must go on to Whitewing, ahead of Tann, and Atikis, and we must accompany you. There can be no delay. Not for Ash. Not for anyone.

The realms are at stake."

Samsen nods his agreement while Kaylin slowly releases me. De'ral seethes. I feel his anger like spears erupting through my spine. The pain has me on the brink of tears, but I bite my tongue until it bleeds instead. "You will go," I say to Kaylin, hating the truth of it. "Find her. Protect her." My breath comes out in hisses. "But first wait for me to procure a Bone Thrower. They will give guidance. They might be able to tell exactly where she is."

"And how long will that take?"

"He has a point, Marcus," Piper says. "It could be hours, or days."

"Seek guidance from the black-robes, if you will, but I'm leaving now." Kaylin straps on his swords.

I grind my teeth. "Then meet us in Whitewing. From there, we'll enter Sierrak by the northern road." I lower my voice to a rumble. "Return with Ash, whatever it takes. I will not have her lost. Not now. Not ever." I straighten up and salute him, fist thumping my chest. "And feel free to end the path of any who get in your way."

Kaylin salutes back. "I'll not need your permission for that, Bone Gatherer." He shoulders his pack and Ash's before pushing the satchel they brought from the library toward Tyche. After a quick nod to the girl, he races out the door without looking back.

The room goes deathly silent until Larseen breaks the spell, clearing his throat. "You're a very dramatic bunch, aren't you?" he says with a smile.

I glare at him.

"Marcus, your loyalty to your followers is exemplary, unless of course there is more going on here than that?" He has the audacity to wink.

Ice settles over me. "If I find you know something of this, Lars, and aren't saying—"

"Never." Larseen shakes his head, the playfulness gone. "I'm here to report to the military advisor, that is all." He looks at the clock on the mantel. "And I'm expected there now. So sorry to hear of Ash's disappearance. I hope she returns, with all due speed." He gives a very slight bow farewell, hands steepled over his heart, and backs to the door. When he reaches it, he turns around. "Say, Tyche, is it?"

The girl looks up.

"Did you find anything of interest in the library?" His eyes go to the satchel.

Tyche hesitates, her mouth half open. "Noth-nothing new," she stutters.

Larseen doesn't look like he believes her and I'm not sure I do, either. "In any case, wonderful to see you all. If I hear word of Ash, I'll send a message."

Larseen grimaces. "Though I must return soon to Baiseen. Anything you'd like me to relay to Master Brogal?"

It's then I realize that without Ash, we have no way to contact the High Savant. "Please tell him what's happened, but rest assured, Kaylin will find her." I grind out the words. "He'll bring her back."

"How can you be so certain?"

"Because he'll turn the world inside out, until she's safe."

"Good to know." Lars bows again and is gone.

60

KAYLIN

I charge down the docks, scanning each ship as I run past them. Gulls take flight, and heads turn at the commotion, but it's nothing compared to the riot exploding in my mind. I know now, after checking the roads in and out of Pandom City, this is the way they took Ash. At least I'll be sure of it the moment I'm in the water.

I need a small, swift, and cheap sloop, a quarter the size of the *Dugong*. It would be faster for me to dive straight in and forget about a vessel entirely, but I can't expect Ash to swim to shore once I find her. Also, swimming to the rescue would be hard to explain to Piper who follows me to procure the vessel I choose. "This one!" I shout over my shoulder when I see a small yacht. I fight my overwhelming desire to run past it to the end of the pier and jump in. It helps restrain me, knowing that the moment my head goes under, Teern will be aware of me. I can imagine the conversation now.

"Kaylin, do you have the six whistle bones?"

"Not quite."

"Then what are you doing here? Where is the Bone Gatherer?"

"Heading for Whitewing; I'm charged with finding Ash."

"You lost her?"

"Seems so…"

"Then, my son, our deal is off."

It's not a conversation I plan on having. Ever.

The yacht looks seaworthy, well maintained, and capable of overtaking a larger vessel, with the right handling. I would happily steal it, and I guess Piper knows that, hence she's following me with a sack of coins.

"Can you catch her in such a small boat?" Piper asks, running up.

"Aye, with enough sail, and if I leave immediately."

"Then do so. I'll deal with the harbormaster." She hefts the coin. "I don't have to buy it, do I?"

"Hire is fine." I tip my head to her and release the mooring lines. "I'll see you in Whitewing, by the Ma'ata's grace."

"Just find Ash!" she calls out, pleading in her voice.

I run up the jib and glide out of the harbor on the still rising tide. With the shallow draw, it matters little if it's incoming or outgoing, but the wind is with me, and we are away in a flash. At the open mouth of the harbor, I head the vessel south, following my gut. It tells me Ash went this way, at least until I hit a snag.

The yacht lurches and I grip the rudder. It takes a moment to realize that the little ship didn't catch on a reef or hit the back of a manatee. It's my chest, caught short of breath from a stabbing pain in my heart. For a second, I think I hear Ash screaming.

"I'm coming for you, lass." While I sense for the direction of her mental alarm, I'm jolted again. This time it *is* the ship that lurches and yanks to the side. I scan the water for reefs and put her back on course. Then a huge wave hits the prow and a flash of long lean limbs porpoises beside me. Salila. Of course it is.

"I'm coming aboard!" She launches out of the sea and somersaults over the low rail in a spectacular move, timed perfectly to miss the mast and land on slippery feet, square in the center of the foredeck. Rosie Red stays in the water, under Teern's enforcement I'm guessing. At least she's following his orders. "Where are we off to, brother? Going to get your girl?"

"What do you know?" I don't want to sound desperate. They will both play on that, but what can I do? I *am* desperate. "Tell me."

"So she is lost?"

I stand, one bare foot resting on the rudder to keep it true. "I've no time for banter. Where is Ash?"

"I assure you I don't know, though I saw her leave."

"You let her be abducted?"

"Of course not. She left with her own kind, guards from Palrio. How was I supposed to know that meant trouble?"

"If I find you had any part in this…"

"Kaylin, you're so theatrical."

"I'm theatrical?"

"Please can we forget about her for one moment?" Suddenly Rosie is on deck next to me. She drops a shoulder and tilts her head, long dark hair clinging to her wet body. She pouts, but the expression falls when I pick her up by the limbs and toss her back over the railing. When she surfaces, I shoot her a glance that hardens her features instantly.

"Fine. We'll talk about Ash. You don't have to be rude about it."

"Where is she?"

"They took her in a Baiseen warship," Salila says. "Heading for the Gap."

I cross my arms and study her. "And why are you two here?"

"Teern, obviously. He said to keep an eye on you, even though I am stuck looking after this Dreaded." She throws her glance toward the sea. "I swear, I will strangle her in her sleep, if she ever closes her eyes. But in any case, I've been following you, walking the promenade, nosing about the shops, entertaining, you know how it is."

"He let you on land?"

"You make it sound as if I'm not capable of passing."

"Oh, you can pass, clothed or not, but tell me this, Salila, in your short time impersonating a lander, how many have died at your hand?"

She clicks her tongue. "It's not my fault they're fragile as polyps." Again, her eyes go to the sea.

"So, more than one?"

"A few more, to be honest."

"That was you, the mess in the alley? Some lander snack before dawn?"

"Can't face the suns without it, and neither can you."

"I don't go around killing them. It's so unnecessary!" I shake my head. "Listen, Salila. I need your help. Help me find the ship that abducted Ash, while they're still on the sea. Before any harm comes to her."

She sways with the swell. "You are so riled, brother." Her eyes are nearly black, all pupils, though the afternoon is sunny. "If you want to know what I think…" She advances until I feel her ocean breath on my face.

I shove her back. "I'm not playing, Salila. You will assist me, or you're going for a long sleep in the Ma'ata. Which will it be?" I clamp both of her wrists, so she can't escape. "Don't think I won't let Teern in on your land-side antics if you refuse my request."

The yacht, finding itself rudderless, veers into the wind. The sails flap, all speed lost. I let her go and fire orders as I return to the helm. Like a belligerent child, Salila obeys.

"This would all be much faster underwater, or have you forgotten your own realm?"

"I agree, but Teern…"

"Ha!" She brightens. "If you think he'd disapprove, you're right, but he's not paying any attention to us at the moment."

"How so?"

She smiles and tilts her head. "He's keeping an eye on Tann."

"I think Tann is going to be out of the game for a while."

"Apparently not." Salila turns serious. "That filthy Sierrak's vessels are over the Ma'ata again. Circling the reef. Might even know what he's looking for, after that mess you made of things."

"That mess was me following Teern's orders." I let go of the rudder, drop anchor, and strip off my shirt. "I'll go south and check the Gap. You and Rosie follow the coast north just in case they took her that way. Tell me the moment you see anything." I drop my eyes to the water and dive.

"The moment I see 'anything'?" she asks as she follows me into the cool turquoise sea.

"Anything of Ash." I bare my teeth and dart at her.

She slips through the bubbles left by her entry and speeds away north, along the coast. In the distance, I overhear them.

"You're right, Salila. He isn't fun at all anymore."

I ignore it, shooting toward the Gap.

"Ash! Where are you, lass?"

61

ASH

Flaming oxkag, my head hurts. It's the only thing I'm sure of. The other pieces won't fit together, like how I got here, where *here* is, or why it's f'qad'n cold and wet. My mind's a sieve, holding nothing but dregs. Soon queasiness erupts up the back of my throat, bringing a vile taste in my mouth. My head pounds and my brow is beaded with sweat. Is there a bucket nearby? I fumble my hands and find them manacled behind my back. I can't put pressure on the points that stop the seasickness. All I can do is rock back and forth, turning darker shades of green.

"Help?" I push my thoughts into the medallion but it's like banging my head on a brick wall. There's no way to orient, no horizon line to watch. Nowhere to rest my eyes in the darkness. The world has become an up and down slosh, my guts moving against the undulations of the sea and the pounding ice picks in my head. "What's happening?" There's no answer from the creaking ship (obviously a ship) and eventually, after throwing up bile, I doze with my chin slumped on my chest.

I don't think I'm out for long, but it could have been hours. On second thought, it *is* hours judging by the way my hands and feet have swollen against the restraints. My fingers tingle, those I can feel. It's going to hurt like stuggs when they cut me loose. Assuming they ever will.

The nausea's compounded by the stifling air and the sideways rocking of the ship. Why are we moving from side to side?

"Anchored, I assume," my ever-sensible inner voice informs me.

Do you *know what happened?*

"Not really. It's very dark in here."

How this inner part of me can be so blasé is inexplicable, but I find comfort in it just the same. Much-needed comfort!

I'm determined to stop this seasickness, so I can think. I wiggle my hands. The iron cuffs are strangulation tight, with one hand locked on top of the other. With a twist, I angle my wrist bone into the underside of the manacle and push until it hurts. It's painful but no worse than anything else happening to me right now, and the pounding in my head abates enough for the question to rise again. How did this happen to me?

"You trusted someone you shouldn't have."

But I'm not sure that's true. And then I remember Talus's warning about danger in places I feel secure. Heat flares through me. Could she not have said it plain? *"Watch out when you are in the Tangeen library."* That would have been much more helpful.

The anger clears my head more and I recall coming up the stairs, asking Lucia for a magnifying glass. Seeing Larseen? That was him, right? The next minute I felt a sharp pain and darkness. If something happened in between, I don't know.

So here I am, in the hold of a ship, no idea where they are taking me. Back across the Black Dart Channel? North to Sierrak? I don't think about that possibility. As the pressure point sends soothing relief through my body, I turn my mind to the shipboard sounds—creaking wood, clanging bells, shouts above me on the main deck. Shouts? I listen harder. It doesn't take long to realize that this ship I'm on, and my captors, are Palrion, shouting, in my native tongue, cries of battle. Great. Now I'm going to drown with my own people who have what? Abducted me? I feel the weight of the medallion around my neck. Could Brogal know? I try to reach out to him again but it only makes my head hurt worse.

If he knows, what good would it do?

"No good at all."

The sound of battle grows louder. Steel hits steel and the slice and cut of honed metal ringing through the air. This just keeps getting worse.

"Or does it?" my inner voice asks.

I don't even try to answer that.

Has Kaylin come to save me? He would have been the first to notice my disappearance unless they have him, too. And Tyche? Are they here with me in the dark? *"Kaylin?"*

There's no answer so maybe this is a rescue.

I listen for a recognizable word amongst the fighting, or any clue as to what's going on. Mostly it's grunts and shouts, but eventually I catch something that makes my heart sink. It's the voice of a Sierrak rising above the cacophony on deck and what he says is easy enough for me to understand.

"Bring up the prisoner."

"Prisoner, single?" my inner voice asks.

I caught that, too.

The hatch flies open, and a shaft of light hits my face. I feel the warmth but can't see clearly. Am I blind? There are comments about the darkness, the mess, and the stink. I can't agree with them more. Despite every intention to remain poised and indignant, tears well. Boots stomp toward me and I squint, making out the silhouettes of men. They have to release the manacles to free me, as the chains are linked to a metal ring in the deck. Sure enough, as soon as the binding around my wrists and ankles are loosened, blood rushes to my extremities, and with it the unbearable pain of a thousand pins and needles driving into flesh. I scream and lash out with everything I've got.

The men grab me with wide, calloused hands. One hoists me in the air and hangs me over his shoulder. I want to point out that he smells worse than I do by far but I'm in too much pain to manage a word. Tears stream and my nose leaks. The captor has his hand around my hip and struggles for a moment to push the length of my skirt away from his face. My favorite lavender dress is in ruins.

"I'd be more concerned about your favorite Self," my inner voice says.

Believe me, that too.

My head hangs down to the Sierrak's lower back, the position doing nothing for the nausea, and to prove it, I unintentionally spew into his boots. It doesn't make me a new friend, I'm sure.

He throws me onto the deck as soon as we're up the hatch. An argument ensues, the gist of which is who will carry me to the other ship and how they will bind me. The good news is, they aren't going to kill me yet. The bad news? Sierraks have me now, and I know how they treat prisoners.

"I'm here. I won't allow harm."

Big words for a disembodied voice.

"Disembodied?" The deeper, sometimes helpful, sometimes disdainful part of me sounds hurt.

I'm sorry, but can I point out that the juxtaposition between us makes you a prisoner, too?

For a moment, I feel the lightness of laughter. It doesn't last long. My head, aching still, is flat against the deck, a goose egg rising near my hairline. At least the deck is clean and smells of wood and pitch and faintly of fish, but there still is no clue as to what ship I'm on. I keep my head down, not wanting to attract attention, but the reprieve is short-lived. Another Sierrak, the loser of a coin toss, replaces my chains with heavier ones, as if I am going to fly away. He hoists me over his shoulder and carries me to the gangplank. While the ship rocks, the deck disappears and all I can see through new tears and snot is my captor's boots, ballooning pants, a very narrow plank, and the choppy blue sea below. The pain in my head is now horrific and I don't trust my vision, but something's there, a fast-swimming shadow below.

A shark? A porpoise? It turns a somersault underwater and stares at me. A Mar? I have the feeling someone is shouting at me, asking me to do something, but the pressure in my head is too much. I can't hear. *"Find Kaylin,"* I beg them, in case they are Mar. In case they can hear my thoughts, in case this isn't a hallucination, but as they fade away, I think they were only a figment of my imagination.

My captor reaches the new ship and I'm passed onto others who thankfully tip me right side up. Now the blood rushes out of my head and my knees buckle. I fall to a heap until a new guard gathers me up, his hands gripping my biceps. As they take me to the hold and chain my ankle to a ring in the floorboards, an order is given—one simple word.

"Fire."

Catapults cut loose and the boom-crack-snap splits my eardrums along with more orders shouted from a distance. Soon the motion changes from rocking to gliding and we are on our way to…where I have no idea. Before I pass out, again in the dark, I wonder briefly if there is any water, and why in all the vis spit'n gorm they took me, a non-savant without bone, phantom, or coin to barter with.

62

KAYLIN

Ash's rescue must be timed perfectly. It's too risky to leap from the waves and snatch her from the guard's hands. There's no boat to whisk her away on. She can't swim to shore from here. Not in chains. I dart after the Sierrak vessel, avoiding the rip created by the sinking Shearwater masts behind me. *"Salila?"*

"You've found her?" Salila's voice is faint. She's traveled far as well, but turns out, in the wrong direction.

"Ash is on a Sierrak ship heading north."

"I'm certain it was Baiseen who took her. Flew the shearwater flag."

I really don't want to explain all this. *"Baiseen had her. Sierrak overtook her. It happened fast."*

"I'll come back."

"Bring the yacht."

"You want me to sail that log? I'm not—"

"Have Rosie tow it with her teeth if you like. I don't care. We're too far from shore for Ash. She's unconscious and in chains."

"Keep her head above water then."

"I don't have her yet." A situation that heats my blood to boiling. *"They carried her across the gangplank, but she was too dazed to hear me, or recognize me in the water."*

"My poor brother. Have you thought that they bound her in rune chains? Likely she can't hear a bull horn next to her ear if that's the case." Salila huffs. *"And what lander girl expects to see her beau under the sea, in the middle of the ocean. Maybe if she knew the truth…"*

"You're an expert on landers now?"

"More than you, apparently." She outright laughs. *"It would make things so much simpler going forward if you told her what you are."*

"I'm going to! But can you hurry along? I'm not far north of the Gap."

"Fine. Please save some Sierraks for me." She smacks her lips.

"I plan on doing this without excessive bloodshed."

"Whyever for?"

I don't try to explain that, either, mainly because it's a valid question. I've no idea why I have tempered my natural approach to such things. All I know is, I don't want Ash to wade through an entire disemboweled crew when I break her out of the hold. Not if there is another way. *"Just bring the yacht."*

"And then what?"

"I'm getting her out of the hold and taking her to Whitewing, as Marcus asked."

"Marcus? I will help." A sigh escapes her lips. It almost sounds genuine.

"A little advice. When you emerge onto land again, try not to kill anyone. Goes for you, too, Rosie."

"Spoilsport." They both huff and are gone.

I swim across the current, staying a few fathoms deep until I rise under the hull, listening for her heartbeat. I hear it, strong and even. *"Ash, lass?"*

She doesn't answer, but I know she is still alive. I feel her presence, vague and amorphous, even if I can't hear her thoughts.

With a knife between my teeth, I climb, crab-like, up the side of the ship. I slink over the railing and into the lifeboat. The sun is soon to set, so I refine my plan. I'll wait until dark to find her in the hold, escaping with minimal noise and harm to the crew.

Failing that, I'll kill every last one of her captors, and sink the Sierrak ship to mark their watery graves.

63

ASH

Shadows jump up the walls. They rise from the single light overhead as it rocks back and forth in time with the floor. We're still at sea, no rescue in sight.

I wait for my inner voice to agree, or disagree, but there's only silence there. I take slow, deep breaths, calming my mind as the seasickness melts away. Now all we have to do is escape.

I try to tuck my feet under me and sit up but am stopped short by leg irons. The metal cuts into my ankles and restricts movement, not to mention blood flow, again. I scoot toward the anchor point of the chain and bend my knees. It brings some relief. The floor is wet and smells of urine. So does the skirt of my torn lavender dress. I groan, realizing my bladder is empty. Does Palrio treat prisoners this poorly? At least I'm not nauseated anymore. There is only so much humiliation I can take in one day, or two.

I manage to lift both manacled hands and push hair out of my face. The ponytail is long gone, though I can't recall if it was in one or not since I last woke up a free person. How long ago was that?

My inner voice, who would know, remains silent.

The voices I catch in the distance confirm the foreign nature of my captors. On the first ship, the crew spoke Palrion, making them *my* people. My own people who betrayed me? It makes me want to spit every curse I know, in every language, which could take all day, but my mouth is too dry to start. I listen harder. Definitely Sierrak.

Footfalls echo down the hold ladder and come this way. Instinct tells me to hide but that's impossible, being chained to the floor as I am, so I do the next best thing: feign sleep.

"Why can't we torture her?" a female voice asks. "She's Palrion and a traveler. Doesn't make sense."

"Orders. We keep her alive and deliver her to *them*." The second voice is slightly slurred, and I suspect a speech impairment or alcohol consumption, maybe both.

"Who's to know if we ask a few questions? Use a little bite, a little gash here and there, where it can't be seen?"

"Too risky. She's dangerous."

The woman laughs, and I stifle one of my own. "Dangerous? Even a High Savant is without their phantom at sea, and this one doesn't wear robes."

Their boots stop in front of me.

"She's a caller, apparently. From Aku."

"Dressed like that?" The woman moves closer.

They think I'm Tyche? That doesn't bode well considering what Tann did to her grandmother and his prisoners from Aku. I wonder if I can reason with them.

"She ain't *calling* anything now," the man says.

A boot nudges my shoulder and I sit up so fast they both step back. My heart's pounding and I have no idea how I managed the move. As soon as my eyes focus, I wish I'd not reacted that way, but it was instinct and I'm up now, alert. No going back.

"Show me your hands," the woman says. She and the man have knives drawn.

I hold up my manacled hands.

The two pull quick breaths and step farther away. "Rune chains," the woman whispers, then snaps her mouth shut as if speaking leaves her vulnerable to attack.

I turn the iron cuffs to the light. They indeed are covered in runes. They remind me of something, like I should know what they mean, but the memory is gone, like so many of them in days' past. It's like walking into a fog. But then, I was struck and have had more trauma to my head.

"I'm hardly in a position to cause any harm," I say. I want to add, *obviously*, but my voice is hoarse and croaky and my throat burns. Besides, no point in aggravating the situation any further.

"Where'd you learn our speech?" the man asks.

Has he not heard of language studies? "I'm a wordsmith, that's all. I think there's been a terrible mistake."

This bit of news has the two of them both talking at once. They chatter over the top of each other, making it hard to follow their speech until one sentence rings out loud and clear. "She's lying," the woman says.

The man agrees.

"I assure you I'm not."

"We said keep your hands up."

Both guards lunge at me and I hit the deck. I cover my head with my arms, but the manacles and chains prevent me from curling into the fetal position as they kick me with heavy boots. My abdomen is fair game, and they concentrate their efforts there. When they stop, my body contorts with blinding pain and a thick metallic liquid drips out of the corner of my mouth and down my throat.

Barbarian vez hole scum. I spit blood. *If I were savant, my phantom would rise, sea or no, and render you into so many pieces, you'd never find the path again.* I shudder at the rage exploding inside me. For a moment, it chases away the pain and terror, so that's good. In the brief space of freedom, I fantasize about what kind of phantom I raise, in this limb-tearing, path-tossing scenario. A *warrior* the likes of the mythical sea dragons of Atlas? It would chew them, and this ship, to bits, and then carry me safely to shore on her back.

But the image doesn't last long. As it melts away like a snowflake in the sun, the pain and fear come running back.

I can't breathe.

Through gasps, I try to analyze the situation as rationally as I can. *Think, Ash. Think!*

Someone has sprung a trap with me in it. Someone who ordered a ship whose crew spoke Palrion. What had been the plan? To shove me overboard and call it an accident? With manacled hands, I would have found it difficult to swim. But why? Mistaken identity? No Palrion would have done that. Whoever grabbed me…they would have seen the three of us enter the library and I am not a golden-brown-skinned, dark-eyed, eleven-year-old orange-robe. So it has to be me they wanted. I'd be scratching my head if I could. I mean, what secret do I keep that's worth killing me for? Or am I just bait to lure Marcus and the whistle bones?

That makes much more sense.

And then, the Baiseen ship was attacked by these Sierraks, who do think I am Tyche. How they got our identities this mixed up, I can't imagine, unless they were simply misinformed or tricked. By whom? I calm my mind with all these ideas, push past the pain, and open to my higher path.

I clear my throat. "If you're quite finished beating me, I would appreciate a drink of water," I say in their native tongue, my voice welling up from my soul.

The woman spits but the man speaks up. "She's to be delivered alive, remember. Go. Fetch water."

She shrugs and disappears, quickly returning with a bucket and ladle.

I want to cry when he leaves the whole thing in front of me, just within reach.

"Make it last," the woman says. "That's going to have to keep you the next few days. We aren't big on serving prisoners in my realm, even one as sought after as you."

I barely hear the words as I take my first sip of the cool, clear liquid. The water is fresh and sweet. Bless the bones for that. Then it sinks in, and I try not to think about how they treat the less important captives. "Long journey, is it?" I ask between sips, hoping for a response, or any clue as to where they are taking me, but the two guards leave without another word, the hatch shutting me into darkness behind them.

Are you there? I call for my inner voice. At least I can discuss this with the other side of my mind.

But I find I'm completely alone in the dark.

64

MARCUS

Kaylin was right. It took hours to find a Bone Thrower, and longer still to negotiate a reading. Do they not understand the word *urgent* in this realm? Meanwhile, I grill De'ral again and again, asking where Ash is, but he still doesn't know.

She's too far away.

"And Salila?" Now would be a good time for her to pop into my head.

Nothing.

What else can I do but seek out a Bone Thrower?

"State your question." The black-robe sits cross-legged, her brown hair falling forward when she smooths down the hide. It is, as with all Bone Throwers, braided with charms, bones, and bells that chime when she moves. The candlelit chamber smells spicy, or is that wafting from the black-robe herself? With her sits a novice, identified by the close-cropped head. Unlike the Sanctuary savants, the level of accomplishment is not marked by robe color but by the length of their hair. This is a teaching session it seems. I don't care; I just want answers.

"Question?" she repeats.

Of course, I can think of nothing but Ash—when I saw her last, what I said to her, my last look. It cuts my soul. I was short with her, anxious about the whistle bones, the quest, telling her she *had* to find answers. That's her last memory of me?

"The more specific, the better," the Bone Thrower prompts.

I rein my thoughts in and take a deep breath. "Where is Ash and is she harmed?" I try to elaborate but the Bone Thrower stops me with a raised hand.

"Silence."

She turns to the novice—going by "young man" or "woman" I cannot say—and tells them to focus on the question, only the question, and allow their phantom to join.

Instinctively, I make to back away until I remember, black-robe phantoms do not take solid form. They are pure energy and light, rising and returning to the savant like a mist over a lake. In moments, the elder Bone Thrower's phantom wafts about her, a deep purple shadow. Immediately, the room feels warmer, and the savant's face begins to glow.

The novice's phantom is harder to see. It's like a shy elemental hiding within the folds of the savant's robes. But the color is striking, like sparkling gold tipped in red. Together, the two black-robes begin a chant as the elder one reaches into the bone bag. She stirs through the content, her eyes closed.

The Bone Thrower retrieves the bones, shakes them in her hands once, and tosses them onto the dark hide. They come to a stop, all but one that skips to the far edge of the hide. Both phantoms disappear for a blink and then return. The black-robes shudder when they do. It's many minutes before the elder stops staring at the whistle bones spread over the hide. "It is done," she says and draws a long, slow inhale, her face now pale, shoulders slumped.

The novice's eyes roll to the back of their head. They keel over as the elder pushes a thick cushion behind them, keeping their head from cracking on the floor. I know that throwing the bones extracts a price from both mind and body, but I didn't know it could knock them out.

"Do you need it written?" the Bone Thrower asks as if it matters little to her either way.

I know how convoluted a bone reading can be, and I don't trust myself or my memory. "Written, if you will, please."

I will remember, De'ral says, but even if so, I want the exact wording.

The elder black-robe pulls a writing board into her lap, pops the cap on her ink bottle, dips the quill and begins to write, thankfully, in Palrion. It's only four sentences but after she fans the scroll dry and rolls it up for me, she smiles. "You already know this, and it's nothing to do with the question, but your bond with this girl Ash lives eternal, before and beyond the path."

Warmth heats my chest. "You're right. That is something I already know." I pay her the coin owed, bow, and take my leave. That was time well spent.

But when I return to our apartments, I've changed my mind. "Curse the bones and throwers, are they not taught plain, simple language in their schools?" I scrub my scalp and read again the list from the reading. But no matter how many times I go through it, I find no real assurances there.

Where is Ash and is she harmed? That was the question, but maybe I should have worded it differently. Would that have brought more clarity?

Too late, De'ral says, matter of fact. He's a coiled wire fit to spring, as am I.

But he is also right. As with all divination, the same question can never be asked twice, unless new information comes to light. In this instance, there has been no news. I read the answers again.

Ash is not alone.

That could mean Kaylin has found her, right? Or it could mean she is surrounded by her abductors.

From sunrise to sunset the distance lengthens.

So they sail, or ride at great speed? Again, good thing I did not detain Kaylin, not that I could have. All this really means is she's not held captive somewhere in Pandom City. I guess that is good to know.

The sea watches her from within.

What the dank waters is that supposed to mean? It makes no sense at all. Is it a metaphor? The irony is, I need Ash's help to unravel it.

None living can stop her.

This is ridiculous. Ash is many things, but unstoppable is not one of them. Unless it means her spirit. Is that saying, peace be her path, she has died? That she walks another way? It takes all my strength not to screw the scroll up into a ball and throw it onto the fire.

The worst part is, even if I knew what any of it meant, it doesn't reveal where she is, and how would I contact Kaylin anyway?

Salila, De'ral says without hesitation. *But we are beyond her call.*

"I wish she wasn't!" My mind goes back to our most recent encounter and heat floods my face.

Tyche pulls on my sleeve, and I tuck the note back into my pocket. Unlike the Bone Thrower, she has presented me with a great deal of valuable information, all that they gathered in the library before Ash disappeared.

I open my mouth to speak but Piper quickly touches the back of my hand and shakes her head, the slightest of motions. Then she taps her ear.

I take her meaning.

On the other side of the room, Samsen, Belair, and Larseen are playing cards. They shout over the music that wafts in from the nearby hall, keeping Larseen distracted as I asked them to. It's past dinnertime and the courtiers of Pandom City dance, again. Do they have music every night in Tangeen? No matter, it should be enough racket to block prying ears, but Piper is cautious. She touches her throat where a small white pearl hangs, striking against her brown skin, and where her two-headed serpent twines as well. Piper raised it to give Belair another healing before his next assignment.

Master Havest is sending him to the Gollnar border to test his *warrior's* skills with a group of yellow-robes and track Tann, if he's gone that way. I never thought I'd say it when we first met, but I'll miss the Tangeen and his brilliant red sun leopard. We all will. But with the realms in upheaval, the assignment's not unexpected. While my mind wanders again, Piper taps me harder. What's she trying to say?

Tyche makes a circle with her thumb and forefinger and holds it against her chest. Then she tips her head toward the poker table. Up go both females' brows, willing me to understand. It reminds me of my youth when my brother and I would communicate in our own sign language at the high table during formal dinner parties. Father, of course, did not share many matters of state with us then, so we made it a point to spy, until sidetracked by the hunting horns or the right moon for fishing. Or a lass. What's wrong with me? I can't concentrate on anything right now.

I sneak a furtive look at Larseen and spot a medallion around his neck and it clicks. He wears a talisman, like the one Brogal gave to Ash. A distance communication device. How long has he had that? I frown and mouth the word *"Brogal"*?

Piper nods and raises her brow again.

Do I understand her right? I count the facts off on my fingers one at a time. Number one, Ash is missing. Number two, Kaylin is off to single-handedly rescue her in a small but hopefully fleet vessel. Number three, we have no idea who is responsible for the abduction. Tann? The red-robe Atikis? Pandom City's Magistrate? Does Belair know something but can't say? He wouldn't hold anything back, not with how close he and Ash have become. Would he?

The way Kaylin accused Lars still sticks in my throat. Is it possible my childhood friend is lying to me? But why would he, or Brogal for that matter, want Ash out of the way when she is so highly skilled? I scribble the question on the back of the Bone Thrower's parchment and Piper shrugs.

Tyche writes the word *knowledge.*

She knows too much? I write back. *Too much about what?*

About the second sun? The Mar? Piper jots ideas down quickly, then scratches them out.

What do Mar have to do with it? I scribble out next and for a moment my mind goes to Salila, and I can't think of anything else.

When I come back to myself, I see Piper doesn't answer that one. Instead, she touches her nose. *"Brogal?"* she mouths slowly.

"What about him?" I put down the quill and ask the question aloud. It's hard to imagine he would order her capture, but at this point, I will rule nothing out.

Piper writes again. *Remember Rowten? He tried to kill Ash, no one else.*

"That we know of," I say aloud again. "I should be searching for her this very moment. Why didn't I go?" I cross my arms over my chest, knowing the answer but asking anyway.

Because you're the Bone Gatherer, Piper writes in her elegant script. *You have no choice but to stay the path.*

So says Brogal.

"So says this." Tyche points at the scroll Kaylin took from the library. It wasn't just Brogal's word about the duty of the Bone Gatherer. It was a truth carried by all the High Savants, her grandmother, Yuki, included. The document attests to that.

I take a moment before agreeing. "That leaves us on our mission to secure the bones and hold them," I say in a soft voice.

"And *call* those we can't collect," Piper adds.

Tyche flinches and I put my hand on her shoulder. "I will not let your blood be spilled."

"But Tann will." She looks down at her hands. "Like he did my grandmother's."

Piper's brow knits as if she is pondering an idea, but doesn't elaborate.

There are whoops and hollers from the table and Belair slaps Samsen on the back. I'm angry at how much fun they're having when Ash could be anywhere, harmed or even gone from this path. "Enough," I boom, a little too abruptly. I motion for Piper to roll up the scrolls.

"Problems, Marcus?" Larseen asks.

"We sail for Whitewing at sunrise. I think it's best to turn in."

"Of course. It is late." Larseen rises and shakes hands with Belair and Samsen. He saunters over to me and grips my shoulder. "Safe journey, Bone Gatherer. I hope our paths cross again soon." He smiles to Piper and Tyche, then hesitates. "Your company is getting smaller, is it not? Do you want me to ask Brogal to send replacements?"

"No need." I give him a casual smile. "Ash and Kaylin will rejoin us in Whitewing, though Belair will be sorely missed."

Larseen doesn't look convinced. "Three savants and a child are hardly enough to guard the whistle bones, especially when you're down a *warrior* phantom and a master swordsman." Apparently, word of Kaylin's skills has made the rounds. Larseen's eyes go to the pouch that hangs on my belt. "I insist on discussing this with Master Brogal."

I control my expression, replaying Kaylin's accusations in my mind. Ash would certainly follow Larseen if asked, under any pretext, but it's all conjecture. I can't prove his involvement either way. "Kaylin and Ash will be with us in Whitewing," I say tightly. "We're sailing at dawn. At any rate, the choice of companions is mine."

"So it is," Lars replies. When I was Heir, he never would have sounded so dismissive.

To your face, De'ral says, which rankles me further.

Lars bows slightly and leaves.

"I must go, too." Belair is up and walking toward us. "I'll miss you, Marcus." He pumps my hand in a strong clasp and then hugs me tight.

Everyone gathers around him, saying goodbye and offering advice for the road. He will travel with a group of yellow- and orange-robes, savants with a mix of *callers, alters,* and one other *warrior* phantom. Hahmen, who raises a *healer,* will go, too, easing the hardship of separation, at least for Belair. He's in good company, and hopefully will find out if any threats are lurking around the borders.

"Farewell," I say, my throat tightening. "Stay the path."

"And you." Belair's eyes well. "I'll pray to the old gods for our recorder's quick return."

"I thought you didn't believe in them."

"For Ash, I find I do."

When he is gone, and the others to bed, I sit in my room, opening the leather pouch Magistrate Riveren had couriered to me this morning. It's the first chance I've had the time, or the mindset, to open it. The gift my father gave the Magistrate glints in the candlelight. A dagger?

No, it's a rondel, four-edged, which is rare. These kinds of blades are not for general purpose, not cutting, but skewering. A battle weapon only. The hilt is embedded with small jade stones, a vivid contrast to the black blade. Did he have this specially smithed?

I pull out the note.

Marcus, I hope these words from your father may give comfort, if not now, then in the future.

To the Magistrate of Tangeen,

All congratulations, Riveren, and best wishes for your reign.

From your true friend, Jacas Adicio.

Long be your path and power.

It's Father's seal, but I've never known him to be genuinely outgoing, or friendly. I look at the date. It was gifted five years before my birth.

Before his firstborn was deemed marred and—

"Sacrificed to the sea."

I stow the gift in the bottom of my pack.

Ash is the only one I want to talk to about this, and I don't even know for certain if she is alive.

65

ASH

I'm dead to this world, lost from the path, paralyzed in the dark unknown. Or this could be a dream. Please, be a dream. That would be a much better option. The sliver of light under the door in front of me, and the lack of manacles, or sensation, has me believing it could be just that. I mean, last I knew I was pegged to the floorboards of a creaking ship, dressed in restraints carved with runes and left completely abandoned.

"Child, open the door."

"Talus?" Her voice is warm and comforting. *"Have you come to rescue me?"*

"Pay attention to what you see."

It occurs to me that the medallion is still around my neck. *"This is a vision?"*

"Open the door."

I focus on the sliver of light. There's no question I'd rather stay in this nebulous realm for as long as possible, not wanting to return to the ship, chained like an animal before the slaughter. When the door pulses with light, I open it.

Emerging from an odorless, colorless fog, I follow a benign shape, a woman, I think, but it's hard to tell if those are savant robes or a non-savant's skirt. I follow, in any case, down a long hallway. It has high windows, revealing nothing but a black night sky, or perhaps my inability to conjure more details in this dream. I'm aware, at least, of that. Candles glow softly, and the floor rocks back and forth. Like the ship. This is so strange.

"As visions often are," Talus says, calm and reassuring.

My medallion lights the way, shining with a warm, bronze light. Around another corner we go, and I know where I am. The Baiseen palace halls.

A woman, for certain, leading the way, her steps clipped. But I'm floating like a ghost phantom, not making a sound, not touching the floor with my bare feet—the feet I know are shackled and chained to a metal ring in the hold.

"Best not think about that," Talus says.

I glide, sensationless. Without breaking stride, the woman, young and purposeful in a glorious royal-blue dress with sunburst trim, whisks into a council chamber as the guard opens the door for her. It closes fast, but I pass right through the wall without feeling a thing. Conversations in the room stop, and everyone rises from their seats. I see her face and understand why. It's Rhiannon.

"Magistrate," Brogal and U'karn say at the same time.

"Magistrate?"

"Pay attention," Talus reminds me.

And I do.

"Here are the maps," Rhiannon says as she unrolls two large scrolls and weighs them down at the corners with smooth black stones.

I lean in to get a better look.

"Now gentlemen and women of the council, this is what we know." She takes out a pouch full of tokens and places a white one in the far northeast of Sierrak, the coastal city of Lepsea. "Tann sailed from his home sanctuary down the coast, at least to Gleemarie in Southern Aturnia."

"Picking up over a hundred warships before he doubled back to attack Aku," U'karn confirms.

"Where he promptly overtook the island Sanctuary," Rhiannon says without a wisp of emotion. "And stole their original whistle bone. It's safe to assume he would have Aturnia's originals as well, but possibly not both of Sierrak's. Reports have it, he left Asyleen in ill favor."

The council nods agreement, but I find myself wondering why he would be out of favor with the largest Sanctuary in Sierrak.

"I'm guessing they didn't want to declare war on the rest of Amassia." Talus couldn't sound drier.

"Right. That makes sense."

Rhiannon places three more white tokens on the map, one each in Northern and Southern Aturnia and one on Aku.

"Then he came to us," Brogal says.

I squint at my guardian. He looks pale and drawn. His white hair thinning. Has he lost weight?

"But we turned him away," he goes on.

"Correct." Rhiannon places a gold token on Baiseen.

"He was reported in Nonnova next," Brogal adds.

"But that bone goes to us as well, so you say." Rhiannon pops a gold token on the Bay of Nonnova, but Brogal reaches across the table and pushes it over to the Isle of Bakton.

"Thank you." She smiles at the correction as if someone just brushed a crumb from her collar. "Now where does that leave us?"

"The Bone Gatherer went to Kutoon, as instructed, and secured the Arrow of Nii. He is in Tangeen now, Pandom City, gathering their whistle bone," Brogal says. "Reports have Tann heading north."

Rhiannon puts a gold token on Tangeen's capital and one on Kutoon. "And where is Tann headed? There are no sanctuaries North of Goll."

The council members rumble, and discussions break out until Brogal stands. "I believe Tann seeks Avon Eyre, holder of the ancient whistle bone, the Mask of Anon."

Rhiannon smirks. "That will keep him busy. Even if Avon Eyre exists, the chances of finding it are—"

"Slim to none," Brogal finishes her sentence. "Marcus must use this advantage and press on. The red-robe Atikis is reportedly on his tail."

"Atikis seeking the bones?" Rhiannon waves the thought away. "I assure you; he is not."

No one dares to contradict her but the tension in the room increases.

U'karn stands up. "Marcus will head out of Tangeen and—"

"Not so fast," Brogal interrupts him. "There's a second whistle bone there."

"You High Savants do keep your secrets," Rhiannon says, a little exasperated.

"Where is this second bone?" U'karn faces Brogal.

"The Sanctuary of Whitewing."

"On the border of Sierrak?" Rhiannon seems surprised.

Brogal nods. "I have it from Larseen in Pandom City that Marcus is sailing there next, but he is dogged by Atikis." Brogal gives Rhiannon a meaningful stare. "I've sent Lars along, to keep me informed."

"You mean, keep *us* informed," Rhiannon corrects him this time.

Brogal doesn't reply. I've never seen such tensions and undercurrents in a council meeting before, at least, not the ones I've attended as recorder. Granted, in those the stakes may not have been this high, but still…is no one in accord?

"That's the ninth whistle bone gathered, three or four in Tann's possession and five in ours, but then what?" Rhiannon asks.

"The Bone Gatherer will have to go to Asyleen," Brogal says, tapping the Sierrak Sanctuary with his finger.

A hush falls over the room.

"What chance will he have there?" Rhiannon looks truly perplexed. "You've made a point to tell me Asyleen is our enemy. They've abducted callers from our outposts. Apparently more than Tann gained in Aku."

"True, but Marcus can't gain the Eye of Sierrak without the leave of Rantorjin, assuming Tann, or Atikis, doesn't have it already."

"Would Rantorjin still be loyal to Tann?"

"It's impossible to say where Rantorjin's loyalty lies. After Tann's actions, their High Savant Zanovine may have reservations. But that's not our only barrier," Brogal says quietly.

Everyone turns to him, waiting.

"Atikis rides and—"

"I told you, I'm not worried about him." Rhiannon dusts her hands.

"You should be. He drives a phantom army before him, the likes of none on Amassia. If he has control of a good enough caller, he's equally as threatening to us as Tann. If not more."

I hold very still, remembering the Suni River escape and the attack on the Nulsea, but Rhiannon shrugs. "Reports?" she asks.

"We finally had a vague description from the Bone Gatherer's recorder."

Vague? I was anything but vague. Told him clear as newly polished glass. My face heats and for a moment, I feel the rock of the boat, the pain of my manacles.

"Steady," Talus says. *"Stay focused or you'll lose it."*

"Atikis is only seen when he wants to be," Brogal says with a shrug. "Larseen was able to communicate a firsthand report from the Bone Gatherer."

"And Ash?"

"Shipboard as we speak. I'm bringing her home where she can attend to more suitable tasks. It's not safe for a non-savant. We already lost the captain of the honor guard to a sailing mishap."

"Mishap?"

"Yes, it was obvious to me from the start that the non-savant wasn't a good choice." Rhiannon's mouth turns down. "But they have Larseen with them now. I suspect he is a better sailor than Rowten, peace be his path."

Sailing mishap? I was a bad choice? This isn't a vision; it's a nightmare. And what's worse, Brogal is lying to the council.

"It's decided then. The Bone Gatherer carries on, and we'll not make a move against Atikis unless provoked." Rhiannon crosses her arms.

"Magistrate, I implore you to take this with the utmost seriousness. According to reports, Atikis has already given much provocation."

"I'll believe it when I see evidence to substantiate the claims."

"Rhiannon!" I focus my whole will on her. *"Listen to him! Brogal might be deceiving you terribly on other counts, but in matters of Atikis, he speaks true."* I want to warn her, but no sound comes out of my mouth no matter how hard I try.

Rhiannon presses her thumb into the spot on the map marked as the Sanctuary of Asyleen as if squashing an insect. "As extra weight, we'll send our troops here and retrieve our callers. I won't have our people turned into slaves at the whim of High Savant Zanovine, or Tann for that matter. If the Bone Gatherer is there, and under duress, we can support him, crushing the enemy, all at once. Thoughts?"

The council room swells with arguments and opinions. Eventually, Rhiannon holds up her hand to stem it. "Thank you for your ideas. The plan holds. All those seeking the whistle bones must pass through this point to gain access to Sierrak's." She looks over the top of Brogal's head at U'karn. "Am I right?"

She waits a fraction of a second for rebuttal and no one dares to speak.

"Good. Now, all we must do is mobilize our combined troops of Tangeen, Nonnova, and Palrio to outnumber Rantorjin's. Send them there, first by ship up the Nulsea. They can ride straight on from Oteb." She slaps a point south of the stronghold of Asyleen. "Let us gather our allied armies and make Sierrak pay for their crimes. When we acquire their whistle bone, it will be a win all round."

So much has changed. I don't understand why Rhiannon is in control. Where is Petén? I put my hand up, desperate to tell her she is wrong, that Atikis is a threat and not to be underestimated.

But the more I try to speak, the darker the room becomes until the light of the medallion winks out, leaving me in the pitch black. As the vision fades, the slow rock of the ocean and the slicing pain comes hurtling back. I wake up to a much worse nightmare, and I'm not sure how much longer I can endure.

A century passes, waiting for nightfall. Whole realms rise and crumble into the sea as I lie under the sailcloth, whispering to her mind-to-mind to no avail. Salila could be right, she is in rune chains. Or unconscious. But I am comforted by her heartbeat, each pulse bringing me a second closer to freeing her. When the dinner bell rings and most of the crew are below, I spring out of the rowboat and creep up the netting like a spider in a web. The sailor on watch walks past and I freeze. When he moves on, unsuspecting, I leap over the railing to land lightly on deck. My bare feet don't make a sound, but I'm cautious. Some of the crew are about, and every one of them carries a long, curved blade.

I can fight my way through all of them, but I'd rather use stealth, for Ash's sake, and then Teern's, who would surely notice a decimated ship at the bottom of the Nulsea. I stick to the shadows, reach the hatch, lift it and swing down. It's my first mistake.

Well, second, if you count leaving Ash to retrieve the magnifying glass by herself.

To be fair, I didn't expect the galley tables to be so close to the lower hold hatch, but they are. No shadows to hide in here as two dozen surprised sailors jump to their feet. They have their weapons drawn as I land. Long and short knives glint in the yellow lantern light. I lean back into the ladder and draw my blades. Already the alarm bell tolls. They are an efficient crew, I'll give them that. I'm guessing my brown island skin and long black hair falling free about my shoulders sets them off. Sierrak warriors braid their hair, and their skin tends toward paler shades. There's no question I'm not one of them. Should have thought that through.

The crew presses in with no hesitation and I abandon the idea that few will be harmed. When the sailors are in my face, I block their strikes and leap over the top of them. The landing is soft, my blades swifter than sight. I'm going to have to kill them all now, so no point trying to hide my Mar abilities. No one will be around to write songs about them.

I whip my sword in a circle, cutting them down, a thresher shark in a school of tuna. After a half dozen lie dead at my feet, I tell them my demands. "I've come for my wordsmith," I say in Palrion. "I suggest you tell me where she is, and then get out of the way."

They look blankly at me, chests heaving, swords raised. Mine is the only weapon wet with blood.

Of course they're blank. They have no idea what I said. I repeat my demand in Sierrak.

They hear but don't retreat. A quick glance behind tells me why. Several have climbed over the rafters, daggers raised above me. I tuck and roll beneath them, coming up with my sword raking across more than one torso. "None of that," I warn. "If you want to live a while longer." I swing my blade around again, my reach dropping more sailors until they all press back. Ash has to be in the lower hold, but I can't see the cursed hatch and my hosts don't offer to show me the way. While I consider the options, the Sierraks attack as one.

It's a demon fight, all hiss and spit and slice. The vessel explodes with the clash of steel on steel, grunts and bellows, and the song of my blades through the air. I take some nicks and stabs but deliver more by far. Sailors double over around me, and the floor turns slippery with blood. As the throng pushes me backward, my toes squish through sliced guts and spongy body parts until my heel slams into an iron ring. The lower hatch. I cut more attackers down, clearing a space.

"Hold!" cries a throaty challenge from the steps. A dozen more swords push their way down and surround me, pointing the tips of their blades at my throat but still smart enough to keep out of my kill circle.

Without warning, I sheath one blade, crouch, and pull open the hatch. Then I disappear into the depths, closing it behind me. I dispatch two guards as I land and scan the darkness. There's a dim light in the corner hanging above a hunched figure. "Ash?" I call, surprised at the emotion in my voice.

Mistake number two, or three, if counting the library.

I splash toward her through the bilge water and stop short.

"Ash is it?" a male voice answers in Sierrak. He comes out of the shadows behind her and clamps a hand tight over her mouth, pulling her against his wide chest. His long knife presses her throat until drops of blood bead in a line.

Her eyes flare wide as she holds her breath.

I lower my weapon. "Don't."

"I see you take my meaning," the guard says. "Spill one more drop of blood and hers will be next."

I let my sword fall.

"That's more like it. Step away from your weapon. Hands where I can see them."

Crew members come cautiously down the ladder, speeding up when they see I'm disarmed. They push me to my knees, cursing and spitting. They lost some friends up there and are keen to pay me back. Also, they likely saw a swordsman more like a phantom than savant. They're scared. And they should be.

My instincts scream to kill them all, but the sailors clamp manacles around my wrists and ankles that burn like molten lava. *Impossible,* I whisper to myself.

My final mistake is underestimating them.

The curs have me in rune chains, draining away my strength.

They drag me to the wall and snake the cursed chains through a ring bolted there, hanging me like a piece of stretched meat.

And then they laugh.

"I guess you have some questions?" I say.

"One or two."

But they don't bother to ask me anything. One by one they pound me until the sound of fists into flesh rings endlessly in my ears. I barely flinch until I see it only invites more abuse. At that point, I go ahead and crumple under the assault. It's not feigned. The last sailor kicks and spits for good measure before tossing the other guard the key. He catches it with the hand that's still clamped over Ash's mouth.

As soon as she is free, Ash screams out a string of curses in a mix of languages even I can't follow. Her face contorts. "Get your filthy f'qad'n ack q'bash hands off of him! By the throw of the bones, you will rue the day you—"

The guard smacks the back of her head, and she hits the deck.

And then, they turn back to me.

67

MARCUS

I focus on the coastline, letting the sea spray cool my face. It helps me ignore the hammer and anvil beating in my head. It's not been a good day thus far, and the sun's only just above the horizon. The first sun, that is. The second sun is higher, like a small red moon climbing toward the midheaven. I flip up the collar of my long coat. The wind bites, along with my thoughts, and my phantom's.

She's been taken, and we sail away like nothing's happened? De'ral's voice is closer to the surface than any phantom's has a right to be over water.

"Remember the throw of the bones? None living will harm her."

That leaves the dead.

"Shades? Shadows? I won't believe it."

Your belief is not required for her to be harmed.

My phantom's words hit hard. *"Kaylin will have her safe by now. He's as motivated as we are."*

She says he hasn't.

I hold suddenly still. *"Who says what now?"*

Salila.

"The Mar woman is bespeaking you?"

Her name is Salila. De'ral corrects me—Saaa-LEE-lah—turning her name into a melody in his deep baritone voice.

I am perfectly aware of her name. Too aware. In my mind, I see her, Salila, dressed in finery, bright and bejeweled. Salila, pressing me against the wall, her lips touching mine… I've not seen or heard a whisper from her since she disappeared from the feast. The wait, the uncertainty, is agonizing.

But it shouldn't be!

I am the Bone Gatherer, tasked with a journey to save our realm. My focus must be unwavering. But if Salila has news of Ash? To stop my whirling thoughts, I shout, "Where is she?"

"Easy does it." Samsen looks up, startled. "We are all concerned."

I realize that my friend and guard has been talking to me. Shouting out random questions about Ash—or was that about the Mar—isn't making me seem calm and in control.

Samsen's blue eyes are beseeching. Like me, like all of us, we're worried about Ash, but each dealing with it in different ways.

I take a deep breath and let it out slowly. I have to calm down.

"Kaylin'll find her. By the bones, he has uncanny skills," Samsen says quietly, his forehead creased.

"You're right." I direct my attention inwardly. *"De'ral, please, what does Salila say?"*

That Kaylin will find her, but will she be alive or dead? De'ral's voice fills my mind again.

"Don't say that!" My eyes shut, heat burning my face.

Samsen clamps onto the railing and leans around to stare me in the face. "You're not speaking to me, are you?"

My eyes remain shut as I shake my head. "No, not to you."

"Struggling with the *warrior* again?"

"Somewhat." I avoid eye contact. "Samsen, have you ever known a phantom to converse with others?"

De'ral chuckles, like it's a joke. On me.

"Other phantoms? It's possible, with training. And very useful for getting messages across. Is he showing signs? This is a good thing."

"No. I mean, with non-savants and Mar."

"Is that what's happening?" Samsen's eyes widen. "How could a phantom connect with a non-savant on land, let alone a Mar in the sea?"

I knuckle my fists into my eyes. "I don't know, but he does."

Samsen takes a moment. "It's new to me, but I can help." He pats my back. "We'll seek counsel in Whitewing, too. There are warrior savants there, Marcus. Orange-robes. They'll have advice."

"There isn't time," I say through clenched teeth.

"We'll make time. You can't rightly raise your *warrior* if there's risk of—" Samsen cuts his words short and turns around. "Larseen, is breakfast in the galley?"

I'm grateful for the alert, not wanting to share the details of my phantom struggles with Lars. I used to trust him, but now there is a window of doubt that won't close.

"A cheery breakfast it is. Bread and berry jam with a particularly rich blend of Ochee. No butter, which I find odd, but this is Tangeen, after all." The orange-robe was on the dock at dawn this morning, waiting to board with us. By Brogal's orders, he is to accompany us as our recorder now that Ash is missing. I protested flatly, saying again that Ash will rejoin us by the end of the day, but Brogal's command is final. According to Lars. He claims to have spoken to him over the distance.

Maybe he did. And maybe not. In the past, I would have believed him without question, but now? It gnaws at my bones.

De'ral and I need to be in accord, watching Larseen's every move, but I don't trust my phantom, either, what with his history of pulling me under when I least expect and locking the mental door shut. It feels like cold fingers tightening around my throat.

"What are we in such deep thought about?" Larseen asks.

"Funny you should ask," Samsen jumps in after whispering to me, "We'll make time to train." He slaps Lars on the back. "Last spring when we were hunting pig on the fringes of the Bone Thrower's cave. Remember?"

"I don't remember anything of that day, past saddling my horse just before dawn," Larseen says and lets out a hearty laugh.

"That's all any of us remember." I take up the thread of the story. "The old black-robes pulled our memories straight out of our heads."

"Must have," Larseen says. "I still think we went through a bone tunnel."

I wave that away. Bone tunnels are mythic thoroughfares said to connect some of the oldest sanctuaries, at least that's the lore. I'm sure if they existed, we'd have some evidence of it. "More likely, we stumbled into a ritual ceremony and were knocked out for the rest of the day, wiped of the recall." I smile despite my whirling thoughts.

Samsen's doing a good job of distracting Larseen. When I have a chance, I catch my friend's eye and nod my thanks.

"We'll scale the great steps of Whitewing tomorrow. It'll be my first time there." Lars stands between us at the rail once the mirth dies down. The orange-robe isn't as broad as me, but he has a hand of height over my head.

I keep my face bland. "Yes, I've been informed." Ash's whereabouts aside, I'm not enjoying this power struggle, subtle as it is, between me and Larseen. Just because I am no longer the Heir.

For now, De'ral reminds me.

A supportive comment from my phantom? I rub the stiffness out of my shoulder wondering what De'ral can really know of politics. This isn't right. Ever since Aku, I've been split apart, of two minds, pulled in two directions, unable to reconcile either. And now De'ral's intense interest in Ash and the affairs of the realm? And the Mar woman?

Salila, De'ral corrects me.

"Fine. Salila. What else does she know?"

More than you think. And Larseen knows more than he says.

My knuckles turn white as I grip the rail, and then I force myself to relax, clasping my hands and stretching my fingers out in front of me, exaggerating a yawn. Maybe De'ral can learn more of what Lars is up to after all. *"Let's test him,"* I say to my phantom.

Let's.

Agreement! I turn to Larseen. "You might be able to help us out."

Samsen perks up, as I knew he would.

"That's what I'm here for," Larseen says with a nod. "To offer my support and counsel."

"Samsen and I were discussing Brogal's position, now that my brother has taken the throne. There must be new mandates coming over from the palace." I keep my voice neutral. No big deal, just speculating on changing policies, something we've discussed amply over the years.

But why bait him like a fox when we could punch the information out of him?

"Because I could be wrong."

We're not.

Larseen smiles, oblivious. "There's much to say on that, but Brogal's asked for discretion, you understand? I really can't discuss the matters between the Sanctuary and Realm with…"

I raise my brow. "Go on. With?"

"With anyone outside the council."

"I used to sit at the head of that table, beside my father, the Magistrate." My teeth snap shut and I force them to ease off.

"You did," Samsen says, laying a calming hand on me. "Marcus and I are under the same restraints, Lars. We are only considering our roles and advancement in light of the current reign. Marcus has much to adjust to, as you can imagine. We all do, but any information would be strictly between us savants." He leans on the last word.

Larseen's voice lowers. "That must have been a blow, coming home to find your throne pulled out from under you."

"I'm relieved, in a way," I lie. "How would I have been able to take up my duties as the next Magistrate and embark on this journey at the same time?" I shrug one shoulder and point to a spot halfway to the coast where whitewater churns and froths. "Did you see that?"

Salila? De'ral says in a quiet tone.

"Is it her?" My heart inexplicably jumps.

Maybe.

"Well talk to her then."

Samsen follows my line of sight. "Mar?" he whispers.

"Surely not," Larseen says and laughs until he sees we aren't smiling. "You don't believe in the Mar, do you?"

Has he been asleep all month? De'ral asks.

"More like scheming, but we can use this." I feel a boost of energy.

"Was that story I heard from Brogal true? I don't believe it." Lars crosses his arms, waiting for a response.

"What did you hear from Brogal?" I ask, brow rising.

The cold wind gusts, rippling our cloaks as we lean on the railing. "Not much. Not much at all. There was talk of sightings unconfirmed."

"Really? That's it?"

Lars turns his palms up. "Basically." He hunches closer. "Tell me what you know, please?"

"It's not meant to be discussed," I say, lowering my voice. "Not at this point." I glance at Samsen, and he dips his head a fraction.

"But it's me. Larseen. A friend to you both all our lives. Tell me if you've seen a Mar. Wouldn't that change everything?"

I wonder what he means by "everything" but don't ask. We have his full attention now.

"I'll keep it to myself," Larseen pleads. "Just between us savants."

Samsen makes out as if he's deliberating, then exhales. "I've seen Mar," Samsen says in his softest voice. The wind lifts his pale-yellow hair as he winks. "I've seen a Mar this far from my face." He holds his thumb and forefinger a fraction apart.

"It can't be true." Lars is genuinely rattled.

"Oh yes. She was—"

"She?" His head shoots to me for confirmation.

She was breathtaking, De'ral says in a whispered tone.

I don't disagree, but *breathtaking*? Phantoms don't speak like this! Yet still, I find myself in a rush of warmth, lost in a vision of Salila.

"She's tall with the longest legs," Samsen continues.

"Legs? I thought they were more like sea dragons, winged water snakes with faces and..."

"Ha!" I shake my head. "They're like us, at least this one is."

"How are you sure she was Mar?"

I laugh, and it's not contrived. "When a woman leaps out of the sea to stand fully naked on the ship's railing, and a second later eviscerates the Sierrak who has you bound and under duress, you know you're in the presence of a Mar." I gather my hair back and tie it.

"Her skin is ivory and her locks a coppery blond," Samsen says.

"Much like Rhiannon's only longer." I know I sound like I'm comparing broodmares in the paddock and Ash would clobber me over the head with a brick if she heard, but we are baiting a trap, and it's working, so I keep it up. Ash said Lars has a weakness for Rhiannon, though I never thought much of it until now.

"What was she doing, this Mar woman?"

"Like Marcus said, saving our lives." Samsen goes on to describe the rescue from our sinking vessel, the one we'd stolen from the docks of Aku after Tann's attack. By the time he gets to the part where we were emerging onto the beach off the coast from Gleemarie, Larseen is entranced.

"And you told this all to Brogal?"

I curl my lip. "We didn't tell him everything."

"What more is there?"

Out of the corner of my eye, I catch Piper and Tyche approaching. Time to spring the trap. I wave them back with the slight flick of my fingers and interrupt Samsen. "Speaking of Rhiannon," I say. "When did my brother declare his betrothal to her?"

"Rhiannon?" Larseen's face turns decidedly sour. "Your brother was played."

"Played?" I keep the concern out of my voice.

"She played us both," Lars says under his breath, but I catch it. "She manipulated Jacas into taking more power from the Sanctuary, leaving us at the mercy of palace rule. It's ruining Brogal's plans, and as for her promise to me —" Lars straightens, suddenly remembering himself. "But between you and me, she made the wrong choice."

"How's that?" Samsen asks.

"Petén's ill."

"He was fit enough when last I saw him sitting on Father's throne." I know my resentment shows but I can only contain so much.

"Not anymore. He's missed every council meeting since you left."

A shadow passes over me. "What kind of illness?"

"I'm not a healer, but the rumors say it's the same as your father's malady, peace be his path." Lars pats my shoulder in an awkward gesture. "Your brother's fallen ill. They try to hide it, but I know. She'll end up alone for her troubles."

Alone on the Phantom Throne, De'ral rumbles.

"Is she sitting in on the council, then, while Petén's unable?" I ask outright. I wasn't expecting that. "Presiding over the meetings in his stead? Not leading the morning hunt, I hope? Chasing after fox and stag?"

"She leads the council, but not the hunt, though she rides with the courtiers." Larseen's lips thin. "Maybe it's nothing. Just the stress of the office. Petén's had a lot to adjust to and he hasn't touched a drop for months. I can attest to that, but he took on too much when he limited the power of the Sanctuary."

"You think he'll be giving it back?" Samsen asks.

"Not if Rhiannon has anything to say about it." Lars looks thoughtful for a moment. "Better she chose Petén than you or I, in any case, don't you think?" He smooths his robes and turns to leave.

"But you're well, I see," I say, hoping for some last bit of information. "If the virulent is catching, there could be an outbreak."

Lars laughed. "The only outbreak to worry about is Rhiannon." His brow wrinkles. "I've speculated too much, Bone Gatherer. Forgive me."

Now he's being respectful?

There's another splash, closer to the ship this time. "Whale after all," I say, though it moved too quickly to be sure. The conversation is over, leaving me convinced that Larseen has an agenda linked to Master Brogal, and that Kaylin might be right. Larseen could have removed Ash to put himself in her place. The good news is, they wouldn't hurt her, surely. Just send her back to Baiseen where she'll be hopping mad, of course, but safer than she would be here by my side.

Perhaps, though I'll miss her, it's a blessing after all.

68

MARCUS

"**G**ods of the Drop, what's that smell?" I cover my nose and mouth as I speak to Captain Anders. It's another brilliant sunrise on the deck marred only by the stink wafting off the water.

"Reefs are dying north of the Fancrest, don't you know?" He wears a bandanna over his face, only his eyes, thick brows, and forehead showing. "The glaciers are melting."

"This time of year?"

"Melting faster than is natural. Each day be like a thousand years."

He goes into so much detail I can barely follow—sea temperatures, rising tides, algae blooms, silt choking the corals, blocking sunlight. "Can't something be done?" I gag on the smell.

"Take deep breaths with your mouth open. Fastest way to acclimate."

Not what I meant, but I follow his advice. It works, a little. "But can't something be done to save the reefs?"

"If there is a cure, I've not heard of it. Ready the others. We'll reach the harbor soon." He waves straight ahead, toward the river mouth.

The *Dugong* tacks to the harbor on the morning tide. I cup my hands to my mouth and blow warmth into them. Another sunrise and still no sign of Ash. The captain calls for the tack again and the boom swings, rushing us forward into the wide-mouthed river. The flowing water is hemmed by white chalk cliffs that race up to the clouds. On the right, the formation tapers, like a giant petrol, wings tucked to dive.

"I guess that's why they call it Whitewing." I've never been to the small city and had thought the maps were an exaggeration. Not so at all.

From the deck, the Sanctuary is barely visible at the top of the right hand cliffs. It's strategic, reached by sailing farther upstream. Again an advantage to the openness of Baiseen. The first mate signals the crew to drop more sail, and soon we're running on only the jib, gliding along the Salmon River. I shiver as we run under the shadow of the cliffs on either side, the water stinking and brackish. Rafts of dark, unnamed lumps bob away from the hull as we glide through them.

Eyes.

"What?" I ask my phantom.

Eyes, watching us, De'ral says again. *To the south.*

I scan the mile-high cliffs on the left side of the harbor as hairs rise at the back of my neck. Before I can question further, Samsen comes up on deck and stands beside me, hand over his mouth. "What died?"

"The reefs. Where are the others?" I ask.

"Not far behind me," Samsen says, keeping his eyes on the horizon. The river narrows, a forest closing in on both sides, but there's still a view of the highest cliff, hundreds of feet above. "Look there," Samsen whispers, keeping his mouth covered. He points up, and to the south.

I follow his line of sight. "What is it?" Then I ask De'ral, *"Can you tell?"*

Not I. It's a moment before he says more. *But Salila can.*

I let out a nervous laugh as heat flushes my face. Great, I'm blushing like a blue-robe at the sound of her name. That will impress.

De'ral cuts into my thoughts, describing what is a dark smudge to my eyes. *It's the red-robe. He's stroking his horse's neck. Talking to it.*

"You can see him?" I ask.

No. Exasperation drips off his voice. *I can't see him, but the Mar women can. It's the same dark horse. She says it's Gollnar bloodstock, his favorite—*

"I don't care about the horse."

You should, De'ral says. *The red-robe does.*

"Wait. Mar women? As in more than one?"

Salila. He savors her name. *And the other. Not a friend. The two of them argue continuously.*

What would they be arguing about? I tilt my head, listening with my inner ears but catch nothing.

Salila says to be careful.

"Salila!" I nearly shout at her. *"You can speak directly to me, you know, through De'ral."* She's done it often enough before. Why not now? *"Please, I don't even know how to understand this message within a message."*

She's protecting you. De'ral says it like no other explanation is needed.

"I don't need protection! Just tell me how far Atikis is from Whitewing Sanctuary?" I speak aloud.

"If it's Atikis, we all need protection, Marcus." Samsen stares into the distance. "Your eyes are better than mine. I thought it was a bear cave, or maybe a moose."

"How far?" I repeat my question to De'ral.

A few hours' ride down the cliff and then up the other side.

"If it's the red-robe, he's nearer than I like." Samsen points at the winding trail, coming to the same conclusion. "It's not the same pinnacle as Whitewing's, though the distance is deceptive, a vertical climb." Samsen squints at me. "When did you become an eagle eye?"

"Best not ask, but good news, we're ahead of him."

I try again to converse with Salila directly, asking for news of Ash, but she doesn't respond. Maybe it's the foul water. No living thing would want to stay in it for long.

We sail farther up the river and the distant peak is swept from view. "Stay observant, Samsen. I don't know what our reception here will be, so close to Sierrak." I turn my gaze to the river's shore.

Wooden boardwalks line both sides of the waterway, built above the high water line. Submerged beneath them, the original pier ripples under the lapping waves. "Sea level that high?"

Samsen shakes his head. "Seems so."

Bloated fish and streams of slimy kelp bump against the pile caps, but the newer boardwalk remains dry.

"Where is everyone?" Samsen asks.

He's right. The place is practically deserted. Understandable, with the stench. With all the algae blooms and dead sea life, the toxins in the air would not be good to breathe. A donkey cart rolls along the other side, and up ahead, a few fishermen play dice in a huddle. Their boats are empty in their moors. Behind the boardwalks are dead gardens. Higher still, buildings stack so close to each other there's barely a gap. As we progress, more people appear until we put into the city of Whitewing proper. There are market stalls and one ship being off loaded, but it's still a desolate place.

"We'll go straight to the Sanctuary?" Samsen asked.

"I should hope so, with our documents, and the letter from Havest. You have it?"

Samsen hands it over but Larseen appears from below and intercepts. "That's my job, Marcus." He coughs. "Is there a dead whale beached below?"

"More than one, I think." My chest tightens at the reminder of the world on the brink, and Ash's absence. Up until now, it was her job to mind the documents. I've nearly surrendered to the fact that she is on her way back to Baiseen, but, selfish as it is, I hope it's not true. Maybe Ash can send a message to Lars via their medallions.

Maybe she has.

The thought does nothing for my mood, or my trust in Lars. If he knows more and isn't saying…

I can't understand it. If Brogal wanted her back, wanted her replaced, why didn't he just say so? Her disappearing without a word doesn't make sense.

Tyche and Piper join us, hands over their mouths. "What reek is in the air?" our healer asks.

I look up to the rose glow of the second sun and she follows my gaze. "Reefs are dying." I repeat Captain Anders. "Glaciers melting too fast, and the sea's warming. Seems it only takes a few degrees to cause grievous harm."

Tyche wrinkles her nose. "The stink is grievous, to be sure."

It takes longer than expected for the ship to be moored. No idea why. By the time we're on the docks, the sun shines high over the eastern cliffs, second sun out of sight. I sweep the deck, doing a double take at the wheelhouse. The cabin boy is staring. When we lock eyes, he slinks away.

"What's that about?" Piper asks before sipping from her waterskin.

"The lad?" Larseen cuts in. "Fascinated by savants, it seems."

He makes excuses for the spy? We can crush them both.

"But we won't," I say in the firmest voice I can muster. But part of me agrees.

"They know we're here." Piper nudges me in the side.

A troop of armed guards arrive at the top of the boardwalk, each in a smart black uniform, including a bandanna around the nose and mouth. They march down the zigzag steps to greet us.

"Havest must have sent word by phantom." I straighten my back as the guards approach.

"Or crow," Larseen says. "They use them to send messages from Pandom City."

"Let's hope it has warmed Whitewing to us," Samsen whispers. He steps forward with Larseen who introduces me as the Bone Gatherer here to meet with High Savant Warcott.

The guard salutes. "The Sanctuary is expecting you." He turns about and leads the way.

"That's our greeting?" Tyche asks. Her hand stays over her nose and mouth.

"At least we're going straight there this time." Piper takes Tyche's hand and shoots me a look.

I know what she means. Stay on guard, eyes open. With that thought in my head, I follow the troop up to the boardwalk. There the entire contingent salutes me and flanks us all like honored guests.

Or prisoners, De'ral adds.

Is my phantom being sarcastic? I'm not sure but I also can't argue the point. As we're marched to the Sanctuary, onlookers might have trouble telling if we are friends or foes. When we reach the highest level, I look back over the harbor. No sign of Kaylin and Ash.

We should be finding her, not visiting sanctuaries. He's angry.

I understand it, I want to bare my teeth, too. But I don't. "*Luckily, we're doing both. Now pay attention. I want this to go smoothly and without a hitch.*"

I listen for a response but hear only the sound of marching feet and my pulse pounding in my throat.

69

ASH

I choke on the taste of my captor's skin, spitting it out of my mouth as soon as I come to. My tongue burns, tar and fishy oil souring it. "Kaylin!" It's a half shriek, half sob as I struggle to right myself.

He shakes his head, the only part of his body he can move. They have him chained to the wall in an X, arms over his head, legs spread eagle. I start to speak but he gives me another no, his head turning side to side.

"Are you shushing me?" I wince as I send the thought, my headache slicing deep as the words form in my mind.

"Don't let them know we matter to each other." His face contorts as well.

"A little late for that." I gasp at the pain. *"You called me by name, not to mention killing the crew to reach me."* I'm panting by the time I finish the sentence. There's something very wrong with my head.

"You might have tipped them off when you threatened to boil them in demon blood if they touched me again."

"I said that?"

"Aye. It'll be hard for me to come off as a mercenary now." The calmness in his eyes, the absence of fear in the face of what I'm thinking must be certain death after prolonged torture, clashes with my rising panic. How does he stay so calm?

I breathe in the rank air of the hold and let it out slowly. He does matter to me. Of course, he matters so much. And I've never told him so.

"Kaylin?" The only sound around us is the slosh of the sea and thumps and drag above. Are they clearing bodies? There had been a lot of fighting. "Kaylin?"

"Speak to my mind."

"I can't. It hurts too much."

His brow wrinkles and fresh blood drips down his temples. "He thwacked you hard on the back of the head, and that goose egg—"

"I don't remember."

"I'm not surprised." He sends me the kindest look, he who is chained to the wall and dripping blood. "Speak Palrion, then," he suggests. "They won't understand."

I wipe tears out of my eyes, the iron manacles scraping my cheeks. "How did you get here? And the others? Is everyone safe? Tyche?" I close my eyes, not wanting to hear the answer, in case it's worse news. The dragging sounds overhead continue. They can't be happy with Kaylin, and the thought makes one word come to mind—retaliation.

Did they beat me again when I was passed out? I feel as if an eight-horse wagon train galloped over my back. I run my tongue around my mouth, making sure no teeth are missing. I swipe up blood but find no gaps in my smile, not that I'm smiling. Feels like I never will again. "Talk to me, Kaylin. While we can. Let me hear your voice."

"You were easy to find, lass, and the others are safe. It's just me, and you, in chains." He tries to shrug but doesn't have enough slack.

"Really?" He might be saying it in case our captors do speak Palrion and are hidden in the hold, listening. But would it be good for them to think there were more of us, or not? I don't know. My head pounds and I can't work it out.

Kaylin confirms it with a nod. Hair falls into his face, and he tries to shake it away. Blood trickles from his nose. He can't reach a shoulder to wipe it.

This is so awful. "And you came here alone?"

"Aye, to rescue you."

I give a furtive glance around the hold. "Thank you. Now what's the plan?"

He doesn't say anything.

"Is there no hope?" I want to ask if there is a Tangeen warship boarding this vessel as we speak, but I already know there isn't.

The walls and floor are thin enough to hear what's going on, and it's nothing resembling a rescue. The thumping above stops and the ship plows silently through the water. Occasionally overhead the sound of tin mop buckets clanking and wire brushes scrubbing back and forth echo in the background. Muffled commands ring out in the distance. Kaylin might have diminished the crew, but there seem to be enough left to sail on and do whatever it is they have a mind to. I don't like our chances.

"There is hope, lass," he says quietly.

I want very much to believe him, which might be the only reason why he says it—to keep our final moments on the path as peaceful as possible. They say how you leave the path has a bearing on how you walk back into your next life. Maybe he's trying to be kind, and at that moment, with it all so hopeless and dark, I love him even more for it.

We are silent for some time and then I say, "They were already mad at me, Kaylin, but I think they're very unhappy now, with you especially."

"That is true, lass."

How long we can live under these circumstances, I don't know. My gut knots in despair, for myself, and even worse for Kaylin. He's only here because of me. "Do you know where we're headed?" I ask to keep from thinking about what happens when we get there.

"North."

"On the Nulsea still?"

"Aye."

"So maybe to South Sierrak?"

"It seems so." His eyes are closed and his voice is only a whisper.

"Are you all right?"

"Reasonably fine." His lips twitch. "You?"

"I'm thirsty." My bucket is empty and there is no sign of them offering to refill it. Biting and kicking my guard might have been unwise, in retrospect.

"I agree. Water would be nice. When we are free from this voyage, and the whistle bones gathered, the Great Dying turned back, I will take you to my home isles of Tutapa. There, we can swim in the lagoons with creatures you've never seen the likes of."

"What creatures?"

"Sea dragons, for one."

Something deep within me brightens. "Sea dragons? Really?"

"Aye, lass."

My heart pounds, knowing that we may never leave this hold alive, let alone survive if we do. I might be able to resign myself to it, but taking Kaylin off the path with me? Because of me? "What were you thinking, coming aboard and attacking a crew when you were ridiculously outnumbered," I ask, heat rising to my head as it pounds, fit to burst. "Tell me what you were thinking, please, so I can understand."

"That's simple, lass. I was thinking of you."

70

T he guards waste no time hustling us along the main thoroughfare, over a stone causeway, and then up a heavily trafficked road. Everyone gives way to them, foot traffic and horses alike. They're a grim bunch, the people of Whitewing, but with the stench on the air, who wouldn't be? When we reach the gates to the Sanctuary, our armed escort salutes and backs away, job done. But they don't go far. The Whitewing soldiers effectively form a blockade between us and the city.

And our ship, De'ral says.

The fact hasn't escaped me. I straighten, my hand nearer to the hilt of my sword. *"It was similar at Nonnova, too, and that turned out well. Probably just visitor protocol."*

The high wooden gates open to a welcoming party of savants. *"See? All good."*

Waiting behind the gate is the High Savant himself, easily identified by his red-robe showing beneath the hem of a long winter cloak. Beside him is an orange-robe, judging by her hem, a woman with soft features and blue eyes that land on nothing for more than an instant. She steps forward. "I'm Mariah, recorder for his excellency, Whitewing High Savant, Master Warcott." She raises her arm out toward the red-robe and bows her head, all very graceful and proper.

"Well met," I say, speaking first before I realize that Larseen is stepping up to do so. Too late now. I nod at him, and he introduces me and the others.

As we stand outside the Sanctuary, still not invited in, more savants arrive, either to greet the newcomers or to guard their master. By the look on their faces, formal and tight, it's the latter. I wonder what reputation precedes us, or if it is the realm we come from that has them cautious.

"It's good to see you are alive, and returned from Aku successfully," Warcott finally says, glancing at my yellow robes below the hem of my long coat. "Welcome to Whitewing Sanctuary. You may enter."

"Thank you." Without further word, we are ushered in.

"Stunning," Piper whispers as she and the others follow.

"And no stink," Tyche says.

"On shore winds spare us most days," Mariah replies to her comment. "And yes, Whitewing is the oldest sanctuary in Tangeen, founded centuries before Pandom City."

I believe it. The Sanctuary is carved from the steep hillside, terraced into many levels out of the sheer cliff, much steeper than Baiseen. It climbs up from the sea and looks, from here, to reach the clouds.

"Each level embodies one of the twelve steps to An'awntia," Mariah informs us as we climb. "We have study and training halls on each one, the landscape evoking the particular level. It helps students immerse."

"Impressive," I say, and it is. But my mind is on other things.

"This is the first level, representing awareness of self, of course." Mariah sweeps one arm out. The grounds are covered with short-cropped grass, gravel pathways, and wooden buildings that are open to view, nothing to hide. Geese waddle near a rock ringed pond. In the trees, blue jays caw. "We've had two thousand years to develop our Sanctuary," she goes on. "Unlike Baiseen which sprung up overnight."

I want to counter that hundreds of years is hardly overnight but hold it back. Get the bone, meet Ash, head on to Asyleen. It's a sound plan and I'm sticking to it.

On the next level, awareness of values, the paths lead to benches under weeping willows and spiral fountains with bronze animal statues. Near one is a wishing well. It's smaller than Aku's but still, I wouldn't mind tossing a coin into it.

"Plenty of places to meditate," I say, in case they expect a comment.

"As there are on all levels," Mariah answers.

By the time we reach the eighth level, renewal, we all stop to stare. The main structure is made of glass framed with dark wood.

"A hothouse," Piper says.

Through the endless windows are flowers and fruits in hanging baskets and savants in summer robes with rolled up sleeves and bare feet. "Are those butterflies in the gardens?" I blink.

"Indeed," Mariah says. "For pollination."

I make a note of adding something like that to the palace gardens, or would it be better in the Sanctuary? It takes a moment for me to realize that I'm blocking the way while I think until Piper pulls me to the side. The traffic up and down the steps increases as we climb, students mostly, their conversations cutting off as they approach only to pick up again as they hurry on.

"Renewal is a favorite level of many," Mariah says. "Especially this time of year." She looks at my wonder and smiles. "Shall we move on?"

Our cheeks are flushed when we arrive at level twelve— the last step to An'awntia, self-acceptance— but not Warcott's. I wonder again how the High Savant knew to meet us at the gates the moment we arrived. Why didn't he send a messenger instead of going all that way himself? I can't imagine Yuki having done so, or High Savant Brogal.

Havest met you with a parade, De'ral reminds me. *On Aku, it was Tyche.*

I smile to myself. *"True."*

"Everyone at Whitewing walks the steps twice a day, including our High Savant," Mariah says as if she can read the curiosity in my face. "No exceptions."

"Excellent for health," Piper says.

They let us study the landscape of level twelve before continuing. The first thing I notice is the tower of the main hall. It's the highest structure I've yet seen, higher than the tallest building in Whitewing city itself.

"Immaculate," Samsen says.

Every path is raked, every hedge and border trimmed, yet a feeling of wilderness surrounds the edges. I wonder how easily it can be protected from the north. I see no wall there.

"I'll bet Ash wishes she could see this," Larseen says.

He makes it sound like she chose not to come. "She already has," I answer, struggling to keep the irritation out of my voice. She talked of it last spring, but I don't remember exactly what she said.

A high-terraced sanctuary with the main hall and training fields at the top of a tableland, De'ral says.

My cheeks burn. Ash is always excited when she returns from travel, and me? I'm usually too deep in my own struggles, with Father, my phantom, a girl, to pay close attention. I can't believe I've been so selfish with her. The realization sticks in my throat like a fishbone. *"I'll be better from now on,"* I vow on the spot.

Maybe try being better at what's in front of you.

"Pardon?"

You said you had a question, my phantom warns. *She wants to hear it.*

I turn to Mariah while the High Savant converses in private with a messenger. "How is it that Whitewing outdoes the capital, Pandom City?"

She curls her lip. "Whitewing was once on Sierrak soil. That's a land that reveres their savants above their Magistrates." She sighs. "A reminder of an era gone by in Tangeen history."

"A time when savants were seen as numinous," Piper says, adding a little wistfully.

"We were born in the wrong century," I say as I follow the High Savant, passing the stone steps leading to the main hall. Warcott is taking us down a different path, toward the trees.

"What's that you say?" Larseen isn't looking at the building. He has his eyes fixed on two young women, green-robes, heading our way. They give us a wide berth, bowing to the High Savant as they pass.

"I was saying, they knew how to respect the sanctuaries back then." I smile.

"And they knew how to build them, too," Samsen adds.

The halls and other buildings are covered with vines all the way up to the peaked timber roofs. Only the windows and doors are trimmed free of the lush growth. As we walk along, music pours out of the halls as do savants in winter cloaks and sheepskin hats and boots. Those walking by us give welcoming nods after bowing to Master Warcott. When a bell rings, throngs of blue- and green-robe students empty out of the hall and break into a run, their legs long and gangly as they head for the training field.

"Morning ritual?" Tyche asks. "On Aku?"

"Or something much like it," Piper answers.

I never thought I would miss the intensive training on Aku, but compared to now, it seems like simpler times. "I wonder if they have an obstacle course here," I say, searching through the tree-lined field.

"Let's hope not," Samsen says as he chuckles.

My face lifts. Everyone on Aku had a good laugh the first day De'ral and I tackled the obstacle course. Finally, I can laugh at it, too, until I remember the island is in ruin now.

Warcott leads us past the training field. On the grounds, young students clustered around their teachers. Like in sanctuaries everywhere, they listen to the orange- and yellow-robe savants who pace back and forth in front of them with their hands behind their backs. Again, I think of Aku, especially when the group closest to us drops to their knees and raises their phantoms. From the lawn comes a spray of dirt as mixed classes of phantoms—a black raven, a cobra, and several short human-like forms along with a lynx and a warthog—erupt from the ground. The students are in good form, and not at all distracted by us, or the High Savant's presence.

Samsen exchanges a look with me as the students are instructed to run the perimeter. It wasn't that long-ago Belair and I did the same, and not very well at the start. The young savants take off and the phantoms follow, some better than others. A few gardeners pushing wheelbarrows rush out of the way to keep from being bowled over by those not paying attention. The orange-robe savants shout encouragement, or in some cases reprimands. Morning training is underway.

High Savant Warcott doesn't slow his pace or comment as he takes a new path toward a cathedral of trees encircled with colored flags, one for each of the robe levels. We pass under the giant boughs and snapping cloth, entering a clearing in the center. There are benches in rows down the middle, made of split logs and set into the ground. It's another good idea to utilize outdoor space.

"Please," he addresses me. "Be seated." The High Savant motions to Mariah who slips away. Then he shucks his cloak and passes it to an attendant. He's a tall man with dark hair and sharp features, very formal, even when his face is relaxed. "Welcome, again, Marcus Adicio and company," he says when we are settled. "It is a pleasure to host Palrio at the Sanctuary of Whitewing."

I stand and bow before sitting back down. Tyche, who is next to me, looks skyward, wrinkling her nose. "Smells like rain," she whispers.

I follow her gaze but can't see a cloud.

Warcott clasps his hands in front of him, the image of patience. "Please, for the records, state the reason for your visit."

I stand again, feeling a bit like a grasshopper, and straighten my cloak, clear my throat. "I, Marcus Adicio, warrior savant and messenger from Baiseen, the Bone Gatherer as assigned by High Savant Brogal, red-robe overseer of the sanctuaries of Palrio, and my company…" I open my hand out to include them, introducing each one by name, phantom, rank, and origins.

De'ral yawns.

"He wants formal? I'm showing him formal." I smile. "We have been charged with the procurement of six of the twelve original whistle bones as written in the ancient Sierrak tablets. The task falls to me at this time in Amassia's cycle of the Great Dying, as only I, who came to Aku over Mossman's Shoals, can accomplish it." I speak the words Brogal instructed Ash to say, but I still don't know if even half of them are true.

From the corner of my eye, Larseen fidgets.

Warcott is about to speak but I'm not finished. "As Master Havest informed us, Whitewing was given charge over the original Mummy Wheat whistle bone, symbolizing the sixth step to An'awntia, the courage and determination to walk the path we must, and by doing so, gain the ways and means to alter it. We are here to collect Mummy Wheat for the allied realms, by your leave, High Savant Warcott of Whitewing Sanctuary."

With, or without, his leave. De'ral shows little appreciation for protocol.

"Indeed, we've been expecting you," the High Savant says and motions for me to sit again.

It makes me wonder why he didn't meet us at the gate with Mummy Wheat and send us on our way. But no. We're wading through the formalities.

"Given the nature of our political climate," Warcott continues, "I have arranged our meeting here, out of doors, away from prying ears and eyes. I hope the safety of this natural cathedral is adequate recompense for a hall with fire and board."

"Safety?" I have to ask because he's saying it like he expects trouble.

"Let's say we're weighing on the side of caution." Warcott picks lint off his sleeve.

"Caution against what, exactly," I ask, my brow creasing.

"Rumors only. Nothing to be too concerned about."

"Spies?"

"That's one way to describe him."

Before he could say more, if he even intended to, Mariah returns. Her eyes shift about, searching the crowd, but that seems to be her norm. Her phantom is up, which it wasn't before. I assume at first it's a *warrior* by the size, near that of a man, and the strong, reptilian jaws, powerful forelimbs, and upright stance. My eyes go to the long-curved nails on both hands and feet, like a raptor's talons. The forelimbs are held oddly, one on top of the other. Maybe *ouster*?

Both. De'ral grinds his teeth.

"Would you relax? She is not the enemy."

Are you sure?

"Quiet!" I'm finding it difficult to concentrate with my phantom close to the surface, and so highly opinionated. It splits my attention and makes my hands sweat. Did I just miss a question from Warcott?

Mariah passes the High Savant a drawstring pouch. It's the shape and size I would expect the whistle bone to be in. Mummy Wheat is from a short piece of Er's arm, the radius, if I remember right, about mid-shaft. *"See? He's going to hand it over."* But as I speak, my forehead prickles.

At the same time, Tyche pulls on my coat, and I scan our setting. *"What does she see?"*

Or smell. De'ral pushes into my head. *The whole place reeks of –*

"Rain," Tyche whispers. "Fresh churned soil and rain."

I take a deep breath through my nose while trying to follow Warcott's speech. Atikis!

The High Savant opens the pouch and, sure as predicted, removes the whistle bone. "And here it is," he says, holding it out for all to see. "Mummy Wheat, the original whistle bone of Whitewing since the dismantling of the crown of bones." He then has Mariah unroll a scroll and melt sealing wax at the bottom. He motions me to him. "Now if you'd be so kind as to impress your seal here." He taps the scroll. "As evidence of receipt. We can make the exchange."

"Exchange?" I say, standing again. "What exchange?" I ask, my mind going in multiple directions.

"Definitely Atikis, unless there's a farm nearby." Piper is up beside Samsen.

"We were further ahead of him," I say, hand going to the hilt of my sword. "Weren't we?"

Not anymore! De'ral roils under my skin.

I turn to Warcott and shout a warning as an arrow zings through the air. It hits with a thwack, striking his hand dead center. The whistle bone flies from his grip and arcs skyward. The High Savant curses then commands, "Savants, defend the circle!" All the while, the arrow is still sticking out of his palm. It would have gone right through if it weren't stopped by the red fletches.

Around us, twenty swords are drawn out of their scabbards and Atikis's ghoulish riders appear. In moments, we are surrounded by the multiple phantoms undulating in and out of the ground. Warcott's guards protect him as he snaps the arrow off and pulls it free of his hand. His focus is on one thing only. Finding the whistle bone. He drops to all fours and searches the grass, ignoring the blood gushing from his hand.

"Raise your phantoms!" I order my companions.

We scramble away from the benches to reach the open space. Tyche is out first, climbing over the back of the seats and landing in the aisle. In a blink, her impala springs from the ground. It lands light, eyes going wide, long neck stretched tall. The speckled brown coat shakes free of dirt and grass. Were the horns always so long?

I draw my sword. Steel clangs on steel as I block the advancing riders. I need more room. This space is hemmed in, too close to raise De'ral. Not yet. "Stay behind me," I shout to Tyche as I block hammering blows. Fights break out all around us and I run the nearest phantom through. "Call that whistle bone!" I tell her.

She's already chanting.

Samsen and Piper have their phantoms up the moment they clear the aisle. Weapons bloodied, they flank me and Tyche. De'ral wants out, but there's still no room to raise him, not in these close quarters. He'll knock our people into the sky. I look for an opening as he roars under my skin, making my head split with the pain of holding him back. "Step away!" I command them. I need De'ral in this fight.

"Tyche," Samsen yells. "Look out!" A slick, wet phantom horse emerges from the ground. Its rider wears a grim mask, twisted into a hideous stare. He wields a scimitar in each hand, high over his head as dirt falls from him and his mount. It quickly morphs into a snake and the rider releases a battle cry.

Tyche stumbles back just in time to avoid a blow while Samsen's eagle, talons extended, cuts in front of her. The phantom rider's throat is slashed, but it advances anyway, head askew on a torn neck. From the ground erupts more riders, circling around, tighter and tighter, closing in. Samsen's phantom swoops again, and Piper stands in front of Tyche, snake heads hissing. She still hasn't retrieved the bone.

"Call Mummy Wheat!" I shout, backing away from my companions. De'ral rakes the inside of his mind, his angst sending shooting pain through my head.

Release me!

"*I'm trying!*"

I head for the perimeter while Tyche and her phantom continue to *call*, its high-pitched voice growing in intensity. It cuts through the sounds of battle and undulating *warrior* phantoms, piercing the air like an invisible spear. Beyond the pulpit, Warcott curses as the whistle bone rises out of the grass a length away from where he searches. It flies out of his reach, arcing to Tyche. I gain the edge of the grove and drop to my knees, waving others out of the way. "Stay back!"

Before Tyche can catch the incoming bone in her outstretched hands, a black condor dives from the sky and grabs it midair. It tries to fly away, but Tyche's *call* is too powerful. The massive bird, whistle bone still in one talon, comes hurling back toward her, all while madly pumping its wings to escape. Whose phantom is it?

I lose sight of Tyche when De'ral tears from the earth. Before I can instruct him, he leaps at the bird, grabs a fist full of tail feathers, and slams it to the ground. Samsen rushes in and plunges his sword through its heart and the condor vanishes from sight. From the corner of my eye, I see Warcott's chest bloom with dark blood. "No!"

The whistle bone drops to the grass, but before it flies to Tyche, Larseen dives, grabbing it with both hands. The force of his momentum sends him skidding forward, and he bangs into two phantom riders thundering out of the ground, swords drawn. Piper jumps to his aid and I charge, De'ral at my side.

Larseen recovers from his fall and his jackal, fierce and bristled, *calls*.

Weapons fly from Atikis's riders and De'ral steps up to pound the phantoms back into the ground, his fists like sledgehammers. Dirt and rubble spray the air with every blow. Samsen and his eagle cut down any phantoms after Tyche, the close quarters working in their favor. I don't fail to notice that the Aku girl is the focus of the phantom riders' attention even more so than the whistle bone. "Protect Tyche," I shout. They don't need reminding.

De'ral shields Tyche, but as he does, a serpent phantom emerges from the ground between Larseen and his jackal. It rears up and swallows the whistle bone in one gulp, Larseen's hand with it.

De'ral lets loose a bellowing challenge and I rush in. The snake has the whistle bone a foot down its throat, and Larseen is up to his arm pit in it. One of Warcott's orange-robes hacks at the phantom as it tries to return to the ground, dragging Larseen along with it.

"Stop the serpent," I call to the savants nearest the creature. I'm not dead sure who is on our side but think of one quick way to find out. "It swallowed the whistle bone."

De'ral pulls a flagpole out of the ground. In a few strides, he's on top of the snake. He skewers it in the middle, green flag still attached, and wrenches it out of the ground while it writhes, impaled. Larseen's eyes bulge as he gasps for breath. His efforts to reclaim his arm, and the whistle bone, fail. It's still stuck, his face red and contorting.

De'ral turns about in a circle and bellows a challenge, holding the flagpole high, Larseen thumping along with it like a limp puppet. Then a new battle cry rings out. More of Warcott's savants pour into the clearing, hacking at the red-robe's phantoms, sending the riders to ground. De'ral lashes out, impaling everything within reach. I engage those attacking Tyche as she calls away their weapons, but I can't run after my phantom, and my control is slipping away.

"Not that one," I say, but it's too late.

De'ral turns back to me with the pole raised over his head, brandishing Mariah's *warrior* lizard, a lynx phantom, and at least two dead savants all squashed together tight. The lynx vanishes, gone to ground, but the lizard still tries to wiggle free. "Stop attacking our allies!" At the very bottom of the stack are a twisting serpent and a dangling Larseen. *"Put them down and get the damned whistle bone."* I stumble, my sword arm going out to catch my fall.

De'ral stares at the lizard for a moment before dropping the pole and stomping on the phantoms to hold them down. That brings a whole new set of cries from Larseen. Undaunted, De'ral takes his massive thumb and forefinger and pinches the phantoms, removing them like pieces of meat from a roasting stick. He sets each gently on the ground where they collapse and disappear.

I wipe sweat from my brow. *"The bone? De'ral, get the bone."*

De'ral throttles the snake and snaps it in half by stretching it from both ends. White ichor sprays into the sky. Both ends of the phantom thrash, then finally go to ground. Larseen falls hard and rolls about in the grass, cradling his arm. The limb is wet and looks like a skinned rabbit, the sleeve of his coat dissolved away. I search for the bone and when I look up, Warcott's guards have their swords leveled at my throat and De'ral's flagpole points at Warcott's chest. No one moves, and the battle recedes into a blur.

"Give me back the whistle bone," Warcott says. His hand is wrapped in a strip of orange cloth while blood seeps through. "I can protect it."

"I don't have it," I say. In my peripheral vision, I watch Atikis's phantom riders dive back into the ground and know exactly who has Mummy Wheat now.

"I don't believe you." Warcott's chest heaves.

De'ral makes a growling sound and I remember he's pointing a weapon at our host and ally.

"De'ral, lower your spear. He is not the enemy."

Are you sure?

"Just do it," I study the row of blades aimed at me. "Atikis took the bone, clearly. It's gone."

"I saw it in your man's hand," Warcott bellows.

He calls you a liar? De'ral's spear inches closer to the High Savant's chest.

Heat rushes to my head. I've stayed out of phantom perspective on purpose because I don't want to be trapped there. I don't want to risk De'ral taking over complete control, especially now, but with my phantom threatening Warcott, I see no other choice. By the bones, we have to go after the red-robe. But first, I must deal with Warcott. *"In a civilized fashion,"* I say to De'ral.

With that thought in mind, I push into De'ral, my arms and legs forcing in as if donning clothes that have shrunk on the line and are now too tight. I plan to drop the weapon threatening Warcott, retrieve the lost bone, and send that red-robe on to his next path to An'awntia. Ready, I push down on De'ral but the instant I do, I'm flipped into the air to land hard on my back. A barred door slams shut and suddenly all I can do is observe as if watching from a bell tower. A vise tightens around my head and renewed pain sears into my mind. The only relief is further down in the cool darkness below. *"You will not trap me."*

But I will. De'ral chuckles.

I blink, and for an instant see my hand in the grass. I've fallen? Hopefully, my limb is still attached to my body. I can't be sure, because I've lost feeling in my arms and legs. I can't move a muscle. *"De'ral. Listen to me. Let me up."* I use everything Zarah, my instructor on Aku, taught me. I focus my mind and force myself to sit up but still all I see is blades of grass and my unmoving hand. The earth jars around me, tearing apart, shuddering under my phantom's footfalls.

"De'ral! What are you doing? You have to let me up!"

71

KAYLIN

I had a plan, and it should have worked. The odds were with me, with Ash, but those odds didn't count on ancient rune chains. Where did they find the wicked things? I can scarcely bear the constant, searing pain. The effort to form a thought is nigh impossible. When I manage, it doesn't reach Salila, or Teern, though calling on them might make matters worse.

Who am I kidding?

Matters cannot be worse.

No! *There is a way out.* I just can't see it yet.

I say so, over and over, until I believe it's true. Ash and I are not going to end like this. Our world is *not* going to end like this!

Find the facts. Work with what you know. The words of a long-ago mentor float back to me.

I can do that. At least, I can try.

My head rings with pain as I concentrate. And in focusing on each breath I find a sliver of comfort. We are still alive. And in thinking on that—mistake number four might have been surrendering my sword too soon.

Was it a bluff? Will they keep Ash alive by all means? I can't dwell long on how it would have gone otherwise. Ash would be dead at the bottom of the sea and no phantom or savant or even the Ma'ata corals would change that.

She's alive, I remind myself, drawing strength. And I am still here. It's a sure sign that they want us for something, but what? As the Bone Gatherer's companions? To lure him, and the bones?

Maybe they took Ash for her knowledge? Maps? Locations? Or could it be that some savant out there thinks she's more than just a wordsmith working for the once-but-no-longer Heir? A simple mistaken identity? The questions make my head spin, and the pain redoubles. The manacles cut deep.

A good splash of water is nowhere in sight, but even without it, I need to resist the runes and regain my strength. I'd take a bucket of my captor's blood in lieu of seawater, without hesitation. If only they would come a little closer.

"Kaylin?"

"Lass? Did you sleep?"

"And awoke still alive. That's good news." Her attempt at lightness pinches my heart.

"I was thinking the same."

We fall silent in the dark, until Ash whispers, "Kaylin, let's not worry."

It's brave. Incredibly brave, what with so much to worry about. "All right. We won't worry, but maybe, somehow, I can explain—"

"No, Kaylin."

"No?"

"I don't care to spend my last moments—"

"Lass, I assure you, these are not." But my strength drains and the burning pain won't stop.

She clears her throat. "I don't care to spend my last moments with the one I love in questions and reasoning."

If we are going to be thrown off the path, this might be the only time to tell her the truth of who I am but as her words melt into me like snow on warm skin, I say the only thing that matters. *Ash, I love you, too…*

But the rune chains take that moment to subsume my mind and I fall into utter darkness before the words can escape aloud.

· · ·

I jolt awake, my body stiffening. A crash rips above us. We both glance to the ceiling as boots thump across the floorboards.

"They're coming," Ash whispers. "Maybe they're bringing water?"

They're most likely bringing the captain and that might mean death, for me at least. I put near two dozen crew members off their paths before losing count. There's no captain on the Ma'ata blessed sea who'd forgive a slaughter like that. "Maybe, but for now, lass, close your eyes. I promise you everything will be all right, no matter what happens." My heart pinches tighter. It's a promise I will die trying to keep.

The hatch opens and down the ladder clomp heavy boots. Ash closes her eyes and I do the same, dropping my chin to my chest.

"That's him?" a level, female voice asks in Sierrak.

"Aye, Captain."

"He's just a lad." She's having trouble believing in my sword skills.

"A lad with a demon inside him."

I smile inwardly. Something like that.

"Was he sent to protect the girl?" the captain asks.

"Without doubt."

"That confirms it. She's the one they want."

"Aye, and we have her now." The sailor chuckles but cuts short when the captain doesn't join in.

"I want her off first when we put into Oteb. Roll her up in a rug, if you have to, but keep the rune chains on, and don't let her be seen."

"Aye, Captain. And him?"

"He goes, too, same way. Keep them alive. Understand? No mistakes."

"Aye, Captain, but the crew won't like it. They're already setting up the keel haul."

Yes! Perfect. Keel haul me! Please! Even with the rune chains, the sea would restore at least some of my strength, and if Salila could hear me, then...

"Tell 'em to put the ropes away. I'll cut any down myself if they try to skewer him. He will be useful, especially if the girl knows him. Any sign she did?"

"He called her by name. Dropped his weapon when I put a knife to her throat."

The captain nods. "Make sure you hold a knife to her then, when we disembark."

A bell rings, only slightly muffled.

"Oteb's on the horizon," the captain says. "All hands on deck."

The sound of their heavy treads disappear up the ladder and fade away. Still, I wait some time before speaking to Ash. I don't want to pull her from peaceful oblivion if she's fallen asleep again.

"Kaylin? Did you hear all that?" she asks, lifting her eyes to me with effort. Her hair hangs limp, a curtain falling to her nose. "What's in Oteb?"

Only one thing. "The road to Asyleen."

"Of course, and what are these rune chains, exactly?"

"Symbols carved with very old incantations."

"Incantations?"

"They keep a savant's phantom from rising."

"That'll have no effect on me."

"They think you're savant, lass."

"And you, too?"

"Seems that way."

She coughs and tries to ease the weight of her restraints. Soon I hear soft snoring as she nods off. "My beautiful lass. We are in a tight place, no denying it. But on my life, I will find a way to save you."

72

MARCUS

I open my eyes but can't make sense of what I see. The ground undulates. Is it the sea? Then I realize. These are not my eyes I'm looking through. They're De'ral's.

"Bring him in!" Samsen slaps me hard across my face. That's definitely mine, not De'ral's.

The sting jerks me back into my body and I grab Samsen's hand to stop the next blow. "I'm awake."

"And so is your *warrior*. Call him in," Piper growls the words out. "Before matters get any worse."

Worse? I squeeze my eyes shut and open them again to blue sky and white clouds, the tips of redwood trees and the backside of De'ral. My phantom sits at the edge of the clearing, pounding the ground with giant fists. My head jars with each thrust and I can only hope he isn't hammering Whitewing savants like nails into the earth. I take a deep breath and call him in, surprised when there is no resistance. I'm back in control, though I feel a cold sweat creep over me. "What happened?"

Samsen helps me to sit. "You and your *warrior* had a bit of an argument when the red-robe started to retreat."

I vaguely remember that much. "And?"

"You won, but your *warrior* made mincemeat out of the remaining phantoms and added a few Whitewing guards in for spice."

He tries to hide it, but I see the concern in Samsen's eyes. Or maybe that's a reflection of my own.

"Where's the whistle bone?" I ask.

"We aren't sure," Piper says. She takes my pulse and examines a gash in my arm.

Before I can protest, her serpent sinks its fangs into my wrist. "A warning. Please!" Healing venom rushes through my blood.

"That's better, isn't it?" she asks.

I can't disagree, so I say nothing. "Atikis must have it."

"Tyche tried to call it back when your *warrior* started dealing with Warcott's guards. It was mayhem after that."

"Any of us hurt?" The serpent retracts its fangs and I struggle to my feet.

"Larseen," Piper says grimly. "He's going to lose his arm."

I curse. "Where is he?"

"In the Whitewing infirmary. They'll have to ship him back to Baiseen as soon as he can travel. It'll be a long recovery."

"What of Ash?" My head snaps up. "Did she and Kaylin show?"

Piper shakes her head no.

The clearing is quiet save for gardeners raking up the mess. The turf and flowers they usually cart around in their wheelbarrows are replaced with bodies and broken weapons. Flies buzz and I shoo them away from my face. "Tyche?"

"She's having a little chat with Warcott," Piper says.

"The girl?"

"She's an orange-robe, don't forget, and the best one of us to convince the High Savant she can call the bone from Atikis, at least at close range."

"And how are we planning on getting that close?"

"Hopefully a forgiving Warcott will furnish us with horses and supplies."

"You left her to manage all of that?!"

"You were out, and the plan seemed best coming from her," Samsen says. "Least threatening among us after..." His voice trails away.

I scan the carnage and nod. "Are we still all on the same side?"

"I hope so," Samsen answers when Piper remains silent. "Your *warrior*, in the end, protected more than he harmed. Warcott would have lost much more without him."

"But their whistle bone is lost." I scrub my face. "What a mess."

Piper hands me a water skin and I drink deeply.

"Excuse me, Bone Gatherer." A blue-robe messenger appears as both suns dim behind thick clouds.

I cork the skin and wipe my lips with the back of my hand.

The blue-robe stops several paces away. "Master Warcott would see you now, if that's convenient." Her voice is high, a child's pitch, but confident. It reminds me of Tyche when we first met. So much has changed since then. "Please follow me." She turns and strides off toward the main hall, looking back several times to see if we follow.

Piper and Samsen move up to flank me. This is when I miss Ash the most. She's the one who can negotiate delicate situations. But if Samsen and Piper sent Tyche, I trust that it was the best course. I turn to gaze at the sea, but that way is only an endless expanse of dark blue. "We need to send a message to the harbormaster, for Ash when she arrives."

"First things first," Piper says. "Let's negotiate our way out of this."

I let my breath out. "Agreed." I take the lead, following the child to the no doubt furious red-robe of Whitewing.

73

MARCUS

Tyche came through, amazingly. It's a relief, or should be, but I can't let myself relax. Something in the back of my mind keeps nagging. The negotiation with Warcott went smoothly, yes, but that's the problem. It was too easy. Wasn't it?

"Thoughts?" I ask Samsen as we saddle the horses, fine animals leased from the High Savant. I keep my voice low in case of prying ears. "Is he telling us everything?"

Samsen straps his bow and quiver to his back. "Warcott believes in the second sun, of that I am sure. You saw the Twin Sun flag flying atop the tower?"

"I did."

"But there is a thorn in his side with Brogal, judging by the way his mouth turned down when he had to say our High Savant's name. Us losing Whitewing's whistle bone didn't help ingratiate him to our cause, either."

"We didn't lose it. It was never fully passed to my hand, what with all his formalities."

"I think he holds you responsible for leading Atikis here. But look at us. We're saddling his horses, heading on with fresh supplies."

"Bought and paid for by me."

"True, but I don't think he's sending us wrong, though his faith in us to recover the bone may be less than he says." Samsen ties his pack to the back of his saddle. "And you're right. There's something he's not saying."

I smooth the saddle pad over my mount's back. They've offered me a strong mare, sixteen hands, a charcoal gray. Her legs, muzzle, mane, and tail are pitch black and her eyes a piercing blue. Striking animal, but a little cantankerous. Her ears pin back when I tighten the girth. "Manners," I say in a mildly chiding voice.

It's something Ash would do, only the reminder of manners would be directed at me, not the horse. She's right. I ease back the girth two notches. "Sorry, girl. Just anxious to get on the road. We'll do it up slowly." I lead her out of the stables, taking a deep breath of cold air while scanning the neighboring peaks. Nothing to be seen, at least, no red-robe rider that I can tell. I'm aware we will be headed inland, leaving the sea. Leaving her behind…

Salila.

She's someone I want on my side.

Before joining the others, I ask Samsen, "They have set a watch on the docks for Ash and Kaylin?"

"I've affirmed that twice already, Marcus. I won't do it a third."

I nod. "Anything of the cabin boy?"

"He was on the docks. Hid when he saw me coming."

"Plenty of time to get to the bottom of that when we return." Right now, more things are pressing.

Like enemy red-robes? De'ral growls.

"Exactly." I turn to Tyche and smile. "Ready to ride?"

She holds the reins of a small black mare while Piper gives her a leg up and shortens her stirrups to fit. Samsen waits next to our healer until she turns and melts briefly into him. Then he mounts his lean liver chestnut and stands sentinel over our party. In the cloudy sky, his gray eagle circles overhead. "All clear, for now," he confirms again.

"But Atikis can't be far," Piper says, mounting up beside him. "We have a compass?"

I pull it out of my pocket and face north. We plan to take the northeast trail to the Salmon River. There we turn due north through a pass that leads to the Asyleen Mountain Ranges. It's a shortcut, one Warcott says is unknown outside the Sanctuary. If Atikis is headed to Asyleen, we might ambush him there. At least, that's what Warcott suggests. I don't know if I can trust him but there's no other choice. Asyleen is where the next whistle bone lies, whether we best Atikis or not.

Once there, we will have the pleasure of meeting Sierrak's most well-known High Savant Zanovine, even if we find the Whitewing whistle bone first and take it from Atikis. Of course, the Magistrate, Rantorjin, isn't a fan of travelers, especially those from neighboring Tangeen. How the leaders of Asyleen will take to my request for their original whistle bone, I have no idea. For the hundredth time, I wish Ash was with us. She always offers a different perspective, and often a better one. And her diplomatic skills, her language skills. "I miss them more than ever now," I mumble.

"What's that?" Samsen asks.

"Just thinking of Ash." I lead my mare forward a few steps, tighten the girth without her protest, and mount up. "Let's move out." With the compass in my right hand and reins in the left, I urge my mare forward. I suspect there are

Whitewing savants watching our progress as we take the long road that winds down the other side of the terraced grounds to the Northwest trail. Who knows. Maybe the boy from the *Dugong,* too, or whoever he works for. I feel eyes on me and touch the leather pouch holding the whistle bones of Baiseen, Bakton, Kutoon, and Pandom City. *"Four in our possession,"* I say to De'ral, just in case he's listening. Not counting earlier grumbles and jabs, my phantom hasn't breathed a word since I brought him back to ground. I listen for a response.

When none comes, I empty my lungs in a rush. It's a strange feeling, the eerie silence in my soul. It makes me want to raise my phantom so I can give him a good talking to. And make sure he's still there. According to Piper, he'd nearly killed Warcott and Mariah, phantoms and all. I claimed it was accidental, tight spaces and writhing enemy phantom, but had it been?

I pocket the compass and lean back in the saddle, the gray mare's hooves clopping down the meandering slope. The last allied sanctuary is behind us, and I still haven't had a chance to talk to anyone about these problems with De'ral. Deep inside I hear a distant chuckle, but as soon as I notice, it vanishes.

"What's wrong?" Samsen asks as he rides beside me.

I shrug. "So much for the warrior training exercises."

Samsen's forehead creases but he's interrupted.

"Get away!" Tyche screams. She brushes madly at her forearm.

"What is it?" I rein the mare up to her.

"An ant bit me." Tyche gasps.

"An ant," Samsen says, keeping emotion out of his face. "Hardly a major wound, after what we've been through." But his mouth's gone thin.

Tyche fixes red, welling eyes on Samsen. "It stings."

"Let's have a look," Piper says. She rides up beside us.

"It's gone." Tyche shows us the red mark on her wrist.

I glance at Piper and Samsen, who look back with expectant faces. There has been no discussion about the strange nature of the disappearing green ants since Ash was taken.

"What color was it?" I have to ask.

Her lower lip trembles. "Green. Same as what Belair stabbed."

"Hmm," Piper says, calm as glass.

"What if it poisoned me?"

Piper examines the bite. She retrieves a tin of salve from her kit and treats the growing welt. "What does your phantom say?"

Tyche's eyes glaze a moment. "She's unconcerned."

"That's a good sign. Besides, if they were dangerous, Belair would have shown signs last year when he was bitten. But he didn't. He journeyed on to Aku and won his yellow robes." She gives the girl's shoulder a comforting squeeze. "We'll keep a close watch. If it turns out to be something more than a simple bite, we will deal with that, too."

It takes her a moment, but she nods.

"Ride with me at the front, Tyche." I raise my fist in the air. "To Asyleen!"

"To Asyleen," they all chorus behind me and we move into a trot, clipping down the trail, heading northwest to the realm of Sierrak and the second sun.

74

ASH

My throat burns like salt on an open wound. What's happening? I can't find my bearings or work out where I am, save for the terrible pain. It's like I am wrapped in chains soaked in acid. Slowly it dawns that the horrid noise ringing in my ears is me screaming. I wake and clamp my jaw shut as the nightmare vanishes. Or does it? I'm not sure which is worse, being caught in dark dreams or waking in the hold of this Sierrak tub. A second later, I find what woke me. Sailors are dragging Kaylin away and another stands over me, a knife to my throat again. "Where are you taking him?"

The guard only grunts but my head clears. For an instant, I feel a powerful surge in my chest. It swells and tightens, pummeling against a fracture line within. Like that moment on Bakton when the shade that tried to consume me from the inside out was expelled. But as the crack now starts to widen, the chains burn harder and it seals up again. The feeling of power drains away, like a wave drawing back from a high sea wall. Two more men come for me next.

"Time to go for a walk, little savant." Hands clamp my arms, and the manacle chains are released from the floor, but not my wrists.

Blood rushes to my feet when they haul me upright. I try to run, but never make it a step. It takes everything I have in me just to remain upright. "Kaylin?" I can't see him anymore but hear the hatch open.

I struggle to turn as the first guard throws me over his shoulder. Like a sack, he carries me up to the galley. The air smells of tar and sweat and grease, a welcome reprieve from the stench below. My guts are completely empty, throat raw and head buzzing. It feels like it might detach from my shoulders and slink to the ground like one of the wretched chains dragging behind me. I can't focus on anything for more than a second, and it doesn't help being upside down, draped over a hulk of a sailor. He carries me across the galley floor and up another ladder to the topside.

The sea breeze hits, and I gulp in the sweet, fresh air. Before I can fill my lungs properly the guard drops me onto the deck in a heap. I lie on my side, wheezing, the chains cutting into my wrists and ankles. The sunlight stabs like knives in my eyes, blinding me. I blink tears, unable to focus on the surroundings. But I can see the runes clearly just inches from my nose. They are carved deep into the cuffs, their shapes familiar. The Retoren symbols are here to haunt me? I recognize two of them, bar and tyr, which mean to descend. To sacrifice. The others I can't recognize. They don't even look like the same language. *"Kaylin, where are you?"* I nearly cry, it hurts so much to send the question.

There's no answer, but I do see two polished riding boots coming into view. A new voice speaks above me. Another Sierrak.

"That her?" Black-boots says.

"Young female journeying with Adicio. We got it right."

They have it wrong, but I don't interrupt.

"And the other?"

I crane my neck, trying to find Kaylin.

"Attempted rescue."

Black-boots has a grim laugh until the other one says, "Killed twenty-two of our crew in short order. Make sure he dies slowly."

"Twenty-two? On the water? Is his phantom still up?"

"No phantom, unless it be his sword which we tossed into the sea."

"That's the end of it then." Black-boots snaps his fingers. "Load 'em in the wagon."

New hands clamp onto my arms and haul me to my feet. The walk across the docks is a whirl, though I try to assess. I'm barefoot, manacles digging into raw flesh. I'm also completely underdressed for the weather in my tattered lavender frock.

I stumble, and my new captor instructs the guard to carry me so over his shoulder I go. This man smells like horse sweat, leather, and manure. Sheepskin, too. As I hang down his back, I lift my chin until I see two guards behind. They each have an arm in a vise-like grip around their own manacled prisoner. "Kaylin," I whisper. My throat is so raw it comes out as a gravely cough.

But he hears me, I'm sure, because he winks his terribly swollen eye. Battered and beaten, hopeless for any chance of escape, the gesture warms me more than anything ever has in my life. It's as if he is saying, "I'll get us out of this, lass. Don't worry."

But how can he? How can I?

When we're clear of the docks and up on the street, I'm thrown into an iron cage in the back of a wagon and chained to the floorboards. I don't know if Kaylin's in the wagon with me because before I have a chance to see, they knock me out again and my world is darkness.

75

SALILA

"*They were what?*" Teern thunders into my mind.

It sends a charge right through me, even though he's leagues away. I right myself and tread water, dead center in the middle of the Oteb Bay. Morning light streams down as I try to explain. I should have made Rosie tell him, but she thought it would be better coming from me. "*Um, Ash and Kaylin were taken prisoner,*" I whisper mind-to-mind, as if that's going to soften the blow.

"*Prisoner?*"

"Prisoners, *with an s. By a Sierrak captain.*"

"*How?*" he booms. Before I can answer, he lets loose an assault of curses that make my ears bleed. "*How did you let this happen?*"

"*Me? Kaylin was the one with her.*" I brush wild hair out of my face but the current pushes it right back at me.

"*Explain.*"

"*It began with Ash being hustled out of the library and onto a Palrion ship. I thought it was official business, her being called back to Baiseen, or brought up-to-date. Some lander protocol with their wordsmiths. How would I know?*"

Teern growls and I continue.

"*I was on my way to tell Kaylin, but the next moment the Palrion ship's gone and he's streaming into the water, demon bent on tearing the ocean floor apart to find her. Rosie and I helped search, of course. And we did find her. Then it gets murky because Kaylin sent us back to watch over Marcus, thinking he could handle it on his own. Clearly an overestimation.*"

"*Go on!*"

"*After Whitewing, Marcus and company left for Asyleen on horseback, so we swam the long way around, to avoid the dead reefs. That's how I discovered the Sierraks have Ash and Kaylin, no Palrions in sight. It seems they think Ash is an orange-robe caller from Aku, which is a bit of a problem. Obviously. I don't know who they think Kaylin is, but rune bands have sapped his strength.*"

"*And you didn't free them yourself?*"

"*They were on the docks by then, and you said not to be revealed, not to*" *expose the Mar, not to sink any ships, not to let Rosie up."*

He waves my words away.

"I contacted you as soon as I saw." I lift my palms. *"Here I am."*

"All right. Enough. Where are they now?"

"Headed to Asyleen." I take a breath. *"And that's not all."*

"There's more?" His voice is chilling, knives down my spine.

"Atikis is on the move. He was in Whitewing where he snatched the Mummy Wheat whistle bone. I think he'll be in Asyleen soon as well, but that's yet to be confirmed."

Teern snarls at me as if this is all my fault. *"Get yourself to Asyleen. Free the girl before Atikis can question her and bring me all the whistle bones you can."*

It's ever so much better in situations like this not to interrupt the Sea King with a question, but I have to be sure. *"You want me to bring you Atikis's skeleton or—"*

"I don't give a parrot fish's ass what you do to his body. Bring me the whistle bones!"

"Fine, but to clarify, I'm to free Ash?"

"Is there something wrong with your hearing? Kill every one of that bone-gathering party, if you must, but retrieve the originals, and Ash. Do you understand? Bring her to me alive."

"What about Kaylin?"

"It's up to you. I'm done with him."

Noodle kelp and urchins, is Teern ever in a mood. *"Got it."* I take off, Rosie at my side.

"Wait!"

We glide to a stop.

"Rosie Red, you're with me."

Of course, just when I get used to putting up with her, she abandons me to do this all on my own.

76

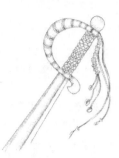

KAYLIN

I'm playing possum, but I think Ash is knocked out for real. My eyes stay downcast as I watch her chest rise and fall. She's all right, as much as a person chained to the back of a wagon can be, but I sense something approaching, and it's not good. I lift my head very slightly, using peripheral vision to locate it.

We are halfway up a winding road, the way to Asyleen. On the right, the foothills rise, their sloping shoulders becoming steeper and steeper. On the left, a sheer drop-off makes me glad the road is five horses wide. But there's no obvious threats, besides the mounted guards with their long pikes and trotting warhorses in matched rows. The likes of them, I can handle, or I could if I was free. No threat from the wayfarer's caravan we passed, or the merchant train we pull over for so it can continue its journey downhill, to Oteb, no doubt. No assassin hides behind the fir trees that spring up here and there beside the road. This enemy I sense is on higher ground, far away, but watching all the same. I feel it, undeniable.

Ash stirs and lets out a sigh.

"Lass? Stay still," I whisper to her. They haven't separated us, which is a blessing. With rune chains on, why would they think they'd need to? But they have that all wrong, for her anyway. For me, they had it right.

She coughs and lifts her head.

"Ash? Don't worry." As the wagon bumps and jerks, I work my right toe into the ankle iron of my left foot. "We're going to find a way out of this."

"It's too late for that." Her voice is hollow. "I think my path is set, and I'm near the end of it. As are you."

The pain in her words hits me. "Ash, don't give up."

She turns to me. Her lips are blue, her body shivering. "Throw of the b'lark'n bones, Kaylin. Look at us."

"I won't let it be the end." I kick straw over her purple feet where the wind has blown it away. "If I can get this—" I stop, listening. Straining to hear. "Someone's coming."

"A rescue?"

I shake my head, a barely perceptible movement. There isn't much time.

I twist my body, working my toe farther into the manacle, pulling on every ounce of strength that will seep past the runes. With a shoulder dropped, I force my weight downward against the inside edge of the manacle. It cracks and then tears free as the wagon, pulled by four horses, rolls over a pothole. The rattle and clank of the iron cage, and the multiple beats of sixteen hooves, masks the sound. I snap the other leg iron the same way, then draw in several deep breaths. Some strength returns. Not much, but maybe enough.

Ash's face pinches. "How did you do that?"

"An old sailor's trick. If you know how the metal is forged."

She looks hopeful. "Can you do mine?"

"Not until I'm completely free."

She frowns and I'm about to say more, but my eyes are drawn to a point up the road. "Do you smell that?"

"Rain and... Oh no."

"Aye, lass." I hold her gaze.

"Atikis," she whispers.

The wagon comes to a halt, the brake grating as it drags along the frozen road. I don't turn my head so it's only out of the corner of my eye that I study the red-robe descending toward us from the foothills. He's mounted on his dark warhorse, the huge beast prancing down the road, his ironshod hooves leaving cracks in the ice.

"Hail Atikis!" our captor calls out.

The entire regiment salutes on the captain's command, the sound of twenty-plus pikes hitting iron shields rings through the air. "I didn't know Gollnar was abroad," the Sierrak captain says. There's a pause, and the captain clears his throat and tries again. "How can we serve you, Lord Atikis?"

Is there a slight cynicism attached to the word "lord"? The man plays with fire. "Keep your head down, lass." I move as close to her as my arm chains allow.

"Show me the prisoners," Atikis commands without addressing the captain by name or rank. His voice is rich and velvety. Persuasive. Though I don't have a clear view of the High Savant's face, I see well enough that he points at us.

The captain speaks again. "We have the Aku caller, Lord, and her guard. Property of Rantorjin, and the High Savant Zanovine." He puts emphasis on the last sentence. "We're delivering them now."

"Since Zanovine is away, I am working with your Magistrate in this matter, it leaves me as the ranking red-robe. I will take the prisoners." It's clear Atikis will not tolerate a dispute.

"Until released by Rantorjin, they are in the care of Asyleen." The captain is a brave man.

A hush comes again as if the air is frozen solid, too cold to breathe in or out. I glimpse the red-robe easing back in the saddle. The leather squeaks and his horse gives a deep *whicker*. "I believe you have that wrong, Captain."

No one moves.

"They are the property of Gollnar now, I assure you. An arrangement you must not be privy to."

The men face each other as the air sparks between them.

"Ash, close your eyes." I drop my chin to my chest and make as if to clap, pulling the chains taut in a sudden move. I call on every fiber and cell to draw more strength through the tiny chinks in the rune, the little pinholes of light that keep me from total darkness. My back straightens against the metal bolted through the hardwood beam. Five horses might be able to break the bonds, eventually. Six for sure. But I pull harder and the framework snaps, the splintering sound crackling through the hillside. The bars jerk free and the chains snake out of the rings. My hands smack together, sending a resounding peal through the air as the entire frame of the wagon shatters, woodchips flying.

I break the bands from my wrists and let out an eerie siren call. The draft horses pin their ears, stampeding over the guards descending upon us. One flings up within reach, and I snatch his arm, biting hard into his wrist. Blood isn't the sea, but it's close, so very close, and for now, that is enough. It slides across my lips and down my throat, infusing me with life-giving strength.

The troops lose all control as the ground begins to shake. In the precious few seconds before Atikis's phantoms fully rise, I yank free from the metal bar and use it to pry loose Ash's chains. Our eyes meet again, hers larger than a night owl's, as is her screech when we start to slide off the back of the wagon bed. I grab her and try to snap the chains, even though the runes sear into my palms. Nothing gives, no chink or pinhole in here, and my hands curl in on themselves, the reek of burnt flesh rising with the scent of newly churned earth.

The road cracks and chaos explodes, phantom horses lunging from the frozen earth.

Shoving the bar at Ash, I hold her gaze. "Protect yourself! This won't take long." It's an optimistic view, I admit, and not completely realistic.

In her eyes is astonishment, and beneath that, fear. I'm not sure if the terror is directed at the guards racing toward us, the red-robe's phantoms, or me.

"Where are you going?" She gasps for breath and takes the iron bar.

"To kill Atikis and set us free."

I leap to the front of the broken wagon, grabbing a shaft of splintered wood. I pull a snake of chain, another useful weapon, and wrap one end around my burned wrist. With the wooden spear raised in the other hand, as quick as lightning I hurl it at the red-robe who still sits arrogantly on his prancing horse. It streams over his carousel of phantoms and arcs down, but an instant before it pierces his heart, Atikis vaults off.

Damn.

That's it, my one easy chance at him, gone.

The only good thing is that the guards back away as the phantom army turns to me.

A raging horse with a gaping mouth rears, its unearthly rider yelling a battle cry. Then another, and another follow. I swing my chain overhead and launch at the closest phantom, the force of impact smashing it sideways. The chain wraps around the rider's neck and I jump to his shoulders to break it with a snap. Phantom horse and rider release a bloodcurdling cry before dissolving back into the ground.

The Sierrak captain orders his guards to recapture me but before they can take a step, more phantoms rise from the road, showering ice and gravel over all. I swing the chain again and the animals contort, altering into long, serpent tentacles. The Sierrak guards lose control of their mounts, the terror driving the animals wild.

Everything slows, as if underwater, as I release the chain and sweep up more wooden shards. With a stake in each hand, I throw myself at the monster phantom, impaling the tentacles, tearing through them like a mountain climber wielding ice picks. Dark blood sprays my face and still I stab and slice, working my way toward the savant whose heart I must pierce to free Ash.

Pieces of severed tentacles lie on the frozen ground, writhing like chopped lizard tails. As I cling to a newly emerged limb, I spot Atikis, safe in the distance. "Coward!" I vault over the top of the thrashing phantom, projecting myself at the red-robe, but midair I hear the words that stop me dead.

"Get the girl!" the captain shouts as he gallops past.

I twist mid flight to spot Ash and as I do, a lashing arm grabs me. It wraps around my chest twice, cinching tight before it goes back into the earth. Mud, ice, and darkness assault as I'm pulled backward through the frozen ground.

Every surface of my body is scored under the weight and pressure of the land, the tentacles squeezing me in half as the earth rips by. With a crack I burst from the dark ground into the sky, my skin raw and bleeding, spine bent and twisted. In the distance, I hear Ash scream.

The pale landscape recedes, and I fly upward. For a moment, I hang in suspension over the road, just long enough to see the guards moving on Ash. Most of the horses are rearing, pawing the air, their military training abandoned in the face of Atikis's monstrous phantom.

My eyes dart back to the wagon. Guards level their swords at Ash and I twist inside my skin, flattening my hand into a knife blade. I slide it between the tentacle and my chest, then with a colossal war cry, I lash out. The phantom limb splits, a fountain of blood gushing, hot and sweet. Its salty liquid revives me again as I hit the ground and roll, my spine cracking back into place.

Sweeping up another chain to whirl overhead, I crouch in the middle of the ravaged road, gather my energy and catapult through the air toward Atikis. The chain tip flicks in front of him and his horse rears back out of reach. I descend on him, chains swinging, as five horses and riders arc out of the ground, earth spewing in a shower of ice. Blasted red-robe! Most phantoms are strong but in only one capacity. This beast, being able to change form at will, is a challenge. I'm slammed to the ground and the phantom horsemen drive their swords toward my chest. I brace to jump free, lifting my head to find Atikis staring down at me. He raises his hand, halting the swords just inches from my body.

"I'd hold still, if I were you, lad," he says above the cacophony around us. "If you can't, so be it, but we'll cut the girl to pieces, one delicate joint at a time." He turns to Ash. "Start with a finger. You may choose which one."

There's the sound of struggle and a muffled cry.

"I promise you," Atikis says. "She will feel every dull slice. That man there's a butcher."

"Stay!" I stop struggling though the ice and rocks puncture my bleeding body. "I surrender." I say it in the Gollnar tongue, then repeat it in Sierrak, for the sake of whoever has a knife on Ash. The butcher.

Atikis smiles and raises his hand. It's almost reluctant, his signal to the wagon. I brace for the sound of terror and pain coming from Ash, but silence falls over us as it begins to snow.

"That's better," the red-robe says. "Your last moments on the path should be calm." He's joined by the Sierrak captain, sitting tall on his horse, though the animal quivers.

"Put these on him." Atikis pulls out a set of thick chains from his saddlebag. "Stronger runes for the stronger savant, eh?" He chuckles.

With his words, luck abandons me.

"Kaylin? Are you alive? I can't see."

I draw in a ragged breath but can't speak. They haul me up, ten blades pressed into my skin. They clamp me, ankles and wrists, in black chains branded with blooded runes. Before they can finish the task, I buckle to the ground, barely able to raise my head out of the snow-covered road. The runes scorch, burning my skin like meat on a grill. Smoke is rising. I can barely see through the haze.

But I see enough. Half a dozen guards are on Ash, ready to run her through if Atikis so much as lifts a finger to signal it. She stares at me with soft eyes, as if we are the only two people in the realm, in this world.

"Kaylin? Whatever happens, know that I love you."

Warmth floods me as I say it back, readily. Easily, because it is truer than the sea itself, but the words will not flow from me to her, and my lass is met only with silence.

"Bring me the girl," Atikis orders. He dismounts, his black boots cracking the ground near my face. "Let's have a closer look."

77

ASH

The scent of horse and sweat wafts up my nose as a guard leans in and yanks me to my feet. He grips my shoulder, hard as a dog bite, but at least we are moving away from the knife-happy butcher. Blood drips from my knuckles to my fingertips where that one made his mark. I could see it in his eyes, the thrill of the amputations he hoped to perform. Fortunately, he stopped.

I wouldn't be much of a recorder without my fingers, would I?

But what has Kaylin done? Surrendered himself, for me? How long does he think Atikis will keep me alive? I'm dragged along by the new guard, my limbs blue and shivering, chains trailing as we walk up the road to the High Savant.

I'm careful to keep my eyes on the red-robe as we approach, but in the periphery I find Kaylin. I can't see much through the pikes pointed at his chest, but he is there. His limbs are manacled, skin bubbling as if the chains were soaked in acid. They've stretched him out taut over the ice. There is no part of him unharmed, but his eyes are alive. They gleam, fierce as a lion's. My breath catches, and tears burn the back of my throat.

I try to gather strength of my own, calculating if I can talk our way free, or kill these captors with my fists. But to succeed where Kaylin has failed? My inner voice would say those aren't good odds. Still, I must try something. *"We cannot end like this. We will not!"* My mind aches with the thought as I send it to Kaylin. And then, a flicker in the distance registers so strangely that I hold my breath. My eyes can't pull away from the hillside, not far up the road.

All heads turn as well when a dozen riders appear as if from straight out of the hill. They gallop down the road toward us. All are brown-robe savants in black armor, their horses snow white, every one of them. Atikis marks them and tightens his jaw, a curse escaping his lips.

That's hopeful, isn't it? If the riders disturb him, it might be good for us. But who are they? The brown-robe Brotherhood of Anon? The ones with Tann, lugging around his blood chest full of bones and Yuki's blood? They are not on our side, at least, the ones with Tann are not.

Clearly Atikis didn't expect to see them emerging from the mountainside.

His face may be bland, but I see surprise in his eyes. *"Kaylin. We are not lost yet."* Again, it stings like needles to speak mind-to-mind with him, but I keep trying until finally I let out a sob. *"I won't let you die!"*

"Be brave, lass." Softly, as if from a great distance, his lilting voice sounds in my head. *"All paths are good, Ash. Remember that. And know that I will always..."*

His last words are lost as the sound of the wind whips them from my mind. But I feel a waft of calming strength from him. I can be brave. I will be. Brave.

My heart hammers hard as I see the riders carry the black-and-white flags of truce. They are here to negotiate? But for what? I steal another glance at Kaylin and the look he gives me, the way he drinks me in, I am certain he feels these are our last moments together on this earth.

"Kaylin. It's going to be all right." The pain exploding in my head as I try to form the words nearly drops me to my knees. I promise him anyway, with all my heart. It will be all right.

Ignoring us, the brown-robe riders ease to a walk, splashing through melting slush until they halt in front of the red-robe. Atikis waits for them to speak. One rider urges her horse forward another step. "Lord Atikis." She nods almost imperceptibly while behind her another rider brings a whistle bone to his lips, poised to play.

I don't know what it means but Atikis seems to. He turns to the Sierrak troops with a warning. "Stand down," he commands.

The brown-robe leader smiles. "Wise choice." She nudges her horse even closer to Atikis. Salt and pepper braids fall to her thighs, and I see her black leather armor is well used, slashed with scars of battle. There are bones of every shape hanging from her waist and saddle. These aren't for augury, I don't think, but sharp as weapons and within easy reach. "I understand you are gathering whistle bones but have yet to procure the Mask of Anon from Avon Eyre." She nods to the Bone Thrower behind her.

"I am indeed the—"

Atikis doesn't finish as the Sierrak captain draws his sword. "In the name of the Magistrate of Asyleen, state your purpose in our realm," he demands as he wedges his horse between her and Atikis. His blade is leveled at her chest.

I look to Kaylin, questioning. Is he thinking what I am? That the captain is an idiot with not long to live?

The brown-robe leader lifts a finger, and the Bone Thrower begins to play. A minor harmonic tune flows from the whistle bone, directed straight at the captain and his Asyleen troops.

Their weapons fall as they quake, suddenly terrified, trying to look away, to run, but their horses stay rooted to the spot. I want to use the distraction to rush to Kaylin's side, but I can't budge. I can barely breathe. The troops fall from their saddles and hit the road hard. Pikes clatter to the ground. Hands clamp over ears as the guards of Asyleen writhe in the mud.

This is our chance, if only I could move my legs, but I, too, am rooted to the spot.

"Enough," Atikis says. "What is it you would like to trade?" The red-robe glances at the whistle bone around her neck, eyebrows raised.

The brown-robe leader dismounts and speaks to him in hushed tones. They both look from me to Kaylin and back and continue talking. I struggle against the chains and whatever has me stuck. Kaylin does the same, but we are both held fast. Eventually, the negotiations end with a handshake. I watch, appalled as the ancient whistle bone of Avon Eyre is given over to Atikis. He dons it over his head, around his neck where it rests against another.

Before I can think of what this means for Marcus, and for Kaylin and me, the brown-robe mounts up again and gives me a fleeting glance. "Bring her," she says without emotion and turns to ride away.

"No! You will not take her!" Kaylin's voice booms as he struggles to break free. The rune chains strain and stretch but before they crack, the brown-robe savant turns back.

"Aren't you a little far from the sea to be giving me orders?" She glances at Atikis. "The rest of the bargain now, if you please?"

"Of course." With that, the High Savant dismounts with a swirl of his red robes, draws his sword, and plunges it straight into Kaylin's heart. The blade sinks deep and dark blood blooms over his white shirt, pooling on the ground before my heart takes another beat.

"No!" I scream, gasping for breath.

The brown-robe tries to lead me away and I swing my manacled arm at him, smacking hard alongside his head. I streak to Kaylin, not caring about the pikes I run over with my bare feet, not noticing the burn and weight of the chains I drag behind me.

"No, no, no!"

His eyes are open, his gaze far away. "Kaylin," I whisper. "I'm here." I press my hand around the wound. There is so much blood. Rivers of bin'ark, so, so much. "Kaylin, stay with me. Please." Tears stream down my face as I cradle his head in my lap. He's so cold it burns my skin. "You must stay the path," I pray. "Stay the path, my love. Please stay the path…"

But Kaylin's eyes no longer see me. His ears no longer hear. I feel the weight of his head, too heavy in my arms, and I know.

He is gone.

"Kaylin!" I wail. Hands grab and pull me away from him, from my last embrace, my last touch. I thrash and try to stop them, but they bind me and hoist me over a horse, belly on the saddle, head draped to the stirrup.

"Let me go!" I choke out the words, unable to move as rope tightens.

They ignore my demand and I hear Atikis order the troops. "Retrieve the chains. We ride to Asyleen."

"No!" A pungent herb is pushed between my teeth and cheek. I nearly gag before I can spit it out but it's too late. The sickly-sweet taste explodes in my mouth, vapors going up my running nose, burning my throat. As I gulp in air, my vision shrinks, darkening at the edges as the horse moves into a rough trot.

I try to see Kaylin, to call his name. I want to touch his lips with my own, to smile and say, again and again, *I love you*, and that all will be well. But my senses fail and slowly, the world with the sailor I love so much drains away.

78

SALILA

"*Damn the Drop, Kaylin. What have you gotten yourself into?*"

I don't like the look of this. As the grade tilts steeper, the road deteriorates. There are signs of a fight. I lick my lips to taste the air. With Atikis. Damn, damn, damn.

I tighten my furs around me, a fetching white ermine coat with contrasting sable brown hood, muffler, and mittens. It's a perfect look for Asyleen, which is where this road is leading. My cheeks are warm from a recent taste of lander blood, and no, I didn't kill the girl who, though shorter than me, turns out to be close enough to my size. It's late afternoon, but the golden sun hides behind the western peaks and the second sun has already set. Clouds dim the way, but not so much that I can't read the story in front of me.

The ground hums with recently living blood. Broken wood and iron stick out of frozen puddles. It doesn't take a genius to imagine Atikis and Kaylin fighting for possession of a whistle bone, or Ash. Likely both. It would be a contest without rune chains—actually, no, a workout, but not a contest. With them? I'm surprised he did this much damage.

"Carry on," I coach myself aloud, warming up my speaking voice. "To Asyleen."

The air is icy, refreshing. It can't burn in and out of my lungs like a lander's, Mar being past such means of respiring, but I do notice my bare feet are no longer cracking the surface of the road as I pad along on two legs. The ambient temperature is dropping. I must do something about it soon or it will raise suspicions. Before I'm in sight of the Sanctuary gates, I stop to the side of the road and pull on the knee-high riding boots the girl wore. They are small for me, uncomfortable and confining, but necessary.

"Hello, guardians," I call out as my feet crunch over the frozen mud at the entrance to Asyleen. The gates are made of iron and stand over the height of four men, double the peak of the wall that surrounded the palace and Sanctuary grounds. There's a guard in attendance, a man dressed in black wool from head to foot, high leather boots, and a thick sheepskin cloak. A hint of orange shows beneath. His hair is dark and cut short to match his close-trimmed beard. Colored flags anchored to the gate posts ripple in the wind. If I blink, I might believe that ten years have not passed since I walked this way. My stomach flutters, feeling a hint of what the landers call butterflies. How interesting.

"Halt trespasser," the guard challenges. Rude man. From the gatehouse several others appear, all dressed the same and carrying pikes. They line up behind the first guard, creating a living barrier.

A barrier to some, but not me.

I push my hood back, beaming a smile as my hair falls about the fur coat. "With whom do I speak?"

The man drops to a knee and my first reaction is to kill him before his phantom's up, but something tells me to wait. Good thing, too. He's not raising a phantom but acknowledging me. Do I know him?

The guard remains on one knee, his head bowed. "Salila," he whispers.

Seems I do.

"I am savant Abtu, orange-robe of the first guards of Rantorjin, and here to serve you." His voice is breathy and deep.

The three other guards look from him to me and back. "Have you gone mad, Abtu?" the tallest guard asked. "She's non-savant."

"Watch your tongue," he warns. "Salila is royalty."

My memory jogs and warmth spreads through me. "Ten years is a long time for the youthful, I see." I click my tongue at the others. "Abtu has not lost his mind, I promise you." I lift my hand to gently tuck a long strand of hair behind my ear. "I am Salila Sovnon, daughter of the ancient and rightful Magistrate of Avon Eyre, here at my father's request." At least that last part isn't a lie, but sadly I've nothing to do with the Sovnon line from Avon Eyre. Although I wouldn't mind that life, I think, if I had to be a lander again.

"Avon Eyre?" one whispers.

"She travels alone?" another guard asks.

"Hardly alone," I answer, having no trouble making my voice sound bored because I'm heading that way fast. "My people remain obscured, camping in the distance as is our custom." I dazzle them with another smile. "The truth is, any number of them are only an arrow's flight away, at all times, no exceptions."

The guards scan the distance, but Abtu turns to me, his face an open book of desire. "Princess Salila is…" He searches for the word.

Ruthless. Cunning. Courageous. Ancient. I can offer up a few dozen adjectives, but none suit the tone he seeks to strike with his companions concerning me. I arch a brow at Abtu.

"Bold," he says.

I'll take it.

"I travel for my path quest." I shrug. "I'm meant to walk it alone, but Father insists I have protection. You know how it is."

"Yes, your grace," the three guards say as one, though they couldn't possibly.

"Now, if you might allow me entrance? I would be pleased to see Magistrate Rantorjin before the ice freezes me to the spot. Will that be too much trouble?"

Abtu scrambles to his feet and opens the gate, motioning the other guards back so I may pass. One of them hesitates for a moment but after a few curt words from Abtu, along the lines of *if you love your life, you'll let royal blood through*, the way is cleared. Abtu sends a runner ahead to alert the Magistrate.

I reward him with a kiss, a brush across his cool lips, but my mind is already elsewhere. *"Are you in the dungeons, Kaylin? You and your girl?"*

No answer.

What he's playing at, I have no idea. One thing's certain, Rantorjin will not be happy with my request to release the new prisoners, unless I can persuade him that it's to his advantage. I take the familiar walkway to the main hall, optimistic. "My, but the blue cypresses have grown," I comment to Abtu, who leads a few steps ahead. The tall, thin pines that line the entrance tower above my head.

He turns. "The color of my robes when we first met."

"You have advanced well along the path, that is clear. Shall we see each other later tonight?"

"I wish I could," he whispers, then shakes his head. "I'm in the Fasting, Princess. It would not be proper."

One less thing to juggle, though I wouldn't have minded. I blow him a kiss. "Next time."

"That is my first and last wish."

Such a dear lander boy.

We reach the palace doors and Abtu bows, taking my hand and kissing it. At his touch, I remember deeply. Not a boy at all, not even ten years ago.

"Until then," I say, and he is gone.

Surprisingly, I sigh, but quickly come back to myself and focus on Rantorjin. He's the project I must navigate. Hopefully, he isn't too old to remember me. Some landers become dotty as the years advance. I'm counting on that not being the case with him.

Down the hall, around the corner, and it turns out there is nothing to fear. The Magistrate indeed remembers. I can see every scintillating detail of our time together pass behind his eyes.

"Princess Sovnon, had I known you were coming, I would have met you at the gates myself."

"I wanted it to be a surprise." I smile, and his heart melts in my hand.

"But you've journeyed on a most inhospitable day. Please allow me to provide refreshments and a close seat by the fire." He pauses and looks behind me. "And your personal guards? Are they on my grounds as well?" His eyebrows go up.

"Camping in the woods behind the wall."

"Ever adventurous, the blood of Sovnon."

"What a high compliment." I tilt my head to the side. "Refreshments would be most welcome, though not too close to the fire." I study the expansive hall from the long dining table to the tall glass windows at the far end. The view of the Sanctuary grounds is stunning. Despite not knowing yet where Kaylin and the girl are, I'm sure this little venture will prove fun.

"Rantorjin, it's been such a long time." I say it as if we are very much in private. "You look older, but not completely decrepit." I squeeze his arms and shoulders. "Still strong enough to lead the might of Sierrak?" My eyes follow the contours of his form, head to toe, returning to his chest where a large pendant hangs. "How the Eye of Sierrak becomes you," I add, noting the Asyleen whistle bone there. "Is this its new place of honor?"

"One can't be too careful." He expands his chest as he speaks.

"So I'm told." I laugh and drum my fingers on his sternum, just below the whistle bone. His heart quickens.

Savants and palace guards hover around us, trying to get a look at me, a woman traveling in thick furs and trailing golden hair that ripples like the sea. The woman who has come to the gates of Asyleen, demanding to see the Magistrate without an appointment. A daughter of Sovnon. Ha! If any had a hint of my real lineage, they'd take a few steps back. If they knew for certain, they'd run for their lives. Ignorance is bliss. "Are you still strong enough for me?" I whisper in Rantorjin's ear, leaning close.

"I assure you, I am," he says, widening his stance.

Rantorjin is a large man, powerfully built, with seal-brown eyes, an angled jaw, and curly gray hair. It used to be black, but he looks good in his years.

"You, on the other hand, my princess, haven't aged a day. What is your secret? Something in the waters of Avon Eyre?" He doesn't let me answer but ushers me into the dining hall with a hand on my lower back. "Please, join us. We were about to take supper."

Something in the water indeed.

Musicians with lutes, drums, and reed pipes play in the far corner. The tunes are tasteful, if not contrived. I prefer the murmur of a gentle tide over a pebbled shore, punctuated by the cry of distant gulls. My mind drifts there until I spot the sideboard laden with food. "I am a tad peckish." I smile brightly while servants come to take my fur coat, scarf, and mittens, not knowing I'm naked as a nudibranch underneath. I couldn't leave the poor girl without a stitch, after all. "Not yet." I wave them away. "Let me warm up first." There's also the chance I might want to make a quick exit and don't plan on leaving a trace of this visit behind.

"Long day's journey then?" Rantorjin asks, not taking his eyes off me. I can see him counting the minutes until we're alone.

"Very," I say and scoop an aromatic salad of beetroots, sunflower seeds, and sheep cheese onto my plate. "Delightful colors, this." I take a deep breath. "It would go so well with fish. Some cod, perhaps?"

Rantorjin snaps his fingers. As he lifts his arm, I watch the Eye of Sierrak ride up. "For you, there is anything, everything. Cooked or raw?"

Anything and everything, indeed. "You remember me well, my lord. Raw, if it's fresh." I bring my plate to the table and sit opposite the Magistrate, eating before he is served. The other guests' eyebrows go up. "Delicious!" I boom. "I'm so relieved to know the quality of your palace cuisine hasn't slipped over time."

"And I'm relieved you think so." He leans toward me. "Salila, don't take this wrong. I'm thrilled you are here, but what do you want?" Rantorjin asks in a low voice. "It's not for food and my company, or even the Sanctuary's young savants."

"You're right. It's for the hot mead." I blow on the edge of my mug and take a sip. "Seriously? There are quite a few things that bring me, you might like to know."

The servants place a plate in front of him. "Starting with?" He attacks his meal for a moment while I consider.

"I want to see the Bone Gatherer." Time to find out what he knows and is willing to say.

"Which one?"

"Don't be coy. I know Atikis is here. I passed the mess on the road not an hour ago and wonder if you have locked up Baiseen in your eagerness to please him."

Rantorjin laughs. His mirth gets the better of him and a servant pats him firmly on the back. He clears his throat. "You misread the signs, Salila. There are screams from the dungeon, to be sure, but they're not from Brogal's Bone Gatherer."

"Ah then, my mistake." I return to my plate, trying unsuccessfully not to smile. "I am sure he is soon to arrive. You might have a grave choice on your hands."

Rantorjin purrs, but then his voice takes on a growling quality. "This is not a game, woman. A Great Dying is upon us! Our High Savant is traveling inland to collect other bones, if Tann hasn't gotten to them first."

So, not aligned with Tann it seems. "Do you plan to hand them over when Marcus Adicio arrives?"

"It is ancient law to hand them over to the Bone Gatherer."

I tilt to look at him sidewise. "That doesn't answer the question."

Rantorjin shrugs. "I suppose it all depends on *which* Bone Gatherer is aligned with Asyleen."

"Atikis? He is here, isn't he?" I take another sip of mead. "Don't hide it. I can smell his wormy phantom as we speak."

Rantorjin keeps eating as if I haven't spoken.

I put my elbows on the table, cradling my chin in my hands. "All right, old man," I say and pout. "I'll play it your way, but I would like to know who broke your prisoners free, destroying what must have been an iron-barred wagon and the first-bones-knows what else in the process? Did you not receive a full report?"

Rantorjin pauses as a servant refills his mug. "That was ineptitude on the part of the captain. He is being dealt with."

"Oh, then...ouch." I dab the corners of my mouth, replace my napkin in my lap, and take another enormous bite of salad. "Ineptitude on the part of the rune chains as well? Tsk, tsk. Who would have thought that the very metals forged by your smiths and marked by your Bone Throwers would be so lax?"

The company within earshot gasps, and Rantorjin slams his mug on the table, making everyone jump. Everyone but me.

"Damn the black-robes, Salila. Stop taunting me with these insinuations." He pushes out of his seat. "If you know something, tell me."

"Relax, Jin." I wave him back down without taking my eyes off my dinner. "You forget yourself. Or perhaps you forget me." My voice is calm, and with a single glance, the other guests go quickly back to their meals.

"That forgetting seems to have gone both ways." But Rantorjin sits, not quite able to look me in the eye for a moment. "You win, Salila. You can have whatever you want, just tell me what you know."

"That's such a kind offer." I reach across the table and toy with his cuff, tracing my finger over the back of his hand. "Let me see those two you've chained in your dungeon, and I will."

"They are important to you?"

"Somewhat."

"Then it pains me to tell you, they are gone."

It takes effort to keep my expression serene. "Gone, you say? How?"

"One taken by your very own savants, and the other, peace be his path."

He doesn't see the shock running through me. I won't let him. But it runs the length of my spine like a razor-backed snake. "Pity." I return to my meal, unable to say more as my throat constricts and limbs begin to vibrate.

"You're staying the night, of course," Rantorjin whispers.

"Mm." Of course I am not. I'm back to the sea the moment I can extricate myself without too much suspicion. Or maybe I'll explode on the spot.

"Good. You can tell me everything in more intimate surroundings."

I rise, losing control. Ready to bolt. But he misreads it and waves me back down. "Not yet, lovely. Finish your meal. There are more courses, and you will want to speak with—ah, here he is." Rantorjin points to the red-robe striding into the hall. "Atikis, come join us. You'll never guess who is here."

MARCUS

"How far?" I ask Samsen. He makes the best sense of maps, more than I do. "At a guess, an hour's ride to the gates of Asyleen."

"That's good news." It's colder than shadows' teeth, and only going to get worse when the first sun sets. The northerlies blow down from the mountain peaks in gusts, freezing the muddy road. Our horses' hooves crunch over the ice, saddle leather squeaking as they lower their heads for the climb. We've abandoned all idle chatter since our first night camping in the foothills. It's too frosty to risk wetting lips more often than necessary or letting out warm breath.

My goal is to reach Asyleen before we freeze to death, and not be killed on sight when we get there. Two separate goals really, but they are in the same vein. Stay alive. Find shelter.

I up the pace until my mount shies away from a pile of wreckage, picking her way along a newly damaged road. "It looks like every phantom in Sierrak rose here."

"Or one very large one." Samsen's brow pinches.

"A squadron of riders as well. Look how these tracks intersect." Piper slows her piebald mare to a walk. The ground is strewn with bent metal bars, splintered wood, and what I am sure are frozen pools of blood. "It looks like someone declared war on a wagon train."

"Atikis?" Piper whispers.

I dismount with Samsen to have a closer look. My boots crack through the thin ice surface and sink up to the laces in slush. I hand Piper my reins and study the tracks. One set leads to the edge of the road and I follow it. "That was a bad end." I spot a carcass at the bottom of the ravine. "Definitely a fight. Maybe Atikis challenged the Sierrak troops."

"Sounds like something he'd do," Samsen agrees.

"Troops guarding a wagon train?" I suggest.

"I think so. Ruined wheel here," Piper says, pointing at the ground. "The team dragged it a fair way." Piper buries her hands in her pockets.

Samsen takes them out and rubs them in his. "What kind of wagon, do you think? Not food or supplies. We'd see the remains."

Piper looks about, her eyes coming back to the bars. "Prisoner cart?"

"A reasonable guess." I can't meet her eyes.

"Did they escape?" Tyche asks and scans the surroundings. "The prisoners?"

I nudge a shackle with the toe of my boot. The iron is stretched and twisted like toffee; the chains snapped in two. "Looks like a phantom broke one free, at least."

"Whatever happened, they were headed to Asyleen." Piper leans into Samsen as she lifts her chin toward the mountains.

I study the lay of the land. "Samsen, send your phantom to scout?" I kick a piece of twisted metal. "It would be good to know what happened here, and what's ahead."

Piper steps back as Samsen drops to one knee. A second later his phantom breaks through the icy ground, spraying mud and gravel, morphing into a bald eagle.

"Is it Atikis?" Tyche whispers.

"No sign of him yet," Samsen says.

Piper pats the girl's leg. "Don't worry. We're safe."

Tyche doesn't look convinced, and I don't blame her. Atikis could be watching us from the top of the next hill. Waiting around a corner.

"He's not on the road," Samsen says, his eyes glazing over as he takes phantom perspective. "I'll follow it to Asyleen." After a time, he shakes his head. "Clear all the way, but farther off than I thought. We may not make it before dark."

That's not good. "Can you leave the eagle up to keep watch?"

Samsen nods. "Accidents happen," he says, mounting back up. "We might be making too much of this."

"Too much of Sierrak troops and likely the red-robe of Gollnar?" I say. "Look here. This horse has hooves the size of dinner plates."

They gather around me and I'm sure we're all picturing Atikis and his dark warhorse. I know I am. "To Asyleen," I say. "Keep your eyes open. We are riding straight into the heart of enemy lands."

Chill wind needles through my coat as my mount's hooves crack the ice-covered cobbles. Terrible weather for a funeral. I can't remember it ever being this cold here in Baiseen. It makes me think there could be truth to some of the stories of the second sun. Brogal explained that day by day, it barrels toward Amassia at the speed of lightning, melting ice caps, shifting currents, flipping the weather on its axis. Rubbish, most likely, but I'd be a fool to dismiss even a remote possibility. And I'm no fool.

The thought has me smiling.

I am the Magistrate of all Palrio, holder of the phantom throne of Baiseen. Woodcutters carve the likeness of my beautiful Chrysel into the left arm of the throne as we speak. She will stand out against all the previous phantoms carved there. Her image will be magnificent. This day is magnificent!

Not so much for Petén, though.

"No, love. Not so much for him." I suspect I'll miss the man, as much as I could miss any.

Don't say that in the eulogy.

"Good advice."

The speech I have prepared, been preparing since our first kiss, in fact, isn't particularly honest, but I will lie to the people for their own good. However, I must be scathingly candid with myself. I won't miss Petén past the potential he offered and maybe a few tricks he had in bed. But his purpose was served. He did his part. *Peace be his path.*

I could never have gained the throne through Marcus, not with his massive phantom, and Ash glued to his side. She's a snake, that one. Analyzing everything. Watching everyone.

I like her.

"Nonsense. She's nothing."

At first, I entertained the idea of Jacas. It would have been possible, though his advisors may have questioned the alliance, especially once his health started to fail. Too risky…but Petén was perfect, and for what he has given me, I am grateful.

For the realm.

"Yes, love. For the realm!"

Jacas was a strong ruler but not immortal. He wouldn't live forever, and his time was running short. Between Marcus with his unmanageable phantom and Petén the non-savant, Palrio would have crumbled under a continued Adicio rule. My father saw this, peace be his path, and I did, too. We would have succumbed, if not to Tann's advancing armies, then to the next power-hungry warlord from Gollnar or Sierrak. I've done them all a favor. My rule will see the realm not just survive, but prosper.

We reach the cremation grounds, the pyre built high and ready to light. At least that will warm me up. I dismount and hand my horse off to the stablemaster. All of Baiseen is present, from the youngest child of the harbor district to the oldest black-robe. Master Brogal catches my eye and I nod for him to begin. The speeches will take time, and no doubt be tedious, but the occasion marks my first public address as Magistrate. I'm going to make it one they will never forget.

As I take up my torch and walk to the pyre, flanked by Brogal, U'karn, and a dozen black-robes, I smile at the synergy. *Peace be your path, husband, and yours, too, Marcus. It is fitting you brothers should leave the world on the same day.*

Are you certain they will?

"I am, little love. All is set in motion. The Bone Gatherer will reach Asyleen, but sadly, the Baiseen troops will be too late to back him up. With Atikis lying in wait, he and his party will not see another dawn."

For the realm?

"For the realm!"

W e dismount at the gates of Asyleen, standing alert, horses by our sides. I take a few steps forward, wishing again that Ash was here to translate. Even Larseen would be better than nothing. "I am Marcus Adicio, the Bone Gatherer of Baiseen. We have come seeking counsel with High Savant Zanovine." I address the gate guards formally, and with more authority than an ex-heir or a yellow-robe has a right to, but my attention is drawn away before I can say more.

There's a loud crack, like the ground splitting, followed by a high-pitched screech. My hand goes to the hilt of my sword. "Was that a phantom?" I turn to Samsen and Piper and ask.

"Maybe, but whatever, or whoever, it is, something is terribly wrong," Samsen replies.

Before the wail stops, the ground begins to shake. The sky darkens as hundreds of blackbirds lift off the palace rooftop. They coo and flap overhead, not seeming to know which way to go.

Tyche puts her hands over her ears.

"What is this?" I turn back to the gate guards. "An earthquake?"

The most worrying thing is the Sierrak guards are as alarmed as we are. They don't answer and the formality of our interview dissolves. Orders are shouted over the sounds of turmoil, all in Sierrak.

I can't follow. Without Kaylin or Ash, none of us can. The horses act out, rearing and snorting. They mince side to side, picking up on our panic and the trembling ground. My mare lets out a shrill whinny and tries to bolt. "Mount up," I call to the others. It's the best way to control the animals, and we can't afford to lose them.

I swing up into the saddle and shorten my reins. Tyche's black pony paws the air, dumping her hard on the ice. I hold my mare to a shivering standstill and stretch my hand down. "Get up, Tyche. Get up!"

She grabs on tight as I pull her up behind me. Samsen's mount lurches, trying to follow the pony. It slams into the piebald's rump and Piper's horse starts bucking. Crazed birds still fill the sky. Have they lost all sense of direction? Some whisk over our heads as the tower bells start to ring. The wind rises, whipping us with icy needles.

"This way," the guard calls in Palrion, waving frantically. "Into the courtyard."

We ride through the gates of Asyleen, a sanctuary so foreign in design that I feel I am in another world. A world that's falling apart. "Surely this is not an everyday occurrence to them."

Samsen's and Piper's eyes are wide. "Can't be," Piper says. "Look at their eyes."

She's right. They are all filled with fear.

As the high gate swings closed behind us, a single thought flitters through my mind amid the panic. Kaylin will keep Ash safe. At least for once, she isn't in the thick of trouble.

I open my eyes, blinking against the bright light and wince at my aching head. *Where am I?*

Icy air burns the inside of my nose and with it comes the scent of snow, pine sap, and wet bark. Not indoors, that's for sure. A horse whinnies in the distance and is answered by two others. More sounds waft into my awareness: crows, a braying donkey, whispering voices. I try to lift my hands but find them weighed down with chains. The links clank together, the metal burning my wrists. "Who's there?"

The whispering stops. "Come on, Initiate. You can do it this time."

"Do what?"

I shift my legs. They are folded under me, on the cold, hard ground. Several savants, all brown-robes, stand around me. *Brown-robes?* Not young initiates, that's certain. These are adult savants, men and women both. "Who are you? What do you want?" I can't remember a b'lark'n thing about how I got here. My head swims as I try to recall where I was last.

One of the brown-robes chants from an open book while others tap wooden drums. What language are they speaking? Both the music and the chanting hovers on the edge of my memory, just out of reach. I startle when one of them kneels by my side. He unlocks the chains, and my hands feel so light I think they'll float away. There are runes carved into the metal. A stab of pain hits me, but not from the manacles.

"Do you want to remember?" My inner voice is suddenly back and not making much sense.

Remember what?

"Where you were last?"

I open the door in my mind a crack and in comes a wave of unbearable grief. I slam the door shut before it reaches me.

As the chains snake away, I lift my head, taking in the surroundings. Anything to divert me from the sorrow in my soul. No wonder I'm freezing. I'm in the middle of a field of hardpacked ice banked with drifts of snow. The cold creeps up from the ground and sucks all the warmth from my limbs, along with the strength. Pines fringe the field. They block the wind as it tosses about in their treetops. Above them, there is no sign of the second sun but the yellow one shines in the west.

I swallow a bittersweet taste in the back of my throat. I recognize it. Piper mixes something like this to warm the body and bring on a restful sleep. I promise, it's not working on either count. I'm dressed in a quilted white-robe and sheepskin boots but still shiver. All I can think is how in the First Bone Thrower's path to An'awntia did I end up here? My mind is gruel down the drain.

"Let's see what you've got, Initiate," a female says to me, then turns to the crowd. And there is a crowd, watching from the sidelines and packed into a stand of tiered seating. They're bundled in long coats and plain, brown robes, faces hidden inside large, pointy cowls. Cheers rise and I feel their expectations, but for what?

"Silence. Let her focus," she says and then to me she whispers, "Initiate, raise your phantom."

"Pardon?" They are about to be badly disappointed if this is what they are waiting for. "Sorry. You have this all wrong. I'm non-savant." But as I think about it, I don't know why I should be apologizing to them. I lift my chin and repeat. "I am non-savant!" It's not like it's an infirmity.

"Raise your phantom!" she says, her voice booming.

I press my palms over my eyes, hoping that when I take them away, the nightmare will end, and I'll be awake, journeying along the road with Marcus, Kaylin, and—

My gut twists. "No," I whisper to myself, but it's too late. The memory floods in with all its cut glass and knives slicing every nerve. *Please. Not this.*

Because, truth be, I don't know where Marcus and the others are, but for Kaylin, I do. He's gone, dead on the road to Asyleen. *Peace be his path.*

My heart pounds, my chest so tight I can't breathe. My limbs go numb and I search the field, looking for some way to escape. I spot a pair of young, sad eyes. A boy's, maybe eleven. He's in a white robe. His hair is golden, like Marcus's when he was the same age.

"Marcus!" I cry out for him. My throat vibrates but the scream never leaves my lips. I bow forward in a heap. *Help me, Marcus. Please. I'm so lost.*

SALILA

"Aminor tremor. Nothing to worry about." Rantorjin is still oblivious to my rage as he waves his people back to their seats. "A commonplace event here."

"Really?" I speak through a clamped jaw. "Commonplace?" I can barely keep from tearing into every throat, breaking every neck in the hall.

"Truthfully, no," he says only to me. "But Amassia's weather patterns are askew."

"That's one way to put it."

He goes on as if I didn't speak. "Have you seen the second sun glowing red in the sky?" He waves out the smaller west windows even though the star set hours ago. "Of course you have."

I can barely contain myself, but first, I'll hear what Atikis says, in case I have it wrong. The red-robe strides toward us but his eyes are on the food.

Rantorjin rises. "Allow me to introduce —"

Atikis, the rude man, interrupts. "Let me eat first before the civilities. It's been a full day."

"And not over yet," I say under my breath as I grip my steak knife. "Where are your prisoners, Atikis?" I lift my chin, spitting the words at him.

"Easy."

The Magistrate's fingers tap mine and I jerk back.

"Lord Atikis," he tries again. "This is Salila Sovnon, of Avon Eyre." The Magistrate speaks formally and with more than a little warning in his tone. It gets the red-robe's attention. "She wishes to hear about the prisoners who were briefly in your possession." The emphasis is on *briefly*.

Atikis nods. "So she will." He goes to the sideboard, not returning to the table until his plate is overflowing. He takes the seat next to me but addresses Rantorjin. I'm very close to reaching down his throat and pulling out his lungs. Let's see what that does to his appetite.

"First," the red-robe says. "It's time for me to collect what's due." He holds out his hand to the Magistrate as if he was owed a few coins.

Every fiber in my being bristles.

Rantorjin clicks his tongue as if about to counter, but instead, he undoes the clasp at the nape of his neck and hands the Eye of Sierrak over to Atikis.

My jaw works back and forth. "So you betray your own High Savant?" I growl.

"My dear, I am sure Zanovine will understand—"

I flip the knife I've been fondling and plunge it into Rantorjin's hand, pinning him to the oak table. It's aimed carefully between the web of his first two fingers, but still, it holds his attention, his face blanching white.

Atikis leaps back, and I rise, pushing the table over, food board and all. Rantorjin rolls with it, still impaled to the wood as he releases an anguished cry for his guards. They rush in, but I ignore them.

"Focus, you imbecile." I pin Atikis with my eyes. "Tell me what happened to the prisoners?"

The Magistrate's guards help him pull the knife from his hand, but they aren't sure who to point their pikes at, me or Atikis.

"Are you mad, woman?" Tears stream down Rantorjin's face as he presses a napkin to the wound. It is quickly turning red.

"Temperamental, is she?" Atikis says.

It's still a joke to him but in a few more moments, it won't be. I'll feel immense satisfaction in that as I swipe up another steak knife.

"Put your weapon away, Princess. I'll tell you what happened."

He still thinks it's funny? But I will be patient. News of Kaylin and Ash comes first. He won't be able to talk without his trachea.

"I traded the young woman, quite successfully."

"Traded her? For what?"

"The Mask of Anon, if you must know." He taps the chains around his neck. "Your own realm's. I'm surprised you weren't aware."

"Where is she now?" I grind out the question.

He shrugs. "They took her with them into the bone tunnel. Perhaps they are back in Avon Eyre by now. Time runs a little differently there, or so I am told."

I ignore the taunt in his eyes and ask my final question. "And her guard? The sailor?" I bare my fangs at the red-robe but he still doesn't seem to know how close he is to his last breath.

"The lad?" He takes a step back, finally registering the rage in my face, the veins pulsing in my neck, the dilated pupils. His next words come as he shifts to his back foot. "A strong one, that. The battle was challenging, even to me."

"And?"

"I ran my blade through his heart. He bled out before the girl stopped screaming. Terrible racket the—"

I raise my knife and lunge, letting loose a war cry.

Atikis is blasted back, hitting the floor hard. Panicked guests jump from their chairs and race for the exit.

"Hold! Both of you." Rantorjin, a brave but stupid man in the end, stands between us, arms warding us off from each other.

"Get out of my way, old man," I say. When he doesn't move, I crack his chest with my fist. He gasps his last breath while watching his heart beat in my hand. I throw the organ to the side and glare at Atikis. "You were saying?"

The guards surround me with pikes as the polished hardwood floor cracks like pealing thunder. Atikis is on one knee, his phantom rising. I leap over the pikes and drive the small knife into his neck. Too late! His phantom is up, a large tentacle jutting up to shield him. My knife sinks into rubbery flesh, not a pulsing artery. I sever the phantom limb from the root as the smell of wet earth fills the hall. Atikis advances on me, sword over his head, multiform phantom busting through the floorboards, upending tables, cracking foundations.

The quarters are too close. "Follow me, Atikis and bring your sea slug."

A tentacle rises toward me, and I run to the floor-to-ceiling windows at the far end of the hall. With hands stretched over my head, I spring into the air and dive through the eighteen-foot plate glass, shattering it into a hundred pieces.

"For Tutapa!" I cry when I land, and turn to face the enemy.

84

MARCUS

There's an explosion inside the palace. "What's happening in there?" It sounds like the earth is tearing apart.

"Look out," Piper cries. Mounted troops rally. Behind them march foot soldiers four abreast. When the tower bells peal, my horse rears. I whip my arm around behind me, pressing Tyche into my back. "Hold on!" I call out as the mare's front hooves slam down on the hardpacked ground. Dozens of troops break off from the main squadrons and head into the palace.

"Look there!" Tyche shouts in a high-pitched voice.

The south window explodes as a woman in white furs dives through it. She hits the ground in an easy roll and leaps to her feet, hands on her hips, facing back the way she came. The splinters in her hair make it sparkle as the setting sun breaks through the clouds. "For Tutapa!" she shouts.

Tutapa? That's Kaylin's battle cry.

Salila! De'ral bellows inside my head, rattling me further.

"Salila?" I call to her but don't think she hears me.

"De'ral! Tell the ex-heir to forget his doubts and let you rise. I could use both of you right now." For a second, she turns my way and catches my eyes.

Heat rushes through me. *"What are you doing attacking Asyleen?"* Is she insane?

Not Asyleen, De'ral booms through me. *She attacks the red-robe. He has your whistle bones.*

Salila's eyes linger on mine while my phantom speaks. *"And I have a score to settle."* She says it to De'ral but I hear her clearly now.

"What score?"

Before she answers, my horse starts to buck. Tyche grips me like a possum, and I take the reins in two hands, keeping the horse's head up. "Steady now," I command all while De'ral slams against the walls of my mind.

Help Salila. His voice is thunder in my head.

I look at her, glorious in the midst of chaos, undaunted by the gathering troops and whatever is behind that shattered glass. *"Of course we're going to help her!"*

As I say it, another blast comes from the palace. Tiles fall from the rooftops, hitting the courtyard like rocks in an avalanche. The jagged edges of the window tremble, then explode outward with a resounding boom. The horses rear and bolt as the entire south wall of the palace sprays out with the blast.

"Salila!" I shout as I fly out of the saddle and hit the hard ice, Tyche right behind me. The girl rolls to her feet, but I've landed on my shoulder, again. Hot pain shoots through it and down my side.

"Tell Marcus to stop playing about and get over here." Salila sounds exasperated.

"I can hear you, and I'm on my way!"

People pour out of the palace like ants from a burning nest and with them comes the smell of freshly turned earth. I kick-jump up, pulling Tyche close to me. A shock wave of stone and demolished furniture, along with a writhing, twisting tentacle, flies out from the broken window. It reaches for Salila who evades so fast I can't follow her motion.

"Well, ex-heir?"

I jump out of my skin, finding her standing right next to me.

"Are you going to help me, or not?"

We're helping! De'ral speaks before I can get my heart out of my throat.

"It's Atikis," Piper shouts. "He's coming!"

Samsen confirms it as the Gollnarian savant, red robe streaming behind him, strides out of the rubble, searching until he spots Salila in the whirl of madness. The red-robe's phantom undulates in and out of the ground, arcing through the air and diving back down, taking the now familiar shape of galloping warriors.

"Distract him, will you?" Salila says. "I'm going after the phantom." In a blink, she's gone.

Distract him?

Meanwhile, Salila is launching herself toward one of the grotesque phantom riders as it erupts from the earth. Its black mane is slick with mud and ice, the fanged teeth gnashing.

"Raise your phantoms!" I command my company and myself. "Tyche, be ready to *call* the whistle bone."

"Mummy Wheat?"

I nod. The instant I kneel, fissures crack in front of me and De'ral busts into dusky light, bellowing a war cry.

"Help Salila with the phantom. I'll distract the red-robe!" It's her plan, so I doubt he will fight me on this. Seems her word is law, unlike my own. Half my mind rips away, flowing into my phantom's perspective. *"And don't trample her while you do."* It's mayhem and we are square in the middle of it.

"Baiseen troops are headed here, at the gallop," Samsen says as his phantom eagle gains height. "The Shearwater rides!"

This is impossible, but I know his phantom can spot the Shearwater flag from miles away. "Are you sure?"

"A full two-hundred ride, archers mostly. More follow from the south."

I hear them! Baiseen's battle horns rise on the wind. There are no other trumpets like them in Amassia. What in dark thunder is Petén thinking?

We're about to be trapped between Sierrak and Baiseen, not to mention the red-robe's phantom. I turn to Samsen. "Hold back, and guard Tyche so she can *call* the bone." The arrogant man wears it around his neck, a decision he's about to regret. I wave Piper up. "You're with me."

She matches my pace as we run.

De'ral leaps ahead, sweeps up a sword, and tosses it to Salila. The last thing I see is him ripping a wrought iron post from the ground and hefting it like a spear. The red-robe's phantom tightens its circle around them.

But it's not so simple for me and Piper. The way to Atikis is quickly blocked by enemy troops, among them callers from other realms, driven forward by Sierrak savants.

"Prisoners," Piper says. "Some from Aku." Her double-headed snake tightens around her neck, hissing as blue tongues scent the air.

I grind my teeth. That means Tann has been here and that we didn't speculate on his path as well as we should have. Where is he now? Where is Ash? I clear my head, and fight.

Piper and I block, cut and strike through every obstacle. Our rampage is relentless, the ferocity I feel exhilarating. When I shift my awareness to De'ral, I find him doing the same: uprooting the enemy phantoms and tossing them skyward as Salila, at a speed unimaginable, slices them to bits. The carousel of grotesque horses are flayed, De'ral hurling the bleeding chunks over the wall and into the woods. They work in a rhythm and grace I only wish I could achieve with my phantom. How is she doing this? I pull my focus back and carry on.

When we break through another wall of troops, *he* stands before us.

"Call Mummy Wheat!" I yell to Tyche, but nothing happens, my voice lost in the chaos of battle.

Atikis, seemingly undaunted by us, is calm. "You, again." He laughs. "They send a pup to track the Bear of Gollnar, but sadly, he is no match."

"I think you underestimate the pup, and his companions." My head tilts toward the slaughter going on behind me while my eyes stay glued on his. That's when I see he wears three whistle bones around his neck, not one.

Atikis shrugs as if it is of no concern. His red robes are spotless save for mud at the hem, and splotches of melted snow. He takes no phantom wounds. So he leaves the fight with Salila and De'ral up to his phantom, not entering its perspective? He must have no idea she is Mar. How could he? Unless he has faced Mar before and they are no match. I don't think so. Even I'm not sure what the sea people are capable of in a fight. From the little I've seen, tooth by claw they are formidable.

"That's an understatement, ex-heir." Salila's laugh rings through De'ral to me and my heart skips a beat. *"Still, keep him busy, will you, lovely?"*

Keep him busy. Right…

Piper and I stand just out of each other's kill circles. Atikis draws another curved blade and lifts his brow. He's a cool summer breeze. I nod imperceptibly at my healer and she lunges first. I move a fraction of a second later, my sword singing through the air as I release a war cry. Piper's blade swipes toward his neck, mine dives straight for his chest. At the same moment, a distant *call* drifts across the battlefield and one of the whistle bones lifts. It strains against the chain and then flies off his neck.

Tyche has Mummy Wheat! But she needs to know there are two others.

Atikis grimaces and swings his curved blades, blocking the double attack in a blur of speed. Steel strikes steel and the reverberation jars me as if lightning cracked through my arms. We attack again, and again, until Piper's sword flies out of her hands, *ousted* by approaching phantoms.

Piper's snake rears and launches from her neck, giving her time to roll away from the red-robe's blow. Atikis's next swing slices the snake phantom in half. It instantly goes to ground.

I spin to check Piper, hoping she jumped out of phantom perspective in time. She's safe, sweeping up a full body shield and sword to face the *ouster,* leaving Atikis to me.

I keep a small part of my awareness with De'ral. "Sierrak archers," I shout at him.

From my phantom's perspective, I note the mounted troops filling the courtyard below, drawing their bows, taking aim. But even these precision-trained riders can't hold their horses within twenty lengths of the phantom battle. The animals rear and bolt, throwing riders from the saddle, arrows firing wide. De'ral turns to sweep the toppled soldiers aside. They skid like empty bottles across the ice. Salila cheers to De'ral, and my perspective falls deeper.

I catch her eye as we fight. Nothing has ever felt like this before. My whole body is alive, on fire without burning.

I feel I could do anything.

And then, Atikis's phantom, in the form of a giant De'ral, strikes at Salila, but his pounding fists can't break the whirling speed of her blade as she shreds it to slivers. *"The red-robe, Marcus?"* Salila's voice is calm, almost sultry, but it snaps me back to my body where Atikis's blade collides with mine.

"Who is distracting who?" Atikis asks, his voice condescending as we parry back and forth.

I don't waste time on a response, but hold the blade in both hands, guard position, drawing up strength from my core. In that moment, I study the two remaining bones, confirming which they are. Then energy, phantom enhanced, bursts from the tip of my sword as I lunge, dropping to one knee. I roll the edge of the blade side-on and cut low, sweeping in a circle a foot above the ground. I feel the slice across his shins as the weapon completes its arc, coming away wet, flinging blood in arcs. As the momentum of the swing pulls me upright, his hot blood spatters my face.

"Whom," I answer finally. It's something Ash would say, and I'm not even sure it's right, but I have cut him deep. The red-robe's arrogance slips.

Sword high overhead, I push the advantage, my weapon slicing toward him.

He evades, and I only nick his forearm, but I see it! Small to start, but certain, bright red blooms across his chest. Phantom wounds, finally. "Now!" I shout to both De'ral and Salila.

But Atikis is already responding.

The horsed riders rush skyward and *alter* into thick, writhing tentacles, feeling blindly through the air. Salila tilts her head back to track them. With a mighty swing, she hacks them off at the ground. They reform into mammoth raptors with razor sharp talons, but just as fast she mows the monsters down.

"Don't stop now, Marcus!" she shouts at me.

I notice the use of my given name as I engage Atikis, zigzagging, dodging, and ducking until he is dripping with phantom wounds. He grunts and gasps. We both do. But he's taking more and more injuries and all confidence is gone.

Salila grasps the remains of the red-robe's *alter* and begins pulling it out of the ground by the roots. The transforming remnants struggle to escape her grip, desperate to return to their savant. She doesn't let them. Salila's eyes are hard as gems as she releases an ear-splitting war cry.

Atikis hesitates at the sound, as if he's recognizing something long forgotten. It's all I need. In a massive blow, I knock the sword from his right hand, taking a few of his fingers with it. "I'll take the bones now, if you please."

He double grips his remaining weapon, blood gushing down the hilt, but his eyes are on me, beseeching. "You have no idea what you are doing. The whistle bones aren't–"

It's no time to pause. I reverse my blade and slice him upward, sternum to chin. Blood, gore and finally the whistle bones fly into the sky, their chains cut free. "Tyche! *Call* Sierrak and Anon!" I let De'ral's voice bleed into mine.

The whistle bones change trajectory, arcing toward her and Samsen. My opponent's beseeching look turns to horror as I run Lord Atikis through, my sword plunging between his ribs and deep into his heart.

Salila is instantly next to me. Trails of blood drip off her fingers as her hands rest at her side, weapon tip pointing at the ground, but I don't think she's wounded. Nothing seems to have touched her, that I can tell.

"You're good with a sword, ex-heir." She doesn't wait for a response but turns her attention to Atikis's corpse. "You took Kaylin from his path," she booms, her voice so strong it tumbles snow from the rooftops.

I nearly fall. "He *what*?"

But her eyes are not on me. "Goodbye, Atikis of Gollnar. May worms consume your tarnished soul." Her words cut through the sound of charging warriors, enslaved *callers*, the horrified cries coming from onlookers and the battle still raging behind us at the gates. There is no mercy in her stance as she reaches out a slender arm toward Atikis and wraps fingers around his throat. Slowly, she lifts his body, tightening her grasp.

"Um, Salila? He's dead."

"Let's make certain, shall we?" Her other hand grasps his hip. In a single motion she raises the corpse overhead. "In the name of the Ma'ata, your path is forfeited. Peace be it, or peace be it not." Salila's face is grim as she stretches his body until it rips clean in two.

Liquid sprays over the snow in a fountain of blood and gore. It spatters our faces, and then the ground of bodies, and churned earth. It splashes against the distant Sanctuary wall and the icy white snow of the rooftops. Salila finally drops the severed appendages and turns to the sea. "Fare thee well, Kaylin. Until we next meet along the path."

An uncanny grief floods me. It washes from my heart, filling my chest and seeping into my limbs. It's her grief, but somehow now it's mine, too. I step beside her, shoulder to shoulder, the barest touch. But close enough, I hope, so that my presence might console her.

She turns to me, her face unguarded. Our eyes meet and something flows between us. No words are spoken, but something deeper. Something true. An understanding that turns grief to awe. We breathe in each other's air and I lean forward. Closer to her, until our lips touch.

In the middle of Asyleen Sanctuary, blood, broken bodies and weapons underfoot, the sounds of battle retreat. Salila rests her hand on my face and melts into me, gives in to me... For an instant there is, what I can only imagine, the experience of An'awntia—the path complete. I am fire and ice, motion and stillness, powerful and powerless. I close my eyes to lose myself completely.

And then she stiffens. "I have to go."

"Stay, Salila." But she's already bunching to run. "Wait!" My head clears. "What of Ash?"

An instant later, trumpets blare and the sounds of battle rush back into my awareness. Baiseen troops break through the main gates and the chant of our *callers* fills the air.

When I look back, Salila is gone.

Samsen catches up to me, panting. "Come on, and get your phantom out of here. We're dead in the crosshairs."

"The whistle bones?"

"Tyche has them. Piper's rushing her into the woods to guard them. Let's go."

We're too late. A wall of *ousters* appear, blocking our escape.

"De'ral, back to me!"

The enemy phantoms conjure an *ouster* wind that strips us of our weapons. My cloak is next and my yellow robes strain at the seams. My skin beads and starts to blister. I grab hold of my whistle bone pouch, ignoring the burn of my flesh, the blood oozing the backs of my hands.

In three bounds, De'ral is with me, arms flailing as if swimming through the snow. He blocks the *ousters'* path, grabs the wrought iron gate, and impales the lot of them like shrimp on a skewer.

Samsen's eagle dives in and out of our expanding circle, talons slicing through shoulders and throats.

A pile of bodies builds, soon to be crushed by De'ral as we defend our ground. Freed from their captors, the enslaved callers join Baiseen, turning the tide. It's not long before the black-and-white streamers of truce are hoisted by Asyleen.

Victory! But somehow it's shallow. When the enemy is completely contained, I gather the others to give them the news. "Kaylin is dead, peace be his path. I have no idea what has happened to Ash."

If only she had stayed. The guttering torches make it hard to see, but I strain into the distance anyway. I keep coming back to the spot where Salila ripped apart Atikis and then vanished when I kissed her. Her speed, with a blade, on foot, is a hundred times the fastest savant's. I can't imagine what she's like in the water, her element. If only she had stayed...

Or if I had thought to ask about Ash sooner. With Kaylin dead, does that mean Ash is, too? Did he find her abductors? But it was Atikis who killed Kaylin. Surely he wasn't the one who had Ash. But if he knows anything, it's too late for me to ask. My mind twists with the possibilities.

Kaylin found the abductors, De'ral says as he hoists a blood-splattered pillar over his shoulder.

I snap back to the present, standing in the middle of the wreckage that but an hour before was the peaceful courtyard of Asyleen Sanctuary. Dozens of Baiseen savants have their phantoms up, working under the torchlight to put things right, as much as you can with so many dead. Mostly it's finding and identifying bodies and sorting weapons from bones.

"*How do you know Kaylin found her?*"

Salila told me.

"*Told what, exactly?*" I wait for him to say more.

"*Kaylin attempted rescue and failed. They bound him in rune chains.*"

"*Rune what?*"

"*Very bad. At Oteb, both were loaded on a wagon to Asyleen. Atikis arrived and tried to claim them.*"

The signs of the fight along the road! Sweat prickles the skin of my forehead. "*Why didn't she tell me?*"

De'ral goes on as if I hadn't spoken. *Anon riders came. They bartered for Ash with their first whistle bone. When they left, Atikis ran Kaylin through.*

"*But what happened to Ash!*"

Anon has her, and you have the whistle bone.

Anon? I punch my hand into my fist. "*The brown-robe Brotherhood took*

Ash? Why? Where?"

Don't know why. De'ral growls. *The "where" is through a bone tunnel.*

"Bone tunnel? Out of myth?"

Out of the side of the hill. De'ral throws down the pillar with a boom, cracking it to pieces. *Salila said it leads to Avon Eyre.*

"What?" The isle that's drawn in a different place depending on which map you read? "How will we ever find her?"

Not by staying here. He begins to pace. *We have to go!*

"Agreed. Is she harmed?" My heart pounds, waiting for his answer.

Are you listening? Kaylin plunged in the heart. Dying as he bled. Ash saw it all.

My hands begin to shake as I scan the grounds. There's only one thing to do. I spot U'karn, Baiseen's head of the War Council, and stride to him. "Commander." I approach, my fists clenched.

The war leader stands next to his black-robe, the master Bone Thrower, Oba, who travels with him on all the campaigns. Her sunset phantom wafts about like plumes of red smoke, appearing and disappearing from view. I'm undaunted, though if Ash were here, she'd tell me to be humbler. More respectful.

But Ash isn't here. That's the whole point.

I stomp up to U'karn, boots crunching over the bloodstained snow and mud. "Commander," I say again, dipping my head to Oba while addressing U'karn. I may not be the Heir anymore, but surely I can make this request. "Is it possible for me to consult with your black-robe?" Strands of hair blow across my face in the wind, escaping the tie at the nape of my neck. There's been no time to clean up.

He studies me and I do my best not to look desperate. "My recorder, Ash. You know her. Master Brogal's ward? She was taken in Tangeen and then by Anon, on the road to Asyleen. She's still missing."

De'ral growls while I speak. He towers high over us, his feet shaking the ground with each footfall, making the torches flare.

"Quiet. Let me do this."

My phantom waves his arms toward the black night sky and cuts loose a holler. We're both outraged, but one of us is better at hiding it. I pinch my brow and wince as savants and troops shy away, eyes glued on De'ral.

"Stop terrorizing these people. They're on our side."

Are they? The first ship that took Ash flew the Shearwater flag.

It's like being slapped in the face with a slab of ice. I'm so shocked I miss some of U'karn's response.

"…can't do it. Magistrate's orders, Marcus. Sanctioned by Master Brogal," U'karn says in his deep, I-rule-legions-of-warriors voice. Most of the commander's face is covered by a bushy dark beard, and his eyes are glinting pools in the torchlight.

"But my orders are to find a way to hold the whistle bones and recover the ones in Tann's possession. Ash is needed for that. If she is alive, I have to have her back." I struggle for a response that will change their minds. "I just want to find my recorder. Please. Her guard was reported dead—"

"Then she's dead, too." U'karn crosses his arms. "They wouldn't spare a non-savant."

I refuse to believe it, until there is no other choice. "Is that what the bones say?" I ask Oba.

U'karn holds his hand up. "As I said, the Magistrate wants us to establish a base here before heading back to Baiseen. Resume the cleanup, Marcus. We still have to stable all the horses and find room for our troops." He makes to move off, but I step in front of him.

"My brother's gone mad if he thinks we can hold Asyleen past winter. When the weather thaws, Sierrak loyalists will pour out of the mountains like meat ants to blood. Their numbers will be unstoppable. And why would he want Baiseen to hold up here anyway? I have their whistle bone. More than I'd hoped to obtain before facing down Tann." I tap my bone bag as evidence, my voice turning into a growl. "We found the lost callers from Aku, at least some of them."

"Marcus? You haven't heard?" There's worry in U'karn's eyes. The Commander whispers something to the Bone Thrower and she walks away without a glance back.

"Heard what?" I ask, my head swimming.

The war commander straightens his broad shoulders and speaks as if delivering a rehearsed message. "I regret to say that Petén Adicio, Magistrate of all Palrio, second son to the throne of Baiseen, brother of the Bone Gatherer, is dead. Peace be his path." U'karn bows his head. "Magistrate Lady Adicio has taken the phantom throne. I'm sorry to speak of it belatedly. I thought you knew."

"Peace be his path," Samsen echoes suddenly by my side.

"Petén's dead?" I whisper.

All the blood drains from my limbs. Images flash through my mind, a mix of fights and arguments. My most recent conflict when Petén usurped the throne out from under me on the pretense that I was dead. Scenes of us hunting in the woods and valleys behind the palace, training young horses, hiding near the lake to watch the girls swim. Two boys, we were, with no mother and a tyrant father, escaping princely duties to explore the realm, getting caught in the tunnels of the Bone Thrower's caves, pinching cream pies from the palace kitchens, falling for the same girl once or twice.

"Petén, peace be your path," I say, my throat thick.

The wind whistles through the broken glass of the palace and I breathe in the glacial air, letting it out in a rush. De'ral drops to his knees, his head level with the others, mirroring my shock. "How did it happen?"

"He's been ill," U'karn begins.

"But he was young. Strong. Our healers skilled."

"Always the first to recover from childhood illnesses," Samsen adds, nodding his head.

"Perhaps he tried to rise too soon in his recovery," U'karn says. "Maybe there had yet to be a recovery at all, and he couldn't stand the confinement."

"I can see that." Petén hated to stay indoors. "What did he do?"

"Joined the hunt and took a fatal fall. It snapped his neck."

Samsen shook his head. "That's—"

"Impossible." I narrow my eyes. "True wouldn't take a wrong step, not with Petén in the saddle. That mare would break all four legs before she endangered his life."

"Agreed, but he wasn't riding True, Marcus."

"Why not? She is, I mean was, his favorite. He never hunted with another, except when she was in foal, which I know for a fact she is not this year."

"Rhiannon." U'karn clears his throat. "Lady Adicio rode True. Petén was on a young stallion. Shouldn't have been outside the training ring, let alone—"

"Insanity," I say under my breath. "Stupid, stupid choice." I scrub my face as more childhood memories rush in, this time featuring Rhiannon. "And how convenient for my new sister-in-law." I don't wait for U'karn to rebuke me. That could see me exiled for treason. "I didn't mean that."

U'karn doesn't speak, but his hand goes to my shoulder.

"Asyleen needs your help, Marcus." Even in the torchlight the destruction is evident. "And her orders are clear. Stay here and establish the Palrion base, fit for her Magistrate's visit. Then return with the whistle bones, to await Tann."

"Await him?"

"The Bone Throwers say you will find him on the fields of Baiseen when the lupin blooms."

"That could be months from now."

"Those are our orders."

From Rhiannon? I want to spit. Instead, I hiss, "So be it," and stretch out my hand to shake his. Oba isn't the only Bone Thrower in Asyleen, and I still have some coin left.

U'karn grips back. "Agreed."

I wince, my hand blistered from the *ouster* wind. I smooth my expression and ignore the pain.

Then U'karn lowers his voice. "Marcus, on your way home, I want you to recruit support whenever you pass through an allied town and city. It's not common knowledge, for morale's sake, but reports have it that Tann's army is shaping up to be sizably larger than first reported. That's the main reason I'm up here, retrieving our callers and keeping Sierrak from joining Tann, while we gather more allies of our own. With Aku weakened and without a fleet, we are disadvantaged."

I don't argue.

U'karn's eyes go to the bone bag at my waist. "You'll do it?"

I nod. "I'll gather support where I can."

"Have them rally in Baiseen unless I send word otherwise. And for the old bones' sakes, recruit Whitewing. We need Warcott on our side."

I'm glad he doesn't ask how smoothly that relationship's gone so far. Not exactly off on the right foot, me and Warcott. "Consider it done."

U'karn brings his fist to his chest in the salute awarded the Magistrate, letting me know his respect is true. "So be it."

I salute back, feeling more honored than I have since losing my throne. But De'ral is another story.

We will not abandon the search for Ash.

"You're right. We won't! If she is on this earth, I will find her." After a few strides, I drop to one knee for an instant. *"To me, De'ral."*

My *warrior* phantom melts into the ground, and I signal Samsen to follow. "We're going to need a new plan."

86

ASH

I'm floating up from the bottom of a slow-moving river. When I reach the surface, I take a breath only to find it's no river at all.

It's a room full of books and I'm sitting in a chair pushed up to a long table. "A library?" I whisper, sending a puff of air out with the question. I love libraries, though the thought makes me inexplicably sad. I don't recognize a thing here, not even myself.

I'm wearing a quilted white robe, not a color I would ever choose, it being impossible to keep clean. Five minutes into my day, with inks and quills and the inevitable drips, the robe would be a mess. Imagine wearing it on horseback, along a muddy road at a gallop. But here I am, holding a book in my hands, not an ink-heavy quill.

It appears I've been reading though I honestly have no idea what, or how I got here, or where *here* is. *Oh no.* My memory gaps are back. What else have I forgotten?

I note the language of the text in my hands. It's Sheb, a common dialect of Sierrak, but still, no bells are ringing. I push my hair from my eyes and frown at the strands sweeping the tops of my shoulders. The color's right, auburn with glints of red, but the length isn't. I don't know much at this moment, but I'm certain my hair was shorter last time I looked.

What is this place?

Balconies run around the cathedral-like room with ladders reaching to the highest levels, like…somewhere else I can't quite remember. The first floor where I sit is full of chairs and tables, some empty, some occupied by brown-robe savants. Men or women, or both, I can't tell. They have the cowls pulled over their heads and lean forward over books and scrolls. I rub my eyes and study the book spines nearest me. It's easy to read the titles with all the natural light pouring in. Every title is about raising phantoms, or the steps to An'awntia, or the way of the savant. It's safe to say this is a sanctuary, but which one?

"Safe to say, yes, but that doesn't mean it's safe." My inner voice speaks in riddles, as usual. At least it's here to comfort me. It feels like it wasn't for a while.

At the head of the table, several unoccupied chairs up from me, sits a man. Like the others here, he's a brown-robe, but his cowl lies back across his shoulders. His features are sharp, his coloring gray. Watching him makes my lip twitch. I know I don't like him but can't remember why. I've never seen him before in my life.

"Really?" My inner voice obviously disagrees.

I can't remember.

"You can. You just don't want to."

Show me.

Images from the past roll in front of my eyes, faster and faster until they blur. When they stop, I fall hard onto the icy road to Asyleen where Kaylin is stretched in chains, beaten so badly I have to keep watching for his next breath, afraid it won't come. They are taking me somewhere, these brown-robes, and I struggle. That's when Atikis lifts his sword and—

Like wounds packed with salt, the pain roils, and my eyes turn to the back of my head. I push against the reliving, push it away, along with all my memories tied to it. They are not worth the agony. Not a single one of them.

"Do you understand what I'm saying, Initiate?"

My eyes pop open. A scream escapes my lips. "I'm non-savant!" I shout. I'm in a library of some kind, and it's dead quiet. There is a man opposite me, in a brown robe. He frowns. Other cowled heads turn to stare, but their expressions are of annoyance rather than shock.

"Non-savant," I say again, this time in a whisper. I don't know why I need to say it, but I do. Sweat drips down my temples as I search for an exit from this unfamiliar place. *How did I get here?*

"Yes dear. Quite stuck in your head, that thought, but we know different. The Bone Throwers foretell—"

"You're wrong." I'm out of my chair but two brown-robes, one on either side of me, clamp onto my shoulders and ease me back down.

"Who are you?" I ask. "Why am I here?"

Other brown-robes in the room shake their heads, all save for one whose eyes linger on me. In them, I see recognition, compassion. Something I'd expect from a friend, only I don't remember making any friends here.

"That's no surprise, since you don't want to remember anything," my inner voice says.

Before I can explore that thought, the man who makes my skin crawl taps the table, calling my attention back to him. "Must I introduce myself to you again, Ash?"

"I think you must." I fold my hands in front of me.

"I've been doing so daily for the last month, and it is becoming tedious," he continues after letting out a huff. "Call me Master Radigan, and with all efforts, try to remember it this time."

A month? I've been here a month?

"Feels longer to me." My dry inner voice is nothing like the way I sound, at least I hope I never sound so condescending.

I remember one thing, I reply to myself.

"Praise the prophecies. Do share."

You gall me to the bone.

"Well, that's something then."

Nothing dampens this part of me, it seems. *Hush now. I need to think.*

Radigan, oblivious to my inner thoughts, crosses his arms. His face is long-suffering and deflated. His gray hair reminds me of wispy, dried weeds in an overgrown pasture. But his accent, that's a puzzler. He speaks more like a Nonnovan than a Sierrak, which is odd for one who raises a reptilian *ouster*, a common class of the realm.

Wait. *How do I know he raises an* ouster? I ask myself.

"Because you've seen it a few dozen times," a young voice says in my head. A boy's? He doesn't add, you *dolt*, but it's implied, in a friendly, teasing way that makes me smile.

I turn around in my seat. *"You?"* I say, spotting the friend I can't remember.

Among several brown-robes, a few tables over, sits a boy in a quilted white-robe with bell sleeves and braided buttons, identical to the one I'm wearing. He's hunched over a book, with blond hair falling forward, concealing most of his face. I'm so reminded of Marcus at that age, save for the book. Marcus wouldn't read without coercion or bribe. I frown. *Have I had this thought before?*

"More than once." My inner voice yawns.

I catch this boy's smile as he steals a glance my way. His blue eyes are like summer skies, several shades lighter than mine, which are more a dark teal. *Unless that's changed, too,* I wonder while twirling a lock of my hair. I must remember to check a mirror when I have the chance.

The boy tries to hide his laughter with a cough.

"Hello," I say, mind-to-mind. *"Are you laughing at me?"*

"Only because you're funny."

Master Radigan clears his throat to pull my attention back. "Can you answer the question?"

There's been a question? "Um…" If he wasn't so aloof, I would try to explain. I would say, *It's true. I'm distracted because I'm whirling in and out of my memories as if they were happening all over again. It's a little disorienting.* I bite the inside of my cheek. I think Kaylin is gone.

"*Yes.*"

He's gone... Tears well, burning the back of my throat as my face heats. Before I cry in front of these strangers, I tuck the grief into a small space inside my heart and close the door, locking it tight. *And you, Master Radigan. Maybe you're my advocate, and maybe you're my enemy. Care to explain which?* But he is unapproachable, like Brogal, so I don't say anything. All I want is to sleep until the hurt and confusion fade away, but Radigan isn't leaving me alone.

"Any time, Initiate."

"I was thinking..." Stalling, really.

"Indeed. Now tell me, Sheb. Yes or no?"

I take a deep breath and focus on Radigan's hound-dog eyes. "Could you rephrase the question please?"

"*Sheb,*" my new friend says. "*He wants to know if you can read it.*" The boy's playful voice is in my head again.

A tic starts up above Radigan's left brow as he confirms it. "I would like to know how much of the Sheb dialect you understand. It would be helpful for you to study the history from the original text, not the translations."

History? This sparks my interest. I scan the row of scrolls tucked neatly into the carved oak shelves. "I'm fluent in Sheb, though I might be rusty. Is there a dictionary handy?" I lift my gaze to meet his stare. "That would be helpful."

Two of the brown-robe savants across the table rise. "This is ridiculous," one says as they walk out.

I don't even try to apologize. "*Why would I?*"

"*Because you're driving them mad today,*" the boy chuckles. "*Worse than usual.*"

"The dictionary is there, at your elbow," Radigan says in a dour tone. "You were just holding it."

"Oh." I pick it up. "Thanks."

He shakes his head. "We'll break for lunch, then train at the usual time."

Train? Everyone stands up, so I do the same and head for the exit. Once out the door, I turn left, hoping it's the fastest way out of here.

Radigan clears his throat. "Initiate." He stops me with his voice. "You forgot these." When I turn back, he places a stack of books in my arms, putting the Sheb dictionary on top. "I expect you to have the text translated by tomorrow. Can you remember that?"

"Sure." Maybe. What text is he talking about? I make to carry on, wondering if I will remember any of this in the morning, or if each day is a new start for me. Their exasperation makes me lean toward the latter.

"Initiate." Radigan stops me again.

I look over my shoulder.

"The dining hall is this way." He motions in the opposite direction and takes off down the corridor, expecting me to follow.

• • •

I look around for my white-robe friend, but he's gone.

"I can walk you there." A brown-robe stops beside me. "It's not far."

"Thanks." I walk beside him, carrying my stack of books. There's no point making a run for it, not until I see the layout of this place. The hallway is lit by high stained-glass windows that splash color over the brown-robe's shoulder. I study his profile, what I can see of it with the cowl up. "I guess I know you, too?"

"I'm Tannson, and yes, we've met." He pushes back his cowl, revealing an attractive face, high cheekbones, dark, gold-flecked eyes, and full lips. A tumble of dark hair falls to his shoulders.

But his name sends a ripple through my core. Surely not related to Tann, the red-robe, could he be? "I'll try and remember you then."

He laughs softly. I like the sound.

When we reach the dining hall, I'm hit by a blast of warmth along with mouthwatering aromas. A huge circular hearth blazes in the center of a room filled with tables and benches, most of them unoccupied. I inhale the scent of wood smoke mixed with roast meat, potatoes and roots, rosemary, and baking bread. My stomach growls and I pat it without thinking.

Tannson nods to me before joining a dozen other brown-robes eating near the fireplace. I follow, and he shakes his head. "White-robe Initiates are over there. You'll feel better after some food in your stomach."

"Thanks." I head for "my" table. There are a few more brown-robes scattered about the room, but I'm the only white-robe dining, it seems.

"Besides me."

I shoot a look at the door where the boy enters. He's young, but there is something grown up about him, a maturity in his posture, and a sadness about his eyes despite the grin. He waves and heads straight for me. I know without a doubt we are friends, even though I can't recall how or why.

"So good of you to remember that much today," he says aloud as he swings his leg over the bench and takes the seat opposite me.

I plunk the books down and sit as well. "I have some missing pieces."

"You always say that."

"I'm consistent at least."

"You always say that, too."

He laughs, and I sigh.

"Don't worry, Ash." He whispers my name when he speaks aloud. "Things got messed up. You know, on your way here, is all."

"The road to Asyleen?" I close my eyes. "Did I tell you that?"

"Yeah. So, no surprise you get muddled." His voice trails off to a whisper again. "This place'll do that to you, too."

"Young and wise," I say, trying to pull myself together. "Where're you from?"

"Dunno."

"Really? Is memory loss this common here?"

He winks and stares longingly at the swinging doors that lead in and out of the kitchen.

"So, I've been here a month?" I ask.

"Since Asyleen fell."

"Asyleen fell?"

"To Baiseen."

"That's impossible. Baiseen didn't attack Sierrak, did they?"

"It's what the Bone Throwers say." The boy loses his train of thought as a young man comes out of the kitchen carrying a tray on his shoulder.

I barely notice. The scene in the road to Asyleen flashes through my mind again. I drop my eyes to the table and hold them there while two bowls of stew and a plate of bread are set between us. The door to my little room that holds my broken heart creaks open and suddenly I'm not hungry anymore. "I lost someone. He was—"

"Kaylin. I know. You've said." The boy stuffs a hunk of bread into his mouth. "You two mattered to each other." He wrinkles his nose. "Whatever that means, and peace be his path, of course."

Tears well until they spill down my cheeks.

"It's all right," the boy puts his small hand over mine, warm and comforting. It's a quick gesture, ending in a pat as he returns to his food. "I think you're getting better." His words are garbled around a mouthful of stew.

I lift my eyes. "Better at what?"

"Grief."

"It doesn't feel better."

"Hurts, I know," he says softly, blowing on his steaming spoonful of food.

My stomach growls, and I gently close the door to the little room and lock it again. "Sorry, but I can't remember your name."

"I'm Initiate, first ranking white-robe." He exhales as if resigned to what will come next.

"That's your name?"

"Here we go again." He takes a moment to chew and swallow his bite. "Initiate is what they call every potential who's ever trained here. Hundreds came before us, but I'll be…" He changes his thought mid-sentence. "You give up your birth name when you arrive. Everyone does. We're all just one long string of Initiates."

"Not me. I'm Ash." Of that I am sure.

"Yeah, best not say so aloud."

"But you called me Ash."

"Because you told me to."

"And what do I call you?"

It is his turn to blush. "My birth name," he whispers. "Tomik. I don't mind as long as they never hear you say it." He points his laden spoon in the direction of the nearest table of brown-robes before popping it in his mouth.

"Tomik is a good name." I take a bite of warm bread saturated with butter. For a while, I'm completely focused on the food.

Tomik laughs. "Now you're better."

"I am." Then I frown. "Do you know where we are?"

"Sure but brace yourself. This always gets you."

"Tell me." I raise my spoon to take a bite of stew.

"Avon Eyre."

I drop the spoon, spilling the load. "You're kidding."

"Nope. Not kidding. This is Avon Eyre, the jewel of Amassia, home of the Brotherhood of Anon, unreachable by any map, save one." He says it like a herald.

There are so many questions arising from that single sentence, I don't know where to begin. "Can I have a tour?"

"Later," Tomik cuts me off. "I'm starving. And we don't have much time."

"What's the rush?"

"Training," he says while he chews. "You better eat up. You'll need your strength." He shovels mouthfuls in as fast as he can.

I do the same, but not as fast. *"Training?"* I ask him mind-to-mind so I don't interrupt his eating.

"*Mine is hard, but yours is basic.*"

"*Why is that?*"

"*Cause you haven't raised your phantom for them yet.*"

I wince. "I'm non-savant."

"*I know that's what you say, but they don't believe you.*"

I finish off my bowl, mopping up the last bits with the bread. I'm not going to argue with the boy. There is something more important I want to ask. "*Tomik, what's this mind speech we have?*"

"*Don't know. Never had it with the others.*"

"What others?" I ask aloud.

He scratches his nose. "Bless the Bone Thrower, this food is good!" He seemed not to have heard my question as he lifts the bowl to his mouth, tipping his head back to get every last drop. Juice runs down the corners of his mouth and I hand him my napkin before he uses his sleeve.

"I'm going for seconds." Tomik jumps out of his seat before I can question him again. He makes his way to a server who is clearing plates from a nearby table. By the time he returns with another bowl, I'm focused on my next question.

"*Tomik, I have to leave. Escape, if necessary. Marcus Adicio, the…*"

"*The Bone Gatherer,*" he finishes my sentence. "*I know. You need to find him. It's urgent.*"

"*Then you also know I might need your help to get away.*"

"*You always ask me this.*" Tomik's face turns serious. "*And you do need me. They'll not let you go willingly.*"

"*All the more reason for me to get out.*"

"*And if you wake up in the wilderness and don't know how you got there or where you are? What then, Ash?*"

I think for a moment. "*I'll write it down in my journal.*"

"*You already do that, and it doesn't seem to be helping much. It takes you too long to think about looking there.*"

That stops me.

"Yesterday, you said as soon as you can wake up and recognize where you are, then you'll go."

"That's a good plan."

A gong sounds and everyone in the hall stands.

"Training?" I ask.

"Right after mid-day devotion." He quickly downs his second helping.

"Devotion?"

"Try to pretend you remember that, at least. They take it very seriously here."

"Devotion to what?"

"The second sun, of course."

"Demon viz in a pot, they worship the second sun?"

"With a passion." He laughs aloud.

We walk together out the main doors. "You're that way." Tomik points down the hall. "Meditation center."

"Oh good. I'm sure I can do that. It'll clear my head."

"Just say the onahas fist."

I stare at him blankly.

"Three times a day. Devotion, remember? Do what they do."

I make my way down the hall and am ushered into a meditation room by none other than Radigan, who's standing by the door, waiting for me. At the sound of another gong, everyone is on their knees, but not to raise phantoms. They turn their faces to the sun, prostrate themselves and chant *onah-shad-onah-matta* over and over again. Once I've fumbled my way through the repetitions, Radigan announces meditation training.

Growing up in the Sanctuary of Baiseen as a ward of Master Brogal—servant would be more accurate than ward, but anyway—meditation is a quiet affair involving soothing, repetitive chants, candlelight, soft drums, and supportive poses. Here, it's another story. I am reminded of the rigorous, heart-pounding Morning Ritual on the Isle of Aku where an obstacle course is traversed along with other extreme hand-to-hand workouts, with and without weapons, all before the breakfast bell.

I soon find myself standing with one foot on a narrow beam raised three feet off the ground, my hands over my head. I take the "pose of the water bird," palms together, eyes closed and hold it until Radigan claps, or I fall, whichever comes first. Mostly, it's me falling. When I ask why I have to do this, he says it will help me gain more control.

"Of what, exactly?"

"Your phantom."

I clamp my jaw tight. If I had a phantom, I wouldn't be here. I'd be with Kaylin, and Marcus, procuring the next whistle bone, not a prisoner in Avon Eyre of all places. "I told you. I am non-savant."

Radigan gives me a long-suffering look. "However long it takes for you to comply. I assure you your phantom will rise."

Then and there, at all cost, I know I have to escape, and soon. I just need to get my fractured mind stitched back together. There has to be a way!

87

ASH

I wake to find a note to myself on the nightstand, instructing me to check my journal but it's not necessary. I remember who I am, where I am. "An initiate of Avon Eyre," I say to the room. And then I frown. There's more to me than that, but this is a good start.

I go to my desk in the corner of the bunkroom and read a short note. *I live in a dorm hall!* It says so right here.

This memory thing is fun. I refer to the whole room as *mine* because, according to the journal, I've yet to share it with anyone. I'm alone, at least when I'm not studying or eating in the common rooms. The space is designed for more occupants, though, with double bunks on each wall, four desks and chairs and plenty of writing materials, quills, inks, and parchments. I wonder, for a moment, if I choose a different desk each morning or if I gravitate to the same one. In any case, I know three days have passed since Radigan put the fear of the old gods in me with his *however long it takes* speech because I marked it in the journal. "And, because I remember." Well, bits and pieces of it, anyway.

I also know that Kaylin is gone. *Peace be his path.*

The thought drains my life away, but it is also something I never want to forget. He deserves to live in my memories, for the rest of this life. No, longer. I vow I will carry his memory with me onto the next path.

I complete today's journal entry, ready to bookmark the page with a white dove feather I found in one of the aviaries. I remember that, too. Up until now, the longest I held my short-term awareness was about sixteen hours, until I go to sleep and wake up blank. But not today.

Like a handful of dandelion puffs that might blow away in a breeze, I guard my memories, rereading earlier entries of the journal. As I thumb through weeks of notes to myself, I find accounts of my life on Avon Eyre. It's sketchy and vague in parts. Not my best writing. But the common thread is how I got here and that I lost Kaylin, even though I don't remember exactly how. The well of sadness opens wide every time I am reminded of him, but I am getting better and better at breathing through it, and then locking it away. *For now.*

"And in the meantime?" my inner voice asks.

We escape to find Marcus. I need him, and the others, more than ever.

"Don't record that, in case they snoop."

Not planning to. I swear my inner self thinks I have a brain the size of a chickpea.

Not today.

I smile. Gaining my memories, no matter how painful, is a step in the right direction along this path because now I can execute my plan.

I'll need warmer clothes, a reliable map, journal, pen and inks, of course, and some of the more interesting scrolls from the library. I would grab their first whistle bone, too, for Marcus, if they hadn't already used it to barter for me.

"You remember that, too." My inner voice is softer now.

I do.

The sadness threatens to drown me, but I keep breathing until it subsides.

"Isn't Marcus gathering the original whistle bones to save us all from the second sun?" a young boy's voice rings in my head. *"He'll have to get the Mask of Anon from Atikis, won't he?"*

"Tomik? I thought we weren't going to listen in on each other without permission. You must knock, please."

He makes a tapping sound in my head before going on. *"I wish you didn't have to leave. But you're the only one left, besides me, and I won't—"* He stops abruptly.

"Won't what?"

Tomik gives a mental shrug. *"Say a word..."*

I'm sure he was going to say something else entirely, but I don't push. *"Come with me then, when I escape."*

For the longest moment, Tomik doesn't reply. *"I can't."*

"Why not?"

"I need more training."

He's so like Marcus at that age. I sober at the thought of my Bone Gatherer, out there traveling the realms without a translator. Or have I been replaced? I must rejoin the campaign.

The thought keeps me going as I continue to pack, throwing in two strikers, a full water skin, and the map I smuggled out of the library.

"I'll pilfer food for you," Tomik says in a way that makes me know he'll have a good time doing it.

It strikes me as a little strange that he's so helpful at every turn. What if he's spying on me? Or maybe I just don't realize how strong our friendship is, since

I'm only starting to remember it. Still, I ask. *"Tomik, why are you helping me?"*

The question stops him short. Then, after a few false starts, he says, *"Because you're good to me."*

"Meaning they aren't?" I feel the flush that goes with admitting it, and something else. Something he is trying hard not to think. *"What else, Tomik?"* I've seen scars on his neck and suddenly I sense they run all the way down his back.

"If I can help you help the Bone Gatherer, why wouldn't I? The fate of Amassia depends on it. Right?"

"That's what I used to think, but they are celebrating the return here." I sigh. *"Tomik, what would the Brotherhood do if they found out you helped me escape?"*

His only response is to mime a knife being drawn across his throat as his tongue sticks out. Then he bursts into laughter.

I trust he's joking. They wouldn't harm their only Initiates, would they? Surely not young, bright Tomik who, so he tells me, can raise a phantom?

"A bright young boy covered in scars," my inner voice whispers.

Chills run through me. *From his past, before Anon rescued him.* Surely.

"Like they did you?" my inner voice asks.

I wasn't harmed as a child.

"Would you remember if you were?"

Don't say such things, I tell myself. Brogal wasn't a warm guardian, but I have no scars from him.

"That you remember…"

• • •

The next morning, with memories still intact, I shoulder my supplies. The pack is bulky, hopefully not noticeably so. I let a few scrolls stick out the top to make it look like I'm simply about the business of learning, not attempting to escape the Sanctuary. I scan the room a final time and head for the massive, unguarded doors that lead out of the temple. There is a lovely, enclosed garden with an aviary to pass through. It's heated, no idea how, and sweat beads my forehead before I'm halfway across the high-ceilinged passage.

Birds flutter in the overhead branches and sunlight streams through the skylight. There are tiny finches with red caps and bright green wings chittering in a bud-covered maple tree, and white pigeons roost high up in a spruce. "It's spring already?" I whisper as I open the top button on my heavy cloak. This won't be as difficult as I thought, if it doesn't rain.

Once I step outside, though, I button straight back up. The north wind stings my face, making me shiver head to toe. How close to the pole are we?

"North or South?" my inner voice speaks up.

It better be North. Otherwise, I'll have to sail back to the mainland.

Try as I might, I have no idea how I got here from Asyleen, save the warm, echoing tunnel lined with massive rib bones. The map details the borders of Avon Eyre, major waterways, mountain ridges, roads and tracks, but it's blank beyond the borders, almost as if it sits outside of time.

"As myth would have it."

Yes, like that.

But the weather isn't mystical. The sun shines overhead, a pale-yellow light with no warmth. The tall pines surrounding the sanctuary are white with snow. The rooftops of the domed buildings are laden as well. They sparkle like diamonds in the milky sunlight. My nose instantly goes cold as I stand in the wind, looking down on the temple square. So this is the fabled Sanctuary of Avon Eyre?

It's nothing like I imagined, not teeming with phantoms of every kind like the Isle of Aku, or even Baiseen. Here there is a solemn air, as if it were once a bustling town, full of life, but now abandoned. Where is everyone? The square is empty of horses and carriages, though there is plenty of room for them. In the midst of the square is a stone fountain, silent and unmoving, the water frozen solid. A dormant tree marks each corner, the branches reaching in all directions like dark, brittle fingers. I can't imagine this place in the spring. Does spring even come here?

As I gaze across the buildings with their tall, narrow windows and closed double doors, my body trembles from the cold. I'm not sure my clothes are warm enough to survive a night in this climate, unless I can manage a fire. In Baiseen, we are lucky to get a light frost, even in the dead of winter.

"You're not in Baiseen," my inner voice reminds me.

True, but bad weather isn't going to turn me back.

I'd had one argument with Radigan about leaving, at least, one I recorded in my journal. He'd said it would never happen, that my purpose would live or die here. That doesn't make me want to stick around to see which. And the purpose he refers to? I don't know what it is. Tomik doesn't either—or won't say. I quizzed him long about it last night and he only shrugged and fidgeted.

"Hurry." Tomik's voice filters into my thoughts.

"Is the cart hitched?"

"Yes, that's why you have to hurry!"

I trot down the many steps and crunch across the snow-covered courtyard, past other, smaller buildings, and on to the stables, trying not to let my teeth chatter. The plan is simple. I'll hide in the back of the cart that Tomik and his master drive to the training field each day. When surrounded by thick trees, I'll slip away unnoticed. Of course, with only a few days' supplies, if I don't find Marcus or friendly shelter fast, the escape will be short-lived. But I will try.

Tomik stands at the stable entrance where a large chestnut draft horse, thick and shaggy with a long winter coat, is hitched to a flatbed cart. The boy waves me in and grabs my sleeve, pulling me behind the door.

"Master Elwen will be back any moment." Tomik is bundled in a full-length coat, hood down, gold curls spilling over his shoulders. "Give me your pack," he says, all business. In moments he replaces the ornamental scrolls on top with a large loaf of bread, a bag of nuts and seeds, and two sticks of dried meat. "I found a compass, too."

"I'm scared to ask where."

"Then don't."

The thievery raises a memory of Kaylin. His shining eyes and pirate smile.

An apple for my lovely lass. The memory surfaces, and with it the pain. It's so swift and heart wrenching, I double over, gasping for breath.

"No!" Tomik grabs my shoulders and shakes them. "Stay with me."

He doesn't mean physically, but mentally. I drag myself back from the abyss. It's hard. At least in the void I'm numb and mindless.

"Focus now. We've no time." Tomik buckles my pack. "Keep it on. You'll only have a moment to disappear."

I shoulder it, watching his face as I do. He looks too young to wear such a serious expression, but judging by the way they treat him, this boy is well along on the path. I haven't seen his phantom, at least, not that I remember, but he calls it kitty, so a lynx perhaps, or a small wild cat? A *warrior*, he says, like Marcus's and Belair's. Maybe akin to a sun leopard! I wonder if its fur is as golden as his locks. I hug him quickly and my heart clenches. "I wish—"

"Are you ready?" Tomik cuts in, his eyes on the distance.

"I only need to get past the gates."

"You need more than that." He unties the covering over the flatbed cart for me to climb in.

I shoot a glance out the breezeway to the main courtyard. Several savants trot up the steps to the library.

"Don't breathe a word," Tomik says and for a moment, his face falls. *"Why am I doing this? If I'm caught..."*

I hear the boy's inner thoughts. "Tomik, I wouldn't betray you," I say, worming my way under the covering.

"I know. You never have."

"What?"

"Quick. Stay down."

"This isn't the first time I've tried to escape?" My heart pushes up to the back of my throat.

"It's lucky third. Now be quiet."

I close my eyes as he flips the cover over my head, leaving me alone in the dark.

88

ASH

My hands are frozen into clubs, my legs wooden stumps. I'm long past feeling my feet as I trudge through the snow. The second sun sets in a red haze. The yellow sun will follow in a few hours, and then I imagine that will be it for me. Ash, wordsmith of Baiseen Sanctuary, unable to keep my place by the Bone Gatherer's side let alone escape Avon Eyre… Ash, the cause of Kaylin's death, will fall asleep, not waking again in this world.

"Ash, the wordsmith who gave up." My inner voice's sarcasm cuts deep.

I'm stating facts.

"Really? You're a Bone Thrower who can see all possible futures? I didn't know one existed."

Stop being mean. I huff out a foggy breath.

"I will when you do."

There's truth to my inner thoughts. I'm not being terribly self-supportive in these last moments of my life.

"Stop!"

But I can't. Things really are this grim. I have no idea how I survived last night. Maybe it was that dream of a second heart beating in my chest, glowing like a golden furnace.

"I mean, literally stop! Get down!"

The urgency drops me to my knees.

From a crouch, I catch the scent of game cooking on a smoky fire. Above the sound of my racing heart, I hear voices. The squeak of leather armor. Horses tamping down the snow, fluttering air out of their nostrils while chomping hay. A lot of horses. Did the Brotherhood send the entire Sanctuary out looking for me?

The decision of what to do next isn't hard to make. I stand, swallow my pride, and take a step forward. Better alive in Avon Eyre than dead in the snow.

"I said, get down!"

On instinct, I drop again, adrenaline coursing through me. *Why? My only choice is to go back. I'll not have it that Kaylin saved me in vain.*

"It's not Anon."

My inner voice has been right enough times in the past for me to pay attention, as much as I want to run to the fire, pull off my wet gloves, and warm these frozen bones that once passed as fingers. And the food smells so good. But, instead, I inch toward a closer row of pines, keeping low. When I reach a trunk ten times my girth, I listen hard. What did my inner self catch that my consciousness could not?

And then I hear it. The voices speak Sierrak, not the tongue of Avon Eyre.

I peek around the tree. A breath later, I snap back, pressing my cheek into the bark as my heart rate doubles. I can't believe it—guards in Sierrak armor posted around a blazing fire. Half a deer roasting on a spit. A sea of tents beyond. Hundreds of picketed horses. And by the fire, standing tall as others remove his armor, the unmistakable profile of High Savant Tann.

He's here?

"Hence the warning."

Tann, here. With his troops. Does he plan to attack Avon Eyre?

"It doesn't look like a diplomatic party."

I risk another glimpse and see them, the brown-robe Brotherhood of Anon. *Why do they march against their own?*

"Maybe they have no choice."

I stretch around the tree a little farther, to see more, but as I do, a phantom in the form of a white wolf lifts its nose and sniffs my way. I duck back, holding my breath until a shout comes from the guards. It's followed by the sounds of phantoms rising, swords unsheathing, and boots crunching through the snow. Toward me.

What now? I ask as panic turns me to stone.

"Run!"

• • •

Air tears in and out of my lungs as they gain on me. *Run faster!* I yell to myself, even though the idea of outdistancing galloping horses is absurd. I'm heading north, I think. In the direction of the Sanctuary. I wish I could be sure, but the compass is deep in my pack and there's no time to search for it now. Thick gray clouds have covered the late afternoon sun, so no help there.

Low branches smack my face, and a rocky outcropping suddenly looms. I duck left and keep running, thinking of Kaylin, the time we fled Mt. Bladon and rafted down the Ferus River Falls. Kaylin, who saved us all that day. Kaylin who gave his life on the road to Asyleen. To save me. My face contorts, and I can't hold back a sob. In my mind's eye, he dies all over again. *Because of me.* I charge out of the woods into a stark, snow-covered clearing, tears freezing on my cheeks.

"Not that way!" my inner voice shouts.

I dig in my heels, struggling to stop. Snow and rock break off beneath my feet and tumble away as I scramble from the brink of a cliff. The edge chips away completely and vanishes, turning into an avalanche as I fall backward. I roll onto my belly and crawl my way to safety.

F'qad'n bones, that was close. As I jump up to run the other way, riders burst into the clearing. Snow flies high in rooster tails as they slide to a halt. I'm trapped.

While the lead mount still skids on his haunches, the rider, in Sierrak war armor, jumps from the saddle. He hits the ground running and races to block my escape. As if I could get away now. Other riders are on the ground as well, weapons drawn. Closing in. I guess I should be glad they aren't archers. It can take ages to die from an arrow wound.

I grit my teeth and begin to drop to my knees, unable to support myself a second longer, but before I touch down, they are at my sides, pulling me up.

"None of that," the guard says in common Sierrak. "Save your phantom for an audience with Tann."

"Idiots," I say under my breath. "You captured a non-savant."

They ignore my comments and muscle me to a waiting horse until we all turn at the sound of whistle bones. The melody wafts into the clearing, causing rock, weapons, and even the horses to lift as if floating in a well. My heart's in my throat. I've seen nothing quite like this before.

In the moments of confusion, the clearing fills with brown-robe riders, their swords drawn, shields up. Behind them follows more riders, all playing whistle bones. The tune warms me, like a soothing blanket over my shoulders. It's so comforting that if I close my eyes, I can imagine Kaylin's arms holding me tight. In that unreal embrace, the striking of swords and grunts of battle disappear. Sadly, the relief doesn't last long.

Again, strong arms grasp me. I'm pulled to my feet, though not roughly. This guard asks after my health, speaking in the dialect used in Avon Eyre. "Tannson?"

"What were you thinking?" he chastises me. "You nearly got yourself killed." He shakes his head. "Give me your hands."

I whip them behind my back when I see he has rune bands. I'll not have anyone torture my mind again, control me again. Imprison me.

But he locks them on my wrists by force.

Blood drains from my limbs and I can barely stand. "I will not be your prisoner."

He looks surprised. "The rune bands are for your protection. Can't have you raising your phantom in the bone tunnel, or out here for that matter, with the rest of Tann's army a stone's throw away."

How many times do I have to say it? "I am non-savant," I hiss.

"Sure, sure." Tannson pushes back his hood and gives a little smile as if he's heard it too many times before. "Would you prefer to stay and dine with Tann?"

They won't let me go, no matter how I respond, so I shake my head no. "We have to warn the Sanctuary." I'm not a monster. No one deserves a surprise attack from Tann, and Tomik is still there.

"Already done."

A horse is brought up for me, and for a moment everything retreats. Tann, the chase, my failed escape, the rising headache from the rune bands. The mare is that extraordinary. Her breath shoots out from her nostrils in puffs of steam. I guess her height at a good sixteen hands, and she's as white as the snow around us save for a splash of ebony down her back, legs, mane, and tail. The coat is so long and thick, my hand disappears when I reach out to stroke her neck, but she flinches away.

"It's the rune bands. Keep them off her skin."

"Sorry," I say to the mare and Tannson boosts me into the saddle. "What's her name?"

"You may call her Star." He brushes the mare's forelock aside as she turns her head around to sniff my boot. Square in the middle of her face is a perfect pentangle.

He hands me a sword and without question, I buckle it to my side. Tann on the loose and all. After a hard gallop around narrow mountain paths, we reach a yawning cave that leads into the side of the mountain. The bone tunnel. Maybe not the one I traveled before, but a bone tunnel, for sure, judging by the giant rib bones that frame the entrance. What mammoth creature left such a skeleton? A snake the size of the Suni River? Small armies could pass through it, no doubt what Tann has in mind.

Tannson dismounts at the threshold and studies the ground. Other brown-robes join him and they converse in low voices.

"What is it?" I ask when he mounts back up, but a sinking feeling tells me

I already know.

"Tann used your little diversion to slip into the tunnel ahead of us."

"He's ahead?" I think of Tomik's sweet face and gentle nature forced to fight the likes of Tann.

"Ahead or behind. Bone tunnels are unpredictable." I want to ask more but he's already leading the way. "Be on guard," he calls out to the others but says no more.

We splash through the mud and enter the dark tunnel. Torches are lit and Tannson calls for silence. He recites a chant, just like the brown-robes did when they took me through the first time. *I remember that!* I want to ask questions, but the air turns thick and still. The sultry warmth makes it hard to keep my eyes open. Chin on my chest, I give in and close my eyes. It could be worse. Out of freezing to death or being captured by Tann, riding back to Avon Eyre is the better option. Though I am nothing more than a prisoner here, too. I clink my manacled wrists together, proving the point to myself. All the same, Star's unfaltering rhythm has me dozing. As I float away, voices come to me in the haze.

"Hail Japera!" The sound of fist-on-armor salutes rings through the tunnel.

"This is the girl?" A woman speaks.

"Should I wake her?"

"Let her rest, but get those rune bands off. What are you thinking? We're near the other side."

The other side of what, I wonder. Maybe I should wake up and find out more. But Star flutters softly out her nose and walks on, and I slip away.

89

MARCUS

Maybe the Bone Thrower was wrong.

I toss another map aside, not even bothering to roll it back up. Ash would hate the negligence, but what I hate more is wasting time searching through the parchments when it's clearly time to mount up and go find her.

What are we waiting for? De'ral's frustration pounds in my head.

"Let me see, fulfilling our duty and responsibility to the allied realms?"

Finding Ash is everything, of course it is, but there are obstacles to overcome first, like supervising Asyleen's repairs, sorting through these bones-be-cracked maps for her location, and taking multiple excursions in search of the alleged bone tunnel. Apparently it's the only way to Avon Eyre. How the same sanctuary can appear in different places on different maps is beyond me. Still, the Bone Thrower gave us coordinates. I just have to find the map that leads to them. Meanwhile, I try to calm my phantom. *"Ash is safe, De'ral. We will mount the search soon."* He sulks and says nothing.

Oba eventually threw the bones to help find Ash, and the results were clear. For once. She is, according to the reading, safe in the Sanctuary of Avon Eyre, immersed in the library, collecting ancient text on the second sun and the whistle bones. Doing as her rank and status demands—the recorder to the Bone Gatherer. The reading also assured that she will rejoin us, though exactly how or when was not specified. But I believe Oba. I must, or I'll go mad with worry.

We head out tomorrow, or I will, without you, De'ral growls at me.

I growl back.

The savant and the phantom are one. Kaylin's words come back to me. Peace be his path, but how could he know that? I have to face that the sailor is right. *Was* right. De'ral's doubts are mine, mine are his. It's just that De'ral worries that if we don't go soon, we'll never find her and I worry that if we go without knowing the way to Avon Eyre, we'll all be lost.

My eyes drift out the window and across the courtyard as they do every day, resting on the place where Salila last stood. She's someone who never has doubts. Never hesitates. It feels like only moments have passed since we were battling the red-robe together and rejoicing in our victory.

It's years to me, De'ral says.

In this, the savant and the phantom have differing views as well.

Do we?

My thoughts halt as Samsen enters the room with another armful of blasted scrolls. It takes a moment for me to pull my eyes from the window and give him my full attention.

He dips his head and piles the scrolls onto the table. "Still no word from the Mar woman?"

Nothing gets by his notice. "I'm not expecting any." I brush it off. "Word of Belair today?"

"Nothing from him, either."

"The Tangeen couldn't have sent a message by now? There have been enough couriers between Asyleen and the south these past weeks."

"Maybe he was detained." Samsen doesn't say what would most likely be the cause of that, nor do I. We've all suffered enough loss. I'm not going to speculate on more.

"And what about word from our Magistrate?"

"Nor her."

I cross my arms tight in front of my chest, hoping it will calm the building rage. As the second sun shines brighter by the day, I'm near to jumping out of my skin. I don't trust what Rhiannon is doing with my realm and I want these whistle bones passed over to Brogal before Tann, or some other red-robe, tries to take them. Will I win those battles on my own? Atikis is dead, yes, but I had help from a Mar.

Salila, De'ral says in the smoky voice reserved just for her.

"Yes, Salila." It's not like I can forget, though I try. Thoughts of her have been haunting me day and night since Atikis fell.

And there are other problems. It seems, though our tally of whistle bones has gone up, we have been duped. My hand goes to the bone bag at my waist as I list them in my mind. The Ancient Shearwater from Baiseen, Tree of Life from Bakton, Arrow of Nii from Kutoon, Ma'ata and Mummy Wheat from Tangeen. We even have the Eye of Sierrak and the Mask of Anon, but when I feel Mummy Wheat, I scowl. "Does Tyche still say it's a replica?"

"She does." Samsen shakes his head. "And Piper agrees. They've pored over the images in Brogal's text. Tested it with precise measurements and *callings.* Safe to say, it's not the original. I wonder if Atikis knew."

"No telling, but it means Warcott was planning to cheat us all along, keeping it for himself? Or for Tann?" Heat rises. It's another betrayal. "We need to double back, and show Warcott he made the wrong choice," I say under my breath.

Samsen stares, but I avoid his eyes.

"You can try to convince Warcott to support us," Samsen says. "Win him over to the allied realms, but we can't declare war on Whitewing Sanctuary, even if he hoards the whistle bone."

"It might be too late for that. Who knows what Rhiannon is up to?" There was nothing about her in any of the bone readings. Usually, if there is an important person along the path, the throw of the bones has something to say about them. But it was almost like she was shrouded on purpose. "I don't know if she's following Petén's plan, or her own."

"It was a terrible accident, your brother's fall. Peace be his path."

"Accident, or murder?"

Samsen's face remains expressionless. "Best keep such sentiments to yourself, Marcus."

"But what is she thinking?" I grumble. "What does she want?" Rhiannon has always been cunning, but to what end? I get up and begin to pace.

"My guess is she wants power."

"Are we talking about Rhiannon again?" Piper nods to me as she enters the room. She seems to be recovering from a nagging illness that neither she nor Samsen will discuss. He opens his arm to her and they share a lingering embrace.

A fire blazes in the hearth but I throw another log on anyway. "Choosing a green broke horse for the hunt? Petén wouldn't have done that."

"If he'd been drinking, he might have," Samsen says.

"Or if he was goaded?" Piper suggests.

Samsen shrugs out of his coat. "Do you really think she orchestrated the accident?" he asks in a low voice. "His fall? His death? It's Rhiannon we're talking about."

I hood my eyes. "I wouldn't put anything past her."

"If so, she did it for the realm," Piper says. "In her mind, it would be justified."

"A twisted mind if that is the case. I'll deal—"

A knock at the door spins me around.

"Who's there?" Samsen calls out, but the door is already swinging open.

I reach for my sword.

"Here you are, lounging by the fire while the others do all the work. I should have known to search indoors first." A man stands at the entrance, his cloak hiding his features until he throws back his hood, freeing shocks of flaming red hair, a fair face, and a wide grin.

"Belair!" I let my sword fall back into the scabbard. "What has kept you?" I crush him in a hug and he *oomphs* out his breath.

"What has kept you from sending a message, he means." Piper kisses him on the cheeks while Samsen hugs him as well.

"Injury." Belair pulls down his collar to show off an angry red scar on his neck, only recently healed. "Didn't have Piper handy to make it as good as new, but I did get these." He takes off his coat to reveal his new orange-robes. "And before you feel left behind, Marcus, High Savant Havest is handing them out to any savant who comes back alive from a battle with Tann. You'd already have yours twice over, in his court."

"I wasn't thinking of that." I wave it away, wishing my words were true. "Congratulations, Belair Duquan, orange-robe of Tangeen." I give him a formal bow.

"Well earned," Piper and Samsen join in. As Piper examines the scar, her brows go up. "If it was the green-robe Hahmen who healed you, he did a good job."

"Yellow-robe now." Belair smiles wide. "I'm not complaining."

"And what of Tann?" Samsen asks.

"He's on the move. Rhiannon's troops—" He pauses. "Peace be your brother's path, Marcus."

"Thanks." I nod for him to go on.

"Her troops, and a very put-off Tangeen contingent, are scouting far to the north. There's no joy in that camp, I promise." Belair hops into a chair and laces his hands behind his head, basking in the heat from the fire. "Tann's pushed into Sierrak, looking for who knows which bone now. I thought he had them all, his six anyway. But he also left a fully-manned Gollnar warship off the coast of Kutoon."

"There again?" I find that hard to reckon. "Why?"

"The focus is under the waves. Maybe he lost something precious when the ship sank? One of the whistle bones?"

"I will send a message to the High Savant of Kutoon." I look at Samsen. "Zakia may know more."

Belair tilts his head toward the courtyard. "I heard the likes of Gaveren the Great destroyed Atikis." He winks. "Did your *warrior* inflict this damage single-handedly, or was anyone else allowed to join in? Samsen? Piper? Kay—"

"Salila actually."

Belair's eyes flare. "I missed too much! But where are the others? I'm guessing Kaylin returned with Ash? What part did the sailor play? He has a wicked blade and…" Belair stops himself, brow creasing. "What's wrong?"

Samsen sighs and lowers his head.

"Kaylin's dead," I say in a flat voice.

"No!" Belair's mouth sags, his cheeky grin vanished. "How?"

I sink into an overstuffed chair, hunch forward and study my hands. "I wasn't there, but it's said that he was run through by Atikis's blade."

Belair covers his face with his hands. "What was he doing fighting Atikis alone? Did he forget he was non-savant?"

"He was trying to protect Ash."

"Atikis had her?" Belair jerks his head back. "Where is she now?"

My eyes lift to Belair's. "Spirited away through a bone tunnel by the Brotherhood of Anon." I sigh.

"Nothing in that sentence makes sense to me." Belair's face contorts.

"Me either, but the Bone Thrower says she's unharmed and will rejoin us soon." I hope with my whole heart it is true. I feel a terrible squeeze in my chest anyway. "We've been searching the road to Asyleen all month for the bone tunnel, and a map that shows the true way to Avon Eyre."

"Avon Eyre?" Belair whistles. "But she's alive?"

"So says the whistle bones."

He frowns. "We've not had great luck with those readings in the past."

"True." I stand, my eyes going to the pile of maps. "Piper, tell Tyche to gather our text, and those blasted maps. It's time for us to pack."

"To seek Ash?" she and Samsen ask.

"Not just seek. Find!"

"Weapons, savants. Ride!" The command jolts me awake. Star bunches her hindquarters and leaps, bursting out of the bone tunnel. We land at a full gallop and in seconds are through the open gates to Avon Eyre's courtyard. "Defend the Sanctuary!" a warrior woman cries above the chaos. The cold slaps my skin; the sun is long past set. Black phantoms fill the sky, blocking the moon with their leathery wings. I cower as they swoop in, and then draw my sword. The night fills with their high-pitched screams.

One flaps near me, so close the tail snaps like a whip in front of my face. When it pumps its wings to rise, a horse and rider squirm in its talons. Avon Eyre's archers fire from the rooftops but all I can think is, we're too late. "Tomik!" I cry out, but my voice is swallowed by the sound of battle and the screeching phantoms.

"Dismount!" Tannson orders as my horse rears. The ground comes up fast. I land hard on my side. A hand reaches to pull me to my feet. A boy's hand. "Tomik?"

"I thought you were dead." He's in dark brown leather armor from head to toe, sword pointed away from me and at the mayhem.

"Not yet." I gasp for air as an *ouster* wind assails us. It rips our swords right out of our hands. "Look out!" I try to warn others.

"Initiates," Radigan calls from behind us. "Raise your phantoms!"

Tomik turns to me. "Are you really non-savant, Ash?" His gaze stays on mine for a fleeting moment.

I nod, tears welling.

"Then stay behind me." He gracefully touches down one knee and leaps back up. The ground cracks. Snow and cobbles fly high into the air. Before I can blink, a huge black lion lunges into the night sky like a starry constellation come to life.

I gasp again, my heart rate quickening.

His phantom is larger than a horse, the broad shoulders rippling as it lands. The mane swings back and forth as he shakes snow and dirt from his coat. The creature bounds forward, then skids to a stop, pushing snow ahead of forepaws like a plow. With front legs dropped to the ground, tail lashing, Tomik's lion throws back his head and roars. The thunderous challenge is matched by screeches from the sky. The lion springs at the nearest phantom diving toward us.

"Weapons!" Tomik shouts. "Don't worry, Ash. I'll pro..." His words are drowned by the turmoil.

A runner must have heard this call because the next thing I know, they appear, replacing the weapons torn out of our hands by the *ouster*. I drop the empty scabbard from my waist and buckle on the new one. It glistens as I draw it and grip the hilt with both hands, raising it over my head to guard against aerial attacks. Giant paws spring into the air as Tomik's lion leaps again, higher than the courtyard fountain. When it lands, a leather-winged phantom writhes in its jaws. I turn away at the sound of breaking bones and spouting blood.

"What did you say, Tomik?"

"He said, don't worry, Ash. I'll protect you."

I shudder as my inner voice turns into Kaylin's and repeats the words, *"I'll protect you, lass..."* It takes me back to the road to Asyleen, where Kaylin died. All over again, I find his sea-green and gray eyes as he lay bound by rune chains. I shake the image away.

Not now. I can't mourn you now.

Tomik and I fight our way across the courtyard, through the stable, and into the field beyond. Another battle. Another sanctuary under attack. Sure, I was trying to escape this one, but it's still another threat I don't know how to stop.

"Always, Ash. Always I will protect you." Kaylin's voice returns. Through the pain, I want to feel it, the protection he promised.

But he's not here now.

I weave in and out of lost memories as I fight. The vision shifts to Marcus pledging his protection, too, only now we are children caught stealing pies from the palace kitchen.

He's not here, either.

And then my memory bursts through a door I didn't know existed. Someone holds me, and cries, *"I am doing this to protect you, little Ash."*

I think it's my mother, but when I look closer, she is gone.

I turn even further inward toward a heartbreaking wail. As the fighting continues around me, Tomik and his phantom clearing our path, the cry inside fades into a keening, a death knell—long and despairing. I follow the sound deeper into the landscapes of my mind where a dark wall is lit by guttering torchlight. The keening comes from the other side.

Hello? Are you hurt? It's a stupid question. No one unharmed makes noises like that. *Do you need help?*

"*We'll die without it.*" The answer settles over me like a thick fog.

I search the wall for cracks in the mortar, but when I look up, it runs for as far as the eye can see. Still, I drag my fingers across it, brick by brick until I feel it. In the far corner is a fracture the length of my arm. I press my eye to the chink in the middle, searching the darkness on the other side.

I see it, the whimpering creature. Trapped in a much-too-small prison. The beast coils tight, as if the walls burn to the touch. The scales on its back pulse a dull gold, but most of its body is charred. My chest caves in, constricting my heart as I count the ribs, visible with each rise and fall of its breath. And then, it calls my name…

"*Ash?*"

I'm here! I dig frantically at the mortar. When I can reach my hand through, I try to touch the suffering creature but my arm's not long enough. *What happened to you?*

"*Bound.*" It gasps mind-to-mind but says no more.

Show me.

The moment I say the words, it feels as if my aching heart bursts open, releasing a thousand black butterflies that spiral into the sky.

91

ASH

The butterflies dissolve, leaving me suspended above a vast space. *Where am I?*

"Below," the creature says.

I drop my gaze and dive like a falcon, pulling up at the last moment to land on a hard wooden chair. My child-size hands fold into my lap and my bare feet swing above the polished floor. *I know this place.* It's Brogal's chambers.

"A memory of it," the creature confirms.

I remember it, sitting in quiet meditation under Master Brogal's guidance. We did it daily for months.

"Do you know what it was for?"

He was helping me.

"Was he?"

In the back of my mind, I hear scraping, like workers rebuilding a wall as the child-me chants. I twist, glimpsing with my mind's eye a barrier that is nearly complete. Something golden is behind it, about to be sealed in. I tremble, suddenly feeling nauseous. *Brogal did this?*

"You both did."

"Pay attention, Ash." Brogal sits at his desk, leaning forward. "Repeat only this chant, no other."

He promised it would raise my phantom, I say to the creature, but I can hear the doubt in my voice.

"Then why did it raise a wall instead?"

I turn to watch the masons whistling as they work. The job is nearly done, just a few more bricks to go. Behind the wall, the golden creature twists and turns, evading the fire that erupts when it tries to scratch and bite its way out. All the while the whistlers keep working and I keep chanting. They tap the final brick into place, sealing the creature away in the darkness. Mortar smooths over the chinks, obliterating every trace. I reach out, but it burns me, and I jerk my hand back, blowing on my fingertips.

From behind the wall are muffled cries.

"Master Brogal? Did you hear that?" the child-me asks.

"Keep chanting, girl. It's nearly done."

I take a deep breath and continue repeating the words Master Brogal taught me, the words that will help raise my phantom.

"Enough," he booms, and I come back to awareness. A shock goes through my body, like a heavy door slamming shut. My jaw clamps tight, mid vowel, and I bite my tongue. The rhythm breaks and I cry out.

Brogal shakes his head. "Ash," he says, so very disappointed. "We must accept that you are non-savant." His words pierce my heart.

"Please, Master. I will try—"

His features contort like melting wax. I see the wall fail for the briefest of moments, coming down in the Sanctuary of Baiseen, only to be built again. This time the binding is done with living filaments, unbreakable strands that come from Brogal himself.

A soul binding?

With that thought, I snap back into the High Savant's chambers, but it's some future, I think. He's so thin, and he babbles, his shoulders twitching from side to side. Something's very wrong.

"Bindings come at a price—as do their breaking. Brogal pays with his mind, as do you."

The next moment I'm on the Isle of Bakton. A shadow phantom clawing at my mouth and barreling down my throat. The *CRACK* resonates through me. I can fell the wall split.

"So it began." My inner voice brings me back to the present.

The wall? Cracking?

"You might say that the shadow was our liberator."

Our? I still can't believe…

"Protect yourself, Ash." My inner voice cuts in. *"Protect us, or we will not survive this battle."*

This battle? Which one is that?

Suddenly I'm back in the field of Avon Eyre, a sword slicing so close to my face the rush of it whips my hair back. I scream from inside a closed mouth, jaw clenched tight as I block the next blow. Somewhere deep inside my mind, a single brick cracks and mortar trickles down in a tiny river of rocks.

"Protect us, Ash. Set me free."

Adrenaline courses through me and I fight back.

Bodies lie scattered over the field as second, third, and fourth waves of the assault roll in. I can't see Tomik and his lion anywhere. And then, a red-robe flashes in the early dawn light. Tann. The High Savant who destroyed Aku, stole their first whistle bone, and tried to destroy Baiseen as well. He catches my eye, and like a storm changing course, he strides straight for me.

Beside him is a reptilian *ouster,* walking upright on hind legs. Its snout is long like a garfish, eyes limpid and round. It begins to twirl its short front legs in a conjuring motion. The wind picks up around him, funneling like a dust devil.

"Set me free!"

I am inside my mind, pulling frantically at the bricks. There's movement, a glimpse of gold as another brick falls. The creature—the phantom!—twists and turns in the confined space, spiked tail lashing, its skin a writhing sea of darkness and light. Large eyes open and shine up at me.

It's like looking into the eyes of everyone I have ever loved.

They brim with uncontainable emotion, but around them, phantom scales tear off and bleed.

I pound at the prison wall and see the crack widen, just a bit. I pound harder, desperate to bring it down. Pain shudders through me and more of the wall splits apart. There's room to reach for a strand of the pulsing blue soul that strengthens the prison. I grab it, pulling until it snaps. I break another, and another. Inside the falling prison, the half-blackened, half-shimmering creature uncoils, reaching out a long, slender claw. *"Free me!"*

I scratch at more bricks, ripping them loose. When I can stretch through far enough to reach the phantom's head, I grasp the last bind, a muzzle cinched tight as barbed wire. Energy rushes up my arm and into my hand and I snap it in two.

The phantom's mouth flies open as it lets out a roar that shakes the rest of the bricks to the ground. She dives headfirst out of the cell. The phantom, my phantom, channels through my body until finding its way into my soul. There she burrows deep, encased and protected, surrounded by all the space in the infinite path.

My eyes fill with tears as she says, *I am Natsari, your phantom, and you are my* savant.

The final brick turns to crumbles as Brogal's tattered blue soul strands writhe about before dissolving—the cursed prison destroyed.

But it hits me. Well, not all of it, because that is too much at once, but the name... Natsari did she say? *"Um, I need to ask—"*

Maybe deal with the red-robe first.

I look up and time slams back into place at high speed. Tann towers over me not a foot away, my white robes suddenly blooming with blood.

"They tell me you are the missing child of the Japera line," the red-robe says in his deep, growling voice. "Deemed marred and drowned. Indeed, we can assume that was a lie."

My body begins to quiver, muscles acting out of sync with each other. "Japera?"

"I wonder what she will say when she finds her scheme exposed?"

I stare at him, uncomprehending.

"Pitiable child." He shakes his head. "You really were cursed to hide in the shadows." He bends closer still. "And it would have worked, if they'd plucked your eyes from your skull at birth and let you live sightless. As it is, they're a dead giveaway. I'm surprised Brogal didn't notice sooner."

I shrink back from his words.

"Or did he?"

"What does he mean?"

Later, Natsari says, replying with a growl of her own. *Let me up.*

Up? I may be a long-lost savant, but there is no way I can raise my phantom, wounded as she is, on the first try, let alone face down a red-robe. My heart is rich with her presence, but I haven't lost all sense. Our reunion will be short-lived. Tann is about to throw us right off the path.

Quick as a snake, he grabs my hair and wrenches my face up to his. As he searches my eyes, he snarls. "Brogal blundered the job." He slams my head to the ground, cracking it on the ice. "But I won't."

"Stop." I gargle the command. Strings of blood fling from my mouth to paint us in red streamers.

He doesn't hear me or notice the energy building in my core.

Heat infuses my body. "Stop!" I shout, using his grip on my hair as a lever to rise to my feet. I strike with my fist, an uppercut to his jaw.

Tann rocks back on his heels. I guess he didn't expect me to have the strength for that. But I fall back down to my knees.

My chin is on my chest, arms hanging limp, face hidden. I'm wheezing as if on my last breath, head bent low but really, I'm struggling to make room for all this…

Power? my phantom says. *Call me up!*

I scan the battlefield with my mind's eye. *"We have to make sure Tomik is safe."*

Natsari huffs. *Be quick.*

"Tomik!" I call to him, mind-to-mind. *"You and the rest of the Brotherhood get behind us, fast."*

"Who's us?"

"Just get behind me!"

Under the building whirl of energy, I turn to lock eyes with Tann. Puffy skin frames his dark eyes, his pupils dilate. The blackness takes up most of the irises, like an animal with their prey. Only I don't think he knows what he's caught in his trap this time.

"Natsari? Are you ready to rise?" I ask, knowing that there has been no time for healing.

I will try. Just like my dry inner voice, the word *try* drips with sarcasm.

It's a good sign.

I've sat beside Marcus a thousand times before when he tried to raise his phantom and hold it to solid form, so this isn't new to me, in theory. But it's different to be the one on their knees, calling up what has been so long imprisoned. I visualize the process, but not with Brogal's chant. Never again will I utter his poisonous words. And there is no telling its true size and strength. Huge in the vision, yes, but it could be a sprite, the size of a house cat, or maybe a hunting dog. I'm fine either way, but...

Will you get on with it?

"This is all new —"

No, it is not. Let me up!

My knees shake as I chant Gaveren the Great's own call, as Marcus used to practice it. *"On-gal-ma. On-gal-ma..."* Heat builds, starting with my feet and coursing up my spine. The fire nearly consumes me until, just before it reaches my head, I whisper aloud, "ON-gal-ma."

"What do you think you're doing, girl?" Tann steps in to grab me.

But he's too slow.

A crack booms through the ground, knocking him over.

"...on-GAL-ma."

Fissures radiate in all directions.

"...on-gal-MA." I pound both fists into the earth in time with my chant. My skin grates on the ice, and my wrists bruise as they connect with rock, but there is no denying my phantom, even in such a damaged state.

Damaged is not always a weakness, she says, and the thought warms me.

The ground shudders, splitting farther, a web of crevices glowing from the depths. I feel the power of Amassia meet me and I sway, gaining my feet.

"Now rise!" I say under my breath.

Everything goes still, and then white light sears across the sky as the entire field from the stables to the feet of the mountain range implodes. A deafening boom follows. Bodies fly high alongside wood, dirt, and snow, catapulted toward the distant trees. Tann is flung away, and for a split-second everything hangs in the air until another impact discharges.

Dirt and ice spray a hundred feet high, momentarily blocking the early morning sun. From the ground leaps a phantom of the purest golden light and blackest shadow. Emerging out of the void, its draconic jaws open in a war cry that I hear only in my mind—a torrent of grief, pain, passion, anger, joy, injustice, freedom, desire, fear, love, hate...an avalanche of feelings that shoot skyward as Natsari springs into the air. All I can think is, she's huge—twice the height and the length of three horses from head to tail. I know I'm supposed to be directing her, but it takes a moment for me to close my mouth. *Um...go get Tann.* No way will I let him escape.

In seconds Natsari gains an impossible speed, a streak of light with a singular intention. Tann is still falling from the initial shockwave and my phantom catches up to him with a force so colossal it rips the fabric of the world. A sphere of dark energy engulfs everything and in that negative space, Tann folds in half, spinal column shattering as the tear in the sky collapses, sealing itself, creating a third, excruciating explosion that knocks me to the ground.

The red-robe Tann joins the streak of light on a new trajectory. My phantom sends him spinning into the trunk of an ancient spruce, uprooting the tree and arcing it through the air. A cloud of particles flows from him. Ants? After a moment's pause, Tann, along with a sky full of debris, comes crashing back to the ground.

Natsari, undulating in the rays of sunrise, turns to me. *What's next?*

92

ASH

Morning light glints off falling snowflakes. I'm near blinded by the brightness, but my hearing is coming back. My vision clears enough for me to realize I am on my side at the edge of a crater covered in growing vines and buds. *"It was always you,"* I say to my inner voice. To my phantom.

It was always me, we just didn't know it.

I lie still, cheek on the ground. Around me plants sprout, leaves opening and their flowers blooming as they turn toward the two suns. It's so beautiful. So peaceful.

Until a high-pitched tone starts ringing in my head and I feel sticky warm fluid trickling from my ears. Blood traces a line across my jaw to drip down my chin. I feel my body again, all at once. Everything aches. *"Natsari?"* I struggle to my knees using my elbows when my bloodied hands and cracked fingers are of no use. *"Where are you?"*

A shadow falls over me. I look up at her, my phantom, a shimmering serpent, like a water dragon with golden scales and flowing tendrils, a creature with infinite worlds rippling behind her eyes. In her claws, she grips Tann, what's left of him. Shivers run up my back as the phantom from my vision, the phantom who seems in this moment to be as real as I, shoves the broken red-robe's body in front of me. *An offering.*

"Um...thank you." I don't know what else to say.

For the last ten years, I was told there was nothing inside me, that I was, like so many others, non-savant. The label carved its way deep into my heart and soul, making this phantom standing, or rather undulating, in front of me, almost incomprehensible. But here she is, a muscular, iridescent, draconic being covered in the glow of both suns, red and yellow, and the darkest, eerie light of pre-dawn. The motion is spellbinding, her wide eyes impossibly loving.

"You are beautiful."

I am Natsari, returned for the next Great Dying.

"It might have helped to know sooner."

I feel a mental shrug as the massive head lowers to me. *The binding prevented me from speaking of it.* Her muzzle tickles my neck. *Show me your wounds.*

The second my crippled hands lift, a stream of her life-force flows into my fingers and through my body. In the time it takes to gain my feet, my eardrums stop throbbing, skin heals over my phantom wounds, pain and weaknesses wash away in a burst of weightless bliss.

"You're a healer?" I stand in awe of the phantom I thought never existed.

I am the Natsari.

"But am I dreaming?" As I look down at my feet, the new vegetation shines up at me. "Not a hallucination?"

Is there such a thing?

I take a deep breath and view the destruction we caused. Troops from both sides whimper and moan as they climb over the rubble that was once the stables and fenced fields beyond. In the distance, vines and trees continue to sprout, growing from lifeless bodies and severed limbs.

"What's happening?"

Energy stored; energy released. We control that now.

"Control?" Her words terrify me as I try to make sense of them. And then I focus on Tann.

The High Savant's body sprouts thin white roots. Mushrooms erupt out of his broken torso. My phantom reaches out a claw and touches his chest. Then, she pushes through to the heart, the red-robe's chest caving in. His mouth opens and twists from escaping air and I have to look away.

Meanwhile, sunflowers and orchids shoot up around us. Hundreds of blue butterflies emerge from the shattered tree trunks and take flight from bodies that turn to lichen and moss. The crater—Natsari's crater—transforms from a graveyard to a kaleidoscope of color. Amongst it all, I search for Tomik.

Turn around.

Relief floods me as he appears, walking toward us, his lion gone to ground. He stops a few feet away, his eyes on Natsari. "I thought you said you were non-savant."

"And I thought you said you raised a 'kitty.'" Before he can answer, I tackle the boy, scooping him up in a bear hug. "I was afraid I'd lost you."

"I'm still here." He hugs me back. "And so is the Sanctuary." *"Which is lucky. Otherwise, I think they would be pretty upset."*

I turn to the tiled roofs, tall trees, and bell tower in the distance. "Who's that?" I point.

"With Radigan?" Tomik squints, hand to his brow to block the morning light. "That's the Bone Thrower, Japera," he says in a whisper. "I think she wants a word with you."

"Looks that way." It's possible I have broken a few hundred of their rules. I check the space where the sky ripped apart. It seems to be staying together. "Japera?" I say when she stops before me.

Her eyes are focused, her head level. It reminds me of Tann and I take a step back. The woman may be a black-robe, but she is a warrior, too, and flanked by a dozen others dressed just like her—black leather armor with swords at their sides, quivers and bows at their backs, whistle bones draped around their necks and even sewn into their armor like wards.

Tomik drops to one knee and bows. He tugs at my sleeve to do the same, but I remain standing. Staring. This is Sul Japera?

Radigan and dozens of the Brotherhood are with her, too. Their eyes are not on me, though. They can't tear their gazes away from my phantom.

As Japera steps closer, Tann's words come back. He's right. Her eyes…it's like looking in the mirror.

"Do I…? Are you…?" I can't get a sentence out. She surprises me even more by dipping her head to Natsari, a quick but reverent bow.

I like her.

"Of course you do." I clear my throat and try again. "I know you?"

"I should hope so, child. I'm Raven Japera."

My heart quickens. "Raven?"

"You were five years old? I came to your house?"

I swallow hard as it falls into place as if it were never missing. "You're my Bone Thrower."

She nods. "One of them."

"But, we're related."

"Obviously."

"How, exactly?"

She sighs like someone who wants to be off but has resigned herself to a longer conversation. "Raven Japera, black-robe of Steepwater, mother of Sul Japera—black-robe of Whitewing, mother of Ashketon Japera—"

I hold up my hand to stop her. "Deemed marred, deceased. But how does this relate to me?" In my mind, I say over and over, *"It can't be true. It can't be true."*

Can't it?

"You are Ashketon Japera." The black-robe clicks her tongue. "The marred bit turned out to be wrong. Good thing we didn't toss you onto a black sailed ship after all."

I look at her, uncomprehending.

She huffs. "Briefly, a Bone Thrower came two days after you were born, as is the custom."

"In Baiseen?"

"No child. In Avon Eyre. Where your mother and father were at the time."

My mouth forms a circle, and a soft whistle flows out.

"The black-robe threw the bones for you, but proceeded to babble as she read them, losing her wits. She swiped the spread back into her bag before any could see and ran, never speaking a comprehensible word again. We were convinced, your parents and I, that you were marred, destined to be sacrificed to the sea. What else would have triggered her so?"

"I was marred?"

I like the sea, Natsari says.

"Hush, love. I'm trying to understand."

"We thought so, but couldn't be certain."

"Because you can't ask the bones the same question twice." I know that at least.

"Hmm. That's when the first deception came, the first and most difficult for Sul."

"My mother?"

"We marked the records as expected—Ashketon Japera, deemed marred and deceased. But we did not hand you over. Instead, she gave you up, her only child. I hid you myself. Sul never knew where you were. It was better that way, but it tore her apart in the end."

"You hid me in Baiseen?"

"Exactly."

"So, my parents were—"

"Hired to care for you until we could read the bones again."

"But my birth parents?"

"Dead now. Peace be their paths." She puts her hands on her hips. "Don't fret. You still have me."

"How, exactly, do I have you?" I feel like my head is swirling in a wash tub.

"Are you listening, child? I came to you when you turned five, the age when the bones would speak again. I broke the rules, for a second time, and read them for you myself." She looks kindly at Natsari. "And they spoke true. You were not marred."

I don't know how to feel about this, or what to say.

Thank you? Natsari suggests.

When I hesitate for too long, Japera lifts her chin. "If it's not clear yet, I am your grandmother, Raven Japera, returned to Avon Eyre to train you. Judging by recent events, it's not a moment too soon." She crosses her arms. "Now where's Tann? I have a question for him."

I swallow hard and point to a scrap of red cloth and mushrooms wilting in the sun. "Under there."

"I see." She clicks her tongue again. It's not hard to tell she does that when annoyed. "Tann's going to be difficult to interrogate then, isn't he, Ash?"

"Interrogate?" I frown.

"He has a number of whistle bones stowed in a blood chest that's nowhere to be seen or *called.* Hence, the interrogation.*"

Now I really don't know what to say.

Oops might do? My phantom laughs.

Before I respond, tambourines sound behind us and dozens more brown-robes appear. Some spread out into the field, looking for survivors. The others parade toward us, cheering and singing praise. Tannson is in the lead and the first thing he does when he reaches me is fall to his knees. He presses his forehead to earth, chanting, "Natsari. Natsari." The others close in, doing the same. My phantom's name, the one that's meant to be forever and always private between her and me, sounds over our heads and across the field. It's not a good start to my life as a savant. *"Did you tell?"*

No, but the Bone Throwers did, she answers. *A very long time ago.*

I start to speak but muddle the words. Between my grandmother snapping orders, the chanting, the bowing crowd, and the stares from Radigan like I have done something incredibly wrong by him, it's too much. My muscles slacken and I falter.

Tomik tries to support me but it's Japera who comes to my side. "Time to bring your phantom to ground," she says quietly in my ear. "She's done enough for one morning, don't you think?"

That snaps me awake. Fire shoots up my spine as muscles tighten and my mind clears. "Not yet." I trusted Brogal who I'd known all my life. I will not trust this woman, matriarch of my line or not, especially on our first meet.

Fourth, my phantom says.

"What?"

First as your grandmother when you were born. Second as your Bone Thrower in Baiseen. Third in the bone tunnel last night and now, on the fields of Avon Eyre. Fourth meet.

"Not yet?" Japera says, but her eyes show a moment of compassion. "Don't worry, Ash. No one is going to bind your phantom ever again."

"How can I be sure you speak the truth?"

Japera's face turns grim as she looks over the battlefield. "You can trust my word, but even if you don't, trust this." Her arm opens out to the field and the devastation there. "You have freed the Natsari and defeated Tann in a single blow. All the red-robes in Amassia couldn't bind your phantom again if they tried."

I want to say that there was a sight more than a single blow exchanged, but I'm suddenly feeling more confident. *"Best come in, love."*

My phantom's undulating skin calms. *I was like a shadow, cursed these many years.*

"That won't happen again." I lower to my knees. *"The wall is down. You don't have to be afraid."*

I feel her rumbling laughter. *I'm not afraid.*

"Then come." I take a deep breath. *"Soon we'll leave to find Marcus, and you'll see much more of the world. But for now, Japera's right. You need to return. We both need a rest."*

Natsari stares down at me, unmoving. A glint of red haze glows, the second sun behind the clouds. It grows closer to the yellow sun every day.

I smile back up into her bright, multicolored eyes. *"Please?"*

I could nap, now that I am free, my phantom admits.

As she melts into the earth a surge of power coils around my core.

"Well done." Japera helps me up, her black leather armor smelling of coppery blood.

I look to the Sanctuary which seems a hundred miles away.

"Allow me," Tannson says. He drops to his knees and raises his phantom, a beautiful piebald horse.

"Star?" I'm vaguely aware of being boosted onto the beast. Tomik is lifted behind me, his arms going around my waist like...like I have felt before. *"The horse I rode through the bone tunnel is Tannson's phantom?"* I ask him.

"You didn't know?"

"There's a lot I didn't know." As we ride back to the Sanctuary, I wonder how in chac'n stuggs I couldn't spot the difference between a real horse and a phantom one.

You'd be surprised, Natsari says in a drowsy voice, *by the differences you've missed.*

"Meaning?" The comment makes no sense, but the familiar, dry voice in

my head lifts my heart. "We have to find Marcus," I say to Japera. "And Tann's bone chest."

"But first, you need training."

"I'm not staying long." I close my eyes, hoping Japera won't try to talk me out of it.

"She won't," Tomik responds. *"And this time, I'm coming with you."*

"What's changed your mind?"

"Are you kidding? Everyone in the Sanctuary will want to be there when you save the world from the next Great Dying."

"You're so funny." Something has been lost in translation if that's what they think.

But on the way back to the temple grounds, I'm not so certain. Brown-robe savants follow us, still chanting and cheering. Others pour out of the halls. They drop to their knees and touch their foreheads to the ground as we pass. Some hold up their wounded for healing or bring children for me to bless. Me? Bless?

Farmers and stable hands, savant and non-savant alike, all press in close to get a glimpse of me. When the second sun comes out from behind a cloud, they raise their faces, expressions transforming to pure bliss. "Nat-Sar-Ree! Nat-Sar-Ree!" they chant.

No matter how many times I blink my eyes, I am sure I must be dreaming.

This is good. My phantom's voice feels warm in my mind, satisfied, and that sensation fills me to the brim, except for one corner of my heart.

"If only Marcus were here to meet you, and—"

Go ahead, Ash. Say his name aloud.

I draw a deep breath. "Kaylin." A tear slides down my cheek. *"If only Kaylin were here to meet you, too."*

My phantom's voice turns wry. *Yes, if only.* Her thought is followed by a deep resonating snore as she falls into a peaceful sleep.

93

KAYLIN

A flurry of sand swirls over my face and I open my eyes to the web of Ma'ata that covers me. Have days gone by? Weeks? Months? I cannot yet think of decades. *"Teern!"*

"Resting well, son?"

"Let me up!"

"It's far too soon to raise your phantom. It took quite a clobbering on the road to Asyleen, I hear."

"Where's Ash?"

"Hate to say I told you so, but she, and her phantom *are on a new path."*

"Her phantom?" I struggle against the entombing corals. *"We had a deal!"*

"We did, and I recall saying that if you let her out of your sight, even for a moment, the deal was off."

I curse him loud and long.

"Calm down, son. It's unfortunate, Atikis sending you to ground, but there's nothing you can do about it now."

"What happened to Ash?"

"So many things… Brogal's bindings, Rowten, the Sierraks, Bakton's shadows, Atikis, Anon, Tann. But the most important thing that happened to her, son, was you."

It doesn't make sense and I struggle all the harder.

"Now, your turn," Teern says. *"How did you allow the Gollnar red-robe to best you?"*

I hold very still, trying not to gnash my teeth at the memory. *"Sierraks captured me when I tried to rescue Ash. They had rune chains. We were loaded into a wagon at Oteb and on the road to Asyleen, Atikis turned up. I was about to put him and his phantom off the path when he threatened Ash's life."*

Teern chuckles. *"I'm guessing that stopped you?"*

"It stopped me dead!" I'm not ashamed of this. I never will be. *"He wrapped me in stronger runes, and when the Brotherhood of Anon traded their first whistle bone for Ash, he ran me through with his sword."*

"I'm sure that was frustrating." Teern tilts his head. *"But well done, all the same."*

I stop struggling. *"Pardon?"*

"You have fulfilled your role, Kaylin."

"What role?" My blood heats as I spit the words at him.

"In releasing Ash's phantom. Tricky enough business, breaking a normal binding. I thought it was done when you returned to Baiseen. I never guessed Brogal would risk a soul binding after that."

"What are you talking about?" I snap. *"I didn't even know she was savant!"*

"It wasn't any one thing you did, Kaylin. Never is. But day by day, your connection to each other drew her phantom closer to the surface. Her thinking she watched you die was most helpful. It got her to the core of her heart. Win–win."

"This is not a win!"

"And Salila and Marcus putting Atikis down, side by side," he continues as if I hadn't spoken. *"You won't see the results, but hopefully it will be worth it, too."*

"Worth what?"

"The planning, of course. So many pieces to the puzzle."

If I had more strength, I would draw my sword and plunge it into Teern's dark and phantom-less heart. *"You made this happen?"*

"Not all of it, but do you think I would leave the events of the next Great Dying to chance?"

My mind spins. *"You sent me to kill them. To kill Ash!"*

He laughs at that. Quite heartily. *"Kaylin, when was the last time you killed an innocent?"*

I frown, still confused.

"Yes, I sent you as an assassin, knowing full well you wouldn't do it. I hoped an attachment would develop but didn't count on it being so strong. I guess I should have. All phantoms love Ash, don't they?"

Rage courses through me. *"You let me believe I was betraying you? Manipulated me the whole time?"*

"Truth is, son, you did *betray me. But, if you knew my mind, it would have freed you to tell Ash everything. She was in your head, was she not? Communing mind-to-mind?"*

I can't deny it.

"So you see, I couldn't have her knowing that Mar are phantoms of the sea, rising from the bodies of their entombed savants that lie eternally aware in the blessed Ma'ata…"

I struggle. It's not feeling so blessed right now.

He pats the corner of my tomb and I scream at him.

"Savants who cannot die but whose phantoms can go to ground. If she had

known, you, and your death would not have had such an effect, would it?"

I try to interrupt but he's not finished. *"Mortality is an essential ingredient for love, Kaylin. Winning another's heart means nothing if you can't lose it just as quickly."*

It hits me full in the face. Ash thinks I am dead. *"You will not survive to regret this!"* I explode in spasms, twisting and straining, but unlike Brogal's binding, the Ma'ata doesn't give an inch. In the case of the Mar, the savant and the phantom are truly one.

"Steady, Kaylin. You must regain your strength before you rise again."

"How long have I been down?" I gasp.

"Not long enough, son."

I wince. *"Let me up!"*

"Can't. You know that. Give it a decade or perhaps two or three."

"When the Great Dying has covered the land? Teern! By the bones, bring me blood and let me rise. Let me go to her now!"

"Shouting in my head won't help your cause," the Sea King says. *"Rest. There's nothing else for it."*

"But Ash! If she survived the bone tunnels, I must find her."

"Oh, she survived them all right, though Avon Eyre will never be the same." Teern leans over my face. *"Raven Japera has her now. The girl needs training and, well, more about that later."*

"You are Teern! You can break the rules." I let out a sob. *"Please. I love her."*

He shakes his head. *"Love breaks many rules, Kaylin, but not this one. Go to sleep."*

I fight the restraints, cursing Teern in every language I know, including my own Tutapan, but he's gone. The current washes over my entombed body and sand, stirred by the Sea King's departure, settles on my Ma'ata covered face. Far above me and to the north, I sense the bright sun shining. Less than an arm's length away from it, the flaring red light of the second sun cuts through the water to reach me.

"Where are you now, Ash? Can you hear me?" I call, but there is no answer save for the whispers of the sea.

When I finally give in to the healing Ma'ata, I make a vow. I will rise again, before Ash leaves this path, and when I do, I will find her. And then nothing, not Teern, not the crown of bones, the second sun, or the next Great Dying will keep us apart.

I send my last thought to her with all my heart and soul, hoping against hope that she will hear. *"Ash, lass. I'm alive. Please don't give up on me."*

GLOSSARY

Aaron Adicio—firstborn son of the Magistrate of Palrio, deemed marred by the Bone Throwers and sacrificed to the sea, an act which has fueled the Magistrate's hatred of the black-robes.

Agapha—a tree-like *warrior* phantom with incredible endurance and strength.

Aku—also referred to as the Sacred Isle of Aku, a politically neutral island realm where all initiate savants go to train for advancement to yellow-robes.

Alters—phantoms who can change shape from one solid form to another. They are most common in Aturnia and Gollnar but can be found in any realm.

Amassia—the third planet from the sun whose seven continents have, over millennia, formed a single landmass surrounded by sea. Alternative spelling is *Amasia*.

An'awntia—pronounced ant-ON-tee-ah—the highest state of mind-body-spirit unity an Amassian can embody, where they have mastered every lot and reached the end of their path.

Ancient Sea Scrolls—historical fossil records, preserved in petrified tablets, that record the histories of the realms prior to the Great Dyings. Only fragments have been found to date.

Ash—orphaned at age eight, wordsmith and best friend of Marcus Adicio, a seventeen-year-old savant raising a draconic phantom named Natsari. Birth name: Ashketon Japera—granddaughter of the black-robe Raven Japera, an infant deemed marred but spirited away to hide in the shadows until called....

Asyleen—the Sierrak Sanctuary in the far north of the continent led by the red-robe Zanovine and the Magistrate, Rantorjin.

Atikis—the red-robe of the Sanctuary of Goll who raises a monstrous, multifaceted *alter* phantom.

Atlan—an alternative name for Nun, Brogal's assistant.

Aturnia—the realms of both Northern Aturnia and Southern Aturnia are to the north of Palrio and hostile. Tann of Lepsea has taken over from their deceased red-robe, peace be his path. Due to political misconduct, Northern Aturnian savants are banned from training on Aku.

Avon Eyre—pronounced ah-von-R. Stories describe it as a small island at the top (or bottom) of the world reached only by an ice bridge in winter but maps from different times and realms mark it in different locations. Perhaps mythical or otherworldly, it is said to host a Sanctuary where the fabled Brotherhood of Anon dwell.

Baiseen—the seat of the throne in the realm of Palrio. Home city to Marcus and Ash where they first raised their phantoms in the initiation trials.

Bakton—the original island Sanctuary in the Archipelago of Nonnova. A now uninhabited, volcanic wasteland with only temple ruins to show for its once magnificent sanctuary.

Belair Duquan—a yellow-robe warrior savant from Tangeen who raises a red sun leopard phantom. Belair continues the journey with Marcus and the others on his search for the original whistle bones.

Black Sailed Ships—outlawed in Palrio, these vessels hoist black sails when they carry a marred child to the Drop to be sacrificed to the sea.

Bone Throwers—those who carve and throw the whistle bones, belonging to a sect of savants whose phantoms never take solid form but remain as wisps of energy and colored light. They wear black robes, no matter their rank, and are oracles, throwing the bones to determine when to sow, harvest, go to war, and most importantly, which child has the potential to be savant, non-savant, or marred.

Bone Gatherer—the savant out of prophecy who will bring all twelve original whistle bones together. The hope is to reform the crown of bones and protect all allies from the ravages of the next Great Dying.

Brogal—the High Savant of Baiseen and Ash's guardian. He raises the most powerful *caller* in the realm that takes the form of a bird of paradise.

Brotherhood of Anon—an ancient sect of savants from the far northern Sanctuary of Avon Eyre who worship the second sun.

Brown-robes—in Avon Eyre, savants of high order, usually black-robe Bone Throwers but can have any class of phantoms. In all other realms, they are children of eight years, allowed to trial and prove themselves savant.

Bucheen—the orange-robe master healer on Aku.

Callers—savants who raise phantoms who use sound (song and chanting) to *call* things to them, such as fish to nets, weapons from a warrior, weeds from a garden bed or in rare cases, blood from bone, or memories from the mind.

Captain Anders—the captain of the *Dugong* who sees Marcus through much of his search for the whistle bones.

Charms—the names of ancient constellations, once called on for their power.

Chrysel—Rhiannon's phantom, a meerkat *caller*. Cute but mind the teeth!

Council members—high-ranking officials of the Sanctuary and Magistrate court allowed to attend policy meetings and vote on the Summits.

Crown of Bones—the group of twelve original whistle bones when collected and played together at once.

De'ral—Marcus's *warrior*, a phantom of massive strength, size, and will.

Destan—an Aturnian green-robe with a *warrior* phantom who trained on Aku and was defeated by Marcus in battle.

Dina—an orange-robe healer savant at the Sanctuary of Baiseen who specializes in herbal medicine.

Dreaded, the—a clan of Mar so horrific in nature and spirit that Teern himself imprisoned them indefinitely in their Ma'ata tombs. They are, by name, Togen, Jenifern, Raymar, Krew, and Rosie Red.

Drop—a deep sea trench along the continental shelf where the black sailed ships take the marred children for sacrifice.

Dugong—Captain Anders's large sloop hired for the first half of the Bone Gatherer's journey.

Elwen—a brown-robe savant in the Sanctuary of Avon Eyre who oversees initiate training with Master Radigan.

Er—King of Si Er Rak (now known simply as Sierrak), the northern realm of Amassia. King Er was thought to be the first known savant and from his skeleton the original whistle bones were carved.

Ferus River Falls—originally named Mossman's Shoals, the fabled falls named in the prophecy of the second sun.

First Whistle Bones—also called the original whistle bones—the first twelve whistle bones, purportedly carved from the skeleton of King Er, but actually stem from much earlier times. Each represents one of the lots or *ways* on the path to An'awntia and were once made into a Crown of Bones. Eventually they were dismantled and sent to the sanctuaries for protection. Each is kept in a place of honor, symbolic of the responsibility and privileges of being savant. In order, they are:

    Crown of Er (mandible)—First Lot—Awareness of Self

    Tree of Eternity (vertebra)—Second Lot—Awareness of Body

    Ancient Shearwater (scapula)—Third Lot—Awareness of Mind

    Ma'ata (femur)—Fourth Lot—Awareness of Feelings

    Water Serpent (coccyx)—Fifth Lot—Awareness of Creativity

    Mummy Wheat (radius)—Sixth Lot—Awareness of Service

    Mask of Anon (cranium)—Seventh Lot—Awareness of Relationships

    Scroll of Hetta (rib)—Eighth Lot– Awareness of Renewal

    Arrow of Nii (femur)—Ninth Lot—Awareness of Expansion

    Jenin Stones (tibia)—Tenth Lot—Awareness of Leadership

    Eye of Sierrak (fibula)—Eleventh Lot—Nonjudgment

    Prince of the Sea (clavicle and scapula)—Twelfth Lot—Self-acceptance

Gaveren the Great—a celebrated Sierrak warrior out of history whose phantom was thought to be the largest and most powerful ever raised.

Ghost Phantoms—a phantom without a savant. In rare occurrences, upon the death of a savant, their phantom becomes untethered from the depths of their being. Ghost phantoms roam for an unknown length of time, lost and confused, always searching for a savant to host them. Also known as shades or shadows.

Goll—the main Sanctuary in the northern regions of Gollnar, once led by the red-robe Atikis and his terrifying, multiformed *alter* phantom.

Gollnar—the realm to the northwest of Baiseen, home of the red-robes Atikis of Goll and Zekia of Kutoon.

Great Dying—the once every twenty-five-million-year extinction that wipes out most of the life forms on Amassia, leaving what survives to evolve along a new path.

Greker—an orange-robe wordsmith at the Sanctuary of Baiseen.

Hahmen—a healer savant from Tangeen. Belair's easy-going friend/love interest. Raises a phantom in the form of a lemur.

Healers—a phantom/savant team devoted to the care and well-being of all life no matter the realm, rank, or species. *Healer* phantoms are found in all the realms.

High Savant—a red-robe savant who has obtained the highest level of aptitude and rank. They usually oversee one of the Sanctuaries.

Huewin—the orange-robe library master on the Isle of Aku.

Initiate—a green-robe savant who has advanced in training far enough to attempt the journey to Aku and earn their yellow robes. The exception is the Sanctuary of Avon Eyre where initiates wear white-robes and do not journey to the Isle of Aku for trials.

Jacas Adicio—Marcus's father and Magistrate of Palrio, orange-robe savant to a *caller* phantom and lord of the throne of Baiseen.

Japera—a matriarchal line of savants: Raven Japera—black-robe of Steepwater, mother of Sul Japera—black-robe of Whitewing, mother of Ashketon Japera—deemed marred and deceased.

Kaylin—a Mar posing as a bosun's mate who guides Marcus and his company when they are stranded on their way to Aku. He also accompanies them on the quest of the Bone Gatherer.

Katren—orange-robe wordsmith in the Sanctuary of Baiseen and Ash's friend and teacher.

Klaavic—Palrion fish stew with prawns, crab, fish, mussels, and clams in a tomato, garlic, and basil broth.

Kutoon—the main Sanctuary in the south of Gollnar, led by the High Savant Zakia and her *alter* phantom.

Landers—a term for those who cannot swim, or when used by Mar, for those who do not live beneath the waves.

Larseen—an orange-robe friend of Marcus who raises a jackal *caller* phantom.

Lepsea—High Savant Tann's Sanctuary on the far northeast of Sierrak.

Lilian—Captain Rowten's sister, a savant friend of Ash's.

Lots or "ways" to An'awntia—twelve in number, they are: receptivity, awareness of body, awareness of mind, awareness of feelings, play, work, partnership, renewal, travel, leadership, nonjudgement and self-acceptance. The journey begins on the eastern point of the great circle and travels like the visible sun around the Earth. Once the first twelve ways are taken, the journey begins again, each lot building on a theme that, over lifetimes along the path, develops to its highest form of expression.

Lucia—librarian in Pandom City Library in Tangeen.

Ma'ata Corals—the ancient polyps that grow from the bones of the old gods and surround the tombs of the Mar. Sometimes written *ma'atta*.

Ma'ata Keeper—a Mar who tends the underwater tomb and oversees the turnings of sacrificed children into Mar.

Mar—long thought to be a mythic race who live beneath the sea but can pass on land as a non-savant, or even savant, under certain circumstances. Some say they are a bloodthirsty race, and possess incredible speed and strength.

Marcus Adicio—the yellow-robe Heir to the throne of Baiseen, Marcus is the third son of Jacas Adicio and raises a *warrior* phantom. He is also Ash's best friend.

Morning Ritual—an early morning practice on the Isle of Aku where all gather for a short meditation followed by rigorous, dynamic exercise.

Natsari—a phantom told of in the ancient sea scrolls who rises to bring balance to the world during the next Great Dying.

Nonnova—the island chain to the southwest of Baiseen, allies of Palrio, led by the High Savant Servine and her *healer-caller* phantom.

Nun—Brogal's enigmatic assistant.

Ochee—a Tangeen spiced tea made from an aromatic mix of ginger, cinnamon, cloves, cardamom, black tea leaf, and dried orange peel.

Old gods—a pantheon of deities said to have been trapped under the earth eons ago, before the last Great Dying. From them the Ma'ata corals, that entomb the Mar, rose.

Ousters—these savants raise phantoms that dispel or vanquish objects, weather, animals, or people. The more advanced ones are very specific. *Ousters* can push away certain types of objects but pass through others. The Aturnians originally used their phantoms to control weather and rain cycles but in the last five hundred years they have been honed for battle. Opposite of a *caller* but can create similar results.

Palrio—the realm south of Aturnia, ruled from the city, and Sanctuary of Baiseen.

Pandom City—the seat of rule for all of Tangeen, the realm across the sea to the west of Palrio. The rulers are the Magistrate Riveren and the High Savant Havest. This is the home realm of Belair Duquan.

Path—the *path* is the road to An'awntia one walks. No one is fully aware of how far they've come along the path with each new lifetime, or how far they have yet to go. It is believed that the savants are closer to An'awntia—further along the path—but it has never been proven.

Petén Adicio—second son of the Magistrate of Palrio, the non-savant brother of Marcus.

Phantoms—a phantom is energy in the savant's inner being and can only rise when the trained savant drops one or both knees to the ground. At that point, the phantom rushes out of the depths of their core, into the earth and rises, blasting from the ground and taking form. In essence, it is a materialization of the savant's shadowed, subliminal, often unknown side of themselves. It is all that is suppressed, and all that is yet to actualize. All that is potential. The savant must come to terms with their own fears and longings if they are to control their phantom, serve the Sanctuaries, and protect the realm.

Phantom Throne—the throne in the hall of Baiseen. In the time of each magistrate's reign, their phantom is carved into the massive wood of this high-backed seat of power. Over the centuries, it explodes with dozens of phantoms, Jacas Adicio's wolf being the most conspicuous.

Piper—an orange-robe, one of the top healers in the Baiseen Sanctuary who raises a double-headed black serpent *healer*. She is the official healer on Marcus's initiation journey to the Isle of Aku.

Potentials—the children the Bone Throwers deemed worthy to try and raise a phantom. They are sent to the sanctuaries at eight years of age, the brown-robes that receive intensive training to see if they are indeed savant. Most will fail and go back to their families, declared non-savant. Those who do raise their phantom will stay on as blue-robes and train up through the ranks, as far as they can go.

Radigan—a brown-robe savant of Avon Eyre who oversees the training of Initiates.

Rantorjin—the Magistrate of the Sierrak city of Asyleen.

Realms of Amassia—see the map and individual realms for details.

Palrio

Tangeen

Isle of Aku

Nonnova

Sierrak

Gollnar

Northern Aturnia

Southern Aturnia

Avon Eyre

Recorders—wordsmiths or scribes, usually savant, who chronicle the initiation journey and other significant events of the realm.

Retoren—an ancient language Ash tries to translate.

Rhiannon—Baiseen's treasurer's most ambitious daughter, yellow-robe to a meerkat *caller* phantom named Chrysel, and childhood friend/once love interest of Marcus.

Rig-tackle Stuggs—a Sierrak football game played with two balls, four teams and four goals, one on each point of the compass.

Riveren—Magistrate of Pandom City.

Robe Colors—indicate rank and training level. See *Savant*.

Rosie Red aka Dreaded Rosie Red—one of the dreaded entombed in the gulf of Kutoon. Teern put her down hundreds of years before the current Great Dying for crimes too horrific to recount.

Rowten—captain of the Baiseen Palace Honor Guard.

Rune bands—also known as rune chains, are manacles or bracelets made from copper, bone, or sometimes gold, etched with runes from the ancient sea scrolls. When worn they are said to keep a savant's phantom from rising and cause terrible pain if they try.

Salila—a Mar woman with extreme appetites, intractable will, and no obvious morals. Her only fear is Teern, known to all Mar as Father, and King of the Sea.

Samsen—a yellow-robe savant who raises a part *caller*-part *alter* phantom that is confined to various forms of birds. He accompanies Marcus on his initiation journey as guard.

Sanctuaries—the temple retreats devoted to the training of savants and their phantoms.

Savant—one who can raise their phantom, bringing forth a manifestation of their being/soul that is either *caller*, *ouster*, *alter*, *warrior* or *healer*, or some combination of two.

> The ranks are:
> **Brown-robe**—children allowed to trial and prove themselves savant (see *brown-robes* of Avon Eyre for exception)
> **Blue-robe**—successful potentials who have begun their training at the Sanctuary
> **Green-robe**—more advanced but haven't held their phantom to form
> **Yellow-robe**—savants who have successfully completed their initiation journey
> **Orange-robe**—highly trained savants that have reached master level
> **Red-robe**—the highest-ranking savant in a given sanctuary
> **Black-robe**—one of the Bone Throwers whose phantoms never hold solid form

Sea Eagle—Captain Nadonis's carrack that sailed Marcus and his party toward Aku.

Second sun (also dark sun or twin sun)—Amassia's binary sun that travels an extremely eccentric orbit. It can be viewed by the naked eye once every twenty-five million years, when it heralds the next Great Dying.

Servine—the High Savant of the Sanctuary of Nonnova, on the main island of the Nonnova archipelago.

Sierrak—the mountainous realm to the far north, main Sanctuary in Asyleen but also sanctuaries in Lepsea, Steepwater, and Morab. Sierriak is famous for their starwatchers and finely made distance glasses.

Summits—meetings attended by council members, usually yellow-robe and higher, to make policies for the realm. A vote on the Summit carries weight as even the Magistrate must uphold Summit decisions, agreed with or not.

Talus—a mysterious white-robe savant from the Isle of Aku. Sometimes referred to as the First Bone Thrower.

Tangeen—the realm to the west of Palrio, whose seat of rule is Pandom City, home of Belair Duquan. Also home realm to one of the most beautiful Sanctuaries in all of Amassia, Whitewing.

Tann—a red-robe, High Savant of Lepsea, Sierrak who raises a reptilian *ouster* phantom.

Taruna—the Ma'ata keeper charged with minding the Mar's underwater tombs off of the coast of Kutoon in Gollnar.

Teern—called Father by all Mar, and the King of the Sea, Teern has the responsibility of ensuring the survival of his people. Some say he isn't Mar himself, but the last of the old gods, surviving many cycles of the Great Dying and remaining unchanged.

Tessellated columns—the monoliths that rise when *called* to protect Baiseen. Over five stories tall, they are carved from obsidian found in the high ranges of Palrio. Ancient legends say they were set by Mar, back when the southwest of Palrio was under the sea.

Twin suns—a symbol found in ancient text to indicate the binary suns of

Amassia. Singular refers directly to the second sun. Tann's ships fly a flag with this emblem, as do some sanctuaries that welcome the second sun.

Tutapa—the island archipelago realm in the south seas. Their Sanctuary, La'hanta, is very small and thought not to host an original whistle bone.

Tyche—granddaughter of Yuki, a twelve-year-old orange-robe savant who raises a *caller* phantom in the form of an impala.

U'karn—head of the war council of Baiseen.

Warriors—Savants who raise *warrior* phantoms that train with their savants for battle, prepared to guard and protect their realm. Seen more in Sierrak and Aturnia but can be found in any realm, though very rare in Palrio.

Warriors' Decree—an ancient chant, uttered before battle, that rouses fighters into a berserker state. Only the first four lines can be written, as the full decree would cause the reader to become enraged:

> *Sing, my blade, fast and true.*
> *Find your mark, through and through.*
> *Take the heart and the soul.*
> *To the core, on you go…*

Whistle Bones—carved from bone, baleen, shell, or tusk, only the whistle bones, thrown by black-robe savants, used for predictions including which child has the potential to raise their phantom, which will be non-savant, and which is marred and must be sacrificed to the sea. Also used to augur best planting time, fish runs, battle tactics, potential alliances and intentions of others, individuals or governments.

Yuki—the High Savant of Aku and Tyche's grandmother.

Zakia—High Savant of Kutoon in Gollnar who raises an *alter* phantom.

Zanovine—High Savant of the Sanctuary of Asyleen in Sierrak.

Zarah—an orange-robe warrior from Northern Aturnia who teaches on the Isle of Aku, Marcus and Belair's instructor.

ACKNOWLEDGMENTS

It takes a unique kind of metaverse to bring a book to life, and I am grateful for all who have participated, not just in the creation of the Amassia series, but to you readers out there who hold this book in your hands. There is no story without you!

Very special acknowledgements go to Aaron Briggs—the A in the AK—for years of brainstorming, cinematic and gaming vision, continuity alerts, action/battle choreography and writing ingenuity. Without your collaboration, this series would only be half a world, half a story. Also, my eternal gratitude goes to Nicole Resciniti whose brilliant insights, tireless contributions (at all hours of the day and night), faith in the story, and never-failing fiction logic are above and beyond all hopes and dreams. If ever there be a perfect agent, it is you, Nic.

I express abundant thanks to everyone at Entangled Publishing, especially Liz Pelletier, Molly Majumder, Heather Holland, Stacy Abrams, Greta Gunselman, Bree Archer, Heather Riccio, Lydia Sharp, Curtis Svehlak, Jessica Turner, Toni Kerr, Meredith Johnson, proofreaders Aimee and Arianne, Jessica Lemmon, and Riki Cleveland. Your work is truly excellent and so appreciated!

Gratitude goes as well to Shawn Wilder, my gorgeous sister, who reads, proofs and comments on anything I throw at her. And, to Katherine Petersen, proofreader/copyeditor and most aligned book buddy. Special thanks also to the authors and influencers who have given me quotes and social media friendship. A boatload of appreciation as well to those on my *Kim's Daily Divination* list (which is more like *monthly* during editing cycles). You make an often-time isolated occupation rich and full.

Not least, a heartfelt thanks to my inner circle who cheer me on (or leave me alone as needed) every day: Aaron, Ochre, Kayla, Kinayda, Son, Shawn, Grayson, the beasts Sinn & Ra and to Sara, Greg, and you, EJ, my bestie forever.

I hope you all love this next addition in the Amassia series!